Praise for *Snakes of St. Augustine*

"I love the snakes in Ginger Pinholster's new novel, *Snakes of St. Augustine*, because the people in her book love them. These snakes do not inspire fear, they do not elicit revulsion; they are powerful, beautiful, strong. As are Pinholster's characters. This big-hearted novel is inhabited not just by dreamers and misfits, but by people struggling with serious mental illness, with addiction, with homelessness, with criminal behavior. Pinholster challenges our assumptions about their lives, without denying their pain or the harm they inflict. Steeped in a singular Florida charm, the novel reads sometimes like a thriller, sometimes like a love story, sometimes like a family drama. Take the leap: fall in love with Jazz, with Serena, with Fletch, with Rocky—maybe even with a ball python or a dusky pygmy rattler."

—Laura McBride, author, *We Are Called to Rise* and *In the Midnight Room*

"Here is a richly textured and compelling novel full of unforgettable personalities who will have you turning pages long into the night. Set in a slice of Florida that exists outside the margins of paradise, Pinholster masterfully spins a tale of humor and tragedy, trial and triumph. A book you won't want to miss."

—Gale Massey, author, *The Girl From Blind River*

"*Snakes of St. Augustine* is a beautifully sensory novel about relationships both broken and built by tragedy. The setting is palpable; this book is a portal to North Florida. Pinholster's characters are vivid (you will swear you know them in real life) and she writes with humor, empathy, and vision."

—Meagan Lucas, author, *Songbirds and Stray Dogs*

"In *Snakes of St. Augustine*, an engaging novel about desperate love and pilfered snakes, Ginger Pinholster writes about neurodiversity with empathy and clarity. Her Florida reflects both the weirdness and beauty of her unforgettable characters."

—Mickey Dubrow, author, *Always Agnes* and *American Judas*

"In *Snakes of St. Augustine*, Serena, a young woman searching for her missing brother, finds herself swept up in a bleak and bizarre world of homeless encampments, drug-addled street jesters, and random pet reptiles. The last thing she needs is to fall in love with one of its denizens, until the charming but manic Jazz appoints himself her deputy. Pinholster's equally wrenching and comic novel takes place against a backdrop of dead-ended despair endemic to northern Florida. Her characters, all of them at loose ends, become bound in a vasculature of feelings that turn them into family. Pinholster is a master of detail, both physical and emotional, and in her masterful hands, even lives tragically touched by mental illness attain poetry and meaning."

—Jennie Erin Smith, author, *Stolen World*

"The eclectic, unforgettable characters of Ginger Pinholster's *Snakes of St. Augustine* wrapped themselves around my heart and refused to let go...most remarkable is Pinholster's graceful and respectful depiction of complex, multi-dimensional neurodiverse characters. Rescue in the novel, or something akin to salvation, arrives through extraordinary acts of courageous love as family is redefined as a circle of those—blood-related or not—who care for one another no matter the demands requested, the heartache endured, or the sacrifice required. Your view of `normal' will be challenged in this novel, and your wrapped heart will grow larger with empathy."

—Mark Hummel, author, *Man, Underground*

"*Snakes of St. Augustine*, Ginger Pinholster's compelling second novel, deals with young men and women emerging from difficult childhoods and struggling with mental illness. The story is told from multiple points of view and the writing is stunning and deeply engaging. The characters are complex and authentic. They will work their way into your heart and as a reader you will feel an intense stake in the outcome. A mesmerizing story that defines `page turner'—you won't want to let go with the last page. Pinholster is a talented novelist to watch and we'll look forward to her next book."

—Carla Rachel Sameth, M.F.A., author, *What is Left* and *One Day on the Gold Line: A Memoir in Essays*

"Pinholster describes wacky Florida with compassion and grace. With an ingenious plot and deeply rendered characters, the novel shows us the power of forgiveness, and the things that really matter in a nutty world: strength, love, humor, and hope."

—Sara B. Fraser, author, *Just River* and *Long Division*

"Pinholster compassionately and deftly creates a cast of characters who live on the margin of our social fabric—people who are suffering from mental illness, who are homeless, who are struggling to get by having grown up without family support; yet these characters, some of whom have become largely invisible to society, find a family among one another. And then there is a story of stolen snakes, a missing person, and drug dealers amid the authentic ambience of a beach community."

—Eva Silverfine Ott, author, *How to Bury Your Dog*

Snakes of St. Augustine

Ginger Pinholster

Regal House Publishing

Published by
Regal House Publishing, LLC
Raleigh, NC 27605

ISBN -13 (paperback): 9781646033829
ISBN -13 (epub): 9781646033836
Library of Congress Control Number: 202294941

Cover images and design by © C. B. Royal

Regal House Publishing, LLC
https://regalhousepublishing.com

Printed in the United States of America

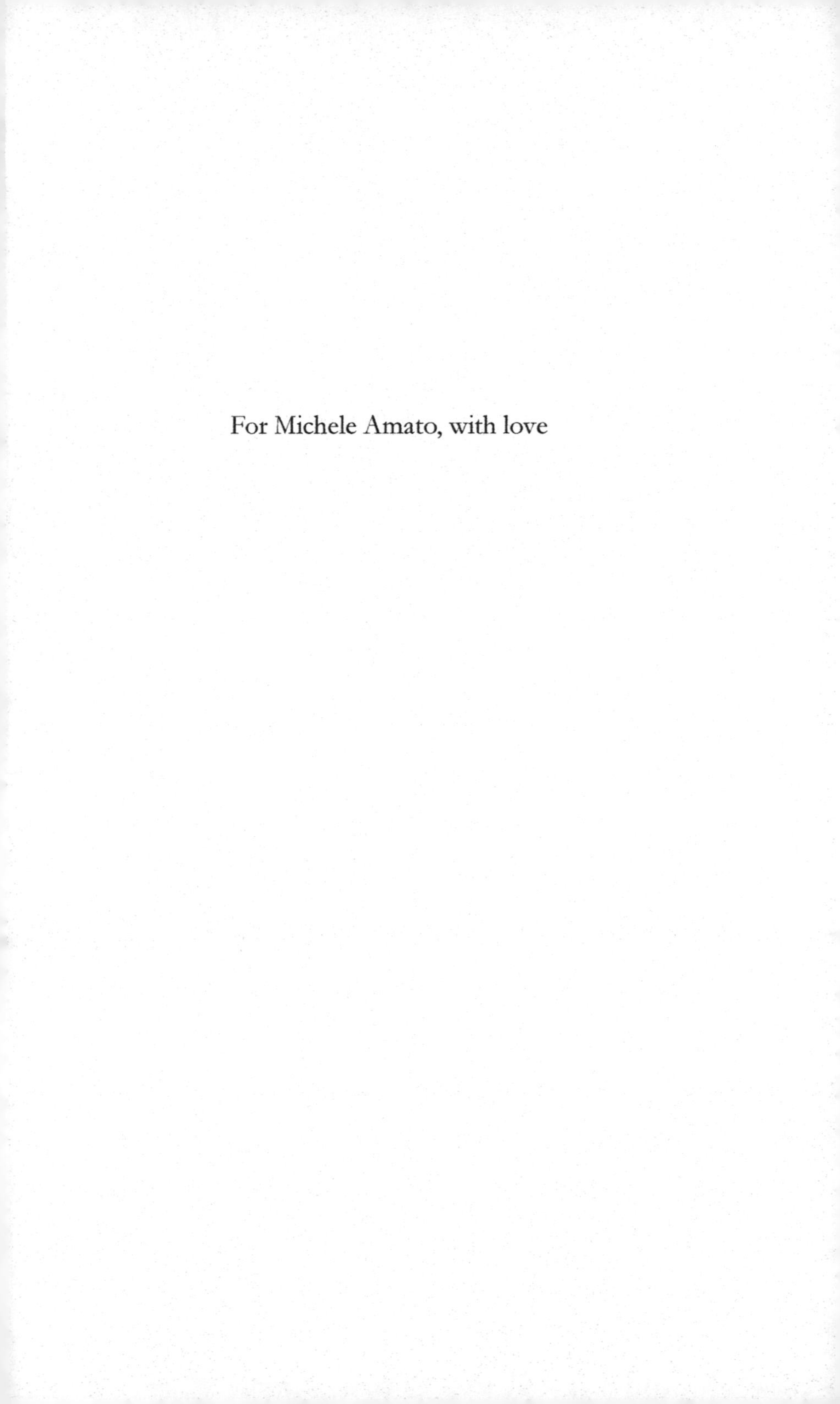

For Michele Amato, with love

1

Trina Leigh Dean

When an intruder triggered the serpentarium's alarm system, water overtopped Trina Leigh Dean's boots and suctioned her into the mud, which prevented a quick escape. The blast rocketed through scrub pines and saw palmettos, traveling at least a quarter mile to reach the shallow pond west of St. Augustine, Florida, where Trina had been searching for an injured snapping turtle. With four hundred snakes in her care—half of them venomous—Trina had invested in an old-school alarm system that sounded like an air raid warning.

No way had she left any of the doors unlocked. After working with reptiles for forty years, amateur mistakes rarely happened—not like in the early years, when Trina had endured one snakebite after another. Also, the alarm wouldn't have gone off unless someone breached the locking mechanism. What category of stupid would cause anyone to break into an animal shelter full of pit vipers and rattlesnakes? An ex-boyfriend had owned a key at one point—her better judgment having been impaired by his lean silhouette and cowboy swagger. For some months after their breakup, Waylon showed up drunk every now and then, but he had moved to Phoenix with someone else. She hadn't heard from him since. He couldn't have set off the alarm.

The turtle with a missing leg, reported to her by a concerned neighbor, would have to wait. Reaching into the muck with both hands, she extracted her flooded boots and fell backward into the water. After much floundering, she scrambled to shore. On the ground at last, Trina took two steps through the pine straw, dropped, yanked off the boots and set off running in wet socks. Sprinting over tree limbs and palm fronds wasn't as easy as it used to be. Her knees, at sixty, felt like a pair of lizards trying to claw their way to freedom. The hot, salty wind burned her lungs.

Trina had entrusted a set of keys to a St. Augustine cop, Fletch Jefferies, on the off chance he might find her some bright morning, paws-up with a red-tailed boa constrictor wrapped around her neck. The serpentarium wasn't within Fletch's jurisdiction, but Trina had been friends with his late wife. He tended to stop by once a month or so to check on Trina. He always called before visiting, though. Fletch could be ruled out as the intruder.

She rounded a bend in the trail. Inside a chicken-wire enclosure, a green iguana cocked his head in her direction. Closer to the serpentarium, two ancient tortoises extended their wrinkled necks over the lip of a pen Trina had assembled from concrete blocks. The alarm, a system purchased secondhand off the internet that wasn't connected to any type of security-response service, let out one last howl and stopped. Beyond a bittersweet cloud of marigolds at the edge of the gravel parking lot, Trina slowed to a walk, breathing hard. A side door gaped open, exposing the shadowy interior of her workroom with its stacks of plastic drawers, all carefully labeled in red ink.

Not wanting to surprise an intruder, she eased around the side of the building. Her fingertips, attached to the brick wall like a terrified gecko, began to throb. The county sheriff was a good thirty minutes away and her snakes could suffocate in the heat by then. Trina needed to get inside, close the door behind her, and adjust the cooling system before the cottonmouths started getting cranky. In the wild, a snake can slide under a rock or into a pond to cool down. The animals in Trina's vast stacks of plastic bins had no such options. If she lost her little scarlet kingsnake, the sweet-natured ball python with its cookies-and-cream complexion, or any of the other harmless snakes she let schoolchildren touch and hold, Trina's meager income would dwindle into food stamps territory.

She tried Fletch's number, but had to leave a message, which she rambled in a breathless way until her final words were snuffed out by a high-pitched tone like an ice pick to her ear drums. In case it might be the last time anyone heard her voice, Trina took a moment to thank Fletch for all his support over the years. After signing off, she crept forward, stopped to pull a painful burr out of her sock, and stuck her head through the door with her eyes closed, resigned to getting clocked unconscious by an unseen blunt object, or worse.

A second passed before Trina opened her eyes and blinked. Except for the steady hum of a dehumidifier, the room was still. Seeing no one, she tiptoed onto the lab's black and white linoleum floor and clicked the door shut. On the wall, a thermostat displayed a temperature that was at least ten degrees too high for Trina's snakes, some of which had once belonged to her parents—roadside reptile hustlers back in the day when Florida was full of kitschy novelties designed to lure tourists.

In its heyday, the Dean Family Exotic Reptile Farm had included a smelly concrete swamp full of bored, overfed alligators, a trio of cobras her father pretended to charm with a cassette tape and a flute he didn't even know how to play, and buckets of baby gators for sale. After her parents died, Trina had cleaned the place up. Working with local teachers and summer camp directors, she turned her parents' weirdly Floridian business into an education and rehabilitation center. For a few years, she had even tried to sell venom to pharmaceutical companies for snakebite remedies, but it was a tough business to break into. Instead, Trina relied on an ever-shrinking number of donations and admission fees.

Up and down the rows of plastic bins in her workroom, nothing looked amiss. Stopping every few feet, she pulled the containers out of their drawers. Tiny crowned snakes, corn snakes she could cradle in one hand, and her brilliantly colored green snakes lay curled and quiet. Near the back of the room, a dusky Pygmy rattler trembled. The air conditioner coughed before spitting a cool current into the space. Trina moved through the classroom where she entertained schoolchildren, into a narrow corridor lined with glass vivaria—temperature-controlled, see-through boxes with informational labels to let visitors know the name of each snake, its habitat, maximum length, and weight. Venomous snakes were marked with a skull and crossbones. Special ultraviolet lights were glowing inside every habitat. Nothing appeared out of order until Trina turned a corner and stopped short to avoid a pile of broken glass.

Banana Splits, the stocky ball python with cheerful yellow splotches, was nowhere to be found—not in her tank or anywhere along the hallway, which was closed at the far end. Side-stepping the glass, grief rose like a suffocating tide inside Trina's chest. Farther down the hallway, she found two more shattered vivaria where nobody was home. Also missing was Bandit, her elderly eastern kingsnake, which was black with elegant, pearly bands. She had inherited both snakes from her parents. Raised in captivity and accustomed to having their meals brought to them, they might not survive in the wild. It was her responsibility to make sure the animals had a long, comfortable, healthy life. They happened to be her moneymakers, too—visually stunning and docile enough to be passed hand-to-hand whenever Trina gave one of her classroom presentations.

Worst of all was the loss of a third snake, Unicorn, her rare eastern indigo, *Drymarchon couperi*—"lord of the forest," in Greek. Trina had rehabilitated Unicorn after part of his tail got chopped off by a bulldozer. Still young but already four feet long and thick, he had been resting in the woods when developers plowed through part of Unicorn's home. The sheriff brought Unicorn to Trina. She had nursed the big snake, lethargic and reluctant to eat at first, until his scales turned an iridescent mix of blue and black, offsetting a sunset-colored throat guaranteed to mesmerize the kids. Trina would never own another eastern indigo—the longest native snake species in the United States, classified as threatened.

Dropping to the floor, she breathed into her hands. Three beloved snakes had been lost. With a roiling sickness, Trina knew why.

She pictured the little girl who had come to live with her family so many years before, when Trina was fifteen. Her parents had fostered the girl, who was left at their doorstep. She was ten, with cigarette burns on her forearms and a purple bruise under one hollow eye. Trina's parents gave the girl a room of her own, and in their own eccentric way, all the love they could muster. Still, Chelsea ran off, again and again. On trips to the supermarket, she latched on to grown men and exposed herself. She beat her head against the wall beside her twin bed with its pink, ruffled skirt, hand-stitched by Trina's mother. Chelsea set fire to the doghouse while the dog was still chained beside it so that he nearly died. Finally, at fourteen, she left one last time.

It would be years before Trina saw her sister again.

2

Serena Jacobs

Serena's fingers felt sticky around the steering wheel, coated with grime from the police station where she had reported her brother Gethin's disappearance to a St. Augustine police officer named Fletcher Jefferies. Beside her, Rahkendra smelled both sweet and sweaty with fear. The funk seemed to pulse up from her pores, stronger and sharper, every minute Gethin stayed gone—two days and six hours, so far. The windshield wipers slapped the glass in double time, dragging arcs of sideways rain. Rahkendra scratched at the misshapen initials tattooed on her bicep: *G + R*. Gethin and Rocky, locked up in a crooked heart.

"My brother's an asshole," Serena said, headed west, toward her neighborhood, away from the clanging tourist trolleys and faux Spanish castles of downtown St. Augustine. "He's done this before. He's old enough to know better."

Rocky fiddled with the silver ring on the side of her nose. "Yeah, well, he's not cut from the same military mold as you," she said.

"What are you talking about?"

In 1991, an Iraqi scud missile had slammed into the US barracks in Saudi Arabia where Serena's father had been stationed. He was one of twenty-eight lost in the blast. Serena was sixteen. The photo, gleaming beside the casket that winter, showed him looking sharp in his Army Reserve uniform.

Up ahead, a train whistled into oblivion. Phone poles blew by. "Gethin and I had the same father."

"Right, but Gethin doesn't even remember him."

A quarter mile ahead, a railroad gate stopped blinking and rolled open. Serena felt gut punched. She sat up straighter, re-aligning her vertebrae. "He was only four when Dad died. Mom was a hot mess. So you're right. Gethin didn't have time to learn the three Ps from Dad."

"Ah yes, the three Ps," Rocky said, exhaling hard. "From your fitness videos on social media."

"Exactly." Serena regretted sounding defensive. "Perseverance, Patience, and Pluck. It all comes down to personal discipline. That's how Dad lived his life. It's how I'm living mine. Gethin missed out on a lot of great lessons when Dad died, but still, he ought to know better than this. I've done my best to teach him."

"Watch out," Rocky said, latching on to the dashboard.

A bicyclist zoomed by Serena's bumper. His orange-striped legs flashed up and down. His helmet had a backward-pointing plastic wing that made him look like the FTD Florist. Serena stood on the brakes and locked her elbows. "Thanks, dude," she said, easing the car's nose over the tracks before turning left. If it had been Gethin and not some random Tour de France wannabe, she would have hit him. Not really, of course—Serena would never hurt anyone—but she could at least fantasize about flattening her brother, after all he had put her through.

Rocky crossed and uncrossed her legs. She couldn't seem to stop fidgeting. Her window rolled down with a consoling hum. "I think there's a bike race or something this weekend. They've been all over the place."

On either side of the road, the space between buildings expanded, giving way to houses with lawns bordered by boxwoods and azaleas, mailboxes decorated with bronze dolphins, and gardening sheds painted to look like barns. To reach her neighborhood of gravel roads and chain-link fences, Serena had to wind her way, with mounting resentment, through a gauntlet of manicured suburbs. The road emptied and turned narrow, squeezed by Spanish moss and sprawling oak trees. The rain drummed a finale, eased up, and stopped. In another minute, they would be back at Serena's house, where she could stop holding her breath, drink a protein smoothie, and search Gethin's computer one more time for any clue to his whereabouts and why he had left them. She stopped the car at a red light, behind a pool of rainwater.

What had happened between Rocky and Gethin to make him run? When he first disappeared, Serena had been out of town, having been summoned to the gated estate of a wealthy bride-to-be in urgent need of a personal trainer. On the passenger seat, Rocky pressed her hands against her face. Her long, beaded braids fell forward. She was a kid, after all, still on the tender, uphill side of her twenties. Gethin, at twenty-eight, was four years older than Rocky. Serena touched the slippery fabric on Rocky's leg—black with red roses running up the seams. She had been wearing the same silky tank top and leggings since Gethin disappeared. "Honey, were you and Gethin fighting about anything?"

Rocky gave Serena a sideways look. "No," she said.

"He seemed pretty mad when you made him get rid of his snakes." For as long as Serena could remember, Gethin had been obsessed with snakes. He tended to introduce himself to strangers by saying he liked music, hiking, and snakes. Rocky couldn't stand snakes. Soon after moving in, she had given Gethin an ultimatum—it was her or the snakes.

"That was months ago." Rocky plucked at her leggings. "He got over it."

"If there's anything you didn't want to tell the police, you can tell me," Serena said. Rocky's thigh tensed up. Serena had held her tongue for two days, not wanting to trigger Rocky, whose temper had been known to flare up, but answers were urgently needed. "Was he using again?"

At another intersection, a red light turned green. Rocky's bottom lip fell open.

Serena pulled her hand back and gripped the wheel, waiting. She inched forward, into the intersection, almost home. She would draw a bath for Rocky, whip up some bubbles, and bring her a snack. The poor kid was exhausted.

"He kept saying—"

A rooster tail of water bombarded the windshield. A voice

called out—"Whoa, whoa, whoa!"—and the car rocked. A grunt was followed by a flash of orange. Legs thumped over the hood. Arms and hands windmilled in a blur. A man, or a boy, flew across her car. When his body hit the pavement, it seemed to make a kind of musical riff like the soundtrack for an aerobics class. Every note pounded inside Serena's brain—palms, knees, hips, shoulder, head. His bike fell onto its side, twisted.

Rocky was screaming.

"Call 911," Serena said. She jumped from the car and dropped to her knees. Without thinking, she scooped up his head like somebody grabbing an injured baby. Immediately, she remembered from all of her first aid training why it might be important to keep his spinal column straight, but she couldn't let go. "You're okay," she said. "You're okay."

His outstretched hands quivered. Red rivers streamed from matching stigmata on his palms. "Am I bleeding?" he said.

His helmetless head was soaked. Ropes of coppery hair stuck to his cheeks, which were hollow and freckled. His eyes, wide open and unblinking, ratcheted around, strangely feline and beautiful—the brightest amber. One of them drifted off to the side. He lowered his hands without looking at them and crossed them over his chest, prayerful. The robin's egg blue of his shirt turned red. "There's a little blood," Serena said. Rocky was out of the car, on the phone, spinning in all directions to get a bead on their location. "You came out of nowhere."

"I just passed my test." He licked a crack in his lips. His chest pumped up and down, too fast. The sky lightened and a few lines emerged around his eyes. In a blink, he seemed to time-travel from nineteen to thirty. Or did he? *Please, God, don't let him be a teenager.*

"It's busy," Rocky said, waving the phone. "How can 911 be busy?"

Serena pulled off her coat, bundled it under his head, and hunkered over her ankles. She craned her head toward Rocky. "Keep trying."

"No ambulance," he said, hoisting himself onto his elbows. "I don't have health insurance."

The word *lawsuit* flashed through Serena's mind. "You need first aid." In Florida, personal injury lawyers regularly achieved celebrity status, advertising on TV, billboards, radio, and buses.

For the first time since she had hit him, or he hit her—*which was it?*—he looked down at himself. His open hands stopped shaking.

Serena thought, *Spinal cord injury.*

From his raw palms, blood oozed onto his lap. His knees had been sandpapered below his shorts. "My hands," he said, and he went horizontal again. "I passed the exam, but now I won't be able to work."

Bankruptcy. Whenever he filed his lawsuit, Serena knew, he would clean her out. It wasn't like she was getting rich from her work as a personal fitness trainer. The ads on her YouTube videos and the occasional PayPal donation from a TikTok fan helped keep the lights on, nothing more.

With the phone still pressed to her ear, Rocky leaned against the car and closed her eyes, inhaling. Serena eyeballed the open car door and touched his shoulder, which felt solid. Under her fingers, his muscles flexed—typical guy; even injured, not wanting to seem flaccid. "Are you a student?"

"Front-end coding, applications developer," he said, meaning—what? "Can you help me up? If the cops show up, they'll haul me into the ER. I can't pay the bill."

Up to that point, Serena hadn't thought about the police. Could she be charged? Who had been at fault? The back wheel of his bicycle clicked off another rotation. Bits of silver and red glass littered the road near his broken side-mirror and a cracked reflector. The front wheel curled skyward at an odd angle. "You can't ride your bike."

His head popped up, and in an instant, he was on his knees, in mourning for his fallen wheels. "Jumbee," he said. Again, he seemed like a kid—shapeshifting between decades. "I'll miss the Hacker's Challenge."

A car with tinted windows rolled toward them, hubcaps flashing to a bass beat. Serena held her breath until it kept going. "Get in the car." Her voice had taken on a low, drill-sergeant tone. "Hurry. I'll grab your bike."

He dove in headfirst.

Rocky turned, mouth opening, and without taking her eyes off Serena, she clicked her phone off. "What are you doing?" she said. "He might rob us."

Through the windshield, his head disappeared. He had stretched himself across the back seat. Serena turned her back to him and whispered. "He's a computer geek, honey. He's injured and outnumbered."

"We should keep trying the police, or flag down the next car."

"No more police today." Serena massaged the back of her neck and stretched it from side to side. Officer Jefferies had yawned without covering his mouth. He clicked his ballpoint pen over and over again while Serena told him about her brother's disappearance. She had been raised to respect all police officers and soldiers without question, but Jefferies had seemed irritable, and he hadn't even bothered to keep his desk clean. She didn't need to be dealing with a traffic ticket—or worse. "We'll drive him to his house. I'll clean his wounds. I'm not some hit-and-run driver. This is the right thing to do."

Rocky pushed the hair off her face with both hands and held it there. "He could have a head injury. Can you give him first aid for that?"

"He's basically fine."

A warbling moan rose up from the back of the car. Serena had been certified in first aid and CPR, for her work as a fitness trainer.

A gray shadow crossed Rocky's face—a fresh wave of grief. Serena had been watching it come and go ever since Gethin left. She needed to get Rocky home. The rain picked up again. Serena clicked a button on her car keys, causing the trunk to pop open. She deadlifted the bike without difficulty. It was the first time she had noticed his helmet—white with yellow and green wings on it—tied to the seat. If he owned a helmet, why hadn't he been wearing it? Why did it look so familiar? Serena's biceps bulged as she shoved the mangled bike through the car's hatch. A sharp edge dug into Serena's thumb. His rain-soaked bike—a yellow one with no tread left on the tires—instantly saturated the inside of the trunk.

The biker's rust-colored face rose up from the back seat like a jack-o'-lantern.

Serena pinched at the gouge in her thumb, which was bleeding. She spoke to him through the open hatch. "Where do you live?"

His eyes drifted, rolling over the road in the direction he had been going. On the front seat, Rocky's head swiveled. "There's a park with a pavilion a little further up," he said. "It's got a bathroom where I can clean up. You can drop me off there."

Serena tried to smile, but her mouth felt too dry. She rolled her tongue over her teeth, closed the trunk, and climbed into the car. For a minute, she sat still, squeezing the steering wheel while raindrops sloughed off her face. "No, I mean, where's your house?" She didn't take her eyes off the road. "You'll need to get those scrapes disinfected."

In the rearview mirror, he pressed his hands against his shirt. His mouth opened and closed. "I'm kind of between houses," he said. "The park's fine."

Rocky's hand slapped down on the edge of her seat. She seemed to be trying to hang on that way.

They could drop him off, as he had asked—he didn't know their names, and given his fear of official involvement, it seemed unlikely he would report the accident. He had the passive eyes of a cat. They looked vacant. He was tapping his palms together, as if preparing to pray. Something wasn't quite right about the kid.

Special needs. The words a kindergarten teacher had slapped on Gethin came back to Serena, and she was a teenager again, listening to her widowed mother cry while she clicked a teaspoon around and around in a cup. At the time, Serena and her mother had no idea what "autism spectrum disorder" meant. It was one of many different diagnoses that were explored and ruled out, in Gethin's case. With no answers, Serena had concluded there was nothing fundamentally wrong with her brother. In her opinion, he only needed to stay off the drugs and focus on a goal, the way their father had taught them to do. Gethin needed to man up, was all.

Serena cranked the engine and adjusted her side mirrors. "This is Rocky, by the way," she said. "I'm Serena."

"Oh, I know." He perked up. "I recognized you from TikTok. I memorized the three Ps."

"Ah yes," Rocky said. "Here we go."

"My name's Jazz."

"Nice to meet you," Serena said, realizing with a jolt that she wasn't anonymous. "You're coming home with us. I'll get you fixed up and then I'll take you wherever you want to go—deal?"

From Rocky, a quick sniff, followed by a cough. Was she getting sick? Probably it was all the stress. "Jazz, huh?" Rocky said. "That's your real name?"

He moved to the center of the back seat, leaned forward, and latched on like a family dog, eager for an outing. His smell surged forward, musky and acrid. "It's Jaswinder—lightning bolt, in Hindu. My mother was a Bollywood star. My father's a McGinness. You see the problem."

Rocky mashed her knuckles against her nose. "Yeah," she said. "Stick with Jazz."

"Lightning bolt," Serena said. "Sounds about right."

"My father helped build the internet in India." Jazz hooked his elbows over the front seat. He seemed to want to climb over it, onto their laps. "When I was little, he—" Jazz stopped talking. In the rearview mirror, his eyes rolled over the car's console, the boxy red numbers indicating the time, a tiny crystal on a string, Rocky's hair beads, and finally, Serena's turquoise bracelet. "Is there any way we could stop for bananas?" he said. "Usually I have a smoothie at about three o' clock every day.

I just cut up a banana, drop it into some milk, and shake it up really well."

Serena flashed on a movie from the 1980s with the actor Dustin Hoffman playing an autistic savant who needed to watch a certain TV show at the same time every day. "I have bananas at my house," she said, pausing between each word. "I like smoothies too."

"Do you have peanut butter?"

Rocky lifted her chin and stroked her neck. One, two, three times.

"I'll bandage you up and take you right back to your spot." Serena was talking mostly to herself. *In and out. Don't get any ideas, kid.* As soon as they found Gethin, they would have a full house again. Also, Serena wasn't sure she could tolerate the smell radiating off Jazz for longer than a car ride across town.

She missed Gethin's smell—the sweet, damp spot under his ponytail telegraphing his presence—the same sweaty-boy perfume from when he was a first grader and she was fumbling through her senior year of high school, bullied and lonely. She always knew, the minute she stepped into the house and inhaled, whether he was home: Her goofy kid brother, leaning out of his bedroom window, lining up peanuts on the ledge, for the birds and squirrels—anything to keep busy while their mom stayed in bed all day. It got so bad after their dad died, Serena took over Gethin's care, even while she was trying to survive adolescence one day at a time.

After their mother disappeared, Serena, eighteen years old, walked into a courthouse with six-year-old Gethin in tow. In her hands, the stack of custody forms had felt icy hot, burning her skin while the room shrank and expanded around her and she knew, like the pop of a frozen lake cracking under her boots, that she was alone. *Abandoned.* Life would never be the same. Serena knew her mother loved her, in the unavoidable way mothers have to love their children, but she didn't particularly like Serena, who took after her father.

Right after her mother left, Serena felt like she had a gaping hole full of fear in her chest. Over time, she filled the void by focusing all her energy on Gethin. Being his caretaker had given Serena a purpose. When he was older, there were beer cans, then hairspray cans with wet towels wrapped around them for huffing, and later, white crystals in tiny plastic baggies hidden in his sock drawer, but Serena and her brother had been buddies, before all that.

The car dipped off the paved road onto a pitted gravel lane, which had turned swampy, as usual, from the rain. Serena eased around a rusty El Camino that hadn't moved for years, in front of her neighbor's homemade cinder-block wall, into her own driveway. In the rush to reach the police station, she had left the garage door open. A foolish error. All three bicycles appeared to be accounted for, wedged between Gethin's work bench, where he had arranged his secondhand tools in rows, and a tower of plastic bins containing Christmas decorations. She rolled the car over an oil spot—troubling because of its recent expansion—until the bumper tapped an antique push mower Gethin had found at a yard sale.

Rocky bolted into the house before Serena had killed the engine. The door slammed. On a shelf above the door, a trio of glass jars trembled.

In the back seat, Jazz sat still and alert. He seemed to be waiting for Serena to acknowledge him.

"I only eat crunchy peanut butter," she said. "More protein."

His smile widened and changed until he was gritting his teeth. "Straight-up bananas would be fine," he said. "If they're not organic, don't worry about it."

Serena threw a leg out of the car. Her sneaker slapped the oily concrete. "I won't."

Inside the house, a stack of plastic-wrapped toilet paper leaned off-center, by the kitchen door. She had been trying to save money at a wholesale club where nothing could be purchased in smaller quantities. Serena didn't like the clutter. Beside a two-pack of toaster-sized peanut butter jars, a fruit fly spiraled up from a crate of tangelos, some of which had begun to shrivel and ooze. On the refrigerator, coupons were pinned beneath magnets featuring good-looking men in different uniforms.

Serena pulled a stool by the sink and turned on the tap. The water sputtered brown before it evened out. Sulfur fumes competed with the leaky tangelos. "Have a seat," she said, reaching under the sink for her first aid kit. Straightening up, she wiped sweat from her face and stopped short. On the stool, Jazz had stripped to the waist. His breath hit the side of her face.

"You look sad about something," he said. Next to the window, his lit-up eyes seemed to change color, taking on more green than amber.

Serena flipped open the box containing the bandages and iodine she always dragged along on her fitness training jobs. "I feel pretty crappy about you being hurt." She said it slowly, careful not to admit guilt. After snapping on a pair of rubber gloves, she cracked open a gauze pad. "Wash your hands, please."

He did as instructed. Serena handed him a wad of paper towels. "No doubt," he said, holding his palms open. "Your whole aura's gray. It's like somebody died."

With the blood washed off, his hands didn't look so bad. The iodine ran over his palm. Although she wasn't injured, Serena felt a pinch. *Like somebody died.* "You're scraped up pretty good." She cradled his hands, prodding them with her plastic-encased fingers. "Fortunately, nothing's broken. You don't need stiches. How old are you?"

"Age isn't really relevant to me."

She pressed gauze over his wounded palm. Her eyes felt tired. For Serena's fortieth birthday, Rocky had made an organic carrot cake, sweetened with apple sauce instead of sugar. "That's because you're still young."

"I'm thirty-two," Jazz said. The second dose of iodine made him suck in a quick breath. "Almost thirty-three, about the same as you, it looks like."

"Ha ha." She said it with sarcasm, but it was a relief to

know she hadn't run over anybody's special-needs kid. He was a grown-up, at least.

When he smiled, his lips made a crackling sound, moving over his teeth. "I'm thirty-two and thirsty."

Serena poured him a cup of water and got back to work. She kept her head down. His sweaty smell seemed to intensify. "Let's fix up your knees next."

He repositioned himself on the stool. "Are you in mourning?"

She stepped back, peeling off the first-aid gloves. Her hands were hot and slick with sweat. *Yes. My brother's missing. The one I'm supposed to be taking care of.* She wasn't about to reveal any secrets to a stranger.

Jazz turned his cheek toward the heart-shaped crystal dangling from a piece of dental floss above Serena's sink. Sometimes, light from the window shot fiery bits of color through it. With the day fading, the crystal was clear and it looked cheap. Serena had teased Gethin about hanging the thing—asked if he had used the dental floss first.

Jazz blinked and braced one hand against the sink. "Whee," he said, swaying.

"You're dizzy," she said. "You should lie down."

He put one foot on the floor and lurched, thumping forward.

Serena caught him under the armpits and hoisted him upright. "Come on," she said, pulling his arm over her shoulder. "This way."

Beyond the kitchen, the little room where Gethin did his schoolwork contained a sagging couch. Jazz reclined on the couch and placed his bandaged hands over his chest. "Wow, you're strong."

"It's my job."

His eyes drifted to half-mast. "You like it?"

"My job? Absolutely. I get to see people change their lives. All it takes is hard work. One older woman I helped, she couldn't even carry her grocery bags. After a few weeks of training, she was doing zot curls with fifteen-pound weights. Now, she's a beast. I had a guy who weighed four hundred pounds, got himself down to half his size."

"Nobody's been this nice to me for a long time."

Serena looked down at him, shifted her weight from one leg to the other. "Oh, nobody's run over you lately?" As soon as she said it, she wished she hadn't.

He closed his eyes, jaw slack, and mumbled something else. "I'm sorry about your brother."

Her body went rigid. Serena didn't remember telling him about Gethin. No, she hadn't said a word. She was sure of it. Had he overheard something she said to Rocky in the car? Had she left her folder of notes open on Gethin's desk? "You should rest," she said, hoping he didn't have a concussion. "Um, maybe try not to fall asleep completely."

On the couch, Jazz closed his eyes. Serena backed away, leaving the door ajar.

In the living room, Rocky stood by her bedroom door, arms crossed, with one foot pointing a kind of accusation. "Call the police," she said, too loudly.

Serena looked over her shoulder, across the kitchen. Jazz had rolled onto his side. His spine jutted through his skin. His rib cage moved in a slow, steady rhythm. He had probably been sleeping on the ground, or on a bench at the picnic area. "Give him a break," she whispered. "He's exhausted. We can take care of him for a few more minutes."

Rocky's eyebrows levitated and stayed there, hovering on her forehead. "What the hell was that he just said? How would he know anything about Gethin?"

On the coffee table, purple and orange goo burbled inside a lava lamp—another one of Gethin's New Age yard sale finds that Serena didn't like. She rubbed the creased spot on her forehead. "He heard us talking."

Rocky put a hand on her hip. "How do you not see what's going on?"

"What do you mean?" Serena reached down and clicked the lava lamp off.

"Remember the first guy who nearly hit us? It's him—same pants, same helmet. It's a setup. He's scamming you."

An old travel magazine was lying open on the floor. Serena scooped it up, closed it, and set it on the table. "He hasn't asked for anything. Okay, a smoothie, big deal. He seems like a homeless guy with some kind of problem. He wanted to go back to his spot."

"Yeah, he's a poor, sweet kid who needs you to coddle him, just like Gethin."

Heat thrummed through Serena's temples. Taking care of her brother had always been her job. She was proud of it. "I left my notes all over the office," she said. "Anybody could have pieced it together."

"He knows Gethin. This wasn't an accident."

"You're exhausted." Serena repositioned the magazine so that it was in the exact center of the little brown coffee table. "Let me draw you a bath."

Rocky flinched and tugged at her shirt, squirming. "No," she said, scratching the back of her neck. "Thanks, but no, I'm fine. I'm going to lie down for a while. Do me a favor. Scream if you're being attacked."

"Will do."

3

Fletch Jefferies

Ten minutes after she called him, Officer Fletch Jefferies found Trina Leigh Dean sitting on the floor of the serpentarium with her head against a wall and her eyes squeezed shut. Blowing wind, he stole a glance at his wristwatch. He had less than an hour to figure out what was going on with Trina and get to the police station. Being late to work four days in a row would trigger another automatic warning. To earn his pension, Fletch needed to survive three more agonizing months of service.

"Trina?"

When she opened her eyes, a single tear slid down the side of her nose.

The sight of his wife's friend, with her gray pigtails and mud-splattered overalls, brought Farah's face back, all at once, in vivid relief. How many Sunday mornings had the two women whispered across Farah's speckled kitchen counter, or sat on the patio together, watching ruby-throated hummingbirds dart around the feeder? Best friends, Trina and Farah would huddle close, laughing while they sipped sugary tea spiked with mint. The memory of Farah's fingers curled around a mug made his chest tighten, as it had every day since the cancer took her. She was wearing a wig at the end but was still smooth faced.

Fletch had been sitting in his driveway, ready to fire up his old Mustang and get to work on time when he listened to Trina's whispery voicemail. "Fletch!" her message had said. "It's me. Farah's reptile-loving pal. Hey, before I forget, I wanted to say thanks for all you've done for me. Man, you've been a rock, truly, and I'm grateful to you. So listen, the reason I called—I was out back and the burglar alarm went off. You know I can't leave my babies in danger, so I'm going in. If you speak at my funeral, please don't talk about that time I married my cousin in Reno. Ha ha!" For a second, the recording captured Trina's labored breathing. "Oh, look, it's probably nothing," she said. "I'm turning into a wuss. I'll call you later, honey bunny."

Moving down a long hallway inside the serpentarium, Fletch sidestepped piles of glass until he was standing next to Trina. He shifted his weight and took a knee. He couldn't get all the way down on the floor. Years of digging trenches for the army, and later, chasing small-time drug dealers for the St. Augustine police department had taken a toll on his spinal column. Also, a vein in his neck kept jumping, which probably meant a spike in his blood pressure that would cause him to keel over and die soon. Fletch touched Trina's shoulder. "What happened to your shoes, dear?" He used his secret, quiet voice, the one he had used only at home with Farah—never when he was on duty.

From Trina, a laugh like the bleating of a goat. "They're stuck in my boots."

After a pause, Fletch tried again. "Where are your boots?"

"Out by the pond. I was knee-deep in muck when the alarm went off. Took me a minute to get free."

The smell of grief rolled up from Trina's skin like something feral and cornered. In his mind, Fletch set a goal to get Trina back on her feet where she could think practical thoughts. Mundane tasks like finding clean socks and a broom could serve as a tightrope for crossing the abyss of grief. Fletch had learned this. "Are you hurt?"

She shook her head and tried for a smile with no teeth in it. "Lost three of my best snakes. The ones I let the kids pass around."

With a groan, Fletch stood up, reached down with both hands, and pulled Farah's old friend upright. "You'll need to call your insurance company. They'll want to see the police report. Have you called the sheriff's office yet?"

Trina ran both hands over her head, looking around at the broken glass and empty spaces. "Nope."

"You know the county's got jurisdiction here. I can't write the report."

"I know, but I don't want anybody else to hear about this. Talk about bad publicity. I'm supposed to be providing a safe space for school kids. Anyway, I don't have insurance. A police report won't help me."

"Wait, what?" *No insurance?* Fletch felt his heart start to race on Trina's behalf.

Her eyes were the color of molasses, but cloudier than he remembered, and heavy-lidded. She nailed him with a stare. Fletch knew the look. It caused him to shut his mouth and keep it shut. Being married for so long, he had mastered a few life-saving tricks. Trina was never one to let anybody tell her how to live her life. He admired her for it. He was also grateful as hell Farah had been Trina's polar opposite.

"You look like crap," she said, banging the last word like somebody punching a hole through a drum.

"Well, thanks, honey."

"No, your face is all red and you're sweating. Are you taking your blood-pressure medicine? What have you been eating? I promised Farah I'd keep an eye on you. I've done a piss-poor job of it so far."

Again, Fletch glanced at the time. *Thirty minutes before work starts.* Out of habit, he tried to run a hand through his hair, but his fingers hit mostly bald skin. The wavy brown mane of his youth was long gone. How so many years had flown by, Fletch had no idea. "I don't quite get it. Is there something more you need to tell me?"

Trina pretended to take a drag from an imaginary cigarette, a pantomime he had seen her act out whenever she was feeling stressed. Farah said it was a weird habit Trina had developed after giving up the real thing. Trina wrapped up the performance by blowing nonexistent smoke rings over her head. "Well, you see, detective," she said, mock-serious, "I know who did it, and it wasn't the butler."

Fletch wiped his forehead with the back of his hand and

stared at his dusty shoes until, somewhere deep in his gray matter, a neuron fired. "Your sister?"

"One hundred percent, no doubt. She took Banana Splits, Bandit, and Unicorn. Those were the snakes she liked best when she helped out around here for two months last summer, before she took off again."

"They were her favorites."

"Exactly." To Fletch's dismay, Trina tapped him in the gut. "Seriously, what's going on with you? Are you still having that compassion fatigue thing?"

The words felt like a frying pan to the side of his head. It was the same term that stupid counselor had used after the boss told him to lower his anxiety level, or else. The ultimatum from his supervisor had been the ultimate stressor, nearly sending Fletch over some unseen but surely fatal brink. "How did you know about that?"

Trina laughed, cocking her head to one side. "Best friends talk, tough guy."

"I've got three months to go." Fletch had his hands outstretched, pleading with the universe to set him free from the job that felt like being compressed by a giant, full-body vise grip. "The counselor said it's more common than people think. Police and soldiers get numb to it, after a while, you know? I'm not the only one."

"Of course you're not."

"My blood pressure shoots up sometimes and I get a little agitated, but you don't have to worry. I'm taking the meds. Thanks for asking." Fletch thought, *Never ask me anything like that again, ever.*

When she patted him like he was a school kid, Fletch had a sudden urge to knock her hand off his shoulder. In an instant, a scorching shame consumed him. How could he be angry at Farah's dear friend, even for a fraction of a second? The lid of his head felt as if it might pop off. It scared him.

Trina pulled her hand back, eyeballing him sideways. He stared at her until her words, blurry at first, came back into focus. "How does all of that work?" she was saying. "What happens when you're agitated and fatigued at the same time? Sounds god-awful."

"Well, for example, two women came to see me yesterday."

"Okay." Trina stretched out the second syllable, urging him to continue.

"They filled out a missing person report on this guy who sounds like a head case." Fletch adjusted his collar, embarrassed by the memory. *Gethin Jacobs, twenty-eight-year-old white male.* "They were upset, you know? Crying and everything. All I could think was, 'Get over it. Grow up. He doesn't want to be found.' I didn't want to deal with them. Later on, I thought, you know, 'What the hell is wrong with me?'"

"You're worn out."

"That's an understatement."

"It's only been a year since we lost Farah."

"I know it's time to call it quits. All I have to do is make it to the finish line. Anyway, listen, sweetie, how can I help? You don't want me to call the sheriff. You want me to help you clean up? I hate to say it, but I'm going to be late for work."

"Can you find her?" Trina's voice had gone quiet and thick as quicksand. "She's a total screw-up, but I feel responsible for her. I owe it to my folks."

Fletch didn't have the first idea where to look for Trina's train wreck of a sister. "Absolutely, I can find her," he said, eager to flee.

"Don't arrest her. Bring her to me. I only want my snakes back. I can't call the sheriff. I know that guy. He'd toss her straight into the hoosegow."

"Yeah, don't say hoosegow. It's not a thing."

"I need to make sure she's okay."

She's definitely not okay, Fletch thought. Instead of saying it out loud, he stuck his hand out for a shake. "Deal."

"Thank you." Trina clapped his hand in both of hers. "Now, I'm cooking some eggs for you, mister."

"No, no. I have to get going."

"Call and say you had an emergency, which you did." Both of them stood, and she gave his sleeve a tug, pulling him toward an antiquated kitchen on the far side of her lab. "I'll make you some eggs with bacon, and if you're a good boy, some orange juice and hash browns."

"I already ate."

"I have cinnamon rolls." She sang the words, trilling the last word.

Mundane tasks. She was latching on to them like a lifeline, and that was good. The daily routine would help her, as it had helped him. He wasn't supposed to eat salty, fatty foods anymore, but he could have a few bites, for her sake. She was dragging him behind her like a corpse on the battlefield. He couldn't help laughing at her persistence. "Okay, okay," he said. He was sick to death of having his chain yanked by The Man. Better to get prodded along, into the culinary cocoon where his wife had spent many happy evenings over a bottle of pinot grigio with her funny, sweet friend, Trina Leigh Dean. "I'll call in late."

4

Rahkendra "Rocky" Wright

After declining Serena's offer of a bubble bath, Rocky stepped into her bedroom, locked the door, and peeled off her clothes. The psoriasis was so painful, a flash flood swamped her eyes. She folded the silky pants and tank top—the only outfit she could stand to wear during an outbreak—and crawled behind the bookcase naked. The scabs on her back had begun to crack and bleed, and she couldn't reach them. Gethin wasn't there to rub cream onto the lesions. He couldn't shine an ultraviolet light onto the thick white and purple patches that itched like a demon under her skin.

Tucked between the wall and Gethin's floor-to-ceiling bookcase, Rocky inhaled the soothing aroma of their commingled schoolbooks. She treasured her collection of chemistry titles. They would be her ticket out of poverty, once she earned her degree. Using a sponge she had rubber-banded onto a long brush, Rocky dabbed her back with a pungent concoction of aloe, coconut oil, oatmeal, and mint—Gethin's invention. It cooled her skin and made it stop crawling for a few seconds, but the sponge wasn't the same as having Gethin smooth elaborate circular patterns along her spine.

Before they met, no one had helped Rocky with her patches. As a kid, she had been instructed to take a hot shower, to "rinse the germs off," as if she could cleanse herself of an auto-immune condition. She wiped her hands on a towel and put the top back on Gethin's jar of ointment. Rocky wondered if her mother ever missed her, or maybe felt relieved to be free of motherhood.

With the blinds closed and Gethin gone, the room felt

gloomy. A few lines of light flickered over the paisley bedspread. Light from the window bounced off a dozen metal buckets. They were everywhere—on the dresser, the desk, and the bedside table, containing Gethin's pens and pencils, hair ties, lip balm, and soap. Each bucket held only one type of thing. He had spray-painted a few of them red, blue, or green, but most of them were silver. Once, she had dropped a pencil into the soap bucket by accident. Both buckets were silver. He had discarded the soap bucket and all its contents on the spot, declaring it tainted.

The buckets had something to do with Gethin's condition, which Serena had described as "maybe OCD, maybe ADHD, maybe autism—nobody really knows, but whatever it is, he's got a very mild case." She had repeated the last part—*a very mild case*—several times, like a kid with a security blanket she didn't want to lose.

Despite his odd habits, Gethin was hotter than chili peppers swimming in Tabasco sauce. At first, Rocky hadn't minded the buckets.

In the kitchen, water splashed in the sink. A cabinet opened and closed. Rocky didn't want to reveal her latest psoriasis outbreak. Only once, she had shared her secret with Serena. The disclosure had triggered a long lecture about eating more fruits, vegetables, and fish rich in omega-3 fatty acids. Serena got on Rocky's last raw nerve sometimes, but she meant well, and nobody had shown more kindness to Rocky, ever. She eased onto her knees and ran her hands under both breasts, wiping the sweat.

Gethin's math textbook was right where he had left it, on the third shelf of the bookcase with a notebook tucked inside of it. For the tenth time, she cracked it open. He had been taking the same class again, trying to pass it. Rocky had aced the course a year before. It wasn't like community college was so hard, except for the student loans. Gethin's loopy, precise handwriting seemed to vibrate off the page: "A variable can assume different values. Random variables happen by chance. Examples—coin toss, rolling dice, banana peel on the sidewalk." He had drawn a picture of each event. The banana peel looked depressed.

Maybe meeting Gethin had been a random variable—nothing more than a cosmic blooper. The wind had been strong that day. She had been racing to clock in at work on time. Her toe hit a curb and her class notes, inked on pastel-colored notecards, went flying. Gethin jumped off a bench, gathered her notes, and asked two questions: "Where did you buy these notecards?" and "Is there any chance you might want my phone number?" After telling him where to find the cards, she scribbled his number only because he was staring at her.

A week later, after being dumped by the latest jerk in a long string, she had opened a bottle of wine before sending a text message. "Hi!" her message said. "Remember me? The ballet dancer from the parking lot?" She kept it vague, having forgotten his name. Right away, he sent back a smiling selfie in which he was holding a batch of colorful notecards. He had bought some for himself. Within a few weeks, she had grown fond of his creased jeans, his sharpened pencils, and his quiet way of asking permission, every time, before putting his hands on her, even for a hug. He understood that her skin hurt sometimes.

Three weeks later, she learned he was a recovering addict. By then, he had mastered the art of curling her toes and she had memorized the smell of him—laundry starch and his ever-present licorice seeds. Also, Serena had invited Rocky to live with them, which was a relief, to be liberated from her mother's claustrophobic apartment.

When her parents divorced, two months shy of Rocky's high-school graduation, they moved into separate studio apartments on opposite ends of town. Her graduation corsage, a pink carnation and baby's breath, hadn't even wilted by the time her mother brought home a guy in his thirties who had a greasy ponytail and no job, which meant he never left their shared room. Rocky had tried sleeping on her dad's couch a few nights, in his room above a dry-cleaning place, but he didn't have Wi-Fi. Also, he seemed so sad, staring at her all hangdog across a bowl of spaghetti. His droopy eyes had turned a washed-out shade of yellow from the vodka.

Beyond Rocky's room, Serena was singing a song about wanting somebody. She was asking them to show her the WAY-ay.

For sure, Serena had shown Rocky the way. The first night Rocky spent with Gethin, Serena had cooked salmon on a plank. There was homemade tartar sauce, a salad with warm goat cheese, mandarin orange slices, and almond slivers. Serena had boogied around the kitchen, listening to music. She said it was nice to have another woman around the place. As her contribution, Rocky bought groceries every other week. Sometimes, she wasn't sure who she needed more—Gethin or his sweet, strong sister.

After spreading a towel over the bed, Rocky eased herself onto it like someone stretching across hot coals. Blinking back fresh tears, she propped herself against the headboard, still naked, and reached for Gethin's laptop. Rocky had always been proud of her smooth café au lait–colored skin. In the waning light, it looked the way she felt—ashy and wilted by fatigue.

A few clicks on the laptop took her to a favorite selfie. She and Gethin had been at a park by the beach, under an oak tree draped with Spanish moss and flowering vines. Classic St. Augustine. Her head was turned toward him, leaning in, smiling. Gethin was smiling, too, but he was staring over the top of her head. What was he seeing, in the distance—a dolphin leaping through waves, a snake in a tree, or a girl in a bikini?

All the pretty girls on his Facebook page had freaked Rocky out at first, until she realized they were mostly New Age types who had discovered Gethin's rambling posts about snakes, music, and hiking. Another category of his online friends plastered his page with religious sayings infused with creepy sexual overtones. Rocky had drawn the line when a woman in India posted a topless selfie emblazoned with a crucifix emoji. Gethin gave Rocky his login after that. She deleted the post and blocked the woman. None of it had seemed to mean anything, though. Or had it? Maybe Gethin had moved to India with Gajri.

But no—he hadn't changed his password after he disappeared. If he had wanted to dump Rocky by running away, wouldn't he lock her out of his account? The messages in his inbox were the usual ones—group blasts about online music events, a couple of flirts from girls leaning into the camera lens. He had answered everyone in the same way: "Thanks! Celebrate nature!" Sometimes, he sent back a smiling snake emoji. Rocky didn't have the login to his email account. She couldn't check his text messages because his phone was missing. Her eyes fluttered shut.

Through the wall, the refrigerator door creaked. Pots and pans rattled. Was Serena making dinner while the Con Man was still in the house? Rocky leaned back on the bed with the laptop under one hand. Gethin or no Gethin, she would be safe. Serena wouldn't kick her out. Or would she? Exhaustion tugged at Rocky's eyelids.

"How are you feeling?" Serena's voice, sweet and full of light, floated under the door. It had a soft twang like a slice of lemon dipped in sugar, a sound that warmed Rocky's brain. She sat up, expecting to see Serena's face, wide-eyed, with her crazy curls going haywire, but the bedroom door remained shut. Serena was talking to Jazz.

"I wondered if you might want me to check his computer." Jazz was wondering, just like Gethin had wondered if Rocky might want his phone number, the day she dropped her schoolwork. Too much freaking wonderment and bogus New Age bullshit to go around. The similarities between Gethin and Jazz smacked her between the eyes. She propped herself up higher, wincing, and looked at her boyfriend's laptop again.

Forks clinked beyond the door. "You didn't rest very long," Serena said without answering his question. *Good*, Rocky thought, keeping two hands on the computer. Letting the Con Man check out Gethin's laptop seemed like the worst of all bad ideas.

"I'm like a dolphin," Jazz said, too loud. "I can only let one-half of my brain sleep at a time, or I'll suffocate."

The gas stove crackled and whooshed. "Interesting," Serena said.

"Even if he scrubbed his files, his hard drive would tell you if he looked up an address on Google Maps or something."

Bastard. Who did Jazz think he was, offering to snoop around on Gethin's computer? That was Rocky's job.

"What are you making?" His voice had moved farther into the kitchen, and it had gone soft. A garlic cloud rolled through the house—leftovers from the previous night's dinner, no doubt. Once again, Rocky opened Gethin's Facebook account, held her breath, and let it out. She wasn't sure if she should feel relieved or sad because it looked exactly the same. He was either deliberately ghosting her, or something bad had happened. Scrolling, she raced through photos of snakes, birds, flowers, and more snakes. His last status update said, "Be your binary self. I'll still admire you."

"I'm just heating up some organic free-range chicken and low-carb pasta," Serena said. "I didn't have lunch."

Nobody had responded to Gethin's pre-disappearance post, probably because they didn't know what the hell it meant, but Rocky knew. It was a dig—at her. They had gone to a party at her friend Yanni's duplex. Some of the math-club nerds were huffing on a hookah, crouched on milk crates in the yard, whispering. Gethin thought they were making fun of him. He started pacing and got too loud. He said he could beat anybody at chess. Everybody smiled little shaky smiles and they cut their eyes at each other or looked down at their feet. On the way home, Rocky had asked why he couldn't act normal for once. "I'm like a binary number," he had said, making no sense. "I've got two modes, zero and one. You always think I'm a zero, but my possibilities are infinite."

In the kitchen, a song began to play—another old tune about loving somebody when they're sixty-four. Serena and her moldy oldies from her dad's vinyl collection. At least Rocky couldn't hear Jazz yammering on about being a dolphin anymore. Had she been too hard on Gethin? He couldn't help being weird.

Most of the time, his weird habits were funny. At other times, they embarrassed her.

Still, she couldn't bear the thought of living alone. He and Serena were Rocky's only real family—a frayed tether, pinning her to a single fragile spot on the planet.

On Facebook, she started typing: "This is Gethin's girlfriend, Rocky. He's been missing since Monday. We've filed a police report. If anybody knows where he is, please send a message to this account."

While she waited for replies, she scanned his list of online friends. The music stopped. From the silence, Serena's voice rose. "You're welcome to stay for dinner."

Rocky let out a sound like a cat with a hairball and she sat up straighter, the better to bang her head against the wall. She would need to get the scammer out of the house. In certain strange ways, Serena the Savage fitness trainer was like a kid, too trusting.

When Rocky got to the J names, she clicked on Jasmine, Princess of Light. Despite the usual selfies in a bathroom mirror, Jasmine appeared to be no threat. She lived in Arkansas and had shared many photos of herself cuddling with a jowly man. After Jasmine, the next name on Gethin's list of friends made Rocky's fingers freeze and hover over the keyboard: Jazz E. Lightning Bolt.

"It's no trouble," Serena was saying. "I'll drive you back after we eat."

"I'm almost glad we crashed into each other." His voice sounded syrupy. "Maybe you needed a jolt, to bring color back into your aura."

There was no mistaking his photo. It was Jazz all right. He was friends with Gethin. His Facebook page was littered with mock-serious selfies—all of them outdoors. She slammed the laptop shut.

Serena's laugh grew louder, masking whatever Jazz was saying to her that was so damn funny. "Wait, wait, no," she said. "You'll electrocute us."

"It wouldn't actually kill us," Jazz said. "I read about a folk artist who used to stick forks in a car battery for inspiration."

From the closet, Rocky grabbed Gethin's white robe, wrapped the belt around her waist, and stomped into the kitchen. Serena was holding the toaster upside down, trying to shake a piece of her brick-like protein bread from the coils. Behind her, Jazz had a butter knife. His arms were looped around her and he kept making halfhearted jabs with the knife, as if he might pry the toast loose with it. *Genius.* Between laughs, Serena kept saying "stop" in a way that seemed to have the opposite meaning.

It made Rocky want to wretch.

She crossed the linoleum and pulled the toaster cord out of the wall. "You lied to us," she said, staring at Jazz. "You're friends with Gethin on Facebook."

Jazz pressed his hand against his chest and coughed like she had knocked the wind out of him. His eyes lost focus. All the red evaporated from Serena's face. She set the toaster down and moved a water glass onto the table.

"I've got so many online friends, I've nearly maxed out the limit," Jazz said. The bloodstained blue shirt looked limp and defeated. "I didn't put it all together before."

Rocky had him penned against the sink. "Right," she said, stretching the word.

Serena adjusted the collar of her workout shirt, blinking. "You know my brother?" The question spiraled up and wobbled, pitiful as a lost kitten.

"I only talked to him in person a few times. I mean—" Jazz rubbed his palms against his shorts. "I saw his photo in the other room and I realized he hasn't been posting anything, which is weird. Usually, he's posting, you know, twenty updates in a row."

"You know him," Rocky said and she looked at Serena, who was holding on to the back of a chair, hunched over. "I tried to warn you."

Serena straightened up and tucked her hair behind her ears. "I don't think I have any pictures of Gethin in the other room."

"This one was behind the futon." Jazz reached into his waistband and pulled out two pieces of paper. "And I found this receipt. It's from Sunday."

Rocky grabbed both items. The photo was torn in half—a binary fragment of Gethin's face, eyes wandering beyond the ragged edge of the image where she no longer existed. It was the same picture Rocky had seen a few minutes earlier on Facebook. She had printed it out at the drug store, thinking they could frame it. Gethin had ripped her out of the print. His hair, blowing around his shoulders, had obscured his frozen half-smile, stopped in time. Pain welled up behind Rocky's cheeks. In her other hand, the numbers on the receipts had gone blurry.

"He bought a coat," Jazz said.

Serena took the receipt and lifted it to eye level. "A parka? Why would anybody need a heavy coat in Florida?"

Jazz reached into his waistband again. "One more thing," he said. "I didn't want it to get sucked up in the vacuum cleaner."

The glint of gold made Rocky's legs buckle. She slid down the refrigerator. The skin on her back felt like it was peeling off. A refrigerator magnet shaped like an eagle crashed to the floor. Serena said, "Oh," and she reached for the bracelet, covering it with her hands. She kneeled beside Rocky so their foreheads touched. "We don't know," she said, whispering. "Honey, listen. It probably fell off his arm."

Rocky knew. He hadn't lost the bracelet she had given to him for their one-year anniversary—fourteen-karat gold, with their names inscribed on it along with a heart and a single word, "Always." He had loved the gift, showered with it, slept with it, made love with it. Gethin had left it behind on purpose.

In his frayed sneakers, Jazz shuffled farther away. "I'm sorry," he said. "I didn't mean to cause you any pain."

Serena stood up, straightening herself, finally taking charge—Serena the Savage, personal trainer to nobody famous. "I should drive you back now."

"I understand," he said.

Rocky didn't understand anything. On the beige linoleum,

black dots swirled and expanded. She swiped at her cheeks. Gethin had meant to leave her, had planned it. Feet *clip-clopped* around her. The door opened and closed, and she was alone.

5

Jaswinder "Jazz" McGinness

Jazz saw every detail—the blue veins on the back of Serena's hands where her skin had grown thin, the milky brown patch on her wrist, her cheeks, lean and sucked in while she drove under an onslaught of streetlights, strobing across the windshield. The flashing burned his eyes. Her silence stung his ears. He closed one eye and then the other, filtering. She slid her hands down the steering wheel, picked at the clasp on her bracelet, and let it clatter into a cup holder. "It's always falling off," she said, waving a hand over the lump of silver and turquoise.

Through the window, a stop sign rose like a red devil, mocking him. The car rolled around its face, which was obscured by graffiti—a word he couldn't decipher—and they crossed a path he knew well, a railroad track headed toward town. At the crossing, someone had painted black musical notes onto the white lines. The sequence created no tune in his head. He lowered his hand over the cup holder but didn't dare touch her jewelry without permission. "I could fix it," he said. "I used to take care of my mother's rings."

Serena leaned forward, peering left and right. Her tongue flicked around her bottom lip. "The lock's bent," she said. "Gethin's must have been broken too. That's probably why it was on the floor."

She hadn't asked Jazz not to touch it. He picked it up in slow motion, giving her a chance to stop him. The stones felt smooth and cool. He spread it across the dashboard, where she could see it. "I'm sure he'll be back soon."

Jazz only wanted her to feel better. He had no idea where Gethin had gone. They had never been close friends. In fact,

Jazz had been royally pissed off at Gethin. After meeting in math class, they had Facebook-friended each other. A day later, Jazz fell in love with Serena as soon as he saw her photo on Gethin's page, and especially after he watched all her TikTok videos. Gethin had refused to introduce her—said she only went out with bodybuilders or some nonsense like that, as if Jazz wasn't good enough. Earlier, when he saw her driving over the railroad tracks, he had wanted to get a better look. He sped up to catch her, took a shortcut through a neighborhood, and wound up skidding on a puddle, right into her car.

Serena spoke without turning her head, as if she might be talking to herself. "We didn't get to eat dinner. My muscles are starting to consume themselves. How about a taco? There's a place up ahead that only uses fresh stuff."

The car banged over a curb. A neon sombrero reflected off the window—purple, red, and yellow. A blast of cold air surged through the vents, making his arms tingle. His injured hands throbbed. Before he could answer, Serena was ordering three dinners at a drive-through window. She counted her change and handed him a paper sack that smelled of hot chicken. He fingered the top of the bag, which warmed his legs. The heat rocketed through his fingertips, into his chest. He felt small and embarrassed—speechless with gratitude.

She turned back onto the road. Jazz opened his mouth to say thank you, but she changed the subject. "Too much salt, but it's clean food," she said. "Where's your mother now?"

The question hooked him through the eyes, causing an explosion as bright as his mother's lost diamond. It had fallen from her engagement ring, which she still wore. She had remained locked in her bathroom crying for two days over the last bit of his father's love for her, lost. Jazz had found the stone buried in a maroon shag carpet. The gold in Meghna's teeth had flashed when she plucked it from his palm. Within days, she had the ring fixed. He didn't want to think about her tiny room at the state hospital, and anyway, Serena had troubles of her own. "Where are any of us, at any given point in time?" he said.

"Consciousness is an illusion. We have the here and the now, and we have love. That's all I know."

Serena glanced at him, half-smiling. "Okay, but where does she live?"

"Ocala."

Her eyebrows rose. Had Serena ever been to the state hospital? On his last visit, Meghna's room had been thick with the smells of baby powder, used diapers, and hair spray. Her black bobby pins were scattered across the windowsill. "A couple of hours southwest of here," she said.

"She moved there two years ago." Jazz peered into the sack, inhaling a cloud of warm salt. Usually, he tried to stick with vegetarian food, but he was hungry. "Some good kayaking over there, I heard. Spanish moss, green pools, and alligators lying around. I've got a student loan, so I stayed here to finish school."

At another crossing, Serena eased to a stop. A horn honked. "The scene of the crime," she said, barely audible. "Which way?"

"Right, then left."

The park rolled into view—a playground covered with rubber-tire mulch, palm trees with the coconuts hacked off, islands of tropical flowers, and finally, farther down the road, his picnic pavilion—white stucco with a bench out front, a colorless awning, and a single unisex bathroom. God willing, nobody had jacked his stuff from under an azalea bush. He had kept everything he loved, including a kid's cartoon toothbrush (a green muscle man), a comb, a dozen shirts and shorts, his favorite books *(Winnie the Pooh* and *Leaves of Grass),* and a photo of his mother—the items he had been able to fit into his backpack, a year after she was sent upstate and the landlord kicked Jazz out. No need to hang on to more than he could use in a week. Serena put the car into gear without killing the engine.

Jazz held up her bracelet. "I could tighten the clasp. I've got a little screwdriver over there with my things."

"I'd better get going." She reached out and closed her fist around the jewelry. "Hope you'll be okay."

"It would take maybe thirty seconds." Jazz remained motionless. He could feel her uncertainty vibrating between them. "I wish you'd let me repay you."

When she looked up, her face was twisted. "For what—injuring you?"

She was smiling, but not in a happy way. The veins in her neck looked like they might snap. "For dinner." He felt guilty, letting her think the accident had been her fault, but at that moment he couldn't bring himself to tell her he had chased her down. He didn't want her to think he was some kind of creepy stalker. It wasn't like he had been riding his bike around her house at night or anything. He happened to see her and he got too excited. That was all.

Her eyes clicked up and down the side of his head where it had hit the ground and scanned his knees and the bloody handprints on his shirt. She gave the bracelet back to him and popped her door open, talking at the same time. "I'll get your bike out."

"Thirty seconds," he said again. He raced for the pavilion, dropped their food on the picnic table, and scrambled for his backpack—still there. He plowed through his possessions until he found the tool, an inch-long screwdriver with a miniature prong, and he ran back to the car, where she was hoisting the bike. He took it from her and closed the hatch, relieved because his hands seemed to be working fine.

The bike wasn't as badly damaged as he had thought at first. Although the frame was bent, the tires hadn't popped. He could fix it. He had assembled the whole thing from spare parts in the first place. Serena looked at the food, eyes sagging. "My head feels light," she said.

He brushed some ants off the bench, taking care not to kill them. He was relieved when she sat down, and he parked beside her, in the glare of a yellow light. Serena spoke from behind her hand while chewing. "How long have you been here?"

Jazz inserted the screwdriver into the clasp, pleased with his surgical placement of the tool. "I've always felt that time is relative." She crunched into the taco again, and he gave the screw another turn. "You were joking with me earlier about your age, but when I look at you, I see you as a child, with a child's heart—a sad one, I have to say. Walt Whitman said age comes after us with grace, force, and fascination."

"Whitman, huh?" She had spread the meal out as if she meant to stay for a while, which made Jazz happy and eager to explain everything flying through his mind. He would have to remember not to talk too fast. People had told him that was a problem. "Do you ever just answer a question?"

The clasp opened and shut with a clean *click*. He tested it three times before sliding the bracelet across the table. "Six months, I think. Before that, I lived at the bicycle repair place where I worked. I've been in transition since my mother moved, but that's okay. Something big's about to happen."

"The Hacker's Challenge?"

"I could win it. I'm the best computer programmer in the country." He wanted to add, *People don't know what I'm capable of,* but he stopped himself. He didn't want to sound arrogant. He only wanted to tell the truth. "Guaranteed job placement. It's a big deal."

She had inhaled her taco so quickly, Jazz thought, the roof of her mouth was probably burning. She left her chips untouched. "How well did you know my brother? Tell me the truth."

Jazz opened his bag, made a little village with a paper napkin and the food—a taco, a small bag of chips, and a plastic container of salsa. No drink. He was thirsty. "I helped him out with a math problem in class one time. He seemed like a good guy. I sent him a friend request on Facebook. We said hello at school a few times. That was it. I think he went to Colorado."

The food sack crackled under her fingers, which were contracting into fists. "Why would you say that? What do you know?"

Jazz pulled a chip out of his mouth without eating it. He folded his hands together, pressed one thumb over the other, and held it down. He needed to be careful. He didn't want to get her hopes up. "It's only a guess. He bought the parka, and a few days ago, right before he stopped posting on Facebook, he added a link about some festival in Boulder."

"He posts a million stupid links to music festivals." She was talking too loudly. To Jazz, every word felt like a laceration. "He wouldn't leave to chase a rock band across the country."

"A lot of people are heading out there to work the weed farms." Jazz kept his tone low and slow, and he nibbled at a corn chip, trying to muffle the crunching sound. He wanted her to feel comfortable disagreeing with him. He was only casting lines to see if some truth might get stuck on one. Gethin could be anywhere. He could be dead. Jazz didn't know.

An ant trundled across her pinky finger. Serena sent it flying. "Gethin's been clean for more than a year."

Jazz chewed and swallowed a bite of taco. "I'm just trying to help you figure it out. I was thinking, you know, how people say Colorado's the latest Gold Rush."

The pale crepe under her eyes twitched. "He wouldn't do that to Rocky and me. He's got more personal discipline than that."

The wind kicked up. Jazz had to hold down his hair. He was losing her. "I'd like to think he went off on an adventure. If he didn't leave of his own free will, I mean—"

"You don't have to say it." She stood up and hiked a leg over the bench. "You either don't know what you're talking about, or you're scamming me, like Rocky said. I've got to go."

"Serena." He grabbed the edge of the table, squaring his shoulders. More than anything, he wanted to bring the light back into her eyes. "I want to offer you a visualization."

She scratched an eyebrow with her pointer finger. "What?"

"An image, for strength." Jazz was on his feet with his hands outstretched, moving forward. "A meditation." *Blue hydrangeas with pink and purple streaks through the petals, like the ones Serena had been holding in Gethin's online photo of his sister—the one that had made Jazz fall in love with her.*

"No, thanks," she said, and she was gone, sprinting across

the sandy playground border, cranking her car. The tires whined. The brake lights flashed. Under the yellow light, next to his uneaten food, her turquoise bracelet gleamed. He grabbed it, tried to chase after her, but stopped at the swing set. Her car was gone and his legs hurt.

He limped back to his spot and ate quickly, gulping chunks of meat, cheese, lettuce, and Serena's uneaten chips like a dog afraid of getting caught with its head in a pantry.

First things first. He would need a plan. Into his phone, he tapped three tasks:

Fix bike
Feed Inca the talking bird
Make Serena love me

He cleaned the table—brushed it with a bandanna, polished it until it was as close to glossy as the old wood would ever be, dragged the bench under an awning in case of rain, picked his teeth with a twig, and stared up at the sky. A sliver of sunlight was shrinking into the horizon, shooting pale orange stripes through a bruised cloud. Jazz dropped to his knees, cringed when his scraped skin hit the grass, and spread his arms wide, inhaling the smell of fresh mulch. "Thank you, thank you, thank you," he said, and he dictated a Facebook status update into his phone. "I am the light and the love, right here, right now, for you. If you agree, reply. If thy name is Gethin, show thyself."

His wounds weren't too bad, and the bike wasn't so heavy, after all, braced against his shoulder while he ran, laughing at the birds that seemed to be calling to him from the trees. He whistled. They whistled back, following him—he knew it. A brown one flapped along the telephone wires, calling his name: "Jazz E., Jazz E., Jazz E." Ahead of him, a cloud shaped like his own face expanded and split in two. With the bike on his back, he ran under the gap in the sky, into himself.

The bike shop was locked, as he had suspected it might be. The owner liked to drink beer with whatever guys showed up at sunset, but he tended to wrap it up well before dark. He would weave toward his truck and rattle off, wasted. Jazz had prayed for Bantam to be free—sober at last, or dead in his sleep. Either way seemed better than the life he was living. Bantam wasn't even his real name, which was Paul. He loved rooster fights, an activity Jazz couldn't bear to imagine. The old man never meant to fire Jazz. He had been drunk and angry, is all, yelling at Jazz to "stop talking a mile a minute about nonsense." Bantam had apparently felt guilty afterward, sent word through one of the guys to let Jazz know he could still pick up his mail and charge his phone there.

Jazz had permission, kind of, but no key. He hauled a ladder from the side of the blue stucco building and pulled himself up to the second-story window. Protected by shutters with a couple of slats missing, the window offered easy access. The upstairs loft was his favorite place, covered with plastic turf, throbbing under red Christmas tree lights. On a ledge overlooking the first floor, a gold-painted Buddha statue sat sentinel. The red light rolled over its crossed legs.

Downstairs, Inca the Toucan let out a riot of old-fashioned swearing, which he had learned from Bantam: "Suck it" was the bird's favorite, along with, "Shove it, shove it, shove it."

Inca was furious with hunger. Jazz unlocked the side door and rolled his broken bike through it, locked himself in, and went into the kitchenette where the old man kept his booze stash and whatever pitiful few bites of food he could hold down in a day. Sure enough, Jazz found a half-eaten cereal bar on the counter. He folded the wrapper over the open end, cracked it with his fist, and carried it out to Inca, who shrieked and stuck out his triangular tongue. "Cracker, cracker," the bird said. Jazz shoved the crumbled granola bar through the slats of Inca's cage. The bird had pecked himself mostly bald.

Finding spare bicycle parts would be no problem. Every corner of the shop was piled to the ceiling with broken or abandoned bicycles, orphaned tires, frames bent beyond all functioning, and handlebars stripped of their steering mechanisms.

Within a minute, Jazz had the wheels, the gear shift, and the pedals off his bike. Building something from nothing, whether it was a computer program, a poem, or a bike, made his blood throb so hard that his temples and wrists began to ache, but he couldn't slow down. He didn't want to stop.

The pain from his injuries had completely disappeared. His fingers flew—screwdriver, wrench, nut, bolt, *next!* While he worked, he talked to Inca, making up rap songs for the bird's benefit. The poor thing was lonely and underfed most of the time. In no time, Jazz had put purple handlebars onto a bright green frame with canary-yellow fenders. When he added a pink seat, Inca squawked. Jazz squawked back. "No, the colors don't match, but cut me some slack," he said, hammering out a toolbox rhythm for his rap song. "Gotta get my lady's brother back."

Inca hooked his talons around the cage, lifted his tail feathers, and splattered poop everywhere. "Shove it, shove it," he said. Jazz had never allowed children into the shop. Any parents who didn't know better than to bring Little Jimmy or Sally around Inca and Bantam were guided to a row of bikes for sale on the sidewalk. Jazz had trained himself to eat less after he got kicked out of his mother's apartment, and he had taught himself to talk less after getting fired. Maybe he could train Inca to say nicer things. "Pretty bird, pretty bird," he said. "I love you, I love you, I love you."

"Suck it," Inca said again.

Jazz finished remaking his bike, rode it around in a few test circles, and made another one from scraps. Again, he chose the brightest colors he could find—orange, teal, red, and chartreuse. He would leave the extra bike as a gift for Bantam, who had given him a prepaid phone for his birthday. When he was finished, he stood back and admired his work, but couldn't bear to stand still. Out loud, he said, "Drop and give me fifty," like a drill sergeant or Serena the Savage, and he laughed. The push-ups hurt his hands only slightly where the skin was raw under the gauze pads. He kept going to one hundred.

His hands were bleeding again after that, and Bantam's rags were greasy, but Jazz used one anyway, took a photo of the bike, and turned on the computer by the cash register. The old relic crackled and glowed like a nuclear reactor. Jazz jogged in place for maybe another five minutes while the screen came into focus one pixel at a time. He posted an image of the bike to the shop's website, gave it the title, "Jazz E. Frankenbike," and logged on to Facebook, still jogging.

On Gethin's page, his profile picture appeared—an extreme close-up that made his nose look like it was surging forward, about to break out of the computer and hit Jazz in the face, 3-D style. Jazz's reflection overlapped and merged with Gethin's picture—eyes wide, mouth pursed, nose to nose. Rocky had posted a sad message, asking for help. A few people had written surprised replies—"OMG!" and "what happened?" and "praying for you," but with no information. Going through Gethin's photos, Jazz found a folder full of shots from Boulder. They looked like internet grabs of landscapes where Gethin might like to go: a green mountain slope dotted with pink and yellow wildflowers, an empty ski lift on a snowy peak, and an outdoor amphitheater with a rock band on stage.

Next, Jazz clicked on Gethin's list of friends. Unexpectedly, a new photo popped up. In it, Gethin wore his trademark giant sunglasses, but also a purple and orange jester hat with spikes dangling in all directions. He had updated his profile photo. He was alive. Either that, or Rocky was online, sending Gethin a sarcastic message about being a joker.

As soon as it appeared, the image vanished like a jack-in-the-box, taunting Jazz. After that, the whole Facebook page went blank. Jazz tried logging on again, but the account seemed to be gone. The guy clearly wanted to be invisible, but why?

Jazz, on the other hand, had been trying for a year to escape the margins, to be seen and heard. Sometimes when he walked by a mother and child in the park, they didn't make eye contact; instead they looked straight through him like he was only some homeless, potentially dangerous ghost, out of focus and wavy around the edges. If anyone asked, he would identify himself as "Jazz in the park." No one ever did.

Without warning, the Tired Dragon slammed down on Jazz, sinking its fangs into his neck, making his head feel too heavy to hold up. Soon, he would lie down and sleep for a day. He punched the cash register open and dropped fifty cents into it, for the half-eaten granola bar. The drawer got stuck when he tried to close it. He had to slam it, which sent Bantam's mail tumbling to the floor. An envelope with Jazz's name on it landed between his feet. The return address had two snakes at the end of it. The letters in his father's name rattled up at him: Terence McGinness.

6

Fletch

His first night back on the beat, Fletch set two goals for himself—Number One, find Trina's stolen snakes and possibly her sister, although in his mind, that objective was secondary to protecting his friend's livelihood, and Number Two, don't kill anyone or be killed. The second goal was proving more difficult than it needed to be, thanks to his rookie partner, Officer Kala Foster. She was a passably good egg, fresh out of school, but with an unfortunate gung-ho streak. All afternoon, Foster had been trying too hard to impress him by pointing out jaywalkers and litterbugs she wanted to "collar." Every gum wad spitter prompted Foster to nail Fletch with a blank, expectant stare, which he tried his best to ignore while driving. Her hard, slightly green eyes and ruddy complexion made him think of two peas in a bowl of tomato soup.

On the patrol car's console, the radio squawked. "Car Four, Car Four, are you ten-eight?"

"Oh," Foster said, lunging for the microphone. "They're asking if we're available."

"Say no."

To his dismay, Fletch had been taken off desk duty the day after his breakfast with Trina Leigh Dean had caused him to be late for work. Two months and twenty-eight days shy of retirement, he was once again being forced to interact with tire thieves, public drunks, and lead-footed drivers. All his case files, including the missing person report on Gethin Jacobs, were handed off to another detective. Worse, Fletch had been assigned to train a newbie.

"But—" Foster lifted her thumb off the microphone's talk button. "We're in service."

"Our shift ends in thirty minutes."

The boss had said they were shorthanded and he needed another veteran on the streets. In a last-ditch effort to keep his desk job, Fletch had even played the crazy card—pointing out that he had been diagnosed with compassion fatigue. "Join the club," was all the boss said, hurling a set of car keys that Fletch fumbled to catch. "Don't shoot anybody." For reasons unknown but probably political, the boss had never liked Fletch. Farah, with her big heart, had come out of the closet, late in life, as a liberal—a risky maneuver in their little wedge of the world. Fletch didn't trust politicians of any stripe, had no particular views one way or the other, and had never felt compelled to defend his wife's Facebook memes to his jackass of a boss. In the car, Fletch gave Foster his best side-eye. "Come on," he said. "Don't leave Dispatch hanging. Tell them we're ten-six. We're busy."

Foster hesitated, apparently trying to decide whether Fletch was joking. He wasn't. "Ten-four," she said, fixing her frozen-pea eyes on Fletch. She never seemed to blink. "We're ten-eight, in service."

From Fletch, a heaving sigh turned into a groan followed by a growl.

Again, the radio buzzed. "Yeah, Car Four, we've got a downtown business owner reporting panhandlers, possible thirty-one, possible seventy-nine—animal control issue."

Foster stared at Fletch with her mouth hanging open.

"There's a drugged-out panhandler blocking a store," he said. "Great. Ask about that last part."

"Dispatch, this is Car Four," Foster began.

"They know we're Car Four," Fletch said. "What's the animal issue? I don't feel like getting dog bit."

Foster continued. "Um, Dispatch, what's the story on that animal issue?"

The radio clicked and the Dispatcher spoke over heavy static. "It's two people, white male and female, late teens or early twenties, south end of St. George Street at Cathedral. The female has a reptile, um, some kind of snake, wrapped around her neck. The business owner said they've been in the sun for a couple of hours. He's concerned about the snake's welfare."

Without taking his eyes off the road, Fletch grabbed the microphone out of Foster's hand. He responded while making a U-turn on King Street, pointing the car back downtown. "Copy that, Dispatch. Car Four is ten fifty-one."

Foster stared straight ahead. She seemed to be stuck to her seat. "We're in route?"

"Looks like." Maybe the snake was Unicorn, the stolen eastern indigo. Trina had given Fletch photos of Unicorn with his chopped-off tail, along with Banana Splits the yellow ball python, and Bandit, the eastern kingsnake that was black with gray bands.

There were no photos of Trina's sister, but Chelsea would be in her mid-fifties, probably with blond hair going gray. Fletch had looked Chelsea up in the system before all his cases got reassigned to an arrogant new detective named Turkington. Years earlier, Trina's sister had been hauled in on solicitation and misdemeanor drug charges, which were later dismissed due to sloppy police work. No known address. None of it surprised Fletch. Trina had shared Chelsea's sad story. Abused as a kid, growing up in a house of horrors, Chelsea couldn't connect with anyone even after being rescued by Trina's parents. "It was like the wires in her brain got crossed," was how Trina put it.

"It's good we finally got a call. I need to practice my training before I forget everything I was taught. I really want to do a good job. I've always wanted to be a police officer. Did I tell you my dad was a sergeant in Jacksonville before he retired?"

"You did," Fletch said. "A few times."

"It's just—" She was picking at the cuticle around her thumbnail, which looked like it got peeled on a regular basis. "I had a bad experience as a kid, picked up a coral snake by mistake, had to get the anti-venom and everything."

Fletch turned the car left, then right. "Why would you pick up a coral snake? Those things are venomous."

"I thought it was a scarlet kingsnake. They look so much

alike. We had kingsnakes in our yard. My brothers used to goof around with them all the time."

"Don't you know that rhyme about how to spot a coral snake—'red touch yellow, kill a fellow'?" Trina had taught Fletch the rhyme. She also said the rhyme doesn't always work because even snakes of the same species have all kinds of different colorations. Amateurs should avoid picking up snakes, period, Trina said.

"Yeah, later I learned it, and that rhyme about kingsnakes too. You know—'red touch black, friend of Jack,' but I was thirteen. I wanted a photo. I was always trying to show my dad I was as tough as my brothers, you know? Damn thing bit me. My hand swelled up and turned black." She held out her hand and stretched her fingers wide to show him a thick white scar down the side of her thumb and wrist. "I'm scared to death of snakes."

Fletch rolled the car onto a curb, called in his location, and unbuckled his seat belt. "Well, sorry about that, but you'll have to woman up, Foster. You can't show fear in this job."

"Maybe I could be an observer on this one? Without getting too close?" Her voice had gone thin. Her face was shining with perspiration. "Dang, I really wanted to help you make a collar today."

Fletch snort-laughed and popped his door open. "That's fine. Pretty sure I won't need to collar anybody. I'm going to have a nice chat with the stoners, get their IDs, and make them move along." Fletch also wanted to lay eyes on the snake, to make sure it didn't belong to Trina. If it did, the stoners were in for a big surprise.

On the pedestrian walkway, the smell of fudge and popcorn overwhelmed Fletch, who was hungry again, four hours after lunch. A man and a woman, both with phones pressed to their ears, pushed matching baby strollers along the row of shop windows. An off-rhythm tambourine rattled and the panhandlers came into view—a couple of scrawny young people, just like the Dispatcher had said. They were doing a loopy dance beside the churchyard's brick wall. Immediately, Fletch knew two things. First, the panhandlers were Brillo Pad, a.k.a. Harry Paddington, whose nickname referred to his wiry mat of red hair, and Melanie Balter, otherwise known as Melon Ball. Second, the snake was not one of Trina's missing reptiles.

"There it is," Foster said, stopping short and sounding breathless. "Don't worry, sir. I can definitely do this."

Fletch patted her shoulder. He could barely remember being Foster's age. He didn't even want to think about being that green. "Relax. See how it's all white? I can tell you from here, it's a leucistic ball python. I have a friend who runs a serpentarium out past the county line. I know a little bit about snakes."

"Is it—" Foster took a half-step sideways and back like she might break into a square dance. "Is it albino or something?"

"I don't think so. I'll bet its eyes are blue, not pink. Let's take a look."

"Is it venomous?"

"Totally harmless." Fletch started walking again while he sized up the situation. Where would Brillo Pad and Melon Ball have come up with the money to buy a blue-eyed leucistic ball python? Trina had eventually sold hers for five hundred dollars. "Come on, Foster. I'll do the talking. Think about what your dad would do."

When he spotted Fletch, Brillo Pad grabbed his money-begging hat off the ground and shoved it over his Raggedy Andy hair. It was a jester's cap made from purple and orange felt with four horns that curled toward his freckled neck, ending in gold jingle bells. Fletch fingered the snap on his gun holster. He knew all about the Jester Heads, an unarmed but unpredictable crew of petty thieves and meth addicts.

By the brick wall, Brillo Pad elbowed his girlfriend and nodded toward Fletch. Melon Ball dropped the tambourine onto a bench and rearranged the snake around her shoulders.

"Afternoon, officers," Brillo Pad said, raising a hand smeared with dirt, presumably from whatever patch of ground he had been sleeping on. Harry Paddington wasn't local and had no known family in the area. He had drifted south from upstate New York, got picked up once for shoplifting food. His face and neck were covered with scabs, no doubt from scratching at imaginary "meth mites." Where the girl had come from, Fletch didn't know. Maybe she had run away from home, or from a sex trafficker. She had been given a warning once before, for loitering and public intoxication. They were both nineteen, legally adults.

With his hands on his hips, Fletch looked them over without blinking or smiling. "How y'all doing?" He yelled the greeting to make sure they understood he couldn't care less how they were doing.

Melon Ball smiled, exposing dark, rotting teeth, another telltale sign of meth use. "We're just fine," she said, stretching the last word and twisting her torso back and forth, high and wild as a flapping power line.

Fletch eyeballed the distance between Brillo Pad and the seashell jewelry shop across the street. "Panhandling's illegal in St. Augustine," he said, pulling out his citation pad as if he might write them a ticket, although he planned to do no such thing. His purpose was to scare them off the street and find out where they got the snake. "So is obstructing a business."

The ball python lifted its weary-looking head, flicked its tongue, and pinned its sapphire eyes on Fletch. Brillo Pad ran his hands over the jester cap, tugging at the horns like he was styling his hair. "Actually, man, it's only illegal if we're within a hundred feet of a school, or twenty feet of a business, a cash machine, a trolley stop, or a public parking lot or restroom. We're at least thirty feet from that business over there."

In Fletch's hands, the citation pad felt like it was transforming into a hammer, rigid and lethal. Heat shot up his neck, inflaming his face, his scalp, and the back of his ears. "Is that right, Harry? You got a tape measure in your pocket?"

"Actually, yeah." Brillo Pad started digging in his grubby pants pocket. "I've got a tape measure app on my phone. I checked it out. I'll show you."

Melon Ball let out a sharp little laugh like a dagger. "You're wrong, officer," she said, singing it. "Brillo's right."

Fletch had his eyes on Brillo Pad's hand, which seemed to be emerging from his pocket at glacial speed. A surge of adrenaline rocketed through Fletch's chest and arms, all the way to his fingertips. When the kid's phone finally appeared, Fletch smacked it to the pavement. "Boy, don't ever point shit at me," he said, shouting so that he sprayed spit on the kid's face. "I don't care what your damn phone says."

"What the hell?" Brillo Pad said. He dropped to his knees and scrambled for the phone.

"Hey," the girl said. "Don't do that."

"Officer Jefferies," Foster said in a hoarse whisper. "Should I call for backup?"

Fletch wheeled on her. "Hell, no. I don't need backup for Mister Know-it-All."

"Sir," Foster said, barely audible above Fletch's ragged breathing, "maybe we should de-escalate the situation?"

Outside the seashell shop, a skinny teenager in a tie-dyed T-shirt was pointing his phone at Fletch like he was about to livestream some choice police brutality. Fletch fought with his heart rate, willing it to slow down. "Yeah, okay," he said, ducking his chin. "Good point."

"You almost broke my phone." Brillo Pad's complaint sounded like a four-year-old who had dropped his ice-cream cone.

"Let's try this again." Fletch was speaking lower and slower, following the approved de-escalation procedures to bring it down a notch. He exhaled and tried to lock eyes with the girl, but it wasn't easy. Her pupils kept swimming all over the place. "Melinda." He snapped his fingers to get her attention. "Melinda? Melinda, look at me. Where'd you get the snake?"

On the back of the poor snake's head, the girl planted a wet kiss. "Who? Snowflake? I'm babysitting her."

From the corner of his eye, Fletch noticed Foster shifting closer, snake phobia be damned, so she could position herself in front of Brillo Pad. Excellent police choreography on Foster's part. She was probably afraid Fletch would deck the kid. Fletch himself was scared of what he might do if the kid mouthed off again. "Who asked you to babysit this animal?"

Melon Ball closed her eyes and dropped her head back. "My friend."

"That right?" Fletch said. "And who's that?"

Brillo Pad hopped from foot to foot. "Shut up, Melly," he said. "You don't have to tell him our business."

Quick as a trigger, Foster flashed a palm, traffic cop-style, and she got right up in Brillo Pad's grill, forcing him to back up. "Hey now," she said, loud but calm. Fletch had to hand it to her. For someone who was five feet tall and maybe a hundred pounds, Foster had some game. "Watch yourself."

Exhaling hard through his nose, Fletch flipped open the citation book again. "That snake's been in the sun way too long. There's been a complaint. You might be more than twenty feet away from a business, but animal cruelty's against the law. Not to mention, I'll bet if I patted you down, I'd find a few items you wouldn't want me to find. I'm going to ask you one more time. Where'd you get the snake?"

"My friend with all the snakes," the girl said.

"Damn it, Mel," Brillo Pad said.

Wiggling triangles of silver light danced in front of Fletch's eyes. The laser light show was the usual precursor to a migraine and a sure sign his blood pressure was through the roof. "What's her name? You're telling me she asked you to look after her snake and you didn't steal it. I'm going to need a name and a phone number so I can check your facts." Fletch was betting Melon Ball's friend was named Chelsea—the abandoned child who had cigarette burns on her arms, as a kid, the day Trina's parents took her in. He doubted anyone could ever get Chelsea off the streets, but Trina was worried about her sister. Farah would have wanted Fletch to try.

"I don't know her name." Melon Ball stepped back and clutched the python, sounding as if she might cry. "We call her Snake Lady."

Brillo Pad blew wind. "Good one, Mel. You're such an idiot."

Fletch slapped the citation pad shut. "Where does she live?"

"I have no clue," the girl said. "She gave us five bucks to watch Snowflake. We'll get five more when she comes back."

"Where'd she go?"

Melon Ball said, "Daytona" at the same time that Brillo Pad said, "Jacksonville."

With his feet spread shoulder-width apart, Fletch rested one hand on his gun and looked down at them. They were both runts. He was doing his best to appear menacing, despite his middle-aged belly and male-pattern baldness. "Daytona or Jacksonville. Which is it?"

"Look, man," Brillo Pad said, opening his palms, "she didn't exactly tell us. She works up and down A1A, if you know what I mean."

Fletch did know. Trina's sister had a past charge for solicitation.

The radio on Foster's shoulder squawked. Dispatch wanted an update. "If they're not going to move along," Foster said to Fletch, "maybe we should write them up for being a public nuisance. What do you think, sir?"

She wasn't half-bad, for a rookie, but hauling the kids in would require calling animal welfare to take the ball python. Trina was a licensed wildlife rehabilitation specialist. He could take the python to Trina instead, or he could use the snake as bait to lure Chelsea. Fletch glared at Brillo Pad. "This snake needs to be in a cool, shady spot. It needs water and food. If you're living on the street, you can't take care of an animal like this. I'll need to seize it."

"Our friend's coming back tonight," Brillo Pad said before Melon Ball could pipe up. "We'll take care of it until then, I promise. I can call you later if you don't tell anybody. We need the other five bucks, man."

Fletch tore off a piece of the citation pad, wrote his phone number on it, and handed it to Brillo Pad. Working an informant was squarely in Fletch's wheelhouse. "Tell you what. If you get out of here and call me as soon as Snowflake's owner comes back, I won't write you up this time. I need to know her name and where she stays. Got it? If I see you tomorrow and you still have that snake, or if you don't call me, I'm going to be all over you. You'll be taking a ride to jail. Understand?"

"Yeah, okay," Brillo Pad said.

"There's a program at the church down the street," Fletch said, "the one with the big steeple. They could help you get clean. You ever want to go there, call me. I'll give you a ride." Farah had volunteered at the church before she got sick.

Brillo Pad cut his eyes sideways, grabbed Melon Ball's arm, and shuffled off.

Fletch waited for them to disappear at the end of St. George Street. The girl's hair was long and light brown, similar to Farah's hair color. For the millionth time, he missed his wife. He would miss her forever.

"Man," Foster said once they were alone. Her small green eyes were stretched wide. "I can't believe you knocked that phone out of his hand. Did you lose it, or what?"

Over Foster's shoulder, a vine of dark pink flowers curled over the brick wall around the churchyard. They reminded Fletch of his wedding day, when he and Farah stood under a trellis covered with ivy. "What if I did?" he said, feeling absent from himself. "You want to sue me? Get in line. Sometimes we have to get aggressive to make a point."

"Look, I can't wind up in a viral video." Foster's high, child-like voice had dropped an octave. "I'm not going to let that happen to me, just so we're clear."

With a strange detachment, Fletch looked at her, feeling geriatric. Two months and twenty-eight days. He only had to hang in there that long, until he could walk away and spend his hours honoring the life he had built with Farah. "Hey, you did good," Fletch said. "Your dad would be proud of you."

"I was scared." Her lips trembled, making her words wobble.

"Our shift's over." Fletch handed her the keys to the patrol car. The dancing pre-migraine aura had left him partially blind.

"We didn't kill anybody or get killed. Let's call it a good day."

Foster looked down at the keys. "I felt a little sick, being that close to a snake, and then you started going postal."

"I'm sorry." Fletch started walking and she followed. "Why don't you tell me more about your mom and dad and all those snake-crazy brothers?"

7

Serena

In the park near her house, Serena's arms burned with exertion. She had finished the fifth repetition on the pull-up bars when her father's old friend Kevin rolled up in his red convertible, causing her to curse under her breath. He called the car his "chick magnet," although he never managed to hang on to a girlfriend beyond the first date. Serena didn't feel like dealing with her father's long-ago military buddy. After her dad's death, Kevin had kept an eye on Serena over the years, tossing her a few bucks here and there. He deserved her respect, and yet, she resented his unsolicited lectures about duty, honor, and country, as if she didn't understand those principles as well or better than he did.

When she could no longer pretend she didn't see him striding across the grass, Serena dropped to the ground, peeled off her sweat-soaked workout gloves, and offered a feeble wave.

"Thought I'd find you here," he said. With each step, he kicked his heels outward, swaggering. He liked to think of himself as a cowboy, although he had never been on or near a horse, so far as she knew. Near the pull-up bars, a scraggly oak tree offered a small circle of shade. Kevin stepped under the branches and waved her over. Around his eyes, long feathery lines made him look older than sixty-something. "I have to say, you're prettier than a speckled bird dog."

"Hi, Uncle Kevin." He wasn't her uncle, but Serena had always called him that to honor his friendship with her dad. For the past year, Kevin had also been Gethin's designated mentor in his twelve-step drug recovery program. In theory, Gethin was supposed to check in with Kevin every day. Serena hoisted her right elbow behind her head, stretched one tricep, and switched arms. Beyond the park's grassy field, cars whizzed through a traffic light. "I have no idea what a speckled bird dog looks like, but thanks, I think."

"It's the prettiest type of hunting dog you ever saw." He hitched up his blue jeans, which had silver spangles running down the outside seams. His off-white shirt had silver snaps for buttons. When he smiled, a dent formed on one side of his cheek, from the time he got cut in a bar fight many years earlier, before he stopped drinking.

"I've seen zero hunting dogs in my life," she said. With the side of her fist, Serena chucked him on the shoulder. "Did you bejewel those pants all by yourself?"

Kevin looked down as if he had forgotten what he was wearing. "Standard issue. JCPenney department store. Ladies want to see a little pizzazz, am I right?"

Her hamstrings pinched when she pressed each knee to her chest. "They don't call you L. L. Cool K. for nothing," she said, repeating one of their standard jokes.

"That's right. Ladies Love Cool Kevin." At the intersection, a horn honked. Someone shouted. From a car window, a middle finger was flipped. Kevin glanced at the altercation and back at Serena. "I'm glad you're working off the stress, sweetheart. Any news about Gethin?"

As fast as she could, Serena started running in place. *One, two, three, four—hop, hop, hop, hop!* "No. I chased down a couple of leads today, filed a report with the police department yesterday."

"I know." Kevin rolled up his shirt sleeves. Both forearms were covered with curly gray shag. "I just came from there."

"Wait—Why? I didn't ask you to do that."

"You never have to ask for my help, honey."

Serena adjusted the straps of her workout bra, shook out her ankles, and planted her hands on her hips. "I know, but it's probably easiest if there's one point of contact with the police."

"Maybe." Kevin put his hands in his pockets and pulled his shoulders up to his ears, turning himself into a question mark.

"The fact of the matter is, as a man, I can get their attention better."

"What? But see, that's just—"

He clapped his hands and braced his palms against the swing set. The muscles in his forearms got bigger, reminding her of Popeye. "It blows me away every time, how much you resemble him," Kevin said, referring to Serena's father. "Only a whole lot better looking."

Tucking her hair behind her ear, Serena fought off the heat creeping under her skin. It wasn't embarrassment that made her flush. She was pissed. Who did he think he was? She knew he fixated on appearances because of all the time he had spent on his physical conditioning in the Army Reserve, but understanding his quirk didn't make it any less annoying. "Somebody close the window," she said, pretending to fan herself. "The wind's blowing."

Kevin stared at her a beat too long. "Are you scared Gethin's dead?"

Serena balanced her weight over both feet, replanting herself. Time had stopped since Gethin vanished. Three clients had left messages, wanting to schedule their fitness sessions. She hadn't called any of them back, which meant she wasn't making money during her brother's latest disappearing act. Serena shifted from side to side, not looking at Kevin, the same way Gethin did when he was nervous. As a kid, he had been unable to keep his legs from rattling the underside of his school desk. That got him sent to the principal, to the counselor's office, and finally, to a therapist on the top floor of a white brick building where Serena did her college homework while eavesdropping outside the door. The therapist had recited laundry lists of nouns, asking Gethin to respond to each of them. "Clown, football, washing machine," the therapist had said. "Funny, no, God," were Gethin's answers. He liked clowns and hated football as well as dirt of any kind.

"Serena?" Kevin said. "You still with me?"

Through the oak tree above her head, an arrow of sunlight

flickered and converged at the edge of her vision, forming a wavy halo around Kevin, who seemed to be short of breath, waiting. "I don't know if he's alive or dead."

Taking hold of her elbow, he guided her onto a bench and sat down beside her, so close she felt entombed by his cologne. "What's your weight these days, kid?"

The park, with its red-and-yellow jungle gym built on a mountain of mulch, seemed to be shrink-wrapping her. Sweat rolled nonstop down the sides of her face. Nearby, a trash can smelled of stale cigarette butts and dog poop. She rubbed her eyelids. "If you're asking how much I can bench press, more than you, old man."

Leaning back, Kevin ran both hands over his white hair, which was still thick and wavy. "Gethin talked about you all the time, you know."

Serena could only imagine Gethin's complaints about his old ball-and-chain sister and her many demands for him to finish school and find a job, any job. "Ha. No doubt. I'm sure he told you I'm an insufferable nag."

"Not at all." Kevin lowered his hands and looked at them. "He loves you."

"I don't think he would have said that. He would have said I dog him all the time about working hard and standing on his own two feet. Love wouldn't be the word."

"Well, you're wrong."

Serena let her lungs deflate. Breathing in and out felt too difficult. "He never uses the word love. I'm honestly not sure if he understands what it means. He might say he admires me."

Kevin's eyes bulged with a frank sadness. "Listen to me. Your brother loves you. Whether he uses that particular word or not, he does."

Serena unclenched her fingers and spoke into them. "You've been so kind to us since we lost Dad. I think you probably know my brother better than I do. Why would he have left us?"

"Honestly, it's a mystery to me." Kevin's knees cracked when he stood up and paced around the mulch-covered playground in his tricolor boots.

"Gethin's a mystery to most people. His brain doesn't work the same way as ours. I used to think, okay, maybe it's a little bit of autism, like the first doctor said, or maybe it's an anxiety disorder, or OCD, or ADHD. We don't know. The fact is, everybody's different in some way, right? But then, it was the drugs too."

"We've got to keep the faith." Kevin's voice churned like an old muffler scraping the road.

"I guess." The clichéd mantra made Serena want to gag. Such an easy, vacuous thing to say. Immediately, she was overwhelmed by guilt. Of all people, why would she direct her anger at Kevin? He had suffered from post-traumatic stress disorder after the missile attack that claimed her father's life. Even so, illness had never stopped him from helping Serena and Gethin, especially after their mother moved on. He had slipped her more than one rent check over the years.

"You know," he said. "Magic happens."

"So does shit," she said.

"Yeah, but"—he pulled a handkerchief from his pocket and mopped his face with it—"I've been sober a long time. Every day's a miracle."

"Amen."

"You said you were chasing down leads. What did you learn?"

In the bright sunlight, Serena's eyes watered. She fished in her backpack for a pair of scratched sunglasses she had found washed up on the beach. "He bought a winter coat at the Army-Navy store. The receipt was in the room where he studies. I talked to the store owner." Hazel. An old woman in fake pearls with eyebrows stenciled into a look of constant alarm. From a gold pack, Hazel had retrieved a brown cigarette, which she stuck behind her ear. *Real polite young fellow, said please and thank you, and so neat and clean,* was what Hazel had said when Serena pulled out Gethin's photo.

"Why would he have bought a coat?"

Inside the store, Serena's lungs had felt constricted by the murky air, the sardine-style clothing racks, glass cases full of knives, and flags covering every inch of wall space. "The store owner asked him that. Gethin said he wanted to look for snakes on Mount Rainier, in Washington State. Rubber boa snakes. He said somebody would pay him good money to count them."

"Rubber boa snakes?"

Under the tree, spots of light shifted over patches of dirt and grass. A used condom lay crumpled by a rock. Serena didn't understand why she felt so cold. She wrapped her arms around her chest. "You were in the same meetings with Gethin. Was he off the wagon?"

"I don't know." Kevin hiked one foot onto the bench, hugged his knee, and stretched his back. "He talks about being in the Recovering Bucket like it's a real place he'd never leave."

"He's got a thing about buckets. He does what they call obsessive-compulsive thinking. Everything has to be in its place, even the thoughts in his head."

"He's unique, that's for sure," Kevin said.

"I don't care what the doctors say, there's nothing fundamentally wrong with my brother, other than being a little bit different. He just needs to shape up and live right."

"I'm not sure I buy the whole Recovering Bucket thing," Kevin said. "An addiction can sneak up and bite us the minute we forget it's there. He didn't call for two weeks, didn't come to meetings, but I can't say for sure what was going on. He doesn't talk much about himself, as you know. He likes to talk about snakes."

"Oh yes. The snakes. He's crazy about them."

"I never quite got that, but hey, to each his own. I know this, he was avoiding me—not a good sign, generally."

"No," she said.

"I would have told you about him missing meetings, but I didn't want to worry you. He's a grown man. He's got to make his own choices and be accountable for them. I appreciated your call when he went missing."

Serena already regretted contacting Kevin. "Do you think he could be headed out west? I've never heard him talk about Mount Rainier before."

"That's a load of bullshit, if you ask me." Kevin switched legs and stretched himself in the opposite direction. "It sounds like geographic rehab—you know, when you try to run away from your problems, but you're the problem? Like, when I was in college and I got into trouble with a girl because I was blackout drunk."

Serena shifted on her seat. "What—what type of trouble?"

"To be honest"—his chest puffed up and he winked, classic Kevin—"the women chased after me when I was at Harvard. I had it going on, you know? Those were my salad days."

"Okay, that's not gross at all." It was weird how he managed to drop Harvard into every conversation, as if he wanted to remind her he still had worth in the world. He had been a lawyer before the bar fight and rehab, after which he had signed up with the Army Reserve. Pulled himself up by the bootstraps. Then came the missile attack that killed Serena's father, the post-traumatic stress disorder, an alcoholic relapse, and finally, recovery again. Serena admired his determination to improve himself and live clean.

"I decided my problems would be solved if I moved to California, but my problems only followed me there. After that, I moved to Florida. Guess what? My problems were waiting for me here too."

Across the yard, a young man in camouflage-patterned shorts pedaled by on a kid's bicycle. His knees cranked up and down, pointing left and right, and he was balancing a six-pack of Busch beer on his lap. A typical Florida scene. The bike's chain squeaked, reminding Serena of Gethin when he was fourteen. His legs had grown too fast. The rest of his body didn't catch up for a few more years. Maybe Jazz had been the same way as a kid—gangly, hyper, and lost. She wondered if Jazz was healing from the bicycle accident.

"Did Gethin want to run away from me?" Her words were

overpowered by a slight breeze that ruffled the contents of the trash can.

Kevin craned his neck, watching the bicyclist. "Listen to me," he said. "It wasn't your fault."

"Was it something between him and Rocky?"

"That's a possibility," Kevin said, rubbing the back of his ear with one finger. "Let's just say, there may have been a little trouble in paradise, you know?"

"I didn't know. I'm starting to get the idea. Why wouldn't he just go ahead and break up with her?"

"You'd have to ask Gethin."

Serena's mouth felt dry. She hauled a water bottle out of her backpack and drained it. Had she trapped her brother in a doomed relationship by offering Rocky a free room? "He could've told me if he wanted her to leave. I would have helped her find a safe place."

"When we get sober, we're about as mature as whenever we started using."

The bicyclist creaked off, sipping a beer. The first time she found cigarettes and cans of Budweiser in Gethin's sock drawer, he was in middle school. Serena was in her early twenties, finished with college, and working as an assistant at a gym. "Gethin was twelve," she said.

Behind Kevin's shoulders, a traffic light turned red. "I was trying to help him live a different kind of life, a clean life."

"You stopped by the police station." Serena cracked her knuckles. "Did you talk to that detective, Officer Jefferies? I wasn't too impressed by him."

"The case got reassigned to another cop, last name Turkington, sharp as a tack. He didn't have any leads yet, but he's working on it. He'll call me with any developments."

"Oh." She wanted to tell him again to butt out and let her deal with the police. Out of respect, she held her tongue.

"I wish I had something more to tell you," he said. "That's all I've got. I've been asking everybody who ever talked to him—not too many people. He posted a ton of stuff online, but in real life, as you know, he didn't have many friends."

"You want to hear something funny?" Serena's eyes filled. "I've been praying for him, like down on my knees, actually praying."

"Do whatever you have to do. Addiction kills. I knew another guy in the program who went missing one time. I wound up at his funeral three months later."

Serena leaned over her knees and expelled all the air from her lungs, stunned by the thought of burying her brother. At her father's funeral, the casket had remained closed. The funeral parlor stank of vanilla-scented candles. The old man had been a high-school football coach and an Army Reservist. "I'd fly to Washington State," she said, "but I wouldn't know where to start looking."

"He probably didn't even leave."

"How can you be so sure?"

"I used to be a lawyer, remember? I've read a lot of criminal cases, and this one's easy. All his old drug connections are here. Why would he leave them?"

Another bicyclist rolled into view. He was commandeering a red bike with antler-style handlebars. He kept his arms locked and his back rigid, the same as Gethin whenever he was feeling anxious. In the midday swelter, the cyclist wore a charcoal-colored coat with a fur-lined hood dangling down his back. A wool cap, sunglasses, and a thin beard covered most of his face. He was jamming to music; wires dangled from his ears. Serena stood up with her mouth open. "He's here."

Whatever Kevin said, Serena didn't hear it. She was running too fast. She didn't think about her abandoned backpack or her new sneakers, plowing through the dirt and grass. She sprinted at top speed and called his name. He never turned to look, but he stood up on the pedals and started moving faster. "Stop," she said. "Gethin. Stop."

In her ears, someone was breathing too hard. Was it her own panic, or Kevin, who had caught up with her? "Hey," he said, waving. "Stop. Hold up."

The red light blinked a maddening shade of green. The bicycle sailed under it and around the corner, out of sight. Serena bent over and braced her elbows against her thighs, breathing. Her knees gave way and she sat on a bald patch of dirt.

Kevin kneeled and wrapped an arm around her. "Whoa, there. That wasn't him. It's just that you miss him so much. You want to see him."

"It was Gethin." Serena scrambled to her feet and squirmed out from under his arm, but Kevin stood up and tugged her closer. She wondered if her side-boob would have little bruises on it later, from his fingertips being mashed into it. In the heat of the moment, he apparently didn't realize he was making too much contact.

"That guy didn't have a ponytail like Gethin."

"He was wearing a hat." Irritation made her voice thin and sharp. "Please. I'm okay. You can let me go of me."

With a final squeeze and a patronizing pat, Kevin released her. "Gethin doesn't have a beard and he's a lot taller."

Between her feet, the soil looked gray, as if it had been mixed with ashes. "He's here," she said again, although she wasn't so sure anymore. "I'm going to find him."

Kevin retrieved her belongings. "Until that happens," he said, easing the backpack over her shoulders as if it might be a velvet shawl, "take care of yourself first."

Serena straightened up. "You're right. Self-discipline's the key to self-preservation. Perseverance, Patience, and Pluck."

"The three P's."

"Thanks for the reminder," she said.

"You've got to keep it together for Rocky too. She's so young, such a pretty girl."

"I'm going to get through this the way my dad taught me."

"That's my girl." Kevin pulled out his car keys. "Why don't you head home and have a rest? Let me take a drive around town. I'll keep talking to folks. Call me later, or I'll call you."

8

Serena

Serena's hands kept shaking as she pulled papers, one after another, out of Gethin's desk while Rocky was at work. Most of it was nothing—school notes on blue index cards and grocery-store receipts with coupons on the back of them, arranged in paper-clipped stacks. Underneath it all, she found a letter, folded in thirds. She recognized the large, curling loops of Gethin's handwriting. "Dear Rocky," it began. "I write more effectively than I speak." Beside his math textbook, Serena's water bottle had left a ring of perspiration on the desk. She took another chug, dried the bottom of the bottle, and kept reading:

> It seems as though we're on two roads running in parallel lines. You're on one road, and I'm on the other. Serena taught me about metaphors, so I decided to use one here because this is a letter. I wish people would say what they mean without trying to trick the mind's eye, but I'm getting better at understanding the weird ways that other people speak. You said I'm an Ophidiomaniac. The word is incorrect in this context. Ophis means snake. A maniac is a crazy person. Loving snakes is not crazy. Snakes eat pests such as rats, although sometimes they might eat a bird, but I don't think that would be their first choice. There are at least forty-four native snake species in Florida, and only six of them are venomous. (I never had a venomous snake, and I would not want one because they might eat a bird.) I am not an Ophidiomaniac. I am a herper, as in herpetologist. To continue with my metaphor, we were

> on two roads that met each other at an intersection. That was some months ago. I can't picture how many months. I would have to look at a calendar and count them up. At any rate, the roads are parallel again. I hope you won't defriend me on Facebook because I still admire you, even if I'm not very good at showing it, but I can't stand the arguments over snakes anymore. There are at least thirty-eight species of nonvenomous native snakes in Florida. I don't even have one species.
>
> —With best regards, Gethin

Serena tucked the letter back into Gethin's drawer and toweled his desk to eliminate all traces of her investigation. He had wanted to break up with Rocky, a sweet kid who had become a dear friend to Serena.

The weight of Serena's sadness felt like it had settled in her bone marrow. She pictured taking a sunset run to get the endorphins flowing, but at the same time, she had another idea, a dark, forbidden one. It was as if the devil himself had flashed an image of Gethin and Rocky's secret stash of jelly beans and individually wrapped chocolates. Serena had spotted it once, hidden in a shoebox in their closet where she had been pillaging for coat hangers. She didn't say anything about it. Everybody has their Achilles heel. A year had gone by since Serena's last sugar overdose. Considering the circumstances, who could blame her for a brief lapse of personal discipline? Her brother was missing and possibly dead. Serena locked the bedroom door, tore open the closet, and sat on the floor with the shoebox full of candy.

With every mouthful, her memories intensified—her kid brother in a maroon cap and gown at his high-school graduation; reading a poem about their father at the funeral; dangling upside down from a tree branch, daring Serena to try and catch him. Serena separated the jelly beans by their color. She ate all the mouth-watering red ones first, followed by the tangy yellow ones.

The chocolates were wrapped in gold foil. Inside, each one was different, ranging from orange-flavored dark chocolate and white chocolate with macadamia nuts, to milk chocolate that tasted like raspberries. Serena bit into a caramel-filled treat that was shaped like a dove. Her mother had moved across the country, taking her menagerie of love birds with her. She had sent a letter a few years later, saying the air was better out west and Serena was all grown up and didn't need her anymore. Gethin, being in grade school at the time and a little bit different from the other kids, still needed his mother, but Gladys had glossed over that point. Serena was left to look after her brother.

Serena was pretty sure she knew the truth about why their mother left. Gladys had never forgiven Gethin for an accident that happened while she was sitting on the patio, staring into space, ignoring him. He may or may not have left the lid off one of his snake boxes. When she finally came back inside, Gethin's foot-long rat snake was curled and bulging on the bottom of the bird cage, which Gladys had left open. She threw herself onto the daybed with its white ruffles, wailing.

With a pang like an echo in her chest, Serena wondered if her mother would care about Gethin's disappearance. She wouldn't know what to do about it. Her last known address was somewhere near Austin. Serena had managed to call Gladys once or twice over the years. Her mother might have moved again, though. No, finding Gethin would be up to Serena.

The only remaining jelly beans were the bitter licorice ones, which Serena wouldn't eat on a dare. On the wood floor by the open closet, she arranged them into a dark serpentine shape. For a while, Gethin had wanted to become a herpetologist, or at least a reptile curator at the Alligator Farm—jobs that would require passing math at community college. He managed to get an internship at the farm once, but they let him go. From what Serena could piece together, the tourists had found Gethin odd. They were unnerved by his lengthy, one-sided conversations about snake tongues, snake digestive processes, and snake sex.

When Rocky moved in, Gethin had owned two snakes—a

shy green one and a tiny black one with an orange ring around its neck, both harmless. Rocky was afraid of them. She claimed to be allergic. Gethin gave in. He chose Rocky and gave his pets to a classmate who set them loose in a field. Gethin locked himself in his room for three days, mourning the loss. Serena had been locked in his room for thirty minutes, having herself a good old-fashioned pity party, but she was ready to get up and out. Empty gold wrappers littered the floor. Her fingers and teeth felt gummy.

Enough was enough.

With a groan of remorse, she gathered her garbage, stuffed the empty shoebox back into the closet, and made her way to the kitchen. Water, and lots of it, was the only way to dilute all the sugar in her bloodstream. She was standing at the sink, refilling her water bottle when a figure appeared through the window.

Jazz.

He stood inert on the sidewalk, less than a dozen feet away, on a spot where tree roots had caused the concrete to surge upward. Behind him, a green, yellow, and purple bicycle leaned against a tree. A bouquet of equally colorful balloons was tied to the bike's handlebars. Jazz didn't look like the same person from the day before. His hair had been washed—brushed, even—and he was wearing green shorts with a matching shirt and a red bandanna around his neck. The colors reminded Serena of an olive stuffed with pimento.

Staring, Serena took another long slug of water and assessed the threat level. Rocky had left to work a double shift at her waitress job, and Kevin, god bless his kind but patronizing old soul, had offered to roam the streets in search of Gethin. If necessary, Serena was sure she could flip Jazz over her shoulder. Despite the muscles, he was skinny. On a scale of one to ten, he represented a threat level of maybe four.

Why did he seem so different? The hair was the main thing, falling over his shoulders, backlit and auburn like some neo-freaking Fabio on the cover of a bodice-ripping romance novel. There was something about his silhouette, too—the unexpected width of his arms and shoulders, relative to the rest of him. She had to respect the work he had clearly put into his physique. In his creased shorts, he could have been a nerdy engineer with an over-eager expression. He no longer looked like the homeless, special-needs case Serena had loaded into her car. She opened the window and yelled. The slight blurring of her words, a result of her tongue going numb from all the jelly beans, should have alarmed her, but didn't.

"What you're doing here?" she yelled, accidentally reversing the verb and the pronoun. She tried again, more slowly. "What. Are. You. Doing. Here?"

He cupped his hands together and held them up without moving.

Serena drank more water, hoping to combat the effects of the junk food. After strictly avoiding carbohydrates for so long, she felt drunk from the sugar binge. Also, she had turned off the air conditioner and opened all the windows to save money. Sugary sweat was popping out of her pores. She wiped her face with a paper towel, laughed, and stuck her face against the ripped window screen. "Dog got your tongue?"

In her mind, Serena was flying over sugary treetops adorned with gumdrops.

Jazz didn't say anything. With one hand, he removed the balloons from the bicycle and walked closer.

The gauze pads on his hands looked ragged. His raw knees were red and bare, not yet scabbed over. "Are you hurt?"

"I didn't mean to scare you," he called out, finally.

Reaching under the sink, she hauled the first aid kit onto the counter and waved for him to come inside.

He shuffled up the driveway, sober faced. The balloons bumped and squeaked over his head. His other hand was cradled against his chest as if he might be bringing her an injured dove or a lightning bug in a jar. The polo shirt was stretched tight across his chest. The sleeves were hiked up over his arms where he was flexing. Serena let out a strange moaning sound that took her by surprise. Probably her stomach ached from all the sweets. She opened the door, trying to look dignified, or at least coherent.

Slowly, he raised one of his bandaged hands and opened it, revealing her turquoise bracelet, which looked shinier than she had ever seen it, strangely elegant for a piece of probably fake jewelry she had bought from a street vendor. The silver plating gleamed against his dingy gauze pads. "You forgot this," he said. "I started to leave it in your mailbox, but I was afraid somebody might steal it."

For a second, she imagined herself saying thank you, grabbing the bracelet, and closing the door, but he was clearly hungry for some sign of gratitude. Under his eyes, blue crescents of skin rippled. Serena opened the door wider. "Come in," she said. "I've been worried about you. What's with the balloons?"

"There was a birthday party at my park." His sneakers, stepping over the threshold, had dried blood on them. He had to lower the balloons to get them through the doorframe. "They forgot to take their balloons. I didn't want them to drift into the pond and choke all the turtles to death. I thought you might like them. I've been worried about you too."

Serena backed up, making way for him. He had an aggressively clean odor, like an open box of laundry detergent. No more trail funk, at least. She leaned against the refrigerator for balance. "Me? Why me, worried?"

At the table, he placed the bracelet beside a salt and pepper set shaped like a moon and star. He released the bouquet of balloons, letting it float upward until it bounced against the ceiling and the motionless fan. "Because of your brother."

Trying to look casual, she crossed one ankle over the other. "Today, I was thinking he's nearby, maybe St. Augustine." Her S's ran together.

Jazz lowered his chin and placed one hand on her waist as if he wanted to steady her. His face was so close, his freckles seemed to be performing a synchronized swimming act. She waited for him to release her. He didn't. "Are you okay?"

"I'm a tit bipsy," she said. "Ha! I mean, a bit tipsy." She let out a barking kind of laugh. When he only smiled, watching her, she stopped and massaged the food baby in her belly.

"Do you drink a lot?"

Her bottom lip had a crack in it. Serena licked it where it was stinging. "No!" She laughed, waving her hands to dismiss the idea. "No, no. I'm completely sober. Believe it or not, this is what happens to me when I eat a whole bag of jelly beans and a box of chocolates. It makes me loopy."

Jazz laughed. His mouth gaped open. "Come on. You? Serena the Savage? You're a fitness guru."

With her palms open, Serena twisted her shoulders into an apology. "Congratulations. You're witnessing a rare event," she said. "I'm usually a fiend about sticking to my nutrition regimen."

"You miss Gethin."

Such a simple statement, yet it ricocheted around her brain, down the back of her throat, fibrous and bitter. It turned into a silent howl that rattled her lungs, causing her blood to vibrate. She heard the sound of his name—*Gethin*—the way she had called for him earlier, the big-nosed baby she had cradled, the silent boy she chased across a moonlit field after he ran away at seven, the long-haired kid she had slapped after finding his sock-drawer stash that first time. Serena lowered the side of her face against Jazz's chest. His arms felt warm, but stiff, forming a precise circle around her back. His heart was beating a bongo rhythm in double time. "Wow, you smell good," she said. "You were so stinky the other day that Rocky and I had to keep the car windows rolled down."

"The community center's got a shower." He didn't move his hands or tighten his grip. "I put the bandages back on after I washed up."

Serena stepped back and tapped her fingertips against her cheeks, willing herself to focus. No more feeling sorry for herself. No more swooning in some random dude's arms. It was time for the three P's—Perseverance, Patience, and Pluck. "We need to change those pads."

His arms were still open. "I'm okay."

"You could get an infection." Inhaling hard, she opened the first aid kit and lined up gauze, iodine, and tape on the counter. The familiar movement of her hands brought a sharper edge to her thoughts. Instantly, she was in work mode, ready to assist any clients who took a tumble during a workout routine.

"Let me help." He peeled off the dirty bandages, tucked them into the trash can, and held his hands up, inspecting them. The wounds looked clean, but one of the abrasions had turned purple around the edges.

Over the sink, she saturated his hands with iodine. "Sorry you had to see me like this."

"Like what?" He turned his hands sideways, letting the orange liquid roll down the drain. "Like a goddess? Like the most beautiful woman who's ever been kind to me?"

She opened her mouth to make a wisecrack—*Right, I'm a supermodel with the Basket Case Agency*—but his eyes were stretched wide and honey-colored, like a sunflower she didn't want to crush with a sarcastic comeback. She taped up his hands again, put antibiotic ointment on his knees, and stowed everything back in the box. "I want to pay you," she said, clicking the lid shut, "for your broken bicycle."

"That's not necessary." He tugged at his shorts, straightening them around his waist, which caused his chest to expand. "I've already fixed it."

"By yourself?" She began wiping down the counter with a Clorox wipe, feeling steadier. "You're a talented guy, aren't you?"

"I try not to brag about it. People would be scared if they actually understood what I'm capable of. Most other guys are jealous of me."

Serena blinked. His jaw snapped shut, sober as a lead gate. He didn't seem to be joking, which could mean he was either crazy, or an arrogant jerk. Crazy, as in, *Likes to do jumping jacks naked* would be fine, and maybe a refreshing change from all the dull gym rats Serena had tended to date over the years. Crazy, as in, *Domestic hostage situations*—not so much. She dried her hands on a dish towel. "What's your story, exactly? Why are you homeless?"

"Is there anything that needs doing around here?" Of course, he wasn't going to answer her question. "I'm the best cook in the world. I'm an excellent housepainter. I could probably go pro, but I get bored too easily. I was in the gifted program in grade school. I could make you a cabinet for all your books if you brought me some wood. I know you'd want to get the sustainable kind. I can fix your plumbing better than anybody charging a hundred dollars an hour."

Maybe it was all the sugar, or the speed of his words machine-gunning her ear drums, but she couldn't keep track of his ideas. They seemed to be electrified—kinetic and forming dangerous arcs. His teeth flashed—white, straight, and clean—and he continued to talk. His fingers ran along the inside of her arm, up and down, slowly. Serena gripped his bicep, maybe to push him away, or to pull him closer. She hadn't decided. "I'm not sure if—"

"My father taught me to do all kinds of things. He's the inventor of the internet. Did I tell you that already? I won't mention his name because you'd know it, and then you'd want my autograph. Ha ha." *Up and down, up and down.* His fingers picked up speed, moving to the back of her neck, under her hair. "I haven't seen him for a long time, but I had a dream three years ago—the twenty-fourth of December, the night before Jesus was born—and I saw God. I woke up, and he was there, surrounded by an incredible light, and he said, 'Your father loves you. I love you.' I try to channel that love. I want to share that light with everybody I meet."

His mouth was pressed against her cheek before she had time to think, which was okay because otherwise she would have stopped him, and she hadn't been with a man in more than a year. That was a well-known fact. Rocky had made a running joke out of it—Serena should join a convent, she said. Even so, a homeless man who was acting manic? Maybe not the best choice.

Jazz moved on to Serena's lips. His mouth was full and warm, nothing like Eddie, who had dated Serena for three years before moving to Oregon for reasons never revealed. Eddie's lips had been thin—moist and cool to the touch, making them feel clammy. Jazz felt as warm as the hot-water bottles her father used to tuck under her toes, to keep them from freezing back when they lived in Pennsylvania.

The kiss continued, soft and full of heat. The circle of his arms no longer felt stiff, but she didn't feel trapped, either. His movements were fluid and reciprocal. She shifted her hands down the hard wings of his shoulder blades. He caressed her face. She pressed the small of his back closer to her sternum. He braced his hips against her belly. Her name rolled toward her in a whisper, from a great height or an impossible distance, faint at first, growing louder. She struggled to surface, blurry but conscious, eager to understand. *Serena. Serena.*

She opened her eyes. "Present."

His eyes were a pair of drills, fully open so that they looked mostly white—blinding. "Do you want to play with me?"

The watery sounds of their breathing stopped. She drew her arms back and pulled her shirt down. He was asking for consent. "Yes, probably, it's definitely time that I—but no. I'm scared."

"I would never hurt you."

"Why aren't you chasing somebody your own age?"

"You're only eight years older than me. I've had three girlfriends so far, all of them my age or a little bit younger. Terrible things happened. Let me tell you. My first girlfriend jumped into the river one night. She said I talked too much. Scared me to death, but she didn't get hurt, thank goodness. I never heard from her again. The next one snorted drugs, which I didn't realize until she held a gun to my head. I don't even know why she did that, but I got away when she fell asleep. The last one was a hoarder. She kept pet rats, but she didn't take care of them. I loved her, but she kicked me out. I hope the rats are okay."

An abandoned dish towel dangled over the faucet, limp. Serena picked it up, folded it, and held it against her stomach. It had been her mother's dish towel, depicting a bowl of fruit. The abandoned birthday party balloons had gotten trapped in a corner of the ceiling. Their multicolored ribbons dangled, limp. The door would need a new deadbolt in case Jazz ever tried to come back. "Another time, maybe," she said, after a long pause, during which she contemplated her long, loveless fate and all the years stretched before her, straight into the grave. "Rocky's coming home soon."

Jazz buttoned his collar and looked out the window. "There's a Jester Festival on Saturday. Would you like to go with me?"

She tucked the towel into a drawer, feeling naked and exhausted. "A jester what?"

His face had transformed back into a nerdy engineer with a smile that seemed smaller than before, but normal—safe. "It's like a clown party at the fairgrounds. It's free. We might see some people we know there."

"Gosh, I'm not sure." Serena pointed at the clock on the wall, a plastic cat with googly eyes and a long tail that switched back and forth. "I've got a million things to do."

Finally, Jazz moved toward the door. *Thank god.* "Understood, and don't worry, I won't try to pressure you. If you want to go out with me, or if you don't want to go out with me, that's your call. It's the lady's choice. That's how I roll. I respect women."

Serena opened the door. "Good to know."

He pushed a business card at her: *Jaswinder McGinness, Weird and Wired In.* "Call me, text me, or friend me on Facebook," he said.

"Thanks for bringing the bracelet back."

His feet moved out the door, but before she could close it, he stuck his head around the frame and kissed her cheek. "I love you," he said. "I love you, I love you."

"Ha." Serena froze.

"I love everybody."

"I'm glad you're feeling better." As soon as his hair had cleared the door, she bolted it shut, ran across the kitchen, and closed the window. From behind a palm tree, Jazz retrieved his multi-colored bicycle, waved, and pedaled off, having left the balloons with Serena.

9

Jazz

Cocooned in the silence of a chauffeured sedan, Jazz unfolded his father's letter—the one mailed to Bantam's bicycle repair shop—and he read it once again:

> Dear son, I need your help with a matter of great importance to me. It would be best if we could speak in person. I realize it's been some time since I last saw you, and I haven't heard from you. Every now and then, I wonder how you're doing, my clever boy. Is your hair still red like mine? Have your shoulders become as broad as mine? My assistant Bruno was able to find an address for you at a bicycle repair shop. I understand that you had worked there at some point. If this letter reaches you, please call me at your earliest opportunity. I will be working nearby for a brief period of time and I would like to see you while I'm here.
>
> —Dad / Terence McGinness

The letter included a phone number, which Bruno had answered. Between grunts, Bruno said only that he would pick Jazz up the next day. It happened to be a day when Jazz had no classes at school. He agreed to the meeting.

As a kid, Jazz had never been to any of his father's offices. Terence had traveled every week. By the time Jazz was ten, they had moved from Oakland, to Dallas, to Atlanta, to St. Augustine. He had usually been alone with his mother, Meghna, first in a brick house with columns and pink azalea bushes, and later, in a one-bedroom apartment, after his father left. Maybe his father needed a good programmer at his company. Probably he had heard how well Jazz was doing in school. Meghna always said Terence was possessed by demons, but she said that about the grocery-store clerk, the laundromat owner, and the landlord too. Jazz didn't blame his dad for leaving. By then, Meghna had taken to sleeping on the floor, curled up behind a cracked leather chair.

Jazz marveled at the softness of the leather inside his father's car as it hummed west on Interstate 4 toward Orlando. Below his shorts, the backs of his legs didn't even stick to the cool tan seat. The car was so quiet, Jazz felt suspended in time. He had tried talking to Bruno, told him the story of his birth, which his mother had described as magical, occurring on the night of a blue moon, and his plans to become a celebrated computer genius. Bruno never shifted his eyes off the road. After a while, he closed the window separating the front seat from the back, leaving Jazz to watch the world go by.

The car rolled toward Sanford, by a white-washed strip mall with a fitness center, and over a lake ringed with palm trees and scrub pines. A red-and-white Dairy Queen sign was followed by the golden arches of McDonald's. Jazz felt his stomach clench. He had run out of coupons for free smoothies at the 7-Eleven, and he had depleted his stockpile of cashews the night before. He could have had dinner at Serena's house, but she had kicked him out. *Beautiful Serena.*

By his elbow, a console held a green water bottle, a triangular red box of chocolate truffles, and breath mints, individually wrapped in crinkly blue foil. Jazz adjusted the fresh bandages on his hands and he tapped on the driver's window. Instantly, the dark glass hummed to half-mast. "Does this candy belong to anybody?"

In the rearview mirror, Bruno's eyebrows converged. "What?"

Jazz leaned forward, pressing his mouth into the small space above the glass. "Is this food for me?"

Bruno's eyes shifted back to the road. "Yeah, who else?"

The window zipped shut again. The car bumped onto a bridge. Three fountains exploded from the middle of a brown lake. Jazz stuffed the chocolates into his mouth two at a time. He tucked the wrappers into his backpack, careful not to litter his father's car. After drinking the water in one pull, he pocketed the breath mints for later.

He checked his phone. There were no responses to the Facebook posts about Gethin. Serena had not been in touch about the Jester Festival, either.

Beside the highway, another lake appeared. Bruno turned left, down a two-lane road flanked by single-story warehouses. Jazz moved to the edge of the seat. His father was bound to hug Jazz around the neck with one arm and fist bump his chin with the other, the way he used to do. The old man would be so happy to see Jazz.

The car rumbled over gravel, into a dirt lot, and around the back of a white building made of wavy tin that had gone rusty in spots. By a dumpster, Bruno parked and walked away without a word. Jazz hauled his backpack across the back seat and scrambled out. He moved quickly away from the stink of trash, toward the back door, which was unmarked and dented as if somebody had kicked it. Bruno punched a few numbers on a keypad. Probably his father was keeping a low profile on purpose. He liked to say it wasn't smart to show off.

A buzzer sounded. Jazz entered a hot black tunnel. The odor of sunbaked garbage seemed to have gotten trapped inside, maybe every time somebody opened the door. His shoes made a sucking sound against the concrete. As his eyes adjusted in the dim light, cigarette butts, bits of paper, and a bandage took shape on the floor.

A door opened and his father's silhouette appeared, backlit by a pale green light. Jazz had forgotten about his father's labored breathing and his bowed legs, which formed an almond-shaped gap between his knees. Terence parked his hands on his hips and spoke. The words curled themselves into fists, around and around the consonants as if they had never wanted to leave

Ireland in the first place. "Ah, there he is now, the prodigal son," he said. "What a chip off the old block you are. My god, but you're a handsome boy still. Bruno, you see my boy? You think the women stand a chance with this red devil around?"

"Good-looking kid," Bruno said before leaving the room.

Jazz felt his jaw lock with a kind of muscle memory from childhood—a tightening that grew more or less intense in relation to the volume of his father's voice. Being called a devil didn't sit well with Jazz. First of all, his hair was more auburn than red, and he was darker than Terence, more like his mother. Also, he tried to be good and kind. *Gentle.* In the arc of lime-colored light by the door, he placed a hand on his father's shoulder, noticing how it was lower than his own. Had the old man shrunk, or had Jazz grown taller? "How are you, Pitaji?" he said, using a term his mother had taught him, to show respect.

Terence yanked Jazz into his embrace so that their chests banged together. He pounded Jazz on the back, shoved him away, and turned toward his desk. "Ah, don't talk that Hindu crap," he said, dismissing Meghna's culture with a wave of his wrinkled hand. "I'm Papa or Dad or Hey You. I don't care what you call me, only today we'll speak English. People ask me, 'Are you Irish American?' What kind of shit question is that to ask a man on American soil? I'm an American citizen. That's all I am. Your mother never loved this country the way I do. So much catching up we have to do. Sit down, won't you? Don't act like you're a stranger. You're my son."

Jazz did as he was told. On cue, Terence grabbed Jazz around the neck. The fist bump seemed oddly limp—weaker than Jazz remembered it. "I was surprised to hear from you," Jazz said, taking in the metal desk covered with paper, the olive-green rotary phone, and a computer that had to be at least ten years old. "I was surprised you're working so close to where I live. How long have you been here?"

"I got here two weeks ago. I won't be staying long." Terence pulled open a drawer, popped a string of black licorice into his mouth, and offered one to Jazz. "This is a temporary shipping location only. I like to fly under the radar. You know what I mean, son? Showing off's for amateurs."

"I've heard you say that." The candy felt warm and slick to the touch. Jazz flicked his tongue against it and then balanced it on his thigh, out of sight. He wasn't hungry after all the chocolates, and the blackness of the candy string, which had already turned the old man's smile into the impenetrable maw of a pirate's cave, surely meant it was loaded with artificial ingredients. "I guess you have competitors looking over your shoulder all the time."

Terence waved the licorice rope and talked with his teeth full of black gum. "Competition, sure. You think Dell, Apple, and Microsoft don't want to know half of what I forget in a day? Did I tell you about the time I met Steve Jobs?"

Down the hall, the door buzzed again. "You did." Feet clopped by. "I remember that story, but you know what's funny? I can't remember the last time I saw you."

"I took you out for a meal—nice place in St. Augustine. You had the veal."

In the corner of the room, a shadow was vibrating near the edge of Jazz's vision. A tiny lizard had gotten trapped inside. It kept craning its neck in one direction and the next, trying to decide where to run. "That was my high-school graduation," Jazz said. He crept off his chair to scoop up the lizard, gently, with both hands. "I'm thirty-two now."

His father's symmetrical face contorted around his jaw where pockets of fat had begun to droop—a new feature since Jazz last saw him. "Put that down," Terence said. "You don't know where it's been."

The lizard kept tickling Jazz. It might have been a gecko or an anole—he could never tell the difference. He opened his fingers and let the poor thing skitter across the old man's desk. Under the green lamp, the lizard froze before darting down the side of the desk, where it spread its toe pads and hung on, panting. "We should put him outside," Jazz said. "He'll die in here with nothing to eat and no friends to talk to."

"You were always too tenderhearted." Terence tapped Jazz on the wrist where a bruise from the bicycle accident had turned a deep blue. "What happened to you?"

Jazz inspected his hands, turning them over as if they might belong to someone else. The gauze pads were still clean, thanks to Serena. He had stopped bleeding. He didn't plan to change the dressings until he saw her again, which might be on Saturday, the day of the Jester Festival, or it might be never. "Mom went to the hospital two years ago. I've been living outdoors, riding my bike to school. I had an accident. What happened to you?"

Until he stopped talking, Jazz didn't realize how hard he was breathing. Inside his brain, anger flipped a switch from green to red. The raspy rhythm of his lungs seemed to fill the room, expanding and contracting. The walls felt as though they were pulsing around him, like a heartbeat. He turned his back on Terence and pressed his injured palms against the wall, willing the concrete blocks to be still. Under his fingers, the wall could have been his father's arterial valve, opening and closing, insistent but fragile.

Anger seemed a logical response to being abandoned, and Jazz felt it, like an unexpected surge in the electrical current that was causing his legs to tremble—loss and isolation, poverty and being invisible, loneliness and his mother's mental illness, fear and rage. Jazz held his breath to slow it down and tame it until he felt a flood of love instead—divine energy!—crackling around his ears like a sparkling whip, urging him toward a higher purpose, connecting him to God and Serena. The energy infused the black opening where his father's smile had been, filling Jazz to the brim.

Turning anger into love was a trick Jazz had taught himself. It had kept him alive.

No words came, only his father's hand, lightly, against his back—a silent apology—and when Jazz turned, an embrace, long and slow so that he knew his Power had worked like an elixir from heaven, softening his father's heart. Jazz squeezed back. The pressure seemed to release a fine, bitter-smelling mist into the room. It leaked from his father's eyes, cleansing him. It was set free in the form of words, which were not, "I'm sorry," or, "I love you," but Jazz knew their meaning, nonetheless, because they were his words, which he had planted like seeds in his father's dirty mouth.

"You want to free that damn lizard?" Terence said, too loud. "Let's do it. Anyway, the walls have ears."

The energy turned and ran between them after that. Jazz could feel the Power—love, God, and light—pouring out of him in words that came nonstop as he collected the lizard and followed his father outside, relieved to escape the rotting lime-colored office, even if they were only moving toward a dumpster surrounded by gravel. Jazz eased the animal through a metal fence near a tree that might have been a large weed. "I'm the best computer programmer in my school," he said, trying to sound casual, and he loped toward the front of the building where he had seen a strip of grass. "Probably better than anyone you've ever met, Steve Jobs included. You can't imagine what I'm capable of. Pretty soon, I'm going to win the Hacker's Challenge. I bet you'll read about it in the papers."

At the road, Terence looked left and right, although the little warehouse was so far from the city, traffic seemed unlikely. Again, his father's hand landed on Jazz's back, urging him forward, across the road to a baseball field knee-deep in uncut grass. Jazz kept talking. He was going to start his own company, maybe go global, show the world what he could do once he finished school. The old man motioned toward a sunken bench—an old dugout for Little League players perhaps. Jazz ducked his head and entered the cool, gritty enclosure, which smelled flowery from all the vines hanging over the roof. White petals carpeted the dirt floor. The bench was thick with insects. Jazz bent down and blew on it, clearing a spot for himself without killing any ants or beetles.

His father sat down and cupped Jazz's face a little too tightly. Jazz wanted to say how much he had missed Terence, and how hard it had been for his mother, but the urgency in his father's eyes stopped him. All he could do was stare back at an older, angrier version of himself while Terence tightened his grip. "I worry," his father said, releasing Jazz.

At first, Jazz was afraid to ask the obvious question, but the silence burrowed holes into his eardrums, which were ringing. "About what?"

Terence smacked his hands against his thighs. "I don't want you to go loco." He shouted it, twirling a finger beside his temple. "Don't go crazy like your mother."

Stop talking nonsense about nothing all the time. How many people had said the same thing to Jazz? *Slow down! I can't keep up.* He couldn't be held responsible—wouldn't be!—by the limitations of other people who were too slow to understand all that he knew, had seen, had read about the world, about all the people and plants in it, the seen and everything that was continuously unseen by everyone but Jazz. Abruptly, the electrical river of love between Jazz and his father ran dry. "You wrote to me." Jazz licked his lips, longing for water. "You said it was important."

Leaning over his knees, Terence propped his fleshy jaw against his fists and stared across the tall grass. "I've missed you."

Meghna's spine had begun to curl after Terence stopped yelling at her to get off the bathroom floor and act like a normal human being. The day he left, the house had gone silent. As the weeks passed and Terence didn't return, Jazz imagined knobs forming on the back of his mother's neck, along her shoulder blades, until her whole body seemed to be permanently curled forward. She was like a dove protecting a clutch of unfertilized eggs that were destined to rot. Inside the dugout, a flower petal landed on the tip of Jazz's shoe. He picked it up and gave it a sniff. It smelled of nothingness—blank, white, and dead. He tossed it up and watched it spiral back to Earth. "I came all this way," Jazz said. "What did you want?"

The old man sat up straight. His palms were open on his lap.

"Things took a bad turn, you know? I did the best I could. I wanted to see you."

The red lights of the ambulance had washed the walls of his mother's small apartment, the night they wheeled her out with an oxygen mask that pressed a red ring around her mouth. "Why now?"

"I got a second chance."

In his chest, Jazz imagined the scratchy wings of an old peacock, lifting. His father needed him, was proud of him, and wanted him back. "What do you mean?"

"I met a woman."

Jazz jumped up and stretched out his arms. A smile expanded until he thought it might crack his face wide open. "I did too."

"Hey, hey." Terrence stuck out his hand and Jazz slapped it. "Eye of the tiger. Who's the unfortunate young lady?"

Pacing inside the dugout, back and forth like a dog going stir-crazy in a kennel, Jazz told his father about Serena's eyes—hazel, with lashes a shade darker than the rest of her hair!—and her smile, with the two canine teeth nearly overlapping the others, but not quite, and her way of helping anyone in need, without question, as if her compassion might be a blanket big enough to cover the whole state of Florida, and her brother, who had gone missing. "I'm going to find him," Jazz said. "Her heart's breaking, and, really, it's the least I can do."

"Why's that?"

"I ran into her car, on my bike. She thinks it was her fault, but it wasn't."

"Smart boy," Terence said. "Don't say a word."

The word *smart* felt like a dart, hitting Jazz in the chest. He didn't feel smart for lying to Serena. "I let her down and she doesn't even know it. I want to make it up to her—make it up to God because he spoke to me on the twenty-fourth of December one year, and I believe it's synchronicity that I'm here with you right now because you know what he said? He said, 'Your father loves you,' and I was given a gift, a calling, and now I have to—"

"Okay, okay, I get it. You're trying to win her over. Don't talk crazy, son." Again, Terence glanced over his shoulder, and straightened the collar of his shirt where a gold cross dangled in his gray chest hair. "So, look, Bruno can find anybody. He knows people."

Jazz pictured Bruno's thick eyebrows in the rearview mirror. "You mean, like a detective or a private investigator?"

Terence made a humming sound. "Maybe we could help each other here—a favor for a favor. My girl needs something too."

The dugout was sweltering. Inside his bloodstained sneakers, Jazz locked up his toes, which were vibrating like hummingbirds near a snake. Sweat rolled down his back. "I don't know many people," he said. "I guess I'm not as popular as Bruno."

His father said he needed a ring, and not some piece of crap from the corner jewelry store—his mother's wedding ring, made in Dublin from platinum, which nobody uses anymore, engraved with his family's coat of arms, now rotting in a lockbox at the looney bin with Meghna. "It belongs to me," he said, finally. "I want it back."

Meghna had been propped up in her bed the last time Jazz saw her, dopey on whatever drugs they were force-feeding her, by the window. Her left cheek and one arm had been sunburned from being left in the same spot every day, forgotten. Terence scratched the side of his nose, which was redder than his cheeks—nearly purple and shot through with spidery red lines. "You could ask her yourself," Jazz said. "Go see her. She'd like that."

"I did. You think I would've gone on a scavenger hunt to find you if I didn't already ride all the way to Ocala for no good reason?" His father was getting loud. The corners of his mouth were wet. Inside his ears, Jazz imagined a series of thin membranes shattering, one after another, into kaleidoscope patterns. "They wouldn't let me take what's mine. You're the next of kin, on their papers."

To keep the shrapnel inside his body from punching through

his rib cage, Jazz expanded his lungs, standing as straight and still as possible. "Right. Because you divorced her, but I'm still her son."

Terence slapped his ankle, cursed, and smeared the bloody remains of a mosquito onto the bench. "That ring came from the old country and ought to be passed down. My girl's expecting. I've got a second chance at having a real family."

"I see." Jazz did see, too: every cancerous freckle lurking in the sparse roots on the old man's thinning scalp, the bumpy wart on the back of his thumb, and the black candy still stuck between the yellow edges of his teeth. Terence was a demon, just as Meghna had said, and not a father at all. He never had been.

"I said I'd return the favor. You want to find your girlfriend's brother, or not?"

"Pretty sure I know where he is, or at least who he's hanging out with." Jazz wrapped his fingers around his throat to keep the bad taste out of his mouth. The Math Nerds at school had a theory that Gethin might be rolling with the Jester Heads. His father's bluster about finding Gethin was just that. Terence had never made good on any of his promises. Also, Jazz didn't want Bruno or his father anywhere near Serena. "What I could use is a job."

Terence leaned his head back against the dugout and stared at Jazz through half-closed eyes. He reached into a battered-looking wallet and handed three twenty-dollar bills to Jazz. "Could you use that?"

Hanging between them, the surface of the bills seemed to be undulating, as if insects were crawling on them. His father shoved the money forward again. Jazz reached for it with two fingers and stuffed the bills in his pocket, unfolded, without a word. He wasn't about to tell the old man about the entrance fee for the Hacker's Challenge and what sixty bucks would mean for his future.

"There's more where that came from." Terence stood up and put his hands on his hips. "Come back with my property and I'll give you five hundred."

"Can you help me get a job?"

"We'll see what the future holds. Bring my ring back."

Jazz turned his head so that he was looking at the old man through one eye. He nodded, turned, and sprinted for the road. No devil could ever make him steal his mother's ring. Jazz was stronger, faster, and tougher than every demon in the world, known and unknown. He ran to a stop sign and beyond it. He ran until he couldn't hear his father yelling anymore. He changed direction, legs pumping, and headed for the highway where he walked up the ramp, panting, and stuck out his thumb. His father's black sedan appeared with Bruno behind the wheel. At the same time, a silver pickup truck pulled into the emergency lane. Jazz ran to it and jumped in.

Serena needed him. He had to help her find Gethin.

10

Fletch

After receiving a breathless phone call from Brillo Pad, Fletch strolled through the police station at the end of his shift. His old chair, newly assigned to Detective Turkington, sat empty. Fletch's jackass of a boss was also nowhere to be seen, thank god. Across the room, a phone jangled. A large, shirtless man in handcuffs shouted behind thick glass. Something about his one phone call. On the other side of Turkington's cluttered desk, Fletch's old friend Ronnie Parson spoke without looking up from his paperwork.

"Turk's in Cancun," Parson said, flipping a page of whatever he was reading, "on his honeymoon."

"You're shitting me. Somebody married Turkington?"

Parson leaned lower over his file folder. The top of his freckled brown head gleamed under the fluorescent lights. "Stranger than fiction," he said.

Fletch looked down at his notepad, which was covered with scrawled, underlined notes from his conversation with Brillo Pad. "I got a lead on that missing person, Gethin Jacobs. Mind if I add it to the file before I forget all the details?"

Parson slapped his pen down and reared back, flashing a twisted smile so that Fletch knew what was coming. A gap between Parson's front teeth was large enough for him to poke the tip of his pink tongue through it, which he liked to do. "What am I? Your boss? What's next, you ask me permission to take a leak? Fletchie want his bot-bot?"

"What was that?" Fletch said with a fake gasp while he pointed across the room. "My interest! There it went."

Parson threw a paperclip at Fletch. "You have some nerve, showing up here after being banished to the streets."

After returning fire with the paperclip, Fletch sat down on his former chair. It creaked and wobbled to the right, the way it had done every morning for many years. He planted his feet and placed his fingertips on the cold edge of the desk, for balance. Instead of Farah's face smiling up from a gold frame, Fletch was confronted by various photos of Turkington curling weights in a tank top with sweat stains under the armpits, posing beside a bicycle with his junk bulging through what appeared to be ballet tights, and shirtless on a boat deck, hoisting a sail so that his hairy back made him look like a gorilla on steroids. No photos of the woman Turkington had just married. When Fletch looked up, Parson was staring at him. "What the hell is this?" Fletch said.

"There's also a mirror in his desk drawer," Parson said, "so he can admire his manly jawline on a regular basis."

Fletch was only a few years older than Parson. They had worked at the same desk for two decades. A pause containing a lifetime of whispered secrets passed between them. "How are you holding up?"

Parson swallowed a laugh and shook his head. "The guy's a legend in his own mind, you know? I've got three more years of this shit, man."

Mentioning his own retirement, which was less than three months away, struck Fletch as needlessly cruel. He clammed up, pulled a drawer open, and fished through Turkington's files until his fingers hit a folder labeled, *Jacobs, Gethin.* His left-handed writing jumped up from the papers, slanting backward. "Come to Papa," he said.

"You know, nowadays you can add information into something called a computer," Parson said. "I don't know if Turkington ever opens that drawer with your old paper files."

"Yeah, well," Fletch said, "maybe some things I don't want in the computer system."

"Where'd you get the lead?" Parson was hunched over his scaly elbows, leaning in, ready for whatever dirt Fletch had dug up. Fletch saw himself, sagging jowls and all, reflected in Parson's smudged eyeglasses. For years, reviewing leads had been one of their more enjoyable daily rituals.

The door to the holding room popped open. A young cop Fletch knew only as Pointy-Headed Guy was directing the shirtless man down the hall. The suspect, clearly a weightlifter, had stopped yelling in favor of crying in big, heaving sobs. On his back, a large blue tattoo of Jesus blessed three people who were slumped on the benches in the waiting area. A door clanged open and shut. "Remember Brillo Pad?" Fletch said.

"Little red-haired punk?"

"That's the one. He was panhandling downtown with his girlfriend and—get this—a snake and a tambourine."

"God, I love Florida," Parson said.

"Remember my friend who runs the serpentarium?"

"Trina? Of course, nice lady. My grandson did a summer camp with her."

Fletch smiled, remembering Parson's polite little grandson, J. J., who had survived a bout of leukemia as a toddler. Parson was too nice to mention that he and Trina had stood on either side of Fletch, holding him up at Farah's funeral. "Somebody stole three of Trina's snakes. She thinks her sister took them."

"Family feud?"

"Junkie," Fletch said.

"Such an old story."

"The sister was a foster kid, went through hell before Trina's family stepped in."

"That's sad." Parson clicked his pen over and over again, something he did whenever he was thinking hard. "So, did Brillo have one of Trina's snakes, or what?"

"No, it was a different kind, but I shook the tree and found out that, sure enough, Brillo got the snake from Trina's sister, Chelsea, and here's the kicker, she's rolling with Gethin Jacobs."

"Huh," Parson said. "The lost brother hooked up with Trina's lost sister?"

"Seems to be the case."

"You know where they are?"

"Dude said they're camping down by the river."

"Homeless City?"

"Sounds like," Fletch said.

"Good work, my man. That calls for snaps in a Z formation."

Fletch attempted to snap a Z shape in the air, but it wound up looking more like the number two. It was another one of Parson's running jokes. Fletch seemed to be incapable of completing the maneuver, but he always tried, for Parson's sake.

"And it's another fail," Parson said, imitating a sports announcer and the roar inside a football stadium. "And the crowd goes wild!"

"Are you done? I'm taking a stroll through Homeless City on Sunday morning while they're still passed out in their tent."

"You work on Sundays?" Parson set his overworked pen down and scowled at it as if it had done him wrong and he wanted to throw the book at it.

"Nope."

"Hey, pal, you shouldn't go down there by yourself. Some of the Jester Heads are living there. They've been a lot more volatile lately."

"I'll be fine. Who's working the Jester Festival this weekend?"

"Pointy-Headed Guy," Parson said.

"Tell him to look for our missing person, okay? There's a photo here."

"Will do. You think Trina's sister and your missing guy are part of that whole Jester Heads thing?"

"Don't know," Fletch said. "Brillo Pad sure looks the part."

Parson hesitated and leaned forward. "Listen, man," he said, "don't walk through Homeless City in your uniform."

"Oh, hell no," Fletch said. "I'm stupid, not crazy."

"Foreman?" Parson raised his palm, addressing an unseen juror. "What say you?"

Ignoring Parson, Fletch rifled through his missing person report until he found a phone number. "I want to call Gethin's sister, let her know what's going on." Fletch would tell Serena

Jacobs everything except for his belief that Chelsea had indeed stolen Trina's snakes. That didn't have anything to do with Serena's missing brother. "She was pretty torn up when I saw her."

"There's a new contact. Older guy, friend of the family, kind of full of himself. He wants to be the point man. I was sitting here when he talked to Turk. He said the sister's too upset to handle it. We should call him with any news."

Turning pages, Fletch found a foreign-looking note at the back of the folder. *Kevin Unreadable.* Apparently, Turkington had opened the old paper file at least once. His handwriting looked like somebody had given a ballpoint pen to a drunk chimpanzee. Fletch strained to read the phone number. He had to consult with Parson on whether the last digit was a nine or a four, but when he dialed the number, Kevin picked up on the second ring.

11

Serena

At the Jester Festival with Rocky and Kevin, Serena felt on edge, overstimulated by the jingle bells, penny whistles, and mandolin music. The humid air smelled greasy. Serena was keeping an eye out for Gethin, as instructed by the police officer who had called Kevin. She was also hoping she wouldn't run into Jazz, given that she had ignored his invitation to the festival.

"Tell me again," she said, glancing at Kevin. "Exactly what did Officer Jefferies say?"

Walking between Serena and Rocky with his chest puffed out, Kevin kept scanning the crowd without turning his head. He seemed to think he was All That, swaggering in his white dress shirt and a turquoise-studded string tie. "He said there'd be a big crowd here, so, um, we might want to, you know, look around for Gethin."

Rocky was stumbling along the mulch-covered path in her flip-flops, scowling. Serena had heard Rocky raiding the pantry at three in the morning, apparently unable to sleep, poor thing. "I guess we can't count on the cops to do their job," Rocky said. "We have to do it ourselves."

Kevin tapped Rocky's arm. "You'd better smile or your face will freeze that way," he said, grinning. Somehow, Serena avoided groaning out loud. Had he always been so patronizing, or was he getting worse with age?

Rocky stopped walking and looked around. On a stage rigged with colorful streamers, a man in green tights began spinning a series of plates on poles. A fiddle player launched into a breakneck solo, backed up by a boy in curly felt shoes who was blowing into a wooden flute. Across the grass, a pig turned on a spit. "White people are so freaking weird," Rocky said.

"What a beautiful day," Serena said. She was trying to change the subject and Rocky's mood, but her voice sounded like a flat tire. She smiled anyway, pointing at a clown on a unicycle. "Ha. Look at that. I'm glad we came. If nothing else, we're getting a little exercise, right?"

Rocky tugged on Kevin's string tie. "You look like Colonel Sanders."

A red patch broke out on Kevin's neck. He stepped back and straightened his collar. "Don't do that, please," he said.

With her pointer fingers, Serena smoothed her eyebrows. She was exhausted by the seemingly endless search for Gethin and the struggle to stay positive. "Colonel Sanders has a bow tie," she said, barely audible, "and a goatee."

"He wears a black string tied in a bow," Rocky said.

A young man with a neck tattoo and a small, stubble-covered head walked by, stopped, and did a double take.

"Hey, Serena the Savage," the man said, smiling behind two finger guns, which he pretended to shoot, complete with sound effects. His front teeth overlapped his bottom lip when he grinned.

Trying to smile, Serena flashed a peace sign. She didn't feel like a warrior and she didn't want to talk to anybody about the relative merits of pushups versus planks. "Thanks for watching," she said, turning her back on the fan.

Kevin wrapped an arm around Serena's shoulder, bodyguard-style. "You're exactly right," he said. "Whether we find Gethin or not, it's a nice day, and I thought some fresh air might do you some good."

"You're always looking out for us," Serena said. She raised an arm and stretched it behind her neck, forcing Kevin to let go.

"We can't stop living life," he said. "We've got to keep the faith. He'll be back."

"Of course." Serena adjusted the straps of her tank top, rubbed the back of her neck with both hands, and cracked her neck from side to side. "But didn't Jefferies have any other information at all? I mean, there are lots of events in St. Augustine all the time. Why this one?"

Kevin motioned toward a kiosk covered with cartoonish drawings of corn dogs, waffle fries, and lemonade. "Who's hungry?" he said.

"Not me." Rocky piped up before he had finished asking the question. She kept scratching the side of her neck and pulling at her blouse like she was uncomfortable in her own skin. Was she having another psoriasis outbreak? Maybe all the grease and salt in the air was irritating her skin.

"Oh, I can't eat that stuff," Serena said. "Do you have any idea how much mouse poop winds up in hot dogs?"

"Yummy," Rocky said.

Serena stopped in her tracks. "I feel like you're stalling," she said, staring at Kevin. "What aren't you telling us? What makes Jefferies think Gethin would be at the Jester Festival?"

Kevin looked down at his pointy boots. "Let me ask you something first." He tipped his head back to eyeball Rocky, who kept reaching under her shirt to scratch her shoulders. "Tell me the truth. Did Gethin relapse?"

Rocky didn't blink, but she waited a beat before answering. "How should I know?" she said. "Gethin never told any of us the truth."

Before Serena could say anything, Kevin piped up. "What do you mean he never told us the truth?"

Serena lowered her chin in Kevin's direction and gave him The Look. It was her trademark Serena the Savage look, the going-for-broke expression she unleashed in her videos before executing a series of insane ninja-style moves called Parkour. The look said, *Back off. I've got this.* Kevin was coming on way too strong. She took Rocky's hands in hers. "Honey," she said, whispering. "Why do you say that?"

"Because I honestly have no idea." Rocky smoothed Serena's hair where it had sprung free from a ponytail. "He was talking crazy all the time."

"Right, but—" Serena got a grip on Rocky's elbows and moved closer until their foreheads were nearly touching. She wished Kevin would take a hike and let her talk to Rocky in private. "Like how, exactly? Gethin always talks a little differently, whether he's high or not."

"He said he needed to be his true binary self."

Serena stepped back and shook her head. "But that's his usual thing. Stuff is either one way or the other, on or off. He doesn't understand if something's not black or white. That's how his brain works."

Kevin let out a heaving sigh. "Pardon me, ladies," he said, glancing at a row of Port-a-Potties across the field. "My prostate's the size of a baseball and nature's calling."

"Yuck," Rocky said. "Way too much information."

"Take your time," Serena said, maybe too quickly. "Don't hurry back."

After Kevin sprinted off, Serena guided Rocky under a tree where the heat was less intense. Maybe she would be less cranky in the shade. They were a few feet from a noisy food station. "Just breathe," Serena said, demonstrating.

Rocky's voice carried well, even over the sizzle of a deep fryer. "What's wrong with Gethin, anyway?" she said. "You told me he was different, no big deal, but obviously, whatever's wrong with him is a big deal. Then, I found out he was in drug rehab. I mean, what the hell?"

Two small girls ran by, squealing in black leotards and skirts made of pink and purple ribbons. "There's nothing fundamentally wrong with Gethin," Serena said, although she felt less certain of it every day. "He thinks in a different way. That's all. When he was little, one of the counselors thought it was ADHD. They put him on Ritalin."

"Sure, because little boys shouldn't be active, right? Maybe he was bored to death in school."

"Maybe," Serena said. "When he was little, maybe four or five, he would get so frustrated, he would scream and throw stuff around his room."

"He was a kid having a tantrum," Rocky said. "He's always been gentle with me."

"It was a little more complicated than that."

"You could have warned me about the drugs." Rocky's voice ricocheted across the lawn, making Serena cringe. "You invited me to come and live with you before you ever said a word about that. Did you need somebody to help take care of him?"

When Kevin reappeared, he was carrying a food box containing a corn dog, waffle fries, napkins, and an insane number of mayonnaise packets. "Hey, there," he said, once again inserting himself between Serena and Rocky. "No judgment if you decide you want some fries. Help yourselves."

Serena ignored Kevin. "Oh, are we playing this game now?" The tips of her ears felt like they were on fire. "Why didn't you tell me about the trouble between you and Gethin?"

"What are you talking about?" Rocky said.

"I found that letter he wrote," Serena said.

"Ladies," Kevin said, easing onto a bench with his box of junk food. "This is starting to remind me of the time I lived in a double-wide with my second ex-wife and my mother-in-law."

Rocky's head reared back. "What letter?"

"The one about Gethin being on a parallel road without his animals."

"You went through my private things?" Rocky snagged two of Kevin's waffle fries, stuffed both into her mouth, and kept talking. "That was months ago. We worked it out."

Serena squeezed her eyes shut for a second and blinked. "I don't think you did. You made him get rid of his pets. They were harmless. Maybe you thought he was okay again, but he wasn't."

"Are you actually saying it's my fault Gethin pulled a disappearing act? How exactly am I responsible for your brother being a snake freak and a junkie?"

"Whoa, now," Kevin said, half-laughing with a mouth full of waffle fries. "Let's bring it down a notch before we cause a scene."

Serena stepped back and smoothed her shirt. Kevin was right. People were staring. A man in a tan polo shirt pulled his son closer. A grandmother cut her eyes and pretended to fix her hair. Hands shaking, Serena sat down next to Kevin.

"Good girl," he said, patting Serena's knee. "Let's all calm down."

"Don't tell us to calm down," Rocky said. "I don't have to be quiet. I want to go home."

"Okay, that's it," Kevin said. He set the food box on the bench and brushed grease onto his pants. "Rocky, please take a seat. I'm going to tell you what I learned from Jefferies."

Serena stood up and offered her hand to Rocky, like an apology. "Actually, I think it would make us feel better to take a walk," she said. "I knew there was more to this."

"There's a lot more," Kevin said. "You're not going to like it, but you need to know."

12

Rocky

Even as her heart bolted from its gate, Rocky's feet felt paralyzed. The possibilities flashing through her brain went from bad to worse. Had Gethin moved out west? Was he in jail? Could he be in the hospital, unconscious and unable to call after being struck by a car? Had he jumped into a snake pit? Was he in the morgue?

She stumbled after Serena, who was obediently plodding behind Kevin, as usual. He led them behind a red barn, down a pine-straw path, beyond a circle of pine trees. On a concrete basketball court, a few kids were learning to ride unicycles of various sizes. A clown in a rainbow-colored wig pretended to chase the kids.

Kevin motioned toward a low brick wall under an oak tree. Once seated, he let his head dangle, limp, so that his white hair drooped. Rocky remained standing, with Serena. She didn't feel like sitting down for Kevin's lecture. "We still don't know much," he said. His voice sounded like water from a burst dam, rumbling from a distance, growing louder. "It's not a sure thing. This is all hearsay—that means secondhand information."

"We know what hearsay means," Rocky said. His constant mansplaining had gotten annoying. "What did the cop say?"

Kevin continued. "Nobody's checked it out yet. I want you to keep that in mind."

Serena pressed her hands into her eye sockets. "I asked you to let me talk to the police." Her voice sounded tiny, more like an apology than a complaint.

"Spit it out," Rocky said.

On the basketball court, a boy of eight or nine fell off his unicycle, onto his hip. He didn't cry, but he didn't get up. The clown loped over and looked at the kid. Kevin watched the drama for a half-second before speaking again. "There's a tent village off the Dixie Highway—"

"By the bridge," Rocky said, shifting her weight. "I've seen it from the road."

"Not that one. This place is farther south. It's a little spit of swamp down along the San Sebastian River, north of the old fishing pier. Some of the homeless folks are tucked in there."

The fallen boy was back on his feet, rearranging the purple spikes on his jester hat. The clown clapped and blew a whistle. Serena paced in a tight circle. "We have to go get him right now," she said.

"Hold on," Kevin said. "Jefferies didn't know for sure. He's going down there tomorrow. He said most of the folks should be holed up in their tents on a Sunday morning. It's a good time to look."

The greasy cardboard box on Kevin's lap made Rocky feel dizzy. "I've read about those places," she said. "They're full of mental patients who want to stab somebody."

"Most of them are harmless," Kevin said, straightening his tie. "We hear about somebody who goes on a shooting spree because they think aliens planted a chip in their brain. We're scared of anybody with a mental illness."

"Well, yeah," Rocky said.

"But the thing is, the head cases are a lot more likely to get attacked. They're different, right? They're at risk. I hear these kinds of stories all the time in my twelve-step meetings."

"Gethin's different," Rocky said. "He's in danger."

"I think so," Kevin said.

Serena stepped to one side, then the other, jumpy as a Texas line dancer. Again, the clown blew his whistle. All the kids hopped off their unicycles. The class was winding down. "Oh my god," she said. "I can't let Gethin get stabbed in some homeless camp. Why are we still here, if we know where he is?"

"The police aren't sure," Kevin said again. "It might be a dead end."

Gethin's tiny hand soaps—salvaged by Serena from hotels she had visited on her work trips—were piled in buckets and arranged in stacks under their bathroom sink: larger to smaller, smelling of vanilla and orange, wild ginger and honey. Every other Sunday, he opened a new one to replace the oatmeal, lavender, or lemon bar that had melted down to nothing in the shower. How was he surviving in a tent in the marsh? Where had he gone to wash and press creases into his jeans? If his fingernails had turned grubby, would Rocky want him back? She wasn't sure anymore, but he was a human being in trouble. "I'm with Serena," Rocky said. The bench, where she was gripping it, felt bumpy with fossilized gum wads. "I don't know what he's doing. Maybe I don't want to know, but he needs help. We're his family."

The silver spangles on Kevin's boots caught the light when he crossed his ankles. "It's not that simple. First of all, it was only a single lead that might be wrong. Jefferies said the informant's a kid—on drugs, of course. Not the most reliable source."

Serena stopped pacing. Her face had turned red. "Who cares? It's something."

Kevin stood and stuffed his hands in his pockets. "See, I hate this." His head was down, like somebody about to throw up over a ship railing. "But I'm a big believer in total honesty."

Nearby, the kids were dragging their unicycles off the court. The clown tugged off his wig, revealing a sweaty, mostly bald dome, which he mopped with a handkerchief. "You don't need to sugarcoat it," Serena said. "I get it. He's probably using drugs again. This isn't my first rodeo with Gethin."

"Maybe," Kevin said, "but here's the deal—"

Rocky crossed her arms and stuck her hands into her armpits. "The police are going to take him to jail if they find him." She spoke in a flat voice, picturing Gethin being handcuffed and stuffed into a cop car. "They know he would never hurt anybody, right?"

Serena stuck a finger under her necklace, rolled the tree

medallion back and forth, and looked at Kevin. "He can barely make eye contact with the cashier at the grocery store. He's got a whole mantra about having respect for living things. He's not a threat."

"No, I don't think anybody wants to take him to jail," Kevin said. "This is hard, but you should know the truth. The thing I want you to understand is, he's not alone."

Rocky reached for Serena's hand.

The point of Serena's chin dropped until it was nearly touching her neck. It made her look like a scared turtle. "Sure, that makes sense. He's got a buddy who's using drugs with him," Serena said.

"He's with a woman," Kevin said. "Chelsea."

"Another addict," Serena said. She was squeezing Rocky's hand too hard.

"Yeah, a pretty sad case from what Jefferies told me." Kevin looked at Rocky. "They're together. Do you understand?"

The ground gave way under the bench where Rocky was sitting. She pulled her hand free of Serena's grip.

Chelsea? Not Mehru, or Maryanne, or The Chosen One, or the Princess of Light, but somebody Rocky had never seen on his Facebook page. She had memorized all of them. No time passed. All time passed. A sound rose from her, muted and sharp at the same time, like an underwater scream—somebody's last words before drowning. What had she said? It didn't seem to be her voice. They were only words that echoed around her, full of horror and shadows, dogging her: "He's a stranger." He wasn't her partner. They weren't a family. He was only a man she had met by accident, a drug addict, a magnet for internet stalkers, a snake worshipper—a head case who might even be violent for all she knew.

A random variable.

"Is she giving him drugs?" Serena croaked out the question.

"I don't—I couldn't tell you," Kevin said. "Remember, we don't know what Gethin's doing, but this woman's been picked up for prostitution in the past."

Serena's eyes darted around. "But why did you think he might be here today?"

After a pause, Kevin pushed a breath out hard. "The word is, Chelsea may be selling snakes to the Jester Heads. That's a group of meth heads. They use snakes to guard their labs, or for entertainment. Maybe it's a sexual thing. The police aren't sure. Nobody really knows."

"Oh," Serena said. "My god."

Jester Heads? Rocky saw but didn't feel her feet hitting the dirt as she ran. Her knees pumped, up and down, back through the narrow passage between the barn and another building. Her shoulder slammed into someone's chest. Bells jingled. A line of green tights got in her way. She kept pitching forward, onto the gravel parking lot, into the street, across the railroad tracks until she no longer knew where she was. The place she had lived seemed suddenly foreign and full of danger.

13

Serena

Serena started running to catch up with Rocky, but Kevin stopped her. "Let me try talking to her," he said. "Meet me at the car."

Her ears burned with fury. Why was he so insistent on giving everyone their marching orders all the time? Did he think she was helpless? Incompetent? Both? Whatever the case, Serena felt too tired to argue. Instead, she nodded. Once he was out of sight, she sat down, tightened the laces of her sneakers, and wiped her face inside the collar of her shirt. For a minute, she held the fabric over her nose and breathed into it.

Is my brother on meth again? Kevin hadn't said it out loud. Rocky didn't seem to know if Gethin was using. Maybe Gethin had done something bad. As a grown-up, he had turned into a person who said *yes, please* and *thank you* with his eyes cast off to the side, always humble. Sure, he had lashed out a few times in his life, but that was way back in grade school. He had been in pain his whole life. Every day, he complained about some mysterious ache in his joints or under his skin. The aches seemed to pop up because he couldn't express his emotions. That was Serena's theory. Words had never come easily to him. Gethin didn't know how to tell Rocky the truth, so he wrote it down and she ignored him, tried to pretend he didn't mean what he meant.

Serena got it. Breaking up was hard to do, but Rocky would need to face the facts. Gethin would need to be a man, talk to Rocky directly, and come up with a compassionate separation plan whenever he reappeared—and he would have to come back. Serena couldn't bear the thought of her kid brother living in squalor with a drug addict.

On her feet again, Serena power-walked past the red barn and around a little visitor's center where the ground was covered with gravel chips. To get her heart pumping, she took the long way around the buildings, eager to distract herself with exercise. Straw and leaves crunched under her shoes. She wasn't in any hurry to get back into the car with Rocky and Kevin, assuming he had even managed to retrieve her. A rusted chain-link fence was buried in mud that gave way under her feet. She kept going, relieved to escape the noisy stage where jesters were still hopping from foot to foot, banging on tambourines, and tipping their mouths toward wooden flutes.

The fence made a loop around the park's periphery. She would feed Rocky, wait for her to head out to school or work, then drive to the old fishing pier in search of tents tucked into the marsh. Screw Kevin's warnings. He wasn't the boss of her. Serena would bring her brother home or get him to the hospital. By herself.

When she rounded a turn, Jazz was there, squatting over his ankles, gesturing like an orchestra conductor at two bleary-eyed kids—a red-haired boy and a skinny girl. Both of the kids were wearing multicolored jester hats.

Serena stopped in her tracks, partially hidden by the corner of a kiosk where an older couple in white aprons were selling dough cakes smothered with powdered sugar. The boy and girl were sitting cross-legged against the fence, taking it all in as if the world might be a giant slow-motion cartoon. Jazz was peppering them with loud questions. His voice sounded nothing like the whispery patter from her sugar-fueled make-out session with him.

"Don't give me that crap," he was saying. "I know about the Jester Heads thing. He posted a picture of himself in one of those hats. I know you've seen him. I'm only asking you where he's hanging out."

Laughter erupted from the red-haired boy—a sunburned guy of nineteen or twenty. His mouth, full of yellow teeth, was hanging half open. His eyes were half closed. "What the hell, man?" he said. "There's no Jester Heads thing. That would be so uncool to have a thing."

From inside the kiosk, a woman with oily cheeks wiped her sugary hands on her apron and smiled at Serena. "Watch out for the grease when it pops," she said. "Might want to step back, doll."

Serena moved behind a tree, a few feet away from the funnel-cake makers. The fence-sitters jostled against each other, grinning and bumping their shoulders together. "Hey, Brillo Pad, this guy's a head case," the girl said. She wore orange tights and a bikini halter top.

"Yeah," the guy said. "Stop harshing our mellow, Jazz. What happened to you, anyway? You used to be fun in math class with all your crazy questions. Now you want us to be narcs."

"Oh my god, yes," the girl said. She leaned onto all fours with her palms pressed into the dirt so that her nipples flashed. "Remember when he started talking about, like, arcs of light and a ladder with numbers on it?"

"Ha ha," the boy named Brillo Pad said. "Oh hell yeah. Classic. The stairway to heaven algorithm. The teacher looked like she might shit herself."

Jazz stood up and straightened his pants: the same green shorts he had worn to bring Serena's bracelet back. "Why am I acting like this?" Jazz was yelling. "Why are you acting like this? There's a guy in trouble. His sister's devastated. Can you understand?" His shouting boomeranged around the fairgrounds. On stage, a fiddle player craned her neck and stared.

"Quiet," Brillo said, uncrossing his legs. "I told you. I haven't seen him, man."

"I'm not asking you to sell him out." Jazz paced in front of them. "I'm asking you to act like my brothers and sisters. Yes, for your information, there are arcs of light all around us, all the time. I can see them. You don't see them because you're trapped in a blackness of your own design. I'm asking you to find the ladder, which, yes, can be expressed by numbers that are infinite, but, no, not beyond your comprehension if you open your minds to it."

His words banged together, faster and louder. At the edge of Serena's vision, a man in a dark blue uniform turned and headed for the fence. Serena stepped out from behind the tree.

"He's crazy, Brillo," the girl said, springing to her feet as the police officer approached. "Look, we don't need a scene."

"There's a higher consciousness that's available to you and to anybody who wants it, but it all starts with love—the love for another human being." Jazz yelled it at their backs as they jumped the fence, one at a time, and loped off toward the trees. His face had turned the color of a freckled carrot, blending with his auburn hair. "It starts with a spark of compassion that turns into an arc of light that leads to heaven and knows no end."

The policeman was young and had stiff-looking hair that had been styled into a brown point. Serena couldn't stop staring at his hand, which was resting on his holstered gun. He hadn't unclipped it. "Hey, now," he said, easing forward so that his shoes creaked. "What's the problem here, son?"

"I'm trying to find somebody," Jazz said. He seemed to be shaking, or vibrating—a wrecking ball, teetering on the edge. "I asked them a simple question. They refused to answer me."

"Maybe that's because you were hollering so loud," the cop said. The people around them had stopped walking, eating, and talking. Those who weren't openly staring were herding small children in the opposite direction. A small, pale woman swept her long ponytail over her shoulder and tugged at it, teeth clenched.

Lower your voice now, Serena thought, or maybe she prayed it. Jazz didn't pick up on her brain waves. He kept right on yelling.

"A woman's trying to find somebody who's missing," Jazz said, waving his arms. "Everybody's letting her down."

"Are you talking about a missing child?" The officer's hand remained coiled, motionless but tighter now, above his gun holster.

"No, he's a grown-up."

"I see." Slowly, the officer's hand fell to his side. "Has a police report been filed?"

Jazz stuck his fingers into his hair and tugged it outward. "I think so, but nobody's doing anything."

"What's the name of the missing person?"

"Gethin," Jazz said. "I don't know his last name."

"Gethin Jacobs," the police officer said. Serena sucked in a big breath and held it, listening hard. "I'm familiar with the case. I'm keeping an eye out for him today."

"Finally." Jazz clenched his head in his hands. "It's been like nobody cares."

"Tell me your name, please."

"Jazz McGinness, but what's that got to do with anything?" Again, his arms shot out, flailing.

"What's your relationship to Gethin Jacobs?"

Jazz punched the air with his fists. "Nobody's helping except me."

Under his uniform, the officer's chest expanded. He took a step backward. His hand drifted toward his belt, fingers dangling. Leather snapped. "Lower your arms, sir," he said.

"Nobody's helping because her voice has been silenced by the cosmic noise that's drowned out everything good in our society, but my voice is the voice of God, and it will be heard. Can you hear me now? Ha ha! Like in the cell phone commercial—can you hear me now? Get it?" Jazz threw his head back and roared like he might be watching the funniest slapstick comedy ever.

"I'm only going to tell you this once," the officer said. "You're disturbing the peace. You need to leave the fairgrounds. Now."

"Can you hear me now?" Jazz said again, still laughing.

Serena raced across the dirt, smiling her biggest smile. She had never met the pointy-haired officer before. "Oh, thank you, officer," she called, careful not to shout and startle him. "You found him. He slipped away when I wasn't looking. I'm so sorry."

With his head tipped to one side, the policeman cut his

eyes toward Serena and back to Jazz. "You know this person?"

"Jazz." Serena pecked him on the cheek, bird-like. "Yes, and I'm so glad you found my cousin. Thank you, thank you. He'll be fine in a minute. He needs his insulin shot. I shouldn't have let him eat that ice-cream cone. He's having a medical emergency, officer. I'll take him to the car now, give him his shot, and drive him home."

Jazz stared at Serena without blinking.

"I see," the policeman said. Again, his arm fell to his side. His name tag said, *Gibbons*.

Serena's arm shot out. She shook his hand, up and down, like she was pumping for water. "Officer Gibbons. I appreciate your help so much, and again, I'm really sorry about all this. I'm Gethin's sister. Jazz has been very worried about Gethin. He gets worked up when he's having an episode."

"A medical emergency, huh?" Gibbons stared at Serena like he was trying to figure out his next move. "Hey, have I seen you on TV?"

"Um, not on TV," Serena said. "I'm on TikTok and YouTube."

Gibbons grinned and pointed. "You're in all those fitness videos."

"Yep, that's me," she said. Occasionally, being recognized by a fan could be helpful. "I'll take him home right now, sir."

"Sounds like a good idea," Gibbons said.

"I'm trying my best." Shoulders at attention, she wrapped an arm around Jazz and shoved him so hard, he stumbled forward. *That's right, officer, I'm a responsible citizen, and I'm the caregiver of this poor, wayward soul.* "I might need to get him to the doctor. I'll remember to keep him away from the ice cream next time."

"You know, my brother-in-law's diabetic," Gibbons said. "He doesn't get agitated when he's having an episode. He gets sleepy, almost like he's drunk."

"That's probably next." Serena couldn't remember the symptoms of diabetes. She had never been a good liar; she was pretty sure a diabetic meltdown didn't involve outbursts of mania.

Gibbons paused, blinking. "Can you just confirm the name he gave me? I didn't look at his ID."

"It's Jazz." Serena smiled harder. "Jazz McGinness."

The officer looked Jazz up and down before turning back to Serena. "Okay," he said, finally. "Take good care of him. I'll keep looking for your brother."

"Thank you." Serena exhaled with relief. Jazz hadn't been shot. Her whole scalp was wet with perspiration. Jazz tried to hug her waist, but she took his hand instead and tugged him along, beyond the gawkers, past the gate and into the parking lot, where she turned and wrapped her arms around him. Waves of adrenaline rolled through her fingertips, onto his back.

He spoke into her hair. "You know I'm not diabetic, right?"

"I know."

"I'm not a little kid, either."

She stepped back and looked at him. Unlike Gethin, Jazz didn't have a problem with eye contact. He was staring burn holes through her. "There's something different about you."

"True." He reached for her hands.

"Anyway, thank you for trying to help me find Gethin."

He inspected the creases in her palms before kissing them. "You're very welcome."

"The police think Gethin's in a tent by the river. They're going to round him up tomorrow morning. It seems like he might be doing drugs. If he's holding, they could arrest him. I want to get there first."

"I'll go," he said. "Yes."

"I didn't ask you if—"

"Take me with you."

Across the parking lot, a car door opened. Kevin was folding Rocky into his car, one hand on her curled back, which looked limp. Kevin rubbed Rocky's neck, straightened up, and waved at Serena. "I could pick you up later tonight," she told Jazz.

"I'll be waiting." Jazz spoke without looking at Serena. He was watching Kevin walk around the car to reach the driver's seat. "You remember my spot?"

"I do."

"Jazz in the park," he said, snapping back to attention.

"Right."

His lips, pressed against her cheek, sent heat to her brain. He jogged off toward a line of bicycles. Serena walked slowly in the direction of the car, exhausted.

Kevin cranked the engine. "You ran into a friend," he said.

"Yes." The word sounded like a rock dropped on an ice field.

The car's air conditioner crackled.

The side of Rocky's head was mashed against the window. "I'm moving in with my dad," she said.

Serena reached over the front seat and touched Rocky's hair. "You're not going anywhere you don't want to go. Just breathe."

Rocky shrugged free and leaned forward, over her knees. Her gauzy blouse rose up, exposing an angry purple patch of skin. Clearly, the psoriasis was back, poor baby.

Kevin reached over and touched her bare skin. Rocky yelped and shoved his hand away, grimacing.

All curled up, she looked small; she was still so young. "You're going to be fine," Serena said. "We're going to get Gethin back, and he's going to be fine too. If he's using and he needs treatment, that's what we'll do." She thought about saying other things, but they all seemed too phony: *Tomorrow's another day. Stay in the moment. Don't lose faith.* Serena couldn't bear to vomit them out loud. For all she knew, Gethin might be sticking dirty needles into his arms.

"I'm due at work in three hours," Rocky said.

Kevin was hunched over the steering wheel. "I didn't mean for things to turn out this way," he mumbled. "Maybe I should have stayed out of it. I was trying to help."

He cranked the car and backed it up. The sedan lurched off the gravel lot, onto the paved road. They rode in silence for a while. He clicked on the blinker and forgot to turn it back off. Serena listened to the blinker tick. The pressure in her head was building up until she thought it might explode. "The good news is, Gethin's not dead," she said. "He's coming home. We'll need a plan to get him well, but everything's going to be okay."

Rocky spoke into her knees. "Nothing's ever going to be the same," she said. "Something's broken. I can't fix it."

14

Jazz

Jazz gripped the dashboard of Serena's car as it bumped off the road and onto a dirt path. The headlights illuminated a sandy trail that disappeared into a tangled mass of scrub pines and saw palmettos with their sword-like leaves sticking out in all directions. To Jazz, they were a bouquet of warning signs: TURN BACK!

He didn't care. For as long as he could remember, he had dreamed of having a woman in his life—first, his mother, who had gathered and lost strength like morning fog, only less predictable, and later, various women he had met on the bike path—the roller-skating divorced mom who jumped into the river one night to escape his nonstop talking, the addicted overweight jogger who held a gun to his head, and the trembling writer on her bench. She had been sweet, though a hoarder, and she'd met someone else. Unsolicited, he had given his phone number to many women. No one ever called. Only Serena with her tired, sudden smile and her eyes flashing sapphire had helped him. She had scooped him off the road, bandaged his wounds, bought him a meal, and made him feel like he wasn't invisible anymore.

Serena stopped the car. The headlights went black, and Jazz clicked on the camping lantern she had set on his lap. If he could, he would bring her all the light in the world: every glowing creature that ever lurked in a darkened tide pool, every drop of sunshine, a freight train full of still-sizzling comets, stars, and moonlight.

"Kevin told me not to come down here," she said for the fifth or sixth time since she had stopped for Jazz at the park.

"You need to find Gethin before that cop does," he said,

helping her finish the thought. "What he needs is a hospital, not jail."

Outside, grasshoppers, bullfrogs, and birds sounded an alarm amid the leaves and mud. Serena peered over the dashboard and into the murky jungle, extending her neck so that the lantern exposed several fine hairs under her chin. "If they're not planning to arrest him, I'm not sure why Kevin was trying to stop me from getting Gethin myself. I guess he thought it would be too dangerous for me."

"I'm here," Jazz said. "I won't let anyone hurt you."

She picked at the skin around her thumbnail. "I was twelve when Gethin was born. Our house had two little rooms with a heating vent on the floor that would leave grill marks on your stomach if you tripped over it. My dad was deployed a lot and my mom worked weird hours, so she set up the bassinet by my bed. He was this pink, gargoyle sort of thing with his scrunched-up face. Never stopped crying. I had to learn how to take care of him, you know?"

Her eyes were wet. Jazz repositioned the lantern so it wouldn't blind her. "It was like you had your own baby, but you were still a kid."

"I loved on that kid like you wouldn't believe. He was my little doll." In the white light, her smile looked translucent and slightly blue like snow nobody had trampled all over yet. "I dragged him everywhere."

"Sounds like a lot of work." He said it slowly, remembering his mother curled under her blanket every day after school. Jazz would open the curtains a fraction, gradually, in case she might be having one of her migraines. She liked tea with mint and sugar. "I had to take care of my mom. Where are your parents now?"

"The last I heard, my mom was in Texas, working on a farm. My dad got killed overseas. He was a soldier."

"What—what happened? Is that okay to ask?"

"It's okay. An Iraqi scud missile hit his barracks, 1991 in Saudi Arabia."

"I'm so sorry." Jazz could feel his heart breaking into several different pieces.

"He used to worry about Gethin," she said. "I told him nothing bad could ever happen to Gethin so long as I'm around."

"You're a good sister."

Serena brushed her lap. Cuticle flakes snowed onto the floor. "I had a job to do. Everybody in my family had a job to do. My dad was always off working. My mom had her hands full. After Dad died, she couldn't handle it anymore. There was nobody else to look after Gethin. Only me."

"And now he's all grown up, and you're still doing it."

Her mouth turned into a hard line. She pocketed her keys. "Looks like a path over there," she said.

Jazz opened the car door and eased a leg out. "Let me walk in front," he said. "There might be snakes." *Or shiv-wielding maniacs,* he thought.

"Or alligators," she said. Her laugh rattled, fragile as rice paper.

The gritty sand crunched under his shoes, which were bloodstained but still salvageable. He tried not to think about all the dust and sticky burrs getting embedded between the laces. He needed to be strong for Serena. How lucky had he been, how blessed to be thrown into her path? Walking the narrow trail, careful to keep his feet inside the lantern's circle, his life seemed to have been reduced to its most essential elements—condensed—strengthened into a single, potent mass of light around his feet. Behind him, Serena's breathing intensified, urging him on. He needed a woman he could protect, to complete him and love him as much as he loved her. Surely he had found the right one. The light radiated from his heart through the armored plate of his rib cage, encircling them. *I am the Maximum Champion,* he thought. *I am your shield, your light, and your path.*

The sandy lane widened. Behind a palm tree, the shadow of a tent emerged, surrounded by tin cans, empty bottles, and overturned crates beside a dead fire ring. The lantern lit up the nylon, exposing a dark figure inside: a man, log-like, lying down. He rolled over and held up a hand to shield his eyes as Jazz crouched down, peering through the unzipped flaps. From inside, a voice rumbled, "Who is it?"

Serena spoke through the opening. "We're not the police," she said, whispering. "I'm looking for my brother. I think he's in trouble."

The man fought off a blanket and poked his head out. His dark hair, shot through with white streaks, stood at attention like a frayed broom. His teeth were mostly obscured by a wet mustache that fluttered into his mouth when he spoke. "I don't know too many people," he said. "I keep to myself, but if somebody's in trouble, I always help out."

Jazz tried not to inhale the unflushed toilet smell coming from inside the tent. "Nice to meet you, sir," he said. "What's your name?"

"Julee," the man said. "Specialist Second Class, Army."

"Thank you for your service," Serena said. "My father was in the Army Reserves. I'm Serena. This is Jazz."

"We both have J names," Jazz said. "Easy to remember."

Serena stared at Jazz for a second before turning back to Julee. "Have you by any chance seen my brother? Young guy with long hair? His name's Gethin."

The man sucked on the ends of his mustache. "What'd he do?"

"Nothing," Serena said. "He's got—well, sort of like a medical problem. I need to get him home tonight. The police are going to be here tomorrow."

"Shit," Julee said, exhaling a boozy dagger of wind that nearly knocked Jazz out of his sneakers. "I'll have to clear out. We don't technically have permission to be here."

It made Jazz nervous, the way Serena kept inching closer to the old guy. "Julee," she said, "I'm worried. Do you know my brother?"

"Not really. He's not a talker."

"That's right," she said. "He's quiet, doesn't look at you when he talks. He's not quite the same as you and me."

"Oh, I think I know what you mean," Julee said. "It's like autism, right?"

"Not exactly. He doesn't really fit into any one category. He's just different. Tall, kind of skinny. You've met him, right?"

Jazz laid a hand on Serena's arm, trying to ease her back. She was coming on too strong. The old guy had recoiled. His dark eyes, so wide at first, had settled back into their sockets. He started tugging the tent flaps together, like a clam at low tide, shutting down. Jazz thought of his mother's eyes, which had been the same way the last time he saw her, under a mountain of blankets at the hospital. Winning the Hacker's Challenge would get him a job with Google or Apple. He would build a castle with a stone wall around it, turrets flying shimmery golden flags, and a bridge across the dunes, aromatic with cedar planks leading to the ocean. He would take care of his mother, Serena, Rocky, and even Gethin if they ever found the poor guy. Jazz could get a driver's license and a car. He could learn how to pilot a seaplane. He could build a community of love and light, right there in St. Augustine, Florida. First up, though, he would need a job.

Julee's waxy head disappeared behind green nylon and reappeared, luminous, gripping something pointed. Jazz sprang to his feet and took hold of Serena's shoulders, ready to pull her clear of any knives, but she reached out. "This was his," Julee said, gray teeth flashing behind the mustache.

"One of Gethin's pencils," she said.

Over Serena's shoulder, Jazz inspected the pencil. The letters of Gethin's name had been stamped in cursive letters along the side, between the pristine eraser and the writing tip.

Serena smiled up at Jazz. The lantern lit up the inside of her mouth. "These were a stocking stuffer last Christmas. He goes through about three a week. He won't use them if they get shorter than four inches long."

"That one's kind of short," Julee said. "Maybe why he didn't want it anymore."

"No," Serena said, handing the pencil back to Julee. "He liked you. He gave you a present."

Julee flipped one leg out of the tent and reached for a pair of battered boots. "Well, actually, it was his friend who gave it to me, not Gethin."

"His friend?"

"Chelsea." On his feet, Julee hitched up his pants. "She said it was payment for looking after her stuff while she's gone. Your brother was with her, but she did all the talking."

Again, Serena looked up at Jazz, mouth open to the sky. "He left?"

Jazz backed up, giving Julee enough space to buckle his belt. "Hey, man," Jazz said, "any idea where Gethin went?"

"We could make it worth your while," Serena said.

Her words seemed to curdle whatever was left of the yogurt Jazz had eaten for dinner the night before. He didn't like how Serena was talking to the old guy like somebody who had stopped by to mow her lawn for tip money.

"That's not necessary," Julee said, but Serena had already plucked a ten-dollar bill out of her pocket. The old man took it, quick as a snake's bite. "Chelsea wanted me to look after her pets while they're gone. She said I could eat whatever food's in there."

Serena asked again. "Where did they go?"

Julee dug the blackened tip of his boot into the sand and looked down at it. "She was going to work some beach gig—you know, planting signs everywhere, handing out water bottles and protein bars—stuff like that. Working the events that come through here is easy money. I didn't catch where."

Serena brushed imaginary sand off the seat of her pants. "We could look on the internet, I guess." She looked and sounded limp. Jazz had a sudden urge to give her mouth-to-soul resuscitation, to wrap his arms around her and squeeze her back to life. He had never been able to bring his mother back from her various head trips. Serena would be easier to revive.

She opened her hands. "Could we see their tent? Maybe they left an address?"

"Yeah, okay, you can see it," Julee said, pointing. "I can't let you take anything out of there. I promised my friend."

Jazz took Serena's hand. She passed the lantern off to Julee, who walked more heavily on one side, as if one leg might be longer than the other one, or maybe all the booze in his body had pooled in his left foot.

"So, tell me about Chelsea," Serena said. "What's her story?"

Julee tossed a tree limb off the path, which nearly caused him to topple over, and he made a noise halfway between a sigh and a song. "She's been around here as long as I have. We call her Camp Mama. She looks after everybody, especially the young ones who roll through here because some idiot said, 'Florida's warm and everybody can just live outdoors, no problem,' like living with all these mosquitoes and alligators is easy, you know? One thing about Chelsea, she can't stand to be alone, likes having somebody around all the time, especially after dark. She gets scared once the sun goes down."

Serena asked Julee if Chelsea had ever been his girlfriend. The question made Jazz cringe.

"I gave it a shot once," Julee said, "but she runs hot and cold. There's no in-between with Chelsea. She's had a tough life, makes her kind of hard to handle, but we're still friends."

Serena muttered something Jazz couldn't quite hear—something about Rocky and her broken heart.

They had reached a shelter closer to the river. Bigger than Julee's tent, Chelsea's home was tall enough for a person to walk straight into it without ducking, elaborately decorated with fluttering strips of red and purple fabric at every corner, staked under a pink tarp that billowed inside a ring of trees.

"I want to go inside," Serena said, too loud. "Please."

Julee rubbed his eyebrows, leaving a moon-shaped smudge on his forehead. "Chelsea would be upset if she knew. She's kind of picky about her stuff. When you don't have a lot, all of it matters. You won't take anything out of there, will you?"

"I'm just looking for clues." Serena had lowered her voice, thank goodness. Through the trees, a flashlight swept back and forth. By the river, somebody muttered. The water splashed. Jazz pulled Serena closer. "My brother needs a doctor," she said.

Bent over with one eye closed, Julee's mouth seemed to be frozen in a kind of half-smile. "Gethin's sick, is he?"

"He needs help," Serena said again. "Do you have any brothers or sisters?"

"I've got a big sister," Julee said. "Haven't seen her in twenty years. Pretty sure she doesn't give a shit where I am."

"I'm sorry to hear that," Serena said. "I care a lot about Gethin."

Jazz put his hand on the back of her hair. He was trying to release the built-up pressure in her skull. It didn't seem to be working.

Julee unzipped the tent, handed the lantern to Jazz, and pulled a cigarette from his shirt pocket. "Help yourself," he said. "I'll stay here and have a smoke."

In the lantern light, the inside of Chelsea's tent reminded Jazz of a dental photo: A bloody sort of pink shade with purple scarves and paisley-patterned tapestries wound around the metal poles. A green blanket covered a mattress on the floor, where the ground crackled under his shoes. Patchwork quilts covered every surface. Cans of corn and peas and bags of rice dangled from a fishnet rigged into the corner. Three translucent plastic tubs were stacked beneath it. Behind the mattress, a jester's hat sat on a box labeled, *St. Augustine Distillery.* No huge surprise there. All the druggies at school were into the Jester Heads scene. Those guys at the festival had been such assholes. They could have told him where to look for Chelsea, the homeless Camp Mama with a sad history and a drug habit.

By the door, Jazz watched over Serena's shoulder as she picked up a large silver crucifix that was holding down a few pieces of paper—three grocery store receipts, a hand-drawn map to a fishing spot, and a picture of two people drawn in pencil. A man and a woman were on the beach with their faces turned in opposite directions. "Gethin did this," she said. "It looks like Rocky's photo of them."

At the edge of his vision, a shadow flickered. The green blanket rustled and bulged like a beating heart. "What in the heaven?" Jazz said.

Outside, a woman's voice called out, "Y'all shouldn't be in there."

"Pipe down, Bea," Julee said on the other side of the tent flap. "It's only a girl looking for her brother."

"Chelsea told me to watch after her babies," Bea said, sounding closer and louder.

"She didn't tell you any such thing," Julee said. "You don't even like each other."

Inside the tent, the blanket moved again. A bright green snake rolled onto the floor. Jazz jumped back. "Oh, hello," he said. "Namaste."

Serena reached down and grabbed the snake by its neck.

"Put that thing back under the blanket," Jazz said. "We don't know if it's venomous or not. Throw it."

"It's a sweet little green snake," she said, holding it up, turning its head one way and then the other. The snake opened its mouth, coiling its slender tail around her hand. "Gethin used to have one. See how its scales are rough-looking? That's why it's called a rough green snake."

"Please don't let it bite you." Jazz couldn't keep his knees locked. His legs wanted to jump as high as possible, up and out.

"It's nonvenomous." She strolled across the mattress with the snake, dropped it into a plastic tub, and looked around with her hands on her hips. "This is starting to make a lot more sense now."

Jazz didn't know what she meant. He would ask her later, after he was out of the tent with its piles of muddy quilts, mysterious tubs, and rusty cans. He ducked under the tent flaps and held them open for her, watching the blankets to make sure they didn't move again. Serena poked her head out. Finally, her feet cleared the threshold. Jazz dropped the lantern and zipped the tent flaps so hard he nearly ripped them.

Julee was smiling through a belch of cigarette smoke. The

cloud expanded and separated to form a coiled crown around his head.

"There's a snake in there," Jazz said.

"Actually, there's three snakes in there," Julee said, and he laughed until he coughed. "She usually keeps them in a box, except when she's gone. Leaving one loose keeps the mosquitoes down. The thieves, too, I reckon. She's not stupid, that Chelsea. Could have been in the military."

Bea was a short, round woman with thorny-looking black hair. "Nobody ought to be in there," she said. "Chelsea's liable to kill all-a y'all."

"We didn't take anything," Serena said.

Jazz didn't like the way Bea's hands were balled into knots. Through oversized glasses, her eyes were magnified and slightly crossed. Her short hair, cut blunt at ear level, formed a bell shape around her face.

To his dismay, Serena pulled another ten-dollar bill from her pocket and she started to fold it, slowly, like she was rubbing baby oil onto it. "I'd like to speak with Chelsea," she said without looking up. She made another crease in the bill, and another. To Jazz, the money looked like a paper airplane of frustration.

Serena held the bill out and spoke. "Any idea where she might be now?"

Julee threw his cigarette, still glowing, onto the sand. "Like I said, she went to work some beach gig, but she didn't tell me where," he said. "I didn't ask."

Bea's fingers twitched open. "You a detective?"

Shaking her head, Serena repositioned the folded cash so that it stuck up between two knuckles. In the same way, Jazz had once held a french fry out for a pelican on the St. Augustine pier. It made his stomach hurt to watch Bea as she leaned in with her neck muscles ruffled up, wanting it so badly. Had Jazz strained forward in the same pitiful way on that ball field in Sanford when his father dangled cash? Jazz didn't think so. He hoped not. "She's with my brother," Serena said.

"She's been with everybody's brother," Bea said. Something

inside her mouth was decomposing. Jazz turned away, not wanting to become infected.

"Oh, come on, that's not fair," Julee said. "It's not very nice, either."

"She was with my husband once," Bea said.

"She's lonely," Julee said, ignoring Bea. "Like I said, she doesn't like being alone in her tent after dark. She told me her folks used to lock her in a closet overnight. Can you imagine treating a little kid that way?"

Jazz couldn't imagine it. Even after his mother got very sick, he never doubted that she loved him.

"My brother's still a kid," Serena said, tightening her fist where the bill was sticking up. Red-and-white lines had formed on her knuckles. "Technically, he's a grown-up, but he thinks a little bit differently. Do you understand what I mean?"

"Sure," Bea said. "Chelsea never met a cradle she couldn't rob."

"Hey, now," Julee said. "Why are you so mean?"

"His name is Gethin," Serena said, staring at Bea. "Maybe you've met him? Kind of tall and skinny, long hair?"

"Yeah, I met him. Sweet fellow—awful quiet, a little off the drumbeat, I think, but real polite. Helped me haul water yesterday. I told him he's got no business being here with a loser like Chelsea. I could see he's a clean, straight kid—no drugs."

Serena's head turned a half-notch to one side. "Are you sure? He's not using?"

"Why the hell would I say it if I'm not sure? I'm sure. He said he got out of the Drug Bucket and he ain't climbing back into it. He feels sorry for Chelsea's snakes, I think is all. Plus, he said he couldn't go home. What'd you do to him, anyway?"

Serena's eyebrows turned into steeples.

"Excuse me," Jazz said, stepping forward, "where did they go, exactly?"

"Daytona boardwalk, from what the kid told me," Bea said. "There's a music show down there. They need workers to set up signs and stuff."

Jazz took the ten-spot from Serena and handed it to Bea. He wanted to give her more, but he was saving his father's dirty bills for the Hacker's Challenge.

Serena tapped Julee's arm. "Remember, cops are coming tomorrow," she said.

"Good to know," Julee said. "Think I'll be out fishing."

Serena looked again at Chelsea's tent with its insides crawling. "I might need to come back if I can't find him," she said. "That be okay?"

Julee tucked a lighter into his shirt pocket. "Honey, you can come back any time."

"Call first," Bea said.

Jazz couldn't tell if she was joking. He placed one hand on his heart, lowering his chin—*thank you*—and he hustled to catch up with Serena, who was already beating a path back through the saw palmettos.

On the path, the line of Serena's back shrank and curled to one side, broken. Jazz wanted to roll his hands over her spine. He could massage love, courage, and a whole rainbow of joy back into her spirit. He lifted the lantern higher and straightened his skeleton, expanding his chest and the long muscles across his shoulders so he could share his full strength with her. Whenever she turned around and locked eyes with him, he would be ready. With his mind, he willed whatever germs had jumped onto his clothes to fly off into the glittery darkness full of hungry snakes. He wanted to be clean, strong, and full of light for Serena.

She didn't look at him again until they were both in the car with the lantern turned off and the engine running. Jazz twisted his body toward her, but he didn't lean in. He would wait for her to stretch her arms toward him for a hug, or extend her hand so he could hold it, or turn her face up for a kiss. He wasn't going to act like some pushy creeper. The situation was delicate. It needed to be her choice. With every neurotransmitter in his brain, he willed her to reach out, but she only put the car in reverse, turned it around, and headed for the road.

Through the headlights, he sent mental telegraphs to the steering wheel and the tires, urging the car toward her house.

Mile after mile, she sank further into her seat, silent. The car turned left, toward the park. She was dropping him off at his spot, not taking him home. "I want to help you," he said, as the playground came into view. "When are you going to Daytona?"

"Tomorrow afternoon." She stopped the car. "I've got to work in the morning. I need the money. This particular client pays cash."

"That's perfect. I've got a class in the morning. I could meet you at one o' clock?"

Serena exhaled with her cheeks puffed out. "I went to Daytona Beach once with my folks, right after we moved to Florida. The Fourth of July. Gethin was a baby. We stayed in a hotel with a water slide in the lobby, played miniature golf, saw some fireworks on the beach, stuff like that. I wanted to ride this thing called the Space Needle. My dad said the old boardwalk was too seedy for kids. We never went down there."

In his mind, Jazz felt a gear lock into place and start spinning too fast. He had never been to Daytona Beach, but he had seen it in photos and on TV. Every detail of it sprang up in vivid relief. "I know Daytona like the back of my hand," he said. "They took down the Space Needle a while back and they've fixed up the boardwalk, but there are still a lot of cheap hotels and bars where the tourists don't hang out. It's like a mouse maze with hiding places for people who live on the street. I know every inch of it. If Gethin's down there, we'll find him."

"Really?"

With his thumb, Jazz rubbed the back of his hand. "Yep."

Serena looked away and back again. "You think Bea knew what she was talking about? I mean when she said Gethin's clean?"

"I'd like to think so."

"This is all about the snakes," she said.

"How so?"

"Gethin loves snakes. Rocky hates them. It was a sore point between them."

A raindrop hit the windshield. *I don't blame Rocky for hating snakes*, he thought. "Love is a gift," he said, not knowing what else to offer. "It's a form of grace. I think love is the whole reason we're here. I hope they work it out."

"Maybe they will." A fine mist, a clap of thunder, and a sheet of rain followed. "I hope Gethin's not outside tonight," she said. "Can you imagine all the mud around Julee's tent? How miserable would that be? I'll never think of rain the same way."

Across the park, water was surely pooling on the cracked concrete pad by the bench where Jazz would be sleeping later. "I'd better put my backpack under the pavilion," he said. "I left it behind the bushes."

Her hand moved toward him, finally—her beautiful hand, throwing bolts of kindness. Jazz took it and reached for the other one too. When her face moved forward, he was ready. He didn't care if his backpack floated into the canal and got ripped apart by alligators or giant mutant catfish. Serena's mouth had called for him.

He answered as gently as possible. The kiss might have continued for a few seconds, or a minute, or an hour. He wouldn't be able to remember later. The rain drummed a rhythm through his ears, into his heart. Time warped to a stand-still.

Her phone rang and rang, but she didn't answer it. The ringing sounded like church bells. She rolled her mouth around to his ear and spoke into it. "You'll have to sleep on the futon," she said, but that was close enough for Jazz, close enough for now.

He got soaked, running to retrieve his backpack from his spot in the park.

15

Rocky

Sixty dollars. If Rocky could make sixty dollars in tips, she would have four hundred total in her bank account—enough to put down a deposit on an apartment of her own, or at least a place she could share with a girlfriend. Maybe Yanni, Rocky's friend with the thick glasses and notebooks full of computer code, might want to share a place. Rocky's knees flashed up and down on the bicycle pedals. She was headed to work, picturing polished wood floors and a view of the river from her new apartment, relieved to be free of the burning skin patches that had made her miserable for three days. The psoriasis outbreak had finally subsided. The ointment had helped.

On the road, somebody yelled from a truck window. "Hey, baby!" Even wearing a trench coat and with her hair squashed under an old lady net, random jerks still hollered, whistling and flicking their tongues. *Disgusting.* As usual, Rocky had buttoned a coat over her uniform of boots, fishnet stockings, a clip-on bow tie, and a black miniskirt she had rigged with a frilly pink hem to cover her thighs. Face forward, neck locked, she kept pedaling. The truck slowed. Rocky had reached the bridge at King Street. She was clear of West Augustine with its winding, unlit streets and chain-link fences, headed into the glare of the tourist district.

"Looking good, darling," the man shouted. His grinning, ruddy face moved by her in slow motion—long, crooked teeth with big gaps between them. Rocky steered the bike to the right, toward the bridge railing. In another minute, she would be under streetlamps and the rust-colored towers of Flagler College, safe. She pedaled faster. The truck sped up, keeping pace.

"Smile, honey," he said.

Rocky lifted one hand, which caused the bike to lurch. Grimacing, she stabbed her middle finger toward the sky, waved it around, and stabbed again.

She knew it was dangerous, but she was exhausted, furious, and close enough to the shopping district to make a run for it if necessary. Predictably, the man screamed The Word. How many times had Rocky heard that awful word with its ancient poison? The man's head—a mullet style from decades earlier, business in the front, party in the back—surged over the sidewalk, nearly striking a phone pole, face contorting and snapping as the truck roared on. "You're not even that pretty."

"But I'm a whole lot smarter than you, asshole." It was another epically bad idea, yelling back. Sure enough, the truck's taillights turned red. Rocky was already sailing by the chocolate shop and a store window full of scented candles. A tourist trolley cruised behind the truck and dinged its bell. She was home free, back in the land of ice-cream cones dropped on the sidewalk, wind chimes made of seashells, and packs of perfumed older women hobbling down brick streets in search of discounted jewelry.

Except for the lack of parking, Rocky liked working downtown. By riding her bike to work, she avoided the parking hassle and saved gas money. If she could get to work fifteen minutes early, before everybody else on her shift, she could tip the hostess for extra tables. Forty bucks was Rocky's average on weekends, but sixty wasn't out of the question on a Saturday night. Money for her own apartment. At the next intersection, Mister Mullet turned right and disappeared.

Evolutionary throwbacks, she thought.

There were still a few good men left in the world. Kevin had been kind, helping Rocky into Serena's house after the Jester Festival trip. He had even left his card with a phone number on it, in case Rocky needed anything or just wanted to talk. Good thing he was strong too. Her legs had collapsed when she tried to step out of the car. Kevin caught her around the waist. His collar had smelled faintly of a tart aftershave that reminded Rocky of her dad. Serena had said, "Whoa" when Rocky started falling. The door opened, spinning, and Rocky's legs went limp. Inside the house, her bedroom was still infused with Gethin's scent, softer than Kevin's aftershave—rich with exotic soaps and the tin of licorice seeds he had left open on the windowsill.

Gethin wouldn't be caught dead yelling at a woman out of a car window. His affection had revealed itself in quiet ways, sliding around her unexpectedly, a hand under her hair, a hug that started off like a scarf slipping across her back but tightened up and gained heat while the plastic cat in Serena's kitchen wagged its tail, ticking off the seconds, a kiss—extra soft, in slow motion.

Gethin. On her bicycle, Rocky turned left into the historic district. Her vision slipped sideways, bed-spinning. She stepped off the bike and walked it down the brick street. The tourists seemed to be swimming by her, dreamlike. Their mouths opened into smiles that expanded, zoomed toward her, and slid by, one after another. Random sentence fragments swirled in a funnel around her head, without meaning: "Pink sea salt," somebody said. "Blistering heat," another voice answered. "That fudge place…white alligator…your mother won't give me credit…anything with peanut butter…the kids will remember…rain on Monday."

Chelsea. Apparently, Gethin was hanging out with a woman by that name. Maybe she let him do meth right in front of her. Maybe they were rolling around buck naked on a bed full of snakes together. Rocky wanted to be furious—she longed for a full head of rage—but every time she thought about his mouth, curling gradually into a smile, coming toward her with his eyes soft, the street shifted under her cheap work boots. She had loved him. Had he loved her? Did he even understand the meaning of the word? Anyway, the incessant recital of pointless snake facts had become annoying, and if he was using drugs again, that was never going to work for Rocky, not to mention that there was no way in hell she could let him touch her again if he had been with someone else.

She had to face the facts. It was over. Gethin was most likely high again. Although she loved Serena, Rocky wasn't going to hang around like a mangled sock that had lost its partner in the dryer. She needed her own place. That would take money. Another sixty dollars, to be exact. Outside the restaurant, she locked the bike and pressed her knuckles against her heart where it seemed to be burning a hole through her coat.

The restaurant's back door was propped open. Through the opening, a pot clanged onto the floor. Dale, the high-school kid who had been bussing tables for the past month, picked it up and put it back onto a stack of clean stuff. Near her bike, the smells of grease, french fries, and seared meat fused with the stench from a garbage can. Rocky smoothed her hair, unbuttoned the trench coat, and went inside. She retrieved the dirty pot as well as a bowl it had been touching, handed them to Dale, and shook her head.

"Aw, come on," he said, laughing. "Five-second rule."

"Don't think the health department would go for that," she said, making her way along a counter loaded with plates ready for delivery—baskets of fried fish and potatoes, tacos stuffed with blackened tuna, little bowls of coleslaw and mango salsa.

A bell dinged. Shelby, another waitress, swept two plates off the counter. *Damn it.* Why was Shelby at work so early? Rocky punched the time clock, tied on an apron, and stuffed an order pad into it. The boss stepped out of his office with a calculator in one hand, wearing a vague smile. "All right," he said, looking sleepy, as usual. He had never concealed his love for weed—he liked to light up in the alley by the bike racks a few times per night. "My whole dream team's here early tonight. You doing okay, Rocky?"

She flashed her biggest smile and leaned over him, using her height to her advantage. Usually, he was a sweet old stoner, except when some newbie couldn't reconcile the night's tickets. Even then, all he ever said was, "Not cool, man," before biting his scraggly fingernails. He had a small crush on Shelby—Rocky was pretty sure of it—otherwise why would he always let Shelby take the best tables? Rocky was faster and friendlier with the customers. Maybe he thought, deep down in a place where he didn't even realize it, that a white waitress would be a better draw than a brown one. "I really need section four tonight," Rocky said, keeping her voice low. "I've got some real shit on the home front. Can you help me out?"

Charlie set the calculator down on the cluttered desk in his office. His eyebrows inched together. He looked up at her and frowned, pure hound dog, like Rocky's father whenever he was hungover. "Shoot, sweetie," he said, "Shelby got here first. You know that's how it works, right? First one here gets dibs."

Rocky did know that, and yet she could only get paid minimum wage for eight hours, no matter what time she punched in. "Just talk to her for me, okay? Tell her it's my turn."

He straightened up, which brought his head to the level of Rocky's shoulder. "Hey, what's going on with you?"

She wasn't about to give up any details. Only once, she had tried to go deep with Charlie. It had triggered a long, rambling monologue on the perils of stress, the tyranny of Western medicine, and the teachings of some Rastafarian dude. "Like I said, some stuff's going on at home." Rocky glanced across the food counter at Shelby, who was serving a table, looking back at Rocky. "I need my own place, basically. Like, tomorrow."

He rubbed his hands together with his shoulders tucked as if it might be cold in the kitchen. "You know I don't butt into any issues between the staff," he said, looking at his flour-speckled sneakers.

"Please talk to her," Rocky said again. She wanted to slap a spine into him. "You're the boss."

"Work it out," Charlie said. "Shelby's a nice kid, just like you. Let me know what you two decide so I can tell the hostess. We've got a new one tonight."

"What happened to Sharon?" Rocky slipped up, letting her voice get too loud.

Sharon had been an ally. She had assigned good tables to Rocky.

"She quit. Left me a voicemail. Can you imagine?" Charlie raised his palms. "Some people don't have the same work ethic as you and me."

The cook, a guy Rocky didn't know by name yet, was staring at them from under his crooked white hat. When she stared back, he looked down at a plate of steak, arranged a sprig of parsley on the side, and shoved it across the counter. "I'll talk to Shelby," Rocky said, feeling defeated before her shift had even begun. She couldn't take another week in the empty bedroom she had shared with Gethin. Sixty dollars and her own place was what she needed.

"Good girl," Charlie said. "I was just about to take a break before it gets too busy. I'll be back in a minute."

Yeah, work that work ethic, man, Rocky thought.

In the dining room, more snippets of conversation flew by her—"thanks for staying gone while I had that chick in there, man," and "left a bra in the bathtub," and "Snake Lady." A table of guys in colorful polo-style shirts were talking about getting high and laid on vacation. "Oh my god," one of them said, "I hope that snake hag comes by here again." They meant the old woman who had recently started bringing a white ball python down to St. George Street. She charged tourists to have their picture taken with it. She sold a little weed on the side, from what Rocky had seen.

Big snakes were crawling all over Florida, thanks to the vast number of clueless rednecks who bought a little one, not realizing it would keep growing, requiring bigger and bigger tanks and a never-ending supply of frozen rats until it tried to eat the family dog and got set loose in a swamp. Gethin had explained this to Rocky, his point being that they should rescue as many discarded snakes as possible. She wasn't about to let him haul any giant constricting machines into their bedroom. Fortunately, Serena had backed Rocky up on that one. No Burmese pythons, and snakes could be kept in the garage only.

Shelby brushed by Rocky with an empty tray on her arm, headed for the kitchen. "I've got a kid to feed," she said before Rocky could say a word. Her skirt was shorter than Rocky's—no frilly hem sewn onto the bottom of it. The backs of her knees were pink and glistening with sweat already.

"I'd pay you back," Rocky said. She had decided not to mention how Shelby snagged section four every single time they worked together. It would make her sound like a whiner. "I've got a situation at home."

There were twenty-four tables in the restaurant. They were divided into four sections, but two of the areas only had five tables with fewer seats, mostly on the sidewalk, which required hawk-like attention in case any drunk or elderly diners wandered off without paying. Another section had six smaller tables inside, clustered around a little stage that was shaped like a ship's prow, adorned by a topless plaster mermaid who had been tangled in a dusty fishnet for at least a decade. Taking orders around the stage on a Saturday night was a surefire recipe for a migraine if the acoustic guitarist showed up to run through his set of 1960s rock favorites over and over again. Only section four offered eight tables in the quiet, more desirable part of the dining room. All those tables had at least four seats. Tips were better there.

Shelby leaned against the glossy bar where seashells had been embalmed under a few million layers of polyurethane, and she rearranged her cleavage. Waitresses at The Spindle could choose one of two approved tops—a white dress shirt with a black bow tie, which was Rocky's preference, or a white V-neck. Shelby had gone for the V-neck in a size smaller than she needed. "Sorry, sweetie," she said. "I've got a situation too. It's called a kid to feed and rent on my trailer lot."

Only three of the tables were occupied so far. In another hour, two more waitresses would arrive and every table would turn over at least three times before closing. "There's a new hostess tonight," Rocky said. "We might do better by working out our own plan before she gets here."

"Sharon split?" Shelby tucked a hair behind her ear.

"It's going to be crazy. What if I picked up two of your tables?"

Shelby licked her teeth and looked at Rocky sideways. "I do try to get out of here on time. My son's eleven. It's not like he's going to burn down the house, but I don't like leaving him alone so late."

Rocky started reeling in her words faster. Shelby had clamped onto the bait. "I promise," she said. "I'll close out every one of your tabs and reconcile it and give you every penny you earned. You know I'm good at math. I won't cheat."

The Spindle's official aprons had strings four times longer than necessary, which meant the waitresses had to wind them around their bodies like straightjackets. Shelby untied her strings, pulled them tighter, and made another knot. "What's your deal, exactly? Anything you want to talk about?"

Above Rocky's head, the lights dimmed, signaling the start of her shift. She blinked. "My boyfriend left. He found somebody else. He's probably doing drugs. I need to move out. I don't have the deposit money."

The cook dinged his bell again. Shelby gave Rocky a quick hug. "You'll be okay," she said. "Tell you what, I'll give you two of my tables after eight o'clock if you close out my tabs at the end of the night and take over with those assholes by the door. You're nicer than me. I was just about to lose my shit with them."

"Deal," Rocky said. She took the order slip from Shelby, picked up the food, and carried it over to the Drunken Polo Shirt table.

"What's this?" A guy with slicked-back blond hair grinned at her when she set a hamburger in front of him.

"That's the blue cheese and bacon burger." Immediately, Rocky slipped into her cheerful customer-service mode.

"No, I mean, where's the other waitress—the one with the shirt?"

Of course, the Polo Shirts had zeroed in on Shelby's cleavage. "She's taking a break, but I'm going to take good care of y'all." Rocky never said "y'all" in her private life; she used it only for the tourists. From a tray, she lowered the last of three plates and surveyed the table—silverware, ketchup, salt—check, check, and check.

Another Polo Shirt spoke up. He had a dimple on one cheek and a gold watch. "That's cool," he said. "We're all fans of Beyoncé, aren't we, guys?"

A hot, salty wind rushed into Rocky's lungs. Several times before, she had heard the Beyoncé comparison, which was absurd. Rocky looked nothing like the singer, but white people seemed to think it was a compliment.

Gethin would never have spoken to her that way. All the air-filled ramblings on his Facebook page about One Love, the connectedness of all beings, and the healing power of the natural world were silly, but he meant every word. He had never forced her to recite her usual Black Spiel about her father's lifelong struggle to get a promotion, to be seen as something other than his skin color, or her mother's obsession with chasing after loser white guys. *Blah blah blah.* Gethin wasn't anything like the dimpled guy in his polo shirt, but then again, Gethin wasn't there. He had abandoned her to live in a tent with an addict.

Gethin was a coward. Rocky was not. She would find her own place, get herself through school, and have a good life without him. First, she would have to deal with the Drunken Polo Shirt table. She moved the ketchup closer to the guy with the hamburger.

He ran a hand over his oily hair.

"Y'all aren't driving tonight, are you?" She asked the question without a smile.

Instantly, Dimple Boy sat up taller, pretending to be sober. His mouth opened.

One of the sidekicks leaned forward, no longer laughing. He was wearing a lime-colored shirt and a baseball cap with an alligator insignia on the brim. "No, ma'am," he said, as if Rocky might be their housekeeper. "We're in a hotel down the block."

She wanted to burst out laughing. She clenched her jaw instead. Total serenity could be used to shame them. "That's a good thing," she said. "I love my customers. I wouldn't want any of them to get hurt or get in trouble with the law. The police are all over this strip, so you know. You might see a couple of the beat cops in here before too long."

"Sorry about my friends," the guy in the alligator cap said. "I can't take them anywhere."

The guy with the dimple looked at his giant watch. "Yeah, sorry," he mumbled.

To make her tip money, Rocky would have to pull them back in. Since she had shamed them, they would feel guilty, which could mean more money, but only if they didn't hate her. "Where y'all from?" Her Southern accent sounded more like Serena than Rocky's mother.

They were from Atlanta—of course. Three rich boys from the big city, on a wilding. All of them were on the verge of cute, except their cheeks were glowing with oil and their fancy shirts were stained yellow under the armpits. Phillip, the guy with the dimple, was unevenly sunburned on the tip of his nose and he had big white rings around his eyes. None of them could pronounce her name correctly—Rah-KEN-drah—but she made them say it several times. They ordered another pitcher of margaritas. Rocky patted Phillip on the back in a maternal way. "I'm so glad y'all came in here," she said, although she wanted to shove his face into his coleslaw. "I'll bring y'all some fresh drinks."

On the other side of the serving window, Shelby was having a silent-movie fit of hysterics, clutching her chest and laughing without any sound. "That was brilliant," she said in a stage whisper. "I've been schooled by the master."

"I'm making my tip money off those piece-of-shit jerks," Rocky said. "I don't care if it kills me."

Shelby's other donated table was a group of older women from Savannah who all wanted separate checks, but that was okay because then at least one of them would drop a five-spot on the table. Rocky closed them out and turned the table.

The Polo Shirt guys were still drinking. "Look, look, look," the guy in the alligator cap said. *Benjamin.* By eavesdropping, Rocky had memorized their names. "There she is again."

"Oh, snap," Phillip said. "Blaine, you've still got some cash. Go see if she's got another bag on her, dude."

Blaine, the guy with pale, slicked-back hair lurched off his chair and onto the sidewalk like he needed to throw up. Outside, the old woman everyone called Snake Lady was posing with a splotchy yellow one instead of her usual white ball python. She was wrapping up a photo shoot with a little boy in red high-topped sneakers. Blaine kept his distance, swaying from one foot to the other until the boy's family paid for the photo and lumbered off. Rocky started cleaning a table near the open door so that she could watch Blaine at the same time. He sidled up to the woman with the snake, tipped his chin, and reached into his pocket.

"Sorry," the woman said, loud enough to be heard inside the restaurant. "I don't have what you need." She packed her snake into a blue-painted box and grabbed the handle. Her skinny arms were bare. The muscles in her biceps popped, weirdly out of proportion with the rest of her body. She could have been forty or seventy, with deep worry lines around her eyes, which were deep-set above high cheekbones and teeth that were so big and white, they looked fake. On her long skirt, gold medallions jingled. Through a mesh window on the blue box, another snake, black and shiny, popped up and disappeared.

"Come on," Blaine was saying. "I've got cash."

"Mazel tov," the woman said, lifting the snake box with no sign of strain. "I'm still waiting for my inheritance. Look, I'm on a very tight schedule. My friend's waiting for me. We can't miss our ride to Daytona."

"Hey, I met you last night," he said, getting louder.

The woman started walking away. One shoulder was lower than the other, from the weight of the box.

"Sure, I remember you," she said. "I can't help you today."

"Hang on." Blaine grabbed her shoulder. "Not even a taste?"

She pulled away, glaring. "Would you leave me alone, please? I told you, I don't have what you need. Also, I don't do business with assholes."

"Thanks a lot, bitch." Blaine's words were slurred.

When she turned around, the woman's face was scrunched up around her teeth. "A bitch is a female dog, so I take that as a compliment, you rich, arrogant douchebag, but for the record, the name's Temptress of Serpents. Remember that after dark when the nightmares start. Remember Miss Chelsea Dean."

Rocky scooped a three-dollar tip off a table, tucked it into her apron, and froze. She had never known Snake Lady's real name. Was it possible? She had to be at least twenty-five years older than Gethin. She didn't look clean, which would freak Gethin out, but she liked snakes and drugs. They had two things in common.

Rocky raced into the kitchen. Shelby was biting into a french fry. "Emergency," Rocky said. "Be right back."

Shelby stopped chewing and her eyes widened.

On the cobblestone street, Rocky's high-heeled boots made running difficult. She settled for a fast shuffle, weaving around tourists who were as round and slow-moving as manatees. They kept stopping unpredictably to stare at ice-cream stores and pizza places, or to lower tiny dogs onto the pavement. Ahead of her, Chelsea turned right, down an alley that was empty by the time Rocky got there. She didn't know what she wanted to say once she caught up with Chelsea Dean, other than, "Have you seen Gethin?" and, "Where is he now?"

Rocky would leave him, regardless, but she needed to know where he had been, why he had left her, and most importantly, if he was all right. She pictured him lying on a dirty mattress in some meth house guarded by snakes, strung out, sick from the drugs or hepatitis, which he would surely catch if he was using needles. Serena's heart would break if her brother died that way. Rocky's heart had already been shattered beyond repair.

Nobody deserved what Gethin had put her through. Definitely not Serena the Savage, queen of kindness.

Rocky turned right again, heard a tinkling sound like the medallions on Chelsea's skirt, saw a flash of purple fabric, and called out, "Wait—Chelsea! Miss Dean! I want to ask you something. I need to talk to you about Gethin." Maybe the woman, crazy as she might be, would know what was going on with him.

At the end of the block, Chelsea stopped. "Quit following me," she said. "What's with everybody chasing me today? I don't know who you are."

"I'm Gethin's girlfriend." The gap between them was shrinking. "My name's Rocky. I work at The Spindle."

Waving a hand, dismissive, Chelsea was on the move again. "Nice to meet you, Rocky. Please go away. I'm on a schedule here." As soon as she said it, she was gone.

Back on the main strip, Rocky heard the sound again and ran toward it. The sidewalk was packed with people. She moved faster, in and out of groups. Through an opening in the crowd, a mass of yellowish-white hair appeared. Rocky darted for it, tripped over a dog leash, and went airborne. There was a yelp, a crack as her knees and elbows hit the bricks, and someone cursing. From the ground, Rocky twisted her head to look again for Chelsea, but she had disappeared again.

A man in red Bermuda shorts and a white belt loomed over Rocky. "Oh, my dear," he said.

Was he the dog owner, or a Good Samaritan? The white dog seemed to have vanished. Had she imagined it? Gethin had told her once to "feed the white dog every day." It was a metaphor he had liked, a recovery program saying Kevin had shared, the white dog being love, or a higher power or something. Flat on her back, Rocky laughed out loud, hoping she had not choked an actual white dog by running through its leash.

"Let me give you a hand," the man said. "That's quite a scrape."

Rocky's right knee was skinned. The man handed her the bow tie that had flown off her uniform. She pulled her skirt down and rocked onto one hip, trying to sit up. "How embarrassing," she said. All she wanted to do was stand up and walk away, drive out of St. Augustine, and never have to see or be seen by anyone there, ever again. She wanted to disappear, magically, into the salty fog, the way Gethin had done, but she didn't have that luxury. She needed to get back to work. She needed another sixty dollars to get her own apartment.

To have any kind of future, she would have to work hard and finish school.

The man reached under Rocky's armpits, tugging her upright. His hands were shaking. His arms weren't strong the way Kevin's had been, earlier. How pathetic—she had been propped up twice in one day by two different men. Irritated, she shrugged off the old guy's embrace and climbed onto her knees. "Thanks," she said. "I've got this."

Walking back to the restaurant, Rocky straightened her back and pinned on the bow tie. She cleaned up in the bathroom, waving off Shelby's questions, closed out Blaine's table for a twenty-dollar tip, which wasn't even 15 percent of the tab, and limped through the rest of her shift.

By the end of the night, she had forty-eight dollars and some change in her apron pocket, not the sixty she had been hoping for. Her knee hurt and she didn't trust herself to ride the bicycle home. She dialed Serena's number three times but got no answer. Ten minutes later, when Serena still wasn't picking up, Rocky pulled Kevin's card out of her purse and stared at the number.

16

Serena

At Serena's house, Jazz lay down on the futon as she had asked him to do, but she didn't leave him there for long. She could hear him rolling around and clearing his throat. The clock's ticking seemed to rattle the walls. The inside of her eyelids felt sunburned. Images of Gethin kept strobing through her head. Each one was more troubling than the next: hollow-eyed and panhandling on the Daytona Beach boardwalk, rubber-strapping his arm, shoving a needle into his veins. Lying in bed, she rubbed her eyes, trying to free them. *Slow down, Serena. We don't know that for sure.* Kevin's words. The old woman by the river had said Gethin was clean. It seemed unlikely, but maybe he had somehow stayed straight.

To distract herself, she picked up her phone. Rocky had tried to call, more than once. Serena hoisted herself upright and sent a text message. "Sorry I missed your calls," she typed. "Everything okay?" Maybe Rocky had found or at least heard from Gethin. Serena's breathing turned shallow until Rocky replied: "I'm fine. Needed a ride—found one. At the diner now. See you later."

On the bedside table, a white lamp illuminated a stack of dog-eared health and travel magazines. Through the wall, Jazz coughed. Serena climbed out of bed. In her extra-long T-shirt, she walked down the hall to Gethin's tiny work room. Jazz was lying on his back with his knees bent and his eyes open. She extended both hands. He took them, stood without a word, and let her guide him back to her room.

For once, briefly, he was quiet—seemingly speechless. Urgently, he kissed her. He kept saying, "I want to be with you," like a battlefield surgeon frantic to stitch up a wound. He stood up, stripped to the waist, which was lean—maybe too lean—and unleashed his hair. The tips of it brushed her cheeks when he bent to kiss her again. "Is this what you want?" He whispered it and waited. Yes, at that moment, it was everything she wanted. *Yes*—the warmth of his skin, the strength of his arms, and his gold medallion, which she hadn't noticed before, tickling her neck.

"I thought you were a giant," he said, "the first time I saw you."

"What?" Serena remembered a mean word-game she used to play on Gethin: *Losers say what?* She would ask the question and wait for him to say, *What?*

"When I got hurt, you were leaning over me, and you looked incredibly tall." Jazz stepped away from her to remove his pants. He folded them into a star shape, like origami, and placed them on the dresser. The quadriceps in his thighs were well-defined, probably from riding his bicycle all over the place, and when he turned, the cheeks of his *gluteus maximus* weren't half-bad, either. A nice, broad shape to the *latissimus dorsi*, tapering down to the posterior *serratus* above his waist.

Serena, on her back and already naked, laced her fingers over her chest. She was staring at the ceiling in order to avoid staring at Jazz. "But I'm short," she said.

"Perhaps, but inside, you're an Amazon with the heart of a giant." When she looked at him, he combed his fingers through his long hair, clearly showing off.

She forced herself to look directly at his face, and only his face. *Must. Look. Into. His. Eyes.* "You say such nice things."

Turning sideways, he flexed his biceps without taking his eyes off her. "I'm the Maximum Champion, you know."

She couldn't help laughing. "Is that right?"

Jazz jumped feet first onto the bed and danced around her legs. "I'm the Maximum Champion! I'm the luckiest man in the world." He let out a whistle loud enough to startle the neighbors, or a bird off its nest half a block away. "I'm with the most beautiful woman I've ever seen."

The bed's shaking made the soft parts of her body jiggle, causing her to tense up.

He dropped onto all fours, grinning, and changed gears, slowing his movements, talking in a low, nonstop murmur that made her feel anesthetized. Nothing hurt. Nothing pinched or burned or itched. He was a warm tide of human touch—relief!—moving over her. Her usual anxiety slid off the bed, onto the floor. He kept moving until she stopped worrying about what time it had gotten to be, how much sleep she would need to meet with a client the next morning, and when Rocky might get home. Afterward, he wouldn't let her go. Even as her breathing leveled out and she slipped into darkness, his voice rolled over her, off and on: "I've been waiting my whole life for this moment. I dreamed about you before I met you. I wanted to be with you before I was born. Beautiful Serena."

Nothing he said was making any sense. Serena didn't care. She had gone too long without a man's touch. Listening to him was like having a white noise machine next to her bed. Three or four times, his words put her to sleep and roused her again.

It was Rocky, banging the kitchen door shut that finally brought Serena back to the light. Her body went rigid. In an instant, she was wide awake. Jazz purred, asleep at last. Across the room, her bedroom door stood ajar. Serena yanked a sheet over Jazz. She managed to cover most of him, but his left flank, pale and muscular as a breaking wave, remained exposed. Rocky stopped at the door, braced her back against the frame, and exhaled. "This would explain why you didn't answer your phone," she said.

Serena said she was sorry and she slid out of bed, still naked—Rocky had seen all of Serena's freckles before—and she walked across the hall, into Gethin's closet. Not wanting to put the same sweaty T-shirt back on, Serena grabbed one of her brother's shirts. His familiar perfume nearly overwhelmed her. She slipped the shirt over her head anyway and kept moving, into the kitchen. Grabbing a tangelo from a stack by the door, she cracked it open. Crescent-shaped strips of rind fell into the sink. A watery orange cloud engulfed her. Juice poured onto her palms. She dropped the pulp and rubbed her sticky hands all over her face, her neck, and her arms.

By the refrigerator, Rocky's eyes had gone glossy. She didn't move when Serena massaged the scent into her braids. "We need a fresh start," Serena said. "Both of us."

Rocky plucked a rind off the floor, chewed it, and spit it into the sink. "Kevin says I should have told you about that letter Gethin gave me. He says if we're family, we shouldn't have secrets."

"You talked to Kevin?"

"He drove me home." From a jar on the counter, Rocky grabbed a stick of vanilla, sawed it across her wrists, and handed it to Serena. "We stopped for a bite to eat. He said he's got a spare bedroom where I can stay for free. It wouldn't be permanent—just until I can get back on my feet. He'll have another renter next month."

The kitchen chair squeaked when Serena sat down on it, placing the vanilla on the table. She wasn't going to stop Rocky, if her heart was set on leaving. The house would be too quiet, though. "I shouldn't have read your private letter."

"I accept your apology," Rocky said, although Serena hadn't exactly offered one.

"Jazz and I are driving to Daytona Beach tomorrow," Serena said. "We heard Gethin's headed down there with Chelsea."

"I can't go with you." Rocky was still standing. "I need to move on."

"If that's what you think is best." On the wall, the cat clock ticked off the time: *one a.m.* "You're welcome to stay here as long as you want. You know that."

"I'll start packing tomorrow." Rocky dug an orange speck out of her teeth. "Chelsea's the Snake Lady, by the way—remember her? From downtown?"

Through the window, the neighbors' mailboxes were outlined in black under the streetlights. On the empty street, they looked stoic, like soldiers at a military funeral, waiting for their marching orders. "That's Chelsea? The panhandler? But she's—"

"Yep. A lot older than Gethin."

Serena blew all the wind out of her lungs. "I think we'll find him soon. Jazz said he knows Daytona Beach like the back of his hand."

"I don't trust that guy."

"I know you don't."

"I think he's a con man," Rocky said.

"He's a sweet, harmless guy," Serena said.

"Do you have any idea what you're doing?"

"No."

Rocky crouched down and lowered her head onto Serena's knees. "Thank you for everything." Her thanks had a bright citrus smell to it. "I hope you find him."

"Oh, Rocky Road," Serena said. "I love you. That's never going to change."

17

Jazz

In Daytona Beach, the boardwalk smelled like beer, popcorn, and cotton candy, all of which stuck to the bottom of his shoes as Jazz held on to Serena's hand and talked and talked. He hadn't slept much—had mainly pretended to rest, lying on his side in Serena's bed, listening to Rocky badmouth him while he tried to work out a series of Big Plans. Three days until the Hacker's Challenge, for one thing. Two days with Serena so far. No time left to make Serena love him by finding Gethin.

The time had come.

Through the soles of his feet, Jazz felt the boardwalk strobing by—salmon-colored pavers interspersed with plain white ones. Children chased each other, squealing. Couples, grandparents, and dog walkers got larger and smaller, walking by, so close Jazz smelled their sweaty sunscreen, perfume, and cigarettes. The waves tensed up and relaxed, in time with the lines on Serena's face.

At a sandy pit, she stopped to look at a long-haired young guy who was watching a group of college kids. They were playing volleyball in their bathing suits and sunglasses. Their skin looked like antique silver, buffed to a high gloss with precious oils. The long-haired guy was propped on an elbow under a few palm trees. His overstuffed backpack lay nearby, and he was wearing too much clothing for the weather—long plumber's pants with a million zippers like portals to another world, a vest, and an orange bandanna. He turned to look at Serena—hazel eyes set in ruddy cheeks—but she had already moved on. Serena didn't seem to notice him; he might as well have been invisible. Jazz wanted to stop and say hello. He knew what it felt like to be inconsequential, always on the sidelines.

Jazz had to jog to catch up with Serena. By another patch of grass and palm trees, she slowed again, eyeballing a man and a woman who sat cross-legged with a shopping cart. They weren't Gethin and Chelsea. Again, Serena was on the move.

Turning in a circle, she pulled out her phone and called up a map. "Where should we be looking?" Her voice strained forward, like a dog trying to lose its leash. Did she feel held back by Jazz? Did she want to get away from him?

At a sidewalk café, a boy of maybe two leaned over the back of a metal chair, reaching for a stuffed turtle. His parents' backs were turned. They were both talking into cell phones, staring out to sea. The boy's arm stretched farther, until his chair pitched forward. Jazz darted between the tables, bumping Serena. Her phone cracked onto the sidewalk. The chair hit the pavement, too, but Jazz caught the boy, who sucked in a big breath before letting out a howl.

"He was falling," Jazz said, handing the boy to his mother.

The woman's mouth hung open. She adjusted a bra strap, put down her phone, and took possession of the boy, mumbling, "Thanks."

Serena looked at her cracked phone. The shattered glass spider-veined between her thumbs. "Wow," she said.

Did she mean, *Wow, you saved a child,* or *Wow, you broke my phone,* or both? Jazz spoke up. "I can fix that. I could be an engineer. I practically am one. I can fix anything, faster than anyone."

With the fingernail on her pinky finger, she picked a loose piece of glass off the phone. "At least I can still see the map." The leash on her voice broke free and whipped around in all directions. On the side of his face, Jazz felt a sudden sting. His cheek burned.

"That's a blessing," he said. "You sacrificed your phone, but that little boy might have busted his wrist, or his head. If I see something that's about to go wrong, I jump in and try to help. I've always been like that."

Her shoulders sagged, no longer straining forward. She

expanded the map and held it under her nose. A man in a parrot-patterned shirt banged into her shoulder. Serena cursed. "Where do people hang out here if they don't have a place to stay?"

Jazz was focused on a red banner, farther up the beach. He closed one eye, to see it better. "What?"

"Where are the hangouts?" Her head tilted. "If you wanted to buy drugs, where would you go?"

Inside the red banner, white letters danced around, expanding and contracting, turning sharp and fuzzy and back to sharp, but Jazz was still too far away to make out the words. Flowing toward the banner, a steady stream of people jostled in green, red, and yellow shirts or bathing suits with stripes and dots. Lifting his arms over his head, he cracked his shoulders and let out a high-pitched scream, releasing the love stuck in his chest. It had built up overnight, phlegmy and unbearable, to the point that it made his breathing fast and shallow. He felt starved of oxygen. He screamed it out.

Jazz looked at Serena through one eye. Her eyebrows had turned into a pair of beautiful swordsmen. He opened his other eye and tried to remember what she had asked him. "I've never been a recreational drug user," he said. "I don't use drugs of any kind."

Serena's chin dropped to her chest. "I'm starting to think you might need drugs."

She had dribbled the sentence down her chest, onto the pavement. The words seemed to splash around her feet like drops of bile. They bounced up, poisonous, and pierced his joints. He cupped his elbows in his hands, squeezing.

You need to be on medication.

So many people had hurt Jazz the same way, with the same words—his father and his mother, his mother's doctor, the counselor at school, and a girl he had known once—as if he would ever agree to anesthetize the light that exploded from the center of his body, forming rainbows around his head, except when it went black. On the boardwalk, the sky seemed to darken. His arms felt chained. He couldn't move. It hurt to lift his tongue, but he did it anyway. "I'll never take lithium."

Serena's top lip peeled back until she looked like a rabbit. Sweat rolled down her neck. "What are you talking about? I didn't say anything about lithium."

"That's what you meant. I've been subjugated by universal animosity my whole life. Satan blackens souls, but it isn't your fault. He takes over our souls when we're scared."

She took two steps backward and looked around in all directions like she was trying to figure out which way to run. "You've got one thing right," she said, and her eyes filled up. "You're scaring the shit out of me."

A bolt of adrenaline nearly knocked Jazz off his feet. What had he said? He couldn't let her be scared of him. He had been put on Earth as a protector of women—the Maximum Champion!—the strongest man alive. He stepped toward her with his arms outstretched. "Beautiful Serena," he said. "Please don't be afraid. I love you. I'm sorry."

She pushed his hands away and kept backing up. "How dare you put me down like that? I've been called a lot of things by random nut cases on social media, but no one's ever actually said I'm the devil."

"I didn't say that. I said—"

Her hands flew up, reminding him of doves. Her fingers got tangled in her hair. "I can't believe I brought you here. What was I thinking?"

"You were thinking you love me?" It was a question, not a statement.

Her laughter had sharp edges to it. She talked at the ocean, not seeming to hear Jazz at all. "I was thinking it's been a long time since I've had sex and here's a guy with a kick-ass body. How stupid could I be?"

More than anything, he wanted to touch her. If she would let him hold her, let him stroke her knotted hair, everything would be all right. If she would tolerate having her hands cradled in his until they weren't balled up anymore, he could stop her from hating him, from leaving like every other woman he had ever known, including his mother, in her own way. "Rocky's wrong about me," he said. "I would never hurt you. I only meant that demons can take hold of us."

Her eyes had gone wild. People were rocketing by them on all sides. "This was a huge mistake," she said. Spit flew from her lips, which had turned white against the red of her face. "I've been stupid. I don't know what made me think I could trust you."

Again, he reached for her. "I'm sorry," he said, moving forward. "I'm sorry, I'm sorry, I'm sorry."

"Don't touch me." She was screaming, flat out. "You said you could help me find Gethin, but you act like you've never been here before in your life. You lied to me. You broke my damn phone, then you have the nerve to insult me."

One more step and she would be in his arms. She would calm down as soon as she felt his heart beating against her cheek. "Serena."

"Find your own way home."

She ran.

Jazz wanted to run, too—he lunged forward, but a large man in a dark T-shirt blocked the path. "Maybe let it go," the man said. His hands were on his hips. He was at least a foot taller than Jazz.

"She's upset because her brother's missing," Jazz said, standing up straighter, and with that, another woman had disappeared on him, lost to the boardwalk and the beach. Serena was somewhere ahead, no longer visible, headed for the river of people and the red banner in the distance.

Jazz sat down on a curb and watched a lizard with a kink in its back leg. The thing looked stunned, as if somebody had stepped on it. It was the same color as the lizard at his father's office in Sanford. Jazz hadn't heard from his father since their visit. Whenever a memory of the old man's dark, gummy mouth popped up, usually right before sleep, Jazz shot it with a bolt of brain light, commanding it to disappear. He didn't have any way to get to Ocala, to see his mother, and anyway, he would never take her wedding ring just because his father wanted to feel like a big shot with his new girlfriend.

Worrying about his father wasn't going to help Jazz find Gethin. He needed to focus. He needed a plan. If he was inside Gethin's head, what would he be doing on Daytona Beach? Jazz sank back onto his ankles, heartbroken and overheated. His stomach felt like a hollow log somebody had set on fire. Across the sidewalk, the same little boy was still playing with the toy turtle while his parents drank beer, ignoring him. Above their heads, in the sign for an arcade, three Jester Heads grinned, menacing the sidewalk below.

Why hadn't Jazz noticed them before? He had been so focused on the kid he had walked right by the place without looking at the sign. *Ice Cream*, it said. *Fun Center*. The heads, molded from white plaster, jutted out from the wall, peering down in green, orange, and blue hats, eyes wild inside pastel-painted masks. It was the kind of place a drugged-out Jester Head from St. Augustine would love—dark as a cave, with people weaving in and out, clutching kids' hands and plastic cups of beer. Jazz climbed to his feet. It was a long shot, but he didn't have any other plan. Serena would have to forgive Jazz if he somehow found her brother.

The dark arcade enveloped Jazz in a sticky coolness that smelled of caramel and dust. Colored lights flickered up and down poles. Electronic chimes pounded a rhythm. A Wheel of Fortune game *clickety-clacked*, silently chanting—*jackpot, bankruptcy, jackpot, bankruptcy*—the story of his life. He could have the most wonderful woman he had ever met, or he could lose it all. His skin crawled from all the microbes that were no doubt swirling in the air, blasting from a heavy boy's blue-stained mouth, bristling on the handles of computerized casino games, a simulated deer-hunting screen, and a pair of miniature basketball cages.

The cacophony of children's voices and musical alarms pricked at his temples, so loud he almost didn't hear the jingle bells at first. The sound grew louder, dancing beyond a table full of popping mole heads, and there he was—a guy in a jester hat. More hats were poking out of a burlap bag slung over his shoulder. Behind orange-tinted sunglasses, the guy didn't speak, but only shook the dangling spears of his hat at kids in his path, to make the bells ring. A blinking neon butterfly flashed around his neck.

Jazz trailed the Jester Head, watching. Purple hippos gobbled up primary-colored balls. Kids yanked long strings of red tickets out of machines, cheering. The hat seller gave off a ripe wind of unwashed armpits and rank underwear. Jazz pulled his shirt over his nose, trying to hold his breath. At a pinball machine that crackled with purple lights, illuminating a dragon, the hat seller turned and locked eyes with Jazz, who let his shirt drop, realizing it might make him look like a bank robber.

The hat seller shook his head. His bells rattled and hissed. In the guy's orange sunglasses, Jazz stared at a jaundiced version of himself. "What do you want, man?" the guy said. The butterfly necklace made his chin look green, then blue, then pink. "Five bucks a hat. Two for eight."

"I've already got one," Jazz said, lying. "My buddy Brillo Pad gave it to me."

The guy looked down an aisle full of kids, at a man behind a glass counter containing pink plastic dolphins, rows of rubber erasers shaped like Star Wars characters, religious stickers, and a hookah pipe resembling a huge penis. "Cameron," the guy said, extending his hand for a shake. "If you know Brillo Pad, we're already friends."

Jazz muttered his name, and he knuckle-bumped Cameron's gray zombie hand.

Cameron sidestepped between two machines where dirty-looking coins piled up and dropped into a pirate's treasure chest. "You need something besides a hat?"

One after another, the coins plummeted off a ledge. "What do you have?"

"Weed." Cameron stood close to Jazz but didn't look at him.

His eyes kept shifting back and forth, shooting darts toward the sidewalk. "Meth. Oxy."

Jazz had to work to keep his neck from flinching. It felt cold and creepy, under his hair, as if one of the kids had dropped an ice cream cone down his shirt. He remembered a line he had heard on the tiny TV set inside Bantam's bicycle repair shop: *Opioids are an epidemic of addiction and suffering.* Parasitic worms seemed to be crawling under Cameron's ragged fingernails. "I'm good," Jazz said. "Looking for a friend of mine. Gethin. Thought maybe you'd seen him."

Cameron's nostrils flared. "Weird name."

"Kind of skinny, tall, about your age—hangs out with Chelsea, the Snake Lady." Serena had told Jazz what Rocky said about Chelsea.

The side of Cameron's face hardened. He smoothed one of his hat spikes and laughed. Two of his bottom teeth looked braided together. "No way I'm saying shit about Chelsea, man. She helped me out when I first moved to Florida. If it weren't for her, I would've starved to death."

"My friend's in need," Jazz said, using code he had learned from eavesdropping on the Jester Heads at school. "In need" meant *in need of drugs.*

On the other side of the Coin Suicide machine, a little girl in a feathered birthday hat screamed, "Conga line!" A red-faced boy latched on to her shoulders. Three others fell in line behind him. "He's not in need," Cameron said. "He's not even cool. I thought he was a narc the first time I met him; he just sits there staring at everybody, never joins in."

Through the shouts of, "Conga, conga," a woman's voice called out, "Cameron!"

"So you have seen him," Jazz said.

Cameron stuck his head into the aisle. The man behind the counter shouted, "You!" and he slammed through a half-sized door, waving a dolphin-shaped baseball bat, which was purple and glowing at the tip. "I told you to stay out of here!"

As he ran for the exit, one of Cameron's bells smacked into

the Wheel of Fortune machine and got stuck, pulling the hat off his head. Behind him, a woman in a green T-shirt and white shorts chased after him, losing a flip-flop in the process.

"Hurry," Cameron yelled. He swiped at his hat, but it was spinning too fast. Without the hat, his head looked small and slightly bald on the top.

Jazz lurched into the aisle, ready to trail Cameron, but he bumped into the empurpled end of the dolphin bat. The arcade manager's pale lips were freckled around his yellow teeth. "Who are you?" the man said. "If you're one of those jester kids, I don't want you here."

"I'm not a Jester Head," Jazz said, thinking fast. "I'm a private investigator, looking for a lost brother."

The man lowered his bat. "Your brother's lost?"

"Not mine. The woman who hired me." Why was Jazz lying? Instantly, a parallel reality had erupted through his brain stem, bubbling into a volcanic explosion of possibilities—a life in which he had a job, a home, a woman, a noble purpose, and enough food to eat.

Conga-line kids snaked by them. "I always cooperate with the police," the man said, fingering a pewter crucifix nestled in the shaggy white hair at his throat. "I run a Christian business."

"I've heard that about you." Jazz was enjoying his parallel reality. His chest felt bloated with authority. He could have been a private investigator, or a police officer, or even a lawyer. He would have been better than any of the ones on TV. He repeated his goal, describing Gethin, Chelsea, the snakes, and the dangers of drug addiction.

The man scratched his back with the dolphin bat. "See it all the time around here," he said, chewing his cheek. "The Lord is my shepherd; I shall not want."

"He maketh me to lie down in green pastures," Jazz said, deciding to roll with it. His mother had sometimes read the psalm over and over again when she wasn't feeling well. "He leadeth me beside the still waters."

The man raised a hand in the air. On his wrist, tiny gold

charms jangled: a peace sign, a cross, an apple, and a naked woman with large breasts. "Snakes, huh?" he said. "There's an exotic pet store two blocks over. Some of the kids hang out there. The owner's a lowlife, not like me at all. Maybe you could take a look over there."

Jazz handed a business card to the man. He had printed a bunch of them at the school library. *Jaswinder McGinness. Weird and Wired In.* "That's my other enterprise," he said, "but it's got the right phone number on it."

Tucking the card into his pocket without looking at it, the man planted the bat between his sandals. "I'll call you if I see anything."

"You've been a great help," Jazz said. "I'll be sure to tell my associates at the police department." He liked the idea of having "associates."

Beyond the arcade's back door, hardened gum wads stippled the sidewalk. A storefront displayed T-shirts emblazoned with obscene cartoons and sayings. To his right, a giant steel slingshot propelled two screaming people into the sky. Cars rumbled by, blasting music. A vendor leaned over her yellow ice-cream cart, smoking a cigarette. Jazz marched to the corner, pumped from impersonating a detective, and turned right.

Two blocks.

Another long shot. If he could find a free computer, maybe Jazz could track the location of Gethin's phone. Then again, Gethin hadn't been answering his phone and he didn't seem to be using any social media. Jazz had checked every day. There were no internet cafés or libraries along the sidewalk—only closely packed pizza joints, souvenir shops, and a "gentlemen's club" with a woman standing outside in a bikini, flipping a cardboard arrow while she danced to whatever tune was blasting through her earphones. Jazz tried to catch her eyes. He wanted to signal to her that he understood her situation—her poverty and boredom—*You are a woman, which makes you a goddess,* was what he wanted to tell her, without words—but she looked straight through him, as if he wasn't there.

Jazz kept going, slightly nauseated by hunger, through an intersection by a parking lot full of motorcycles, until he saw a small brick building with a strangely proportioned painting of an alligator by the front door. The sign looked homemade, as if somebody's cousin had sketched the gator in acrylic shades that were more blue than green. The place was well-lit but deserted. The dirt parking lot sat desolate. A small front door had been propped open with a brick. Jazz had to duck his head to get inside, which made him feel like he was crawling into a rabbit's hole.

The place smelled of cedar chips and bird poop, urine and chlorine. The aisles were narrow, crowded by shadowy towers of motionless lizards and snakes, a pair of baby alligators lying prone in a muddy pool, a nearly featherless parrot that didn't blink when Jazz stopped to say hello, frogs clinging to a sawed-off tree branch, and an aquarium that was empty except for two dead goldfish on a clump of algae. Under the hum of traffic, the shop was quiet, with no one else in sight. Jazz walked to the end of the aisle, where a back door had been propped open, probably for the breeze.

Across a stretch of grass, a man sat hunched over his knees with his hands folded together. A brown ponytail fell down his back. His ear was ringed with so many freckles, they looked like piercings. It was the main thing Jazz remembered from sitting beside Gethin in math class. He had lost weight. He was dressed oddly. His beard was growing out, but the freckles were unmistakable.

Jazz was certain.

His fingers were damp from the heat. He had to wipe them against his pants before he could fish out his phone and send a text message to Serena. With shaking fingers, Jazz typed, *I found him.*

18

Serena

Surrounded by the raucous beach party, Serena didn't hear her phone pinging, but she felt it buzz inside her pocket. Reading the first three words of a message from Jazz—*I found him*—she dropped to her knees in the sand, blinking hard. The rest of the message described a pet shop many blocks northwest of her location. *Will wait for you*, Jazz wrote.

Stealing a bicycle, even one that had been tossed onto a sand dune like rusty garbage, would have shocked Serena's father. Fat fingers of dune grass had a grip on the bike's crumbling frame, suggesting it had long since been forgotten by its owner. Still, her dad would have been disappointed to see Serena yank the bike out of the sand, hop aboard, and start pedaling hell-for-leather in case anyone tried to stop her. Sergeant Jacobs had raised a good soldier and an athlete—a daughter who followed the rules and kept her promises. She had promised, above all else, to take care of her brother. Jazz had found Gethin. Serena's car was miles back up the beach. She had no time to waste.

The tires on the old bike were nearly flat, which didn't make riding it through sand any easier, but all of Serena's strength training paid off and her adrenaline was pumping so hard, she had to spit the metallic taste out of her mouth. Her hat was gone—lost when she ran away from Jazz. Her upper lip and scalp felt scorched from milling around the music festival for an hour, scanning the crowd for Gethin. All she saw were boys playing beer pong with red plastic cups and girls with tattoos on their backsides wearing bikinis that looked like American flags. Kids with no self-discipline, going nowhere, making nothing of themselves. Was Gethin the same way? Serena had tried to show him how to live by their father's mantra—Perseverance, Patience, and Pluck.

She had failed.

Standing on the pedals with sweat singeing her eyes and clouding her vision, Serena barreled up a ramp full of people and onto the street, shouting a few lame apologies over her shoulder. A guy with a large silver eyebrow piercing said, "Hey!" and jumped off the sidewalk. Serena pushed harder, thighs flexing, six blocks north and three blocks east until she saw the pet shop sign with a lopsided drawing of an alligator, exactly as Jazz had described it. He hadn't said whether Gethin was high, injured, or alone—only that they would wait for her.

With the shop in sight, Serena poured on the speed, so close to ending the nightmare of her brother's latest disappearance. Her greatest fear—being alone for the rest of her life, without her parents or even her brother—would stop rearing its desperate head every night if only she could get Gethin back to her tiny house in their rundown neighborhood, safe in his own bed. Through the open door of the pet shop, Jazz was shouting, "Stop!" and "No."

Gethin rose up in front of Serena's handlebars a split-second before she recognized him, before she could hit the brakes or swerve. She clipped his heel and he fell forward, arms outstretched with his mouth open, making no sound. He hit the asphalt with his chin and shouted with his mouth full of blood, all of which Serena saw in slow motion as she flew off the bike and onto her ass.

She scrambled to her brother's side, whipped off her shirt, and pressed it against his face. His smell was foreign—dusty and sour—not Gethin's trademark soap-and-licorice aroma. Dark stubble obscured his flushed face. Remembering her first-aid training, Serena groped inside his mouth with two fingers, feeling for any loose teeth that might choke him. The scrape on his chin, covered with blood from his sliced tongue, looked worse than it was.

"Eew, stop it," Gethin said, sitting upright. "Why did you hit me?"

Jazz dropped to his knees beside Gethin. "He ran," Jazz said. "He was holding a snake that was sick and it died. He freaked out and ran off."

Serena had one hand around the back of Gethin's neck. She was pressing her shirt against his mouth with the other. In her sports bra and shorts, she was wearing more clothes than most of the people on the beach, but she felt exposed. As usual, Gethin sat rigid, tensed up but not struggling. "I've been so worried," she said, ignoring Jazz. She looked around at the stolen bicycle sprawled on its side, two little boys who gawked from the back seat of a blue minivan that eased around them, and an overweight couple smoking cigarettes across the street. Probably no one had called the police, it being just another Saturday in Daytona Beach. Still, a patrol car might roll by at any time. Gethin didn't like loud, sudden noises. "We need to get you off the street."

"I don't want to go home," Gethin said. "I want to help the snakes."

"Okay, show them to me, buddy," Serena said, playing along, and she turned toward Jazz, whose face had the stunned, blank look of an empty dinner plate. "Give me a hand."

She tucked her bloody shirt into the waistband of her shorts. With a minor assist from Jazz, she hauled Gethin up by the armpits. He felt heavier than he looked. Once he was standing, Serena walked beside him, keeping a firm grip on his arm. He had longer legs, but Serena was stronger than him, by far, and she wasn't letting go. Jazz walked behind them with his hands outstretched as though Gethin might fall backward.

Inside the pet shop, the smell triggered Serena's gag reflex. A cloud of gnats made slow circles over see-through boxes full of lethargic snakes, frogs, lizards, and turtles, all of which were in dry shadows—no carefully arranged reptile lamps or foggers like the ones Serena had seen Gethin use. At the opposite end of the room, an open door revealed part of a patchy lawn.

"Who's minding the store?" she said, peering around and seeing no one.

"Nobody," Jazz said. "It's pretty weird."

Gethin slid onto the floor, touched his open mouth with one finger, and stared at the blood on it. His face, no longer flushed, was as pale as the beach and it looked dry, ready to blow away. His eyes were black, moving backward in his skull to a place Serena had never understood. "She died," he said as if he couldn't believe it.

Serena eased onto the floor beside him. "Who died?"

"The little snake," Jazz said. "He was holding her when I got here."

"Let him tell me," Serena said, waving Jazz off. Gethin would be better if she could get him talking. She had to get him out of his head.

"She was right there in my hands," Gethin said. "Then she wasn't."

Jazz remained standing at a distance. "He wasn't surprised to see me. He remembered me. Brillo Pad told him we were looking for him."

"Let him talk," Serena said again. "Please."

"It's not right," Gethin said. His hair was uncombed. He was wearing a shirt Serena had never seen before: red with the same logo as the music festival banner on the beach.

Serena had to resist the urge to touch him. Gethin wasn't big on being patted or hugged unless he saw it coming and had time to brace for it. Almost anything could spook him when he was upset. "What do you think happened to the snake?"

"They get high and forget all about these animals all day long," Gethin said. "Chelsea and her Jester Head friends. Nobody's watching them. Nobody's feeding them. They don't even have dome lights or foggers. Before you know it, they're dehydrated and eating each other. It's disgusting and abusive."

Beyond the front door, a group of motorcycles coughed by. Exhaust fumes floated through the shop. "Where's your friend now?" Serena said. "Chelsea."

"I need to bury her," Gethin said.

Serena inhaled, too quickly, realized he meant the snake, not Chelsea, and exhaled. His feet looked dusty inside canvas sandals that were too big for him. "How about if we say a prayer? Remember the prayers Dad taught us?"

"They have no respect for living things, all of these people in Chelsea's orbit." He was talking to himself, not responding to Serena's question, tapping his thumb against his pointer finger. "I know she loves the snakes, deep down, but she's too tangled up in bad thoughts from the past. She's in the Drug Bucket. That snake was a living creature, a beautiful ribbon snake, no threat to anyone."

"So, that's not a thing anymore?" Serena said. "You and Chelsea?"

Gethin's face bunched up. He put a hand over his stomach and whispered. "She tried to have sex with me last night. She said she didn't want to be alone in the dark."

"I see."

"I rejected her overtures."

Serena felt sick and relieved at the same time. "Good choice," she said.

"This morning, she ran into an old friend on the beach. I guess he'll take my place in her tent. I need to find someplace else to go, but she's got all my money."

In the moment that passed between them, Serena thought of her father's gentle, patient gaze. "I love you, buddy."

Gethin brushed the dirt off his hands. "You've always been kind," he said. "Unfortunately, going back to your house is not an option. I'm sorry if that makes you cry, and that's not sarcasm, by the way. I regret how I've treated you—genuinely, as they say. It isn't something that I enjoy, being away from soap and hot water."

She wasn't sure what he meant. It didn't matter. She only needed to get him home. "Is this about Rocky?"

"Yes." Gethin pinched a crease into both legs of his slacks, which were beige and pulled up above his waist—the kind she had seen on older men who liked to take strolls through her neighborhood every morning. The red T-shirt was too small and didn't quite reach the top of his pants. "It's more about me, I suppose. The binary nature of who I am has never been appreciated. Snakes don't kill themselves, you know. Birds don't eat themselves."

Serena leaned forward, peering into the blackness of Gethin's eyes. A wormhole seemed to open up and pull her closer, until Serena could see their father in his casket and their mother driving away. "I don't understand," she said, speaking slowly. "Are you talking about your thing with the buckets?"

"Everything's binary," he said. "It's in one spot or the other. Things can't get mixed up. Rocky was in the Safe Bucket with me, but she moved out of it. I really wish she hadn't done that. It was her decision."

Serena didn't blink. Her eyes burned. "She's been incredibly worried about you."

Gethin stared at his hands. "I admired her very much. I can't explain how much."

"I need to ask you something." Serena said it without moving a muscle.

"That's fine." Gethin tipped his head to the side, quizzical.

"Are you high right now?"

"Of course not. I'm in the Recovering Bucket. I've tried to explain this so many times. Anything in the world can be put into a bucket. Once it's in there, it will stay in there unless someone deliberately takes it out and puts it someplace else. That causes chaos. I don't move things out of their buckets. I prefer precision. No way would I go back into the Drug Bucket."

Behind her, Jazz shuffled his feet and made a noise like he had something to say. Serena shot him a warning glare, shook her head, and waited, hoping he would stay quiet.

He didn't take the hint. "Hey, man," Jazz said, "I noticed—I mean, I saw how you posted a photo of yourself in a jester hat. It's none of my business, but I was wondering—"

"That wasn't my choice," Gethin said. "They stuck a hat on

me and grabbed my phone. As soon as I got my phone back, I deleted my Facebook page. That hat was filthy. I had no shampoo."

"So you're fully present," Serena said, staring at her brother although he almost never made eye contact. "You're still in the Recovering Bucket. I want to believe you, but it's not easy."

Except for balling up his fists, Gethin didn't move. "I didn't kill Mom's bird."

"I know you didn't," she said. "Mom killed Mom's bird. We've been over this."

"I didn't set the snake loose."

"She left the birdcage open. You were just a kid. She wasn't looking after you."

"Sometimes I wonder if we'll ever see her again," Gethin said.

"The bird?"

"No, Mom. The bird died, obviously."

His gaze left Serena feeling hollowed out. Staring at him felt like looking through a tunnel with nothing on the other side of it. He didn't look high. He only looked sad. "You need to come home now," she said.

"I can't leave until Chelsea and her friends come back. We can't leave these snakes here all alone. One of them already died. We have to feed and water them, but there's no food in this place they call a pet shop. I looked."

Serena stared down the aisle of the pet shop. "Bring them with you."

"Rocky wouldn't like that."

"She might get over it," Serena said, standing up, "or she might not. It's my house. You're my brother. Let's go."

19

Jazz

From the animal tanks, a tropical musk drifted uncertainly through the shop. "I could help," Jazz said. The line swayed with uncertainty, like a bridge made of rope.

In her pocket, Serena's keys chattered, as brittle and excited as the kids in the arcade had been. She tossed them, underhanded. He made the catch. No fumbling. "You remember where we parked, right? Bring the car around. We'll get some of these animals ready to go."

We. *She said we, she said we, she said we.* A bright wind circled his head and lifted his hair, filling it with glitter.

"I'm a better driver than anybody at NASCAR," Jazz said.

Gethin laughed. Serena did not.

With the keys digging into his palm, Jazz ran. His feet popped and sparked. They seemed to pound indentations into the pavement. He hadn't been behind the wheel of a car in three years—his mother's old Chrysler had been sold for groceries before she left—but Serena's perfumed sedan cranked as soon as Jazz turned the key. He let it idle for a minute. While the engine evened out, his phone rang.

Answering it in Serena's car, with its dangling crystal on the rearview mirror and the padded back seats where he had first smiled at her made his shoulders feel big. His phone displayed a number without a name. Maybe his old boss Bantam was calling to say he needed more help at the bike shop. Jazz could get his job back. "Hello," he said, pushing the word out into the world as a gift to the person on the other end of the line, giving it a brightness like a green shoot popping up through the mud.

"Mr. McGinness? Jaswinder?"

He recognized the slow twang right away. It was his mother's social worker. Mrs. Spencer. *Corinna.* "Hello," he said again, wilting. "Is she all right? Is she sick? Did something happen?"

Corinna said his mother wasn't sick. "She's on a new medication and doing much better. She wants to see you."

Jazz ran his hands down the steering wheel, which felt clean and cool—not the least bit contaminated. Serena had wiped it with a cleaning cloth, twice, on the way to Daytona Beach. "I've had a little trouble with the transportation issue," he said. "I'm kind of between jobs."

The other end of the line went quiet. A couple wearing blue cowboy hats walked in front of the car. The man tipped his hat, smiling.

"You're all she talks about, son," Corinna said.

Her words felt like an ice cube, swallowed whole. The jagged edges of her meaning made his throat hurt. Jazz had no home of his own, no money, and no car. He had nothing to give his mother, nothing besides love.

"Part of her recovery plan is to reestablish ties with her family," Corinna said when he didn't answer.

"Don't let my father anywhere near her."

"I understand that situation. We'll keep her safe. Do you think you can visit?"

From his father's temporary office in Sanford, Jazz had hitchhiked all the way back to St. Augustine. He was sitting in a car that Serena might or might not let him borrow. "Tell my mother I love her," he said. "I'll see her soon."

"Soon, as in this week would be excellent," Corinna said.

"God willing," Jazz said.

"You need to make a specific plan."

A brief silence crawled across the dashboard, guilty. "I'll be there this week."

Corinna thanked him and hung up.

Jazz had no trouble with the car's steering or the brakes, which he kept tapping. Behind him, someone honked. A stream of sweat rolled down his neck, but he didn't know where to find the air-conditioning button and he didn't dare take his eyes off the road or his hands off the wheel. His driver's license was still valid, but he didn't want to risk getting pulled over in Serena's car. He turned left and then right until the crooked alligator sign came into view.

They were outside, waiting beside three clear plastic boxes. Serena had her arm around Gethin. His head was resting at a stiff angle on top of hers. She was smiling, and when she saw Jazz, the smile widened.

She waved. *She waved, she waved.*

Jazz, the Maximum Champion, had found Serena's brother. He had rolled up in a perfumed chariot to carry them home. Through the windshield, the flat blue sky cracked open, shooting rainbows that expanded and surrounded him. Jazz eased the car to a stop.

The boxes contained a fat yellow snake, a dark one with pearl-colored rings, and a long black snake with a stubby-looking tail. Once they had loaded the boxes into the car, Jazz climbed into the back seat, letting Gethin sit up front, next to his sister, where he belonged.

For a while, Serena drove in silence, leaning forward with her hands wrapped around the top of the steering wheel. Jazz wanted to give her a box of chocolates and a bouquet of flowers—anything to make her smile. Instead, he told a lame joke about a pirate. "A pirate walked into a bar. He said, 'Ouch'… because he had hit his head on the bar after walking into it." That one made Gethin laugh. An invisible door cracked open. Jazz stuck his head through it, leaning over the front seat.

Gethin was watching phone poles flash by. "Rocky's going to be angry with me," he said.

"You need to apologize," Serena said, "even if you're breaking up. She's suffered. I have too, by the way."

"Take her some flowers," Jazz said. "Do you know what my favorite flower is?"

Gethin turned his head and blinked at Jazz, deadpan. "Let me think about it for a minute," he said. "No, I don't know what your favorite flower is."

"Passion flowers. *Passiflora incarnata.* Some Spanish priests named them after the crucifixion. There are a whole bunch of them by my park. You know the park with the pond that's almost a lake, behind the Baptist church? Every time I see those flowers, I feel like I've been transported into the clouds, straight to heaven with a choir of angels singing around me."

Serena leaned back against her seat. She turned her head to talk. "Those are the purple, wiry-looking ones, right? I didn't know that about the name, but now that you mention it, the middle does look kind of like a crucifix. They've got all those crazy filaments and everything."

"There's an island in the middle of the pond. You have to swim to it, which I've only done once because I saw an alligator on the bank one time. I don't think an alligator would actually try to bite me—I mean, who would bite the Jazz Man? Even an alligator would know better than that—but anyway, once you get there, the place is covered with passion flowers and butterflies."

"That's pretty cool," Serena said.

Maybe she was so happy to see her brother, she had forgotten all about her argument with Jazz. He hoped so. If he talked long enough about all the brightness in the world, maybe he could scrub his words about Satan and demonic possession right out of Serena's brain. She would have to forgive him then. He tapped Gethin on the shoulder. "Do you know what I mean? Women love flowers. Women *are* flowers."

The muscles in Gethin's neck went stiff. "Let me get a pen so I can write that down," he said, and he fumbled in his pockets for a second or two.

When they finally reached Serena's house in St. Augustine, Rocky wasn't there.

Gethin unloaded the trio of snakes and fussed over the lighting, fog machines, and ventilation in the garage. Jazz did his best to help, gathering towels and bowls of water. Serena cooked a package of chicken breasts with brown rice, and she set the kitchen table for three. Jazz sat in Rocky's place. After dinner, he held his breath, waiting for Serena to grab her car keys and drive him back to his spot. She never did. She let him stay.

She let him stay, she let him stay, she let him stay.

20

GETHIN JACOBS

At the kitchen table later, Gethin pressed his elbows against the metal surface until his skin turned red. He listened to the clock tick and Rocky's shallow breathing, in and out, like a dove being constricted. Across her cheekbones, the beautiful smooth skin was stretched too tight, forming crinkles around her eyes. She stared at him sideways and looked away. Gethin's knees bounced up and down. The metal table bounced too. Rocky kept both hands around a mug of tea. Inside, the pale green liquid trembled. To calm his legs, he pushed one foot on top of the other. The tips of his fingers tapped together in a pattern: trigger, middle, ring, pinky, trigger, trigger, pinky. The trigger finger needed extra taps, to keep it from pointing.

Serena had said he owed Rocky this much: an apology and a chance to speak her mind, "to find some closure." He pictured the whiteboard in his math class, littered with a long column of backward-facing numbers, adding up to nothing.

"I didn't have sex with her," he said.

Rocky dropped a spoon against her saucer. The noise sank its fangs into his eardrums. "You expect me to believe that?"

Gethin leaned forward until his shoulders were nearly touching the table. "I wasn't wasted, either."

"You lied to me. You lied to Serena. Why should I believe you're telling me the truth now?"

Behind her, the kitchen wall seemed to bounce forward. Serena had painted it a deep rose color, darker than the rest of the room, and in Gethin's mind, as it bounced, pulsing in time with his heart, it formed a frame around Rocky's head. Some of her braids had come undone on the top. The tendrils waved, searching under the slow, circular breeze of the ceiling fan. Her eyes were red at the bottom but still glowing brown, enriched by red velvety shadows, warm enough to swim in. "A lie would be an error," he said. "It's a dropped stitch, a mutation, or the wrong chord. I admire precision. You know this about me."

Her eyes scanned each corner of the table: one, two, three, four. Her fingers expanded, stretching flat across the metal. Gethin stopped tapping. Back when he used to hold her hands, they had fit inside of his completely, like a baby bird wrapped up and waiting inside an egg. He could tell it wasn't the right time to reach for her, though. Her thoughts had moved into a different bucket on another shelf. "That's the thing I don't understand," she said. "You left your soap collection here, not to mention your iron. I know you can't stand putting on pants that don't have a crease."

A suitcase leaned against the back of her chair. The bag was printed with a red leopard pattern. Rocky also owned a red leopard dress. He had always enjoyed seeing her in it. The pink handle of a toothbrush poked through a green-mesh pocket. "I left in a hurry," he said. "It wasn't easy."

"That woman smells bad." Rocky's face shriveled up at the center. "She's wearing the same clothes every time I've seen her downtown. How could you be with her?"

"I wasn't with her." Gethin sat up straighter. He pictured his vertebrae uncoiling and clicking into place, one after another, in slow motion. "I wouldn't. Pretty sure that's why she told me to leave at my earliest opportunity. More accurately, she told me to 'get lost' and she walked away, left me in the middle of that crowd in Daytona. I walked back to that horrible pet store because the snakes needed care."

The tips of Rocky's fingers—long and pale, forming exquisitely parallel lines—smoothed and smoothed her eyebrows. "None of this makes any sense."

"I could help with your braids." He loved twisting her braids together. She had so many braids, set in rows from top to bottom. Each braid ended with a tiny rubber band covered by a fragment of aluminum foil, which was hidden by a bead. Fixing her braids involved precision and counting. "Sorry I wasn't here to do that."

Her cheeks turned a dark red color. Her eyes closed and she pressed her fingers into them, to stop the leaking. *Pain.* Not in her eyes, but inside her chest. Serena had told Gethin when he was still small what it meant for a person to cry. "We filed a police report," she said. "I thought you were dead. I pictured you on a morgue slab, and you're worried about my messy hair?"

"I didn't say it was messy. Actually, it's lovely—you're lovely. You always are. You can't help it."

"Was this all about some stupid snakes?"

"I don't appreciate the word stupid in reference to living creatures, but no. You and I are living creatures too. Snakes are God's creatures. So are you, and so am I. My mother taught me that before she left."

"I told you about my allergies. I'm pretty sure snakes make my skin break out."

"That's why I always kept my snakes in the garage."

For a second, Rocky's head jerked, as if Something Unknown had flicked against the back of her neck. Her forehead creased and her mouth opened into the shape of a howl. "Why then? You're sitting here telling me it wasn't about getting high, getting laid, or your snake hobby that I've never liked. If you just decided you hate me, why didn't you tell me, straight up, 'Hey, Rocky, you need to move out'—or something? Why'd you torture me with all that worry?"

The floor, ceiling, and walls felt like they were coiling around him, choking him. The clock's ticking sounded too loud. "That's incorrect. I don't hate you. What I feel for you is the opposite of hate, which is love, but you didn't want me anymore. That's not uncommon. Other people have wished I would disappear. My mother, for instance. I don't blame you, but I am who I am, both ways—light and dark, on and off. Binary. I could either disappear or die. I didn't want to die, so I disappeared. I really don't like it when your eyes leak. I wish they'd stop."

"Why would you think I didn't want you around anymore?"

Gethin rocked left and right. He looked at the ceiling fan, which had dust on it. To the left of the motor, one of the speckled ceiling tiles had come loose. He would have to put that problem on his list of Things to Fix. Serena couldn't afford a handyman. Jazz seemed like the type to start a project but never finish it. "You know," he said, "if you want to discuss the truth versus lies, or errors, as I like to call them, you could begin with what you wrote to my sister."

"What?" Rocky shook her head. "When?"

"She doesn't want me here, either. She feels sorry for me, which I must say, I strongly dislike."

"Are you kidding me?" Rocky's voice climbed up the wall until it sounded like it was punching a hole in the broken ceiling tile. He pressed his hands over his ears. "You chewed up her heart when you left, Gethin. Where do you come up with this bullshit?"

"On the computer. You left your email open, after that party where people were making fun of me at Yanni's house."

A crease formed between her eyebrows. She stared at the floor. Gethin stared at it too. The floor looked clean. "I don't remember what I wrote." She had switched to whispering.

"I'll tell you what you wrote. I memorized the message. You said, Number One, 'I don't know if I can take this anymore,' and Number Two, 'He embarrasses the hell out of me sometimes,' and Number Three, 'Tell me what's wrong with him before I go crazy.' That's what you wrote. Three sentences, like three blind mice, or three little pigs. Three strikes and you're out, Gethin. I didn't want to be put in the Trash Bucket. I left before that could happen."

Rocky watched him without blinking. Her eyes had stopped leaking, finally. "People told us all kinds of things. Were you talking about a trip to Mount Rainier?"

"I was going to take a bus to Jacksonville and a plane to Seattle," Gethin said. "They're studying rubber boas on Mount Rainier. They pay people to count them. I read about it on Facebook."

"Why didn't you get on the bus?"

He told Rocky what had happened next. The bus station had smelled like potato chips, a few of which had crunched under his shoes when he walked toward an open bench. Before he could reach it, a woman latched on to his elbow. "The bus was delayed," he said. "While I was waiting at the bus station, I met another person. That person was Chelsea. She had the yellow ball python with her. Its name is Banana Splits. I could see it wasn't in the best health."

"You were worried about her snake."

"Yes, and we started talking. Quite a number of words were exchanged. She told me how it was when she was small."

"What do you mean?"

"People hurt her. Her mother was not there. Her father did bad things."

For a moment, Rocky stared at him without speaking. "What kind of things?"

"Burns on her arms. No food to eat. A monster who came into her room after dark. She couldn't see to fight. She doesn't like to be alone at night."

Again, Rocky was quiet. "Did she hurt you?"

"No, no," he said. "She gave me some crackers and part of a Mountain Dew."

"What else did you talk about?"

"We were eating the crackers. I asked when the snakes had their last meal. She said it had been a while. She didn't have money for food. She had other snakes in her tent, starving. She had a very pretty kingsnake and an eastern indigo, if you can believe it. I had never seen an eastern indigo before. They're quite rare. Such a beautiful creature, although its tail got chopped off somehow."

Rocky swallowed. "How much did you give her?"

"Five hundred. She took me to see the snakes. I wanted to assess them. Her friend owns a pet shop in Daytona. She took me there too."

Rocky left the room. When she came back, she was carrying

a bucket full of hair picks, beads, and oil. She pulled her chair closer and handed him the comb.

Gethin ran his hands down her back first, removed the beads and foil and rubber bands, and started untying her hair. The ends touched her hips. The silence felt brittle, like something he needed to wriggle out of. "Will you be staying here? I could unpack your suitcase. Your clothes probably need ironing by now."

Three more braids fell loose and curled down her back before she answered. "I'm going to stay in Kevin's extra room for a while. He's got a tenant coming next month, but that gives me two weeks to figure things out. We'll see how we feel by then, okay?"

He rubbed oil onto her scalp until it was shining and pink, but Rocky didn't go limp under his hands, the way she used to do. "So, it's over."

"No, I'm saying, let's see how we do. It's been hard for me. I had another breakout while you were gone."

For a moment, he was quiet. "Who helped you?"

"No one. I helped myself."

"I'm sorry I wasn't here to help you with the ointment." He loved smoothing the cream over her rough patches, loved healing her until she uncoiled with relief and laid her head on his shoulder.

A red bead dropped to the floor. She picked it up, handed it back to him. "I need some time," she said.

"Things are either black or white," he said. "I'm either in, or I'm out. You're here, or you're not here."

"I'm between two places." Her voice had gone thin. She leaned back against him until he couldn't braid her hair anymore. "You're in the middle, where it's gray. It's not black or white. I'm feeling pretty confused right now, but I'm not blowing you off. I'm not your mother. I would never ghost you. Do you understand?"

The weight of her body pinned his arms. He slid them out and wrapped them around her, gently, so she wouldn't become afraid and coil up again. She smelled like the lavender soap he had bought for her birthday. "I understand," he said. "I have two weeks to convince you."

Rocky turned her head and pressed her cheek against his chest without saying anything.

The screen door creaked open. Kevin's big silhouette, backlit by the garage light, filled the frame. Rocky sat up straight and smoothed her braids back.

Kevin parked his knuckles against his belt, elbows out, trapping triangles of air under his armpits, traffic cop-style. He was wearing a blue polo shirt and slacks with creases in them. The creases weren't very good. One of the lines veered off to the left instead of going straight up and down. His black loafers looked newly oiled. He smelled sweet too, like he had dressed for a funeral, or a date. Gethin cocked his thumb back, but he didn't tap it against his pointer finger.

"You had us awfully worried," Kevin said.

Rocky stood up, gave Kevin a pat on the back, and reached for her suitcase as if she couldn't wait to be gone. Some of her braids dangled, undone.

Behind Kevin, the snakes were quiet in their boxes, probably recovering from the car ride, happy to be in the garage with water, food, and a fan. "You shouldn't be here," Gethin said.

Rocky's teeth turned into icicles, hanging from a fake smile. "I'm leaving the car for you," she said, looking at Gethin.

He had paid for most of the car—87 percent of it—so that seemed fair, yet it didn't feel right. The car was a tether that would keep her close to him. "You'll need it to get to work."

"I can take the bus from Kevin's place."

Gethin knew where Kevin lived. His house was in Lincolnville, across the river, near downtown. "You'll have to get to school somehow. I could pick you up."

"Thanks, honey, but that's also an easy bus ride."

Clearly, she didn't want to be tied to him anymore. Gethin stood up, repositioned his chair, and checked the time. He would feed the rescued snakes again in forty-three minutes. On the drive back to St. Augustine with Serena and Jazz, they had stopped for pet food. Kevin still had his hands on his hips. "We were talking," Gethin said, staring at Kevin. "You could have just honked your horn."

Kevin took the suitcase from Rocky, who had her head down. "I wanted to ask if you'll go to the four o' clock meeting with me," he said. The invitation came out stiff and formal. "You'll start your recovery all over again, one step at a time."

"I don't need to start over." Gethin's voice had a rattling edge to it. "Rocky can fill you in. I never got out of the Recovering Bucket."

"We've been over this. It doesn't work like that. We're always still recovering. It's a spiritual program. You have to work it."

"You're taking my girl away. She'll be in the Gone Bucket."

"That's not what's happening at all," Kevin said. "She asked for my help. Somebody calls for my help, I answer."

"I'm not gone," Rocky said. "I'm taking a break."

Gethin stood in the middle of the kitchen, shifting his weight from foot to foot, staring at Kevin. "I'm firing you as my recovery sponsor," Gethin said.

Kevin lowered his chin and exhaled into his collar. His mouth bunched up and he didn't say anything for a minute. "That's your choice. I'll see if I can find you a temporary sponsor."

"I don't need one." Through the open door leading to the garage, one of the snakes uncurled itself and lifted its head. They were getting hungry. Rocky would need to eat too. He touched her elbow and let it go. "Come back for dinner," he said. "On Friday. I'll make something special."

She turned her head and looked around the garage. "Maybe we could go out somewhere. This feels—"

"I'll make everything perfect." He didn't have the money to take her out. "I'll pick you up on Friday at six o' clock in the evening, not the morning."

"Okay." She stepped into the garage and blew him a kiss. "I'll see you then. Take care of yourself."

"I love you," Gethin said. He had never told her before. It hadn't occurred to him.

Kevin backed out of the room and put his hand on the doorknob. "Anytime you want to go to a meeting with me," he said. "Think about it."

"Okay, let me think," Gethin said, looking at the ceiling while stroking his chin. "No." He wanted to throw a chair at Kevin.

"Suit yourself." Kevin tried to close the door, but Gethin held it open.

"Sorry about the mess in here," Rocky said as she sidestepped the snake boxes.

That was when it happened. Kevin's hand unfurled like a plume of poison gas and he set it on Rocky's back. Beyond the garage, sunlight bounced up from the sidewalk, slamming into Gethin's eye sockets. It ricocheted painfully around his skull. Lightning bolts, too fast for human sight, seemed to strike the exact spot where Kevin was still touching Rocky, and not even through her blouse, but high up on her shoulder blades, where her skin had always been as shiny as caramel, under the lovely braids Gethin had tried to repair.

21

Jazz

Jazz drove Serena's car west on Route 207, beyond St. Augustine, past the edge of town and the fairgrounds until he was careening through flat farmland. Inside a thick fog, tractors and portable irrigation machines turned into gray silhouettes. Serena hadn't asked too many questions. He had explained the purpose of his trip—to see his mother. Serena dropped the keys into his hand, kissed his cheek, asked him to be back in time for her to get to work. Again, she thanked him for finding Gethin.

Would Jazz find his mother lying alone by the window again? Or sleeping with her mouth open and her hands crossed, like a corpse?

Onward he drove to Palatka, lined with tidy, two-story brick stores, and he turned left toward Ravine Gardens Park. He drove with the windows open. The hot wind flew into his face, his ears, his nose, infusing his brain with freedom, power, and hope. A reliably working car with a full tank of gas struck him as a beautiful thing. He could keep driving, beyond Ocala, but he was on a mission. His mother needed him.

Saw palmettos, palm trees, and lives oaks encroached on the two-lane road. Turning from one small highway to another, the car bumped over railroad tracks and into Citra. Three wooden crosses—one yellow and two white ones—rose up between a Baptist church and a dollar store. The road widened, spanning four lanes. He passed sweeping horse pastures. Suddenly, the hidden rural landscape gave way to lots for sale, antique malls, and fast-food restaurants, followed by a couple selling all of their possessions by the side of the road. Tractor, RV, and car dealerships popped up until Jazz passed a Welcome to Ocala sign.

He would not ask his mother about her wedding ring. He would never give the ring to his father.

One more turn and he finally found the place where his mother had been living for the past two years, behind a gas station, a church, and a strip mall. He pulled through the circular driveway and into a parking lot. The low-slung building was shaped like a horseshoe. Farther off, a larger building advertised rehabilitation services. Leaves littered a tennis court. Tendrils of Spanish moss fluttered from oak trees. Would Meghna hug him and say hello? Would she remember his name?

Inside, the social worker was waiting for him. Corinna Spencer's buoyant cheeks had fallen, leaving hollow pits under her droopy eyes. The formidable breasts were gone, too; her shoulders sagged inside a navy-blue dress with a white bow on the front. Jazz hugged her, feeling bone and sinew, brittle gaps and feathery skin: death.

"You're sick," he said. "What's wrong?"

She peered at him over her glasses. "I didn't tell you that. Is it obvious?"

The reception area contained four beige armchairs, a lacquered coffee table, and an oversized bouquet of plastic flowers. The room smelled synthetic, as if someone had scrubbed it with bleach before spraying perfume—a cross between a swimming pool and a department store. Jazz pictured the toxic plume eating holes through his nasal passages. "It's probably only obvious to me." He inspected her hands, which were shot through with blue veins that shifted under his thumbs. "I see everything. I see things no one else sees or wants to see. The things I see would give most people nightmares. Sometimes, I close one eye if it gets to be too much. I have dolphin vision."

Corinna pulled her hands back. "How old are you now?"

"I'm thirty-two." Jazz leaned over the plastic bouquet, separated two rubbery stalks, and rescued a child's forgotten toy—a miniature Superman figure with his arms raised for flight. "Almost thirty-three. I see the whole world." Superman got tucked into a pocket of Corinna's dress.

"They've got a Lost and Found box," she said.

"How's my mother?" Jazz peered over Corinna's shoulder, down the hall. A woman looked up from a desk, removed a pen from behind her ear, and turned away. A door opened and closed. "How are you doing with your illness?"

"Your mom's much better, but she needs to start transitioning. The state won't pay her hospital bills after next month. There are state-run assisted living places, but she doesn't want that. Honestly, I don't want that for her, either. We need a plan."

"I see." Powder-blue jumpsuits were everywhere—on an orderly who was pushing a patient in a wheelchair, on a man parked next to the reception desk, on a nurse who also wore paper shoes tied with strings. No one whistled or played music or snapped their fingers, which Jazz urgently wanted to do. With every breath, Corinna's chest rattled. "You didn't tell me how you're doing," he said.

"I'm done with the radiation and chemotherapy." Her knees were shaking. She listed to one side. "I'd like to get your mom squared away. She's such a sweetheart."

Jazz pulled one of the armchairs closer. "We should sit down."

Corinna's hands wobbled, reaching for the armrests. "I need to know if you can help your mother."

The fake flowers seemed to elongate, turning into spears with tentacles. He pushed the vase to the far side of the coffee table where it couldn't sneak up on him. "Do you think my mother will recognize me this time?"

"Yes." In the big chair, Corinna reminded him of a wormhole in space, sucking everything into its center. "Last time we talked, I asked you to get into treatment. Did you ever do that?"

Jazz stood up and walked toward the automatic door until it opened, bathing him in heat and light, which made him think of Serena. He turned around. The door closed. He walked toward it again, forcing it to open. He repeated this process three times. "I met the most beautiful woman. Being in love is the best therapy I could possibly imagine. Have you ever been in love?"

"You were supposed to start taking lithium," she said, ignoring his question. "I sent you to a doctor who gave you a prescription. Did you ever get it filled? Are you taking the medication?"

His neck, when he swiveled it around, let out two loud cracks. He got two more cracks out of his shoulders. He started to crack his knuckles, but her eyes, still staring, had iced over. "I don't need medication," he said. "I'm the luckiest man alive. I have God. I have light. I have a beautiful woman."

"Do you have a home?" The back of the chair was higher than her head. She let it fall back and she looked at him sideways. "Something permanent?"

"Yes." Outside, the light shifted, boring into him. After he found Gethin, Jazz had spent the night at Serena's house. She had loaned her car to Jazz, maybe as a kind of repayment for locating Gethin. Would she take Jazz back to his spot in the park when he returned her car? Jazz didn't know. "I live with my girlfriend."

"How many people are in the home?"

"Four." He pictured Rocky's suitcase, red and spotted like a leopard. "Next week, maybe three."

"How would your girlfriend feel about your mother moving in?"

Jazz locked his fingers together like a prayer. He turned them over and looked at all the pink and white lines on his palms. His love and life lines intersected in a confusing tangle. "I don't know."

"Your mom's on disability and Medicaid." Corinna's voice strengthened, buzzing around his ears. "She's got a little bit of financial support and health insurance."

"I'm not sure," Jazz said again. His ears were ringing. He wanted to see his mother. As soon as he saw her, he would know what to do next. He could bolt down the hallway—nobody could stop the Maximum Champion, certainly not the skinny orderly in his sky-colored uniform, but Jazz didn't want to be rude. Corinna had been a true friend to Meghna. Corinna was sick and she was trying to help.

"You know, Jazz, it's genetic." Her words buzzed around his head until they stung him. He wiggled his fingers inside his ears, trying to release the poison. "Some people think that what you have is on the same spectrum as your mother's condition, but it's just like you said. You're lucky. Unlike schizophrenia, bipolar I is fairly easy to treat. You have to agree to be treated. Do you still have that doctor's prescription, or not?"

His brain felt as though it had shot through the top of his head, out of his body. His arms and legs went rigid. "I want to see my mother now." The sentence came out heavy and cold as a shroud. Yes, he had the doctor's dirty prescription, wrinkled at the bottom of his backpack. "I came to see my mother. I'm going to her room. I'm sincerely grateful to you. You're a genuinely kind person. You're very beautiful too. There's a sweet, pure light that comes off you. I'm going to pray for your good health."

"I could help you," Corinna said. Her eyes reached up, open like hands.

Blood rushed back into his limbs. He felt rubbery, as if he could dance on the ceiling. He kissed her cheek, hugged her, and walked away. She called him back.

"Keep this," she said, handing him the Superman toy. "Remember what I said. You told me once you're the Maximum Champion. You're a hero, but heroes need to take care of themselves too. They have to be brave and take medicine even if it's scary."

Jazz thanked her and pocketed the figure, annoyed. Superman's hands dug into his leg. "I heard what you said."

"I have another appointment now, but I want you to call me after you visit your mom. Let me know how it went and what kind of plan will work for the two of you."

He remembered where to find his mother's room, down the corridor, around a corner, beyond the dining room with its padlocked refrigerators, to the left, facing the road. Along the way, he greeted everyone, shaking hands: "How are you today? My name is Jazz. What's your name? I love that shirt. God bless you. Have a beautiful day."

At her doorway, a small gray dog cocked its head. Silver tags jingled on its collar. Its tongue dangled through a smile. Jazz crouched down to pet it. One of the tags said, *Pandora.* From inside the room, Meghna softly called for Jazz. His name sounded dreamlike. *She recognized him.*

In the center of the room, she remained motionless for a second, smiling and tentative in blue slacks and a lilac-colored blouse that reached her knees. She grabbed her throat with both hands, staring, and Jazz moved forward, pulling her into his orbit, a little bit at a time, until her cheek was pressed against his chest, and finally, her hands touched his back. "You'll have to excuse my little friend," Meghna said, barely audible. "She can't say hello properly."

Jazz spoke into his mother's hair, which had a bright, clean smell. "Why not?"

"They cut her vocal cords to make her stop barking." Meghna pulled away but locked her fingers around his elbow. Her eyelids looked heavy. "Can you imagine?"

Pandora clicked across the room and sniffed Jazz. He picked up the dog, cradled her, and set her back down. She sat down at his feet, wheezing. "Who would do such a thing?"

"Whoever left her outside the shelter." Meghna's hands moved back to her throat. "She can't breathe very well. Corinna says vocal cords can grow back sometimes. I'm hoping Pandora will find her voice again."

Meghna's room was full of sweet, heavy smells: perfume, shampoo, and baby powder. The smells had begun to latch on to Jazz. He wasn't sure how to help his mother, or if he could, or what Serena would say about another roommate. He had just met Serena. There was no way he could ask her such a thing.

On the dresser, beside a silver-plated hairbrush Jazz remembered from childhood, a framed photo showed Meghna holding him by the hand when he was six years old, headed to school for the first time. His hair had been more orange then, coiling in all directions. Meghna had tried to slick his hair back with oil, which only made it look wet and messy. The kids had made fun of him, calling him Lard Head, Carrot Top, and Freckle Face. From the beginning, he knew he had been born different. "I'm glad to hear your voice again," he said. "You were asleep last time I came to see you."

"I'm on a new medication."

He had to keep bending forward to hear her. Meghna had learned English by whispering it, after she got married and moved to America. In India, she had been an actress—a reader of great works. She couldn't stand the idea of fracturing any language. Because she wasn't sure about English words at first, she said them quietly. "I was about to take Pandora for a walk. Would you like to help?"

"Yes."

Beyond a back door, after Meghna had signed herself out and promised to remain at least ten feet away from the gate, the air moved slowly, but it moved, sending a sticky breeze under his collar. The outside smells were a neutral green; they took no sides, made no claim on him. Jazz began to feel better. They walked around the tennis courts, into a circle of oak trees. He wrapped an arm around his mother's shoulder. Pandora's tail bounced up and down.

"I'm going to buy you a castle," Jazz said, picturing the sun bouncing off a series of gold domes. "There's a computer contest coming up, the Hacker's Challenge. When I win the prize, we can build a place on the ocean with a walkway down to the beach. I was thinking it should be a boardwalk, but then I thought, no, a stone bridge would be more beautiful, but the top would have to be polished flat so we could wheel our chairs and umbrellas down to the water. What do you think?"

"It sounds like the home where I grew up, before my father died. It wasn't on the ocean. It was in the mountains. There was a river below."

"I remember." They had reached a muddy pond, which was dotted with lily pads and surrounded by chunks of granite.

"You were never there."

"I remember my dreams from before I was born," Jazz said.

"I remember all the songs that were sung before I came into this world," she said, repeating a line Jazz had heard many times, usually while she was reaching for invisible shapes in the air. This time, her eyes were clear.

"The song of bubbles in your mother's womb." Jazz could picture it. "The light and the waves."

"The doctors don't like it when I tell them the story, but it's true. I didn't hallucinate it."

They had reached the far side of the pond. The hospital was barely visible around the bend, through the trees. He leaned over to unlatch Pandora from her leash. "I believe you," he said. "I understand."

"I don't think that's safe." Meghna's voice had turned sharp. Pandora raced a circle around the pond, coughing. "There are rules here."

"It's okay, Mātā." Jazz smoothed a strand of hair off her face, and he kissed her cheek. "There's a fence around us. She wants to be free."

Meghna leaned her back against a tree trunk. Pandora sniffed at the water where it met a sandy patch of grass. The pond was still except in the center, where water burped from a rusted pipe that might have been a fountain at some point. "Where do you live now?"

"I live in the world." He stuck his hands into his pockets, repositioned Superman, and jingled Serena's car keys. Pandora pawed at the water, testing it.

"You're not in the apartment anymore?"

"No. I'm in school."

"Did your father help you find a job?"

It was a promise the old man had repeated like a prayer when Jazz was younger and the three of them still occasionally ate dinner together at a table with flowers on it. *I'll put you in touch with people. You won't ever have to worry in life.* Bravado and bluster. Lies from a blackened mouth. Fake offers from an outstretched hand that snapped back unexpectedly.

On the backside of the property, the fence was no more than four feet high, and it was slack in spots. For Jazz, it was a symbolic restriction—a ridiculous warning. Getting his mother and the dog over it would be awkward but easy. "We should leave," he said. His joints burned. "Nobody owns me. Nobody owns you. It's not a crime to be free, to be happy in the world. I could lift you up, Mātā. I have a car. We could be gone in two minutes."

She reached for a tree branch and hung onto it. "My doctors are here. I've made friends. I need my medication."

Pandora had waded into the water up to her neck. She smiled back at them. On the far side of the pond, the water rippled. "Do you? Is being different a crime? Do you think this life is better, being locked up and anesthetized, unable to talk about your dreams?"

"I'm happier now." Meghna didn't look at him. She was walking toward the water. "You worry me. Corinna says you need medication too."

In the water, the ripple was dark and moved at a steady pace. It reminded Jazz of how his mother had sometimes danced with long scarves in the unlit house, after his father left—all swirling circles and deliberate movements. He recognized the shape a second too late. A large turtle with a pointed head surged forward. Pandora wheezed and turned for the shore, but the turtle snapped at the dog's tail.

Meghna screamed. Jazz plunged into the water and grabbed Pandora, hauling half of the turtle out of the water at the same time. The turtle refused to let go. Jazz didn't want to hurt it. He held its neck without squeezing, applying just enough pressure to make the thing open its mouth, which looked like a hawk's beak. As soon as its jaws opened, Jazz pushed it away, threw Pandora onto the grass, and scrambled out.

The dog let out a series of raspy squeaks. Meghna clipped

the leash back onto it. "Pandora says she was scared," Meghna said. "She didn't know the pond was dangerous. She wants to know why I didn't take better care of her."

Jazz inspected the dog's tail. It took all his strength. His arms felt weighted down. His hands moved only in increments. "She's not hurt," he said. "It just caught her fur."

He expected his mother to pick up the dog and cradle it, wailing. He expected her to scream and shake her finger, but she only stroked Pandora's head. "I won't blame you if you don't want to live with me," she said. "Maybe you don't think you can. I know it was bad before. Corinna says you just need to tell me the truth so I can make plans."

The Truth. He had never liked the word. Whose truth? Wikipedia's truth, subject to a million perspectives? Media truth? God's truth? His own truth had been complicated—full of dark turns, magical smells, and sudden gifts too precious to put into words. He could never be sure how many of the moments in his life had been real versus dreams. Serena, for example, could retreat into his dreams the moment he returned with her car. "The truth is that I'm homeless," he said. "I've been living in a park because I couldn't pay the rent on the apartment, but I hope to win this contest I told you about. The Hacker's Challenge. I've met a beautiful woman. I love her."

"Oh, how wonderful," his mother said. "If you love her, I love her too."

"I want you with me more than anything, but I can't see into the future right now."

"I understand," she said.

"All I can give you is this moment and all my love."

His mother reached into her pocket. When her hand reappeared, it sparkled. The diamond in her wedding ring caught the light, sending out flares as she turned it between her fingers. "I had another reason for bringing you here."

"I don't want it." It came out quickly, as fast as the backside of his father's hand, smacking Jazz across the face when he was six and didn't want to go back to school because he couldn't stand to be teased anymore. If Jazz took the ring, it would be like having a loaded gun in his pocket. His father would find him and use the ring against him. "That belongs to you."

She pressed it toward him. Jazz put his hands behind his back. Pandora curled herself at his feet, whimpering. "You could sell it and get enough money for an apartment. When I'm with you, I can help. I get a disability payment every month."

He took Pandora's leash from his mother, picked up the dog and pressed her wet imprint into his shirt. She smelled like mud mixed with fish and rotting leaves. "I can't sell your wedding ring. It's part of your history."

"Pawn it, then, and get the cash." Meghna pushed the ring at him again. "You could buy it back later. Don't let your father near it. He's already been here, trying to take my things, but you're my next of kin, so he got nothing. Anyway, they say I'm competent to handle my own affairs now."

"Congratulations."

Pandora's funk had seeped through the waistband of Jazz's pants. "We should go back," he said. He was no longer thinking about jumping the fence. He set the dog down. "I should have a shower before I head back."

Meghna pushed the ring into his hand and wrapped his wet fingers around it. "Please. Take it. I've got nothing else of value. Make a plan for us."

His plan, which had been so bright in his mind the day before, like a flat highway stretching straight into the horizon toward Serena, turned shadowy and geometric, full of dead-ends and trick doors. Jazz pocketed the ring, reluctantly, just as he had accepted his father's cash. With Pandora's leash in his hand, Jazz guided his mother back to her room.

22

Serena

With Jazz in possession of Serena's car, she was on her bicycle, pedaling circles around a labyrinth of curling streets, hitting gravel, asphalt, and more gravel, sailing through patches of light and the shadows of oak and palm trees, searching for Gethin.

Again.

How many years had she spent looking for her brother, trying to understand him and keep him safe? Maybe he had only gone to the grocery store in his old car. Serena had gone on a walk, mostly so she could call Fletch Jefferies, the police officer, to let him know Gethin had been found—saved, along with several snakes. Jefferies said the snakes were most likely stolen. He planned to take a look on his way home, but when Serena got back from her walk, something was wrong. The kitchen table, chairs, cleaning supplies, stacks of magazines, coffee table, half-empty paint cans, gardening tools, and Gethin's buckets were lined up on the driveway. The three snakes they had rescued in Daytona Beach were safe, curled up in their boxes inside the garage.

Gethin wasn't answering his phone. No answer from Rocky, either. Serena dragged everything back into the house, hopped onto her bicycle, and went looking.

Sweat poured down Serena's face, stinging her eyes. Her hair and shirt were soaked. She hadn't brought her water bottle. The street seemed to throb with heat. She didn't realize how far she had traveled until she saw the little pavilion where Jazz had been camping.

Did he sleep mostly on the grass or on the concrete? Which would be worse—dealing with bugs and a back ache, being hungry all the time, or the constant threat of getting mugged?

She had been happy to loan her car to him so he could see his mother. He had told her about Meghna. Serena wanted to help, of course, and even after his strange outburst in Daytona, she was surprised by how much she missed him. She pictured him running alongside the bike, flexing his lovely muscles. He could use his weirdly supernatural powers of observation to zero in on Gethin again. He would take one look at the wet hair plastered to her face and say, "You're beautiful," and, "I love you," over and over until she didn't care if he was crazy or not, which probably made her crazier than him, in her own way.

Serena steered the bike under the pavilion and let it crash onto the grass. She imagined Jazz smiling with his arms outstretched, running toward his mother, who had been sick for a long time—too sick to help him. Serena's mother had no such excuse. Gladys had no excuse at all, in fact, except that she was self-centered and had always wanted to live in Austin. She had sent Gethin a T-shirt for his birthday with the town motto on it: *Keep Austin Weird.* No card or note inside the envelope—only her return address on the outside. Gethin had never worn the shirt. Serena hobbled toward the picnic table. "Thanks for nothing, Mom," she said. "Great T-shirt."

Although Gladys hadn't seen Gethin for years, she was still his mother. She had a right to know what was going on. Pulling out her phone, Serena looked up the farm where Gladys had been working the last time she got in touch. Serena wasn't sure what she would say, but whatever came out, she wasn't going to cry. A stranger with a deep, drawling voice answered the phone. "Gladys hasn't lived here for at least a year," he said. "Not sure where she went."

Serena hung up.

It was a stupid idea. Even if Serena could find her mother, what could Gladys possibly have to say for herself after so many years away? Serena dug her knuckles into her burning eyes. She tried to imagine her mother saying, "Well, hello, darling. Are you doing well?"

Maybe Gladys would talk about organic farming or the

weather in Texas. One wheel of the bicycle ticked slowly in the wind. Serena thought again about Jazz and the wounds on his hands and knees, after she had accidentally knocked him off his bike. "I can't find Gethin." She said it out loud, as if her mother might be standing next to her. "He keeps disappearing. I'm pretty damned strong, but I could use some help here."

Serena laughed in a sour way. She started imitating how her mother used to sound, whenever she was talking trash about somebody. "Gethin's always lost and found," Serena said, using a high, drippy tone. "That's what he does, remember? Why are you being so dramatic?"

After a minute, Serena answered herself. "Yeah," she said, "but I'm afraid he's going to die." The fear, finally expressed, felt as though it had lifted her off her feet, levitating her above the pavilion. *He says he's not on drugs, but he's in rough shape. He's upset about Rocky.*

Overhead, a mottled cloud floated by. Gethin had always been different. So many labels had been tossed around. ADHD. Something the doctor described as "Autism Light"—Visual and Auditory Processing Disorder. OCD. A slight developmental delay. Anxiety, depression, addictions. The truth was, Gethin was just Gethin.

"He's going to piss somebody off and get himself killed." In the empty park, saying it out loud seemed dangerous, as if the words themselves could cause something horrible to happen. Serena remembered something epically stupid her mother had told her once. "You have to let him go with love."

Never, Serena thought. *I promised Dad.*

The bush where Jazz kept his backpack seemed to house a family of chipmunks. They darted in and out of the leaves and poked their heads up, hypervigilant, on edge. In the stream behind the park, something splashed. Serena wandered around a swing set and a climbing gym that looked like a miniature log cabin. Across the water, somebody was crab-walking over rocks along the bank. He was partially hidden by mangrove branches.

I love my brother.

An oddly familiar shout bounced across the water. The man stepped down, into the water. He flashed his mostly bare body only briefly, but it was long enough for Serena to see her kid brother in his underwear, no longer a boy, submerged in the muddy pond where Jazz had seen an alligator.

Gethin seemed to be in a trance, as usual, focused only on what he wanted at that moment. Immediately, Serena understood his plan. Toward the middle of the lake, the little island was exactly as Jazz had described it, with a tree at its center. The tree was surrounded by bushes she recognized as seagrape, thick with paddle-like leaves and green berries. Even from a distance, she could see brown-and-yellow-striped butterflies floating, here and there, over the wiry purple flowers—the crucifixion flowers Jazz had talked about when they were in the car coming back from Daytona Beach.

Her brother's face was shiny and transfixed. Filaments in his shoulders moved from side to side. Had he removed his clothing to avoid getting it dirty? Typical Gethin, always worried about cleanliness. If anyone else saw him at that moment, nearly naked in a murky pond in Florida, they would surely call the police. He would be seen as a predator, a crazy person, a danger to children in the park. Removing plants from a public park was probably against the law. Anyone else would be afraid, but Serena understood. He was gathering passion flowers for his dinner date with Rocky.

Pink with exertion, Gethin rose out of the water and tilted his ears to the ground, twice on each side, maybe to let the water roll out. After circling the island, he stood under the tree with his eyes closed and stretched out his arms. Was he enjoying the sun on his wet skin, or was it another one of his physical tics—a ritual without meaning, except to him? He lowered his arms, counted to three on his fingers, and stretched them again, moving in the same sequence as before. Again, he counted.

He had gotten too thin. She tried not to look at all of him, exposed, but she couldn't help seeing her brother, fully revealed and imperfect, with his asymmetrical rib cage and the funny star-shaped patch of hair on his chest. He had grown up tall and broad-shouldered. Serena could understand why Rocky loved him, or had loved him. He was a good-looking guy, even if he was wearing Superman boxer briefs and he couldn't carry on a conversation without tapping his fingers together.

Serena was seeing Gethin, finally—her baby brother with his peculiar special needs no one had ever been able to define. As he told everyone who met him, he liked music and hiking and snakes. Apparently, he still liked Rocky too—enough to get covered with mud by wading into water where an alligator might be lurking. He wasn't lazy or undisciplined, as Serena had always thought. He was different—so different, it didn't matter whether he persevered, or had patience and pluck, their father's most cherished virtues. Gethin probably wasn't ever going to hold down a regular job or "make something of himself" in the way that Serena and her dad had dreamed about it. The best Serena could hope for was to keep her brother alive, safe at home.

That was all. That was enough.

She would never, as her mother had proposed, "let go with love." In Serena's case, letting Gethin go wasn't a loving choice; her love for him would always require hard work, sticking around, and being responsible for another person. She watched Gethin for a half-hour while he gathered flowers. She waited as he slogged back across the stream and up the rocks, where he disappeared into the trees again.

For the first time, Serena saw Gethin as he was.

He left without seeming to notice her.

Remaining in place for another few minutes, Serena's mind raced into the future, to a time when she might not be around to take care of Gethin. It wasn't like Serena had any money. All she had was her little house, but maybe if she kept working hard—*the three P's!*—she could set Gethin up so he would always be safe, no matter what happened. With Serena's help, Gethin might be okay. He might have a life.

The ghost of Serena's mother vanished, maybe for good,

and all at once, her father was standing beside her instead. He wrapped an arm around Serena, speaking in his low, quiet way.

I'm proud of you, was what he said.

23

Fletch

"I've got a present for you," Fletch said and he placed three lumpy pillowcases onto a table in Trina Leigh Dean's serpentarium. He had put the pillowcases into the trunk of his patrol car soon after her snakes were stolen. "Merry Christmas."

Her eyes expanded and she shook her head, half-laughing. "It's not—what is this? It couldn't possibly be—?"

"Yes, ma'am," he said, grinning so hard he felt like his tired old face might crack open. "It could be, and it is indeed your three babies."

Trina lunged at him, squeezing his neck and talking into his ear. "You sweet man. I love you for this. Thank you, thank you."

Heat crept up his collar. To shake it off, he laughed a little too long. "Now, I couldn't tell what kind of shape they're in, honey. I was scared shitless. I just stuffed them into these pillowcases and I drove them over here right away."

"Come to mama," Trina said, untying the first bag. Banana Splits was coiled in a tight ball at the bottom of it, still a luminous yellow with cheerful splotches. Trina lifted the ball python onto the table, holding its head as well as its body. The snake blinked and flicked its tongue when she gave it a peck on the side of its face. A tear rolled down Trina's face. She didn't bother to wipe it away. "She looks a little tired, maybe dehydrated, but she's okay."

Fletch opened the second pillowcase, prompting Unicorn to surge out with such force, Trina had to catch him before he slid off the table. She cradled the big snake's head for a second and wrapped him around her neck so that his stubby tail hung down over her belt. "He seems to be in fighting form," Fletch said, laughing.

"He's healthy, but you found him just in time." Trina lifted Unicorn's face and inspected his eyes. "See how his scales are a little bit dull? He's getting ready to molt. His habitat needs to be extra humid."

"He's in good hands now."

After lowering Unicorn into an extra-large bin, Trina eased the old eastern kingsnake out of its cotton sack. "And here's my handsome Bandit," she said. "This is too good to be true. Tell me the whole story. Where have they been? How did you get them back?"

While she zipped around the serpentarium, placing each snake in a separate vivarium with water and a dead, defrosted mouse, Fletch followed her, talking a blue streak. "Remember my missing person, Gethin—the guy whose sister was so upset?"

"Yeah." Trina repositioned the ultraviolet light in one of the habitats. "Your blood pressure was giving you fits the day she came to see you at the station."

"That's right. Serena. She's his sister."

"You tracked him down?" Trina stood back, smiled, and put her hands on her hips. "Good work, detective."

"I had an informant," Fletch said, softening his tone. He didn't want to tell Trina the bad news about her sister. "I found out who Gethin was living with."

"Who was it?" She was still smiling, as if they were playing a guessing game.

"Your sister, honey. You were right. Chelsea had your babies, tried to sell them in Daytona Beach. Gethin didn't like the way she was treating them. He and Serena brought them home. She called to tell me all this. When she described the snakes, I was pretty sure they belonged to you, so I rolled over there to take a look. There was nobody home, but the garage was wide open. Your snakes were right there, safe and sound."

Trina's bright face, so happy a second earlier, began to collapse. She stepped back, coughed, and squeezed her eyes shut. "But why—where's Chelsea? Is she all right? Can I see her?"

Instead of answering, which would have required telling Trina the truth about Chelsea's way of life, Fletch hugged her. "I'll find her," he said, not at all sure that would be a good idea for anybody.

24

Gethin

Downtown on St. George Street, Gethin stopped and scanned the cobblestone walkway for an alley, an open door, or any other escape route when Brillo Pad's red hair popped through the crowd, unmistakable. The shops were all packed. Gethin cracked his neck, *left-right-left,* and he pinched sharper creases into his long-sleeved shirt, which felt too warm for the weather. Brillo Pad never rolled without his skinny girlfriend, Melon Ball. Also, Chelsea was almost always somewhere nearby.

Gethin didn't want to see Chelsea. He didn't want to go back into the Danger Bucket. Finally, the red hair disappeared into a bar. Gethin was safe. He counted to ten and made his way forward again.

A white lovebird, like the one his mother had owned, was all he needed to make everything perfect for Rocky's return on Friday night. He had mopped and dusted the whole house. While he was out gathering the passion flowers, a police officer picked up the three snakes. Serena explained how Chelsea had stolen them from the serpentarium. Gethin missed the snakes, but he was happy they were back where they belonged, receiving good care. He had been to the serpentarium many times. It was a happy place. Anyway, Gethin didn't have time to keep thinking about the snakes. He needed to buy a lovebird downtown, then get back home to finalize his plan. If he could execute all the steps of his plan in the correct sequence, Rocky would be back in the Safe Bucket. She would be back in Serena's house.

A surprising thing happened on St. George Street. As he approached the pet store, it was gone. The Wild Things sign, with its spray-painted art-deco lettering that looked like graffiti, had been replaced by the red-and-blue logo for a chain store called Companion Care. Gethin's chest thumped. Had his friend Rahman lost his job? Unknown people made Gethin sweat and talk too fast or shut down. He wiped his hands on his pants and went over the plan in his head. He ticked it off on his fingers, whispering the steps into his shirt collar.

One, ask to see their bird collection.

Two, buy a lovebird.

Three, ask Serena to go out for a movie. (This one would be tricky.)

Four, wash clothing.

Four-B, press clothing.

Five, cook meal.

Six, open wine, preferably the pink kind beginning with the letter Z.

Seven, spray more lemon oil.

Eight, play music, but not the loud, rhythmic kind—something with a woman singer and an up-and-down melody.

Nine, light candles.

Ten, win Rocky back.

When he stepped inside the pet shop, the door made a loud buzzing sound. The place smelled like cedar chips and wet dog fur. Inside a small glass enclosure, a poodle was getting hosed down. Hamsters ran on wheels. Green birds with yellow heads hopped around their cages, squawking. Along the back wall, rows of fish tanks shimmered, blue, orange, and lavender under spotlights. Towers of pet food lined the aisles.

A young woman approached him. She had a green streak in her pale hair and a headset attached to a black box on her belt like a singer on stage, or a secret service agent. Her name tag said Austin—the same as the city where Gethin's mother had decided to live. Austin the Person had several merged freckles across the bridge of her nose. She asked if she could help him.

"Blessings," he said. His fingers felt wet.

Austin adjusted her headset without smiling. "All God's creatures are blessings." She said it robotically as if she had been forced to memorize a brochure for new employees. "That's like our motto."

"It's an excellent motto. Very few people understand."

"Cool." Austin was chewing gum. She looked him up and down, maybe assessing the creases in his slacks and the shine on his shoes. "Let me guess. You need to register an emotional support animal, am I right? There's a form on the counter. You need a psychologist to sign the form, but you can pay somebody to do that online. We've got a list. It's pretty easy."

"Emotional support?"

"It's super convenient because then you can take your companion on planes and stuff. It's thirty-five dollars, plus the shrink's fee."

Gethin rocked onto his left heel, then his right. If he stuck his hand into his pocket, he could jingle a few nickels around his paper money. "Is Rahman here?"

"Who?"

Behind Austin, a man wearing a rust-colored uniform pulled a dead fish from a tank. He dumped the creature into a plastic bag and slammed the lid shut. "Rahman Abdelsayed. He's got long hair, which you might call blond or brown, although maybe more brown, I would say. He's got a tattoo of an eagle on his right hand. He's in charge of reptiles, amphibians, and raptors."

"Sorry, there's no one here by that name." Austin fiddled with the black box on her belt. "How can I help?"

"Please." He couldn't think of anything else to say. "May I speak with the store manager?"

Her face went flat. No more crinkly lines through the freckles. "You're doing it."

Gethin looked at his reflective brown shoes, which were tied in a double bow, the way his mother had taught him when he was four. He plucked at an eyebrow. "I apologize. Are you in charge of reptiles now?"

"We don't keep exotics anymore. Domestic companions

only. Hence the name, Companion Care. You sure you don't want the support animal registration?"

The lights were too bright. Gethin preferred more subdued lighting. With a pinch, a hair came out of his eyebrow. Gethin inspected it. He wanted to make a wish and blow it away, but she was staring at him, still chewing gum. He dropped it and tapped his thumb against his middle finger: *one, two, three, four, five, six, seven, eight, nine, ten.* Ten steps to get Rocky back. "Do you sell lovebirds?"

By the cash register, a pair of teenage girls laughed behind their hands and bumped their shoulders together. "You mean like doves? No, we sell parakeets only," Austin said. "Fifteen dollars per bird, and we require that you buy at least two. They do better that way."

Gethin had to open his mouth for air. He was breathing too fast. "I don't believe that I ever introduced myself properly. My name is Gethin Jacobs. I like music and hiking and snakes."

Austin pressed her lips together. "Pleasure to meet you, Gethin." She had a soft, sing-song voice as if she might be talking to a child. "Sorry we don't have what you wanted. You have yourself a nice day, okay?"

When she walked away, Austin had the same kind of rolling stride as Rocky.

The lights had made him blind. The lights were blackness.

It was hotter outside, but not as bright. He moved under the shade of a tree and stood still, counting off the steps of his plan now that his plan had no lovebird in it.

He heard Brillo Pad before he saw the red hair again. It was too late to run. Gethin felt pinned in place.

"Whatcha doing there?" Brillo Pad's real name was Harry, like the British prince—the young one who would never be king. Gethin had overheard some guys at school teasing Harry about his name once. No one ever called him Harry, which seemed like a shame. Maybe Brillo Pad's crinkled-up face would smooth out, turning kind, if people treated him like they expected him to be noble. "Hey, how come you took Chelsea's snakes from Daytona? She wants them back."

Gethin shielded his eyes with one hand. He needed to protect himself from the sun and the jagged look in Brillo Pad's eyes. The clock tower ticked off another minute. "I rescued them," Gethin said. "They would have died. They're God's creatures."

Brillo Pad's gaze shifted back and forth. He wiped the back of his hand across his nose and let out a laugh like a nail gun going off. "Man, you're a weird one."

On a bench nearby, Brillo Pad's sort-of girlfriend, Melon Ball, shifted from one hip to the other. During roll call in class, the teacher had used Melon Ball's real name, Melinda. Her skin looked too thin to hold her bones. One of her shoulder blades had a scab on it. "Hey, those snakes didn't belong to you," she said in a voice like a toy with a pull-string in its back. "Those were Chelsea's property."

"I didn't steal anything," Gethin said. Sweat dropped from his sternum to his stomach, making him want to scratch. His arms tightened.

"Dude," Brillo Pad said. He moved closer, whispering. The exhaust blasting out of his mouth smelled like hot garbage and cheap weed. "Nobody said you stole anything. Listen, what's your story? You're jumping out of your skin. Speaking of skin, what the hell's wrong with your face?"

Gethin fingered a scab that had formed on his chin where he couldn't stop scratching it. "Allergies."

Melon Ball hauled herself off the bench, one limb at a time. A long ponytail sprouted from the top of her head. She separated it, tugged both parts, and flipped the end over her shoulder. The pieces of her hair fell in six lines: *One, two, three, four, five, six.* Her hips rolled and her skirt dragged on the ground. The fabric made a sound like a scolding at bedtime: *Shhhhhh.* "Ha ha," she said. "Somebody's got meth mites."

"I don't take meth," Gethin said.

"Uh-huh," she said. "Then what the hell's that thing on your face?"

"Whoa, nosy Melly, chill out," Brillo Pad said. He wrapped his elbow around her neck and knuckle-rubbed her head until she wriggled free. "We don't care what he's up to, do we, babe? Lookit, my man's been shopping. He's probably got a little cash on him. Am I right, man? You got a twenty on you?"

The words were spinning around like a roulette wheel: *Clackety clack-clack-clack.* Gethin exhaled against the sound. *Once, twice.* He had a ten-dollar bill, two fives, a one, and some coins in his pocket. About twenty-two dollars. "I wasn't shopping," he said. "They didn't have what I needed."

Brillo Pad's upper teeth jutted forward when he smiled. "So," he said, scratching his head, "no speed, huh?"

"No," Gethin said. "I'm in the Recovering Bucket."

With his head tipped back, Brillo Pad laughed so that the dark underside of his teeth showed. "What's that supposed to mean?"

"It means I'm safe," Gethin said. As they talked, he counted the number of people who walked behind Brillo Pad: fourteen. Too many people. "Rahman doesn't work at the pet store anymore. Rahman was my friend. The new manager doesn't sell lovebirds."

The wind blew Melon Ball's skirt open, exposing her wrinkled knees, which made her look like a very old woman with a sparse patch of pubic hair. No underwear. At the top of the skirt, a long sash wrapped around her waist. She untied it and made a new knot that seemed to be a slipknot but it could have been a half-hitch; Gethin couldn't see because her hands moved too fast. Her fingers trembled. "Change the subject all you want, but you took Chelsea's snakes," she said. "You need to bring them back."

Gethin decided not to mention the police officer who had relocated Chelsea's snakes to the serpentarium, where they would have a better life.

"Yeah," Brillo Pad said. "Those snakes are her livelihood, man."

A dog barked, low and slow. Gethin turned his head toward the sound. Outside the ice-cream shop, a familiar shape came into focus. Kevin was leaning against the wall with one hand in his pocket. He raised the other hand without smiling. *Hello, Gethin,* the hand said. *I see you.*

Brillo Pad tugged at Gethin's sleeve. "Can you help me out, man?" His voice had a curl to it and a hook at the end. "Got a little cash? Maybe we could make a trade?"

Melon Ball rearranged her skirt, her hair, and her sash again. She rolled her tongue over her chapped lips before speaking. "Chelsea's really upset."

Gethin shifted his feet so they were pointing in the other direction. "I see a person I know." He didn't say, "My friend's here," because that would have been incorrect. Kevin wasn't his friend anymore. Kevin was the guy who was trying to steal Rocky. In the distance, Kevin started walking away.

"We haven't had anything to eat all day," Melon Ball said.

"There's a place down the street," Brillo Pad said. "Pizza slices are two for one. Whatever you've got, man, really."

It wasn't like Gethin needed his money anymore. The pet shop wasn't selling lovebirds. "How much does a slice of pizza cost?"

Brillo Pad licked his lips, bouncing. "Five bucks, fully loaded."

A folded ten-dollar bill came out of Gethin's pocket. With his fingers, he sharpened its creases. "Five plus five is ten dollars," he said, handing the money to Brillo Pad, who crushed it in his fist.

Melon Ball smoothed her skirt, ready to go.

Brillo Pad had water in his eyes. "Thanks, really," he said. "We've been starving. Nobody's helped us all day. Hey, if you have another ten, we could get a whole pie."

"I have to go," Gethin said, pivoting to leave. Between the strolling tourists, a police officer walked by, licking an ice-cream cone covered with rainbow-colored sprinkles. Two sprinkles were stuck to his chin—blue and green. On his sleeve, the St. Augustine town patch said, Founded in 1565.

"Please," Brillo Pad said.

Gethin handed over two five-dollar bills.

"Hey, man," Brillo Pad said, grabbing Gethin's shoulder. "I feel bad. Let me pay you back. Just a taste to keep it real."

"I don't need anything," Gethin said. From behind, he felt a tug at his jeans, like his back pocket was being ripped off. He kept moving. Kevin's back appeared once or twice, whenever a seam opened in the crowd, but he was gone by the time Gethin reached his car. Probably Kevin had gone home to Rocky.

Gethin's plan to buy a lovebird had failed. He still had the purple passion flowers. Too late, Gethin realized he no longer had enough money to buy a bottle of wine starting with the letter Z. Maybe Serena would have a bottle of something in the refrigerator. Either way, Gethin felt certain he could still win Rocky back. He could get her back into the Safe Bucket, with him.

25

Rocky

To lace up her boots in Kevin's tiny guest room, where she had been staying, Rocky had to hairpin her legs on the twin bed. She couldn't sit on the edge of the bed and bend over her knees without banging her head against the wall. After two days, the acrobatic act had gotten old. Venturing into another part of the house to pull her boots on or off felt awkward; she was bound to run into Kevin, who was constantly lurking. She didn't have time for another one of Kevin's long-winded lectures. Rocky needed to get to school, which would require a sprint to the bus stop at the end of the street. After class, she would take another bus back into town to work her shift at the restaurant.

Kevin let recovering addicts stay in the guest room; inside, the white walls were decorated with a crucifix and the Serenity Prayer cross-stitched on a yellowing piece of linen. The house dated to the turn of the century. Kevin had sectioned off the original kitchen, turning the back part of it into an extra bedroom room where Rocky slept. She could spread her arms and touch the beaded-wood paneling on either side of the room. Also in the space were a free-standing porcelain sink and an old mini fridge that hummed all night long, right by her head. Near the end of the room, off the kitchen, a door led down some steps and into the backyard.

Rocky was in another kind of recovery. Or was she? Did she want to go back to Gethin, or not? The question kept flipping over in her mind like a perpetual coin toss. *Heads, tails, heads.* Could she ever accept someone she had no hope of changing?

She had fallen for three things about him: his ability to create order out of chaos, which Rocky had never learned to do, growing up in her parents' loony-bin house; the way his deadpan proclamations made her laugh, even if he didn't get the joke; and his body. She wasn't ashamed to admit it. Gethin had a killer body, broad at the shoulders and rippling across the middle. Rocky had worked hard since she was fourteen—old enough to get a Social Security card and a job. Why shouldn't she have a little fun for once in her life? It was impossible to take him anywhere, though. He embarrassed her by acting weird. Also, for Rocky, the honeymoon had ended when he disappeared.

She checked her phone and groaned. Another five minutes had slipped away. Her boots were still only halfway laced. On her back, at least she could see part of the sky and the top of an oak tree with its ancient, tangled branches. She otherwise couldn't see out of her room's ship-style portal without standing on the bed, which she had done a few times, trying to shake off claustrophobia. Kevin's yard was a small plot of well-tended grass and two trees with a swinging bench strung between them. On either side, two-story houses hugged the lawn, giving it a closed-in feeling, nothing like the jungle behind Serena's house where she had revealed the river by bushwhacking her way through the saw palmettos. Rocky had loved to walk Serena's homemade river trail with Gethin after they first met, before he started collecting snakes again.

Gethin said he had stayed clean. He hadn't slept with Chelsea, the woman who wandered around Hypolita Street, selling weed and photos of herself with a ball python wrapped around her neck. Rocky believed him. People took advantage of Gethin all the time. His mind was always spinning in concentric circles that tightened and expanded like gravitational fields in a universe inhabited only by Gethin.

One more loop in her laces and Rocky would be ready to run for the bus stop. From the kitchen, the air conditioner clicked on. Within seconds, her small room turned icy. The floorboards in the old house slanted from the front door to the back. Three or four times an hour, all the cold air in the house got trapped near Rocky's bed, whenever the window unit chugged to life.

She swung her feet onto the floor and inspected the laces. Her mind felt knotted. Would he hold her back forever? *Yes.* Did she love him? *Yes.* Rocky wanted to run to the bus stop and keep going. She wanted the tiny bed to collapse and swallow her into a sinkhole.

She bounced up, eager to leave.

Kevin blocked her exit. His creased face was illuminated on one side where sunlight was blasting through the back door. "Headed out somewhere?" He was always smiling. At first, Rocky thought he was a rare species: a genuinely friendly guy, a sturdy safety net. Lately, Kevin's friendliness had seemed more like a tangled fishing net that had snagged her ankles.

"I've got a class and work after that. I'll be back late." She didn't say she would be home—only that she would be back. Kevin's frigid prayer room didn't feel anything like home.

His chin bobbed up and down while he looked around the room at her open suitcase and her sneakers tucked under the bed. "You've got a key," he said.

"I know. Thank you." The hair on her arms stood at attention, either from the cold or because Kevin kept staring at her without blinking. How long had he been standing there? She would have moved into the kitchen and through the living room, but he took up the whole door frame. "I really appreciate you helping me out."

He leaned against the door with his hands in his pockets as if he had all the time in the world. "You give any thought to what we were talking about before?"

Rocky removed her backpack from a hook on the wall. "Sure, I guess." If he started another sermon about acknowledging her desires and living with honesty and integrity, Rocky was pretty sure she would barf. A wave of his rolled across the room, coiling itself around her. Maybe she was wrong, and Kevin was only being his usual unbearably paternal self, but at that moment, he was giving her the creeps. "Seriously," she said, "I can't thank you enough, but I'm going to miss my bus."

"Let me drive you."

"No." It came out too fast. Rocky wasn't sure why. Something about him seemed off. "The bus is easy."

She moved forward, hoping he would step aside and let her pass. He spoke again without moving. "I saw him downtown," Kevin said. "Gethin, talking to that drug dealer with the red hair."

The air conditioner coughed and roared louder. Rocky's fingers had gone numb.

"Gethin talks to everybody he meets. He always says the same thing about how he likes hiking and music and snakes."

"No, honey." Kevin took his hands out of his pockets and grabbed both sides of the door frame, preventing escape. "This was something else. I know a drug deal when I see one."

The wind felt squeezed out of her. She swallowed, trying to get more air. "Why are you telling me this? I thought you were Gethin's friend. You were his recovery sponsor."

"I'm not his sponsor anymore." His hands dropped to his sides. "I'm more concerned about you now. I want you to move forward with your eyes open, so you're not fooling yourself about a future with this guy. We can't judge him, but we've got to be realistic here."

Rocky charged for the door, hoping to disappear before her eyes filled up. Kevin caught her and squashed her against his chest. It wasn't a Dad Hug. His hands, moving down her back, weren't the hands of an uncle comforting his niece. "Shh," he said, whispering into her hair. When she stared up at him, his eyes had glazed over, like an animal in some weird mating trance. "You're okay."

"Stop," Rocky said, struggling to free her arms. "I have to go."

"Come on," Kevin said. His breath smelled sour. "Stay with me."

"Stop," she said again. "No."

Kevin cupped her face with both hands and laughed. "The diva act is getting pretty old, kid," he said. "You really need to smile more."

His fingers, circling her neck, felt rough against the tender part of Rocky's skin where her psoriasis had begun to flare up again. "Don't touch me." She twisted her head, trying to break free. "You're practically Serena's uncle."

In one quick move, Kevin crushed her against his body. "Take it easy," he said. "You're always so stressed out."

Too many times, Rocky had been in the same situation. She knew what to do. There was no point in fighting. Kevin was bigger and stronger. Instantly, she went limp, surrendering all resistance, putting on an act like the snakes Gethin called "drama noodles"—little gray hognose snakes that flip over with their tongues hanging out, playing dead if anybody messes with them. Kevin's tart aroma overpowered Rocky, making her feel dizzy. She thought of Gethin's licorice seeds and his collection of sweet-smelling soaps. When Kevin pulled back and looked down at her, she ducked under his armpit and ran, bee-lining it for the front door. She didn't bother closing it behind her. Her sneakers, all the clothes in her suitcase, and her toiletries could stay where they were until she could retrieve them, sometime when Kevin's car wasn't parked outside.

She should have seen it coming. Danger wasn't always as obvious as a slippery hand making its way under the covers, courtesy of her mother's latest drunk boyfriend when she was twelve. It was more nuanced than the red-eared guy leaning through his truck window while she swerved on her bicycle. Sometimes, danger smiled. It pretended to be a friend. A hero with a hard-on. She was sad, but not surprised to see danger in Kevin's face. For Rocky, danger was everywhere, always.

If she had a car, she could sleep in it, but she had refused to take the rusty old Honda she owned with Gethin. She didn't want to be tied to him that way. Not anymore. She didn't want to be tied to any man.

26

Rocky

The bus dropped Rocky off at the northernmost tip of campus. It was a ten-minute hike from there to the quad and the chemistry building. She scanned the concrete benches and the grassy lawn, half-hoping to see Gethin, relieved because the Math Nerds were alone under a palm tree, passing a hookah back and forth.

The Biochem 211 teacher was an adjunct. Almost all of them were adjuncts. It was cheaper than paying full-time faculty. The teacher, Stan, rattled on about DNA methylation in space—genes turned on or off to make life's blueprint older or younger—the astronaut who spent a year on the International Space Station while his twin stayed home eating potato chips—the twisted double helix and cosmic radiation. The whiteboard trembled like it might come crashing down every time Stan banged on it with a marker, as he liked to do. The class dragged on.

And on.

And on. Rocky checked her phone for messages. No word from Gethin or Serena—her family. Or were they? She scrolled through Gethin's Facebook page, which he had reactivated, but without updating it. Immediately after class, Rocky would call and tell Serena about Kevin.

"Marie Maynard Daly," Stan said, too close to Rocky.

She looked up, recognizing the name—dreading it. Stan stared through her.

"She was the first African American woman to earn a PhD in chemistry," Stan said, eyes locked on Rocky, as if he was the first person in the entire universe to know this fact. "She pioneered the way for other women in the field."

Swiftly, Rocky lifted her phone to her face, furious. Marie Maynard Daly, daughter of an immigrant, who rose to greatness studying enzymes. *Blah blah blah.* Rocky had heard the tale at least six times already. Each time, she had been the only woman of color in the classroom. Every recitation seemed orchestrated for her benefit.

Two guys on the front row glanced over their shoulders, presumably checking to see if Rocky looked inspired yet. She wanted to crawl under her desk and out the door. Fortunately, class was over. Stan's big windup about game-changing Black women chemists had been his grand finale.

The bus was late. She had to run to reach the restaurant on time.

Inside, the night's entertainment—a slender sixty-something woman and a white-haired guy with a guitar—were crooning and plunking their way through a soft jazz version of an old hookup song. For Liz & Taylor, who performed twice a week, it was once again a marvelous night for a moon dance. In the kitchen, a dish banged onto the floor. The french fry grease smelled particularly viscous. In the dimly lit room, Rocky blinked her eyes into focus. Shelby was nowhere to be seen. Rocky had made it to work first. She approached the hostess podium to put dibs on the best tables. Emmaline, the current hostess, traced a laminated map of the dining room and marked the prime sections with an R for Rocky.

The apron with Rocky's name tag pinned to it felt slick with grease. She tied the strings too tightly, as if she could bind all her courage with a double knot. The memory of Kevin's sickening cologne made her heart thump twice in one beat. She got straight to work, knocking off a four-seater for a ten-dollar tip within the first hour. The next diners were stingier. Rocky had heard them making fun of Liz & Taylor's rendition of "Islands in the Stream." The woman's hamburger had too much mayonnaise. Rocky's tip was only 5 percent of the couple's meal.

When Shelby finally showed up, she bumped Rocky's shoulder, sending a hot plate of barbeque ribs flying across the kitchen. Brown streaks splattered the white walls, the metal countertop, and part of Rocky's apron. "Oh no," Shelby said in her sneaky-fake way. "It's tough working the busy section, huh? Let me know if you want to do a switcheroo, hon."

During rush hour, Rocky's two largest tables, arranged side by side, were (A) five drunk white boys bellowing their political views for the whole restaurant to hear, right next to (B) an elderly man in a blue linen shirt who was obviously treating his grandkids to a vacation dinner downtown. The man kept one hand on the back of a tiny girl's high chair while he fed her french fries and did coin tricks for a boy who flinched every time the drunk guys yelled for more beer. As she moved from table to table, Rocky had to keep changing roles, from wisecracking Party Mom to Polite Professional.

"Give me all your loving," the drunk guys roared, singing along with Liz & Taylor. Rocky set a third round of beer on the Drunk Guys' table and she leaned down to whisper to the apparent ringleader—a thirty-ish surfer type with white rings around his eyes and a spiky shock of bleached hair. "Hey," she said in her most soothing voice. "This is the last one, okay? We've got kids here tonight."

She hadn't expected the ringleader to move so fast. He wrapped his wiry surfer arms around her. Rocky lost her balance, falling hard onto his lap. "Aw, c'mon, beautiful," he said. "Don't give me a hard time."

An ugly wave of growling laughter rose from the table. Rocky felt the ringleader's belt buckle against her hip and his fingers digging into her arms. "Let's get this party started!" one of the others yelled, raising a glass that sloshed over his fingers.

Rocky struggled to get her boots on the floor. What a shit-eating day. It was almost enough to make her go running back to Gethin. Sweet, crazy Gethin.

The ringleader squeezed her bottom and pressed his wet mouth against her ear. "You feel good," he said.

Across the dining room, the older man stood up with a napkin tucked under his chin. "That's enough," he said in a surprisingly loud voice that sounded like a bullwhip. "I've had just about enough of this nonsense."

Behind him, his grandson whimpered. "Baba," he said. "No."

Liz & Taylor ended their song after the second verse. A sudden silence greeted them. Rocky felt everyone's eyes on her. She dug her thumbs under the surfer's hands, freeing herself. Baba's hands were balled into liver-spotted fists. Behind him, his grandson sat up straighter. The baby in her high chair had stopped banging her spoon.

"All right, all right, pops," the surfer said, laughing with his hands raised, surrendering. "We're good here, right, guys?"

"Sorry, sir," Rocky said as she passed the older man's table. How many times per day did she say "sorry" to somebody for something that wasn't her fault?

The drunk guys left a few minutes later, tossing cash on the table that barely covered their bill. With his hand on the doorknob, the ringleader yelled, "Make America white again!" The door chimed like a siren in Rocky's head.

Liz & Taylor launched into their second set, kicking it off with an ambitious rhythm-box version of "You've Got a Friend." They followed it up with a hopeful song about living in paradise that sounded more like a question than a statement.

Hidden behind the prep table, Rocky was wrapping silverware in paper napkins, taking a breather by the back door when someone spoke through the screen. Rocky jumped and turned to look. It was Chelsea, looking gaunt and pale with a white snake draped over her shoulders. Her eyes were caked with makeup.

❧

Despite the heat, Chelsea couldn't stop shaking. Icy peaks had formed on her arms. She was broke and hungry. More than anything, she didn't want to be alone in her dark tent in the woods. Chelsea was afraid of the dark—always had been, ever since she was locked in a closet for hours on end, as a kid. Also, her snake needed help.

In the alley behind The Spindle, she adjusted the ball python around her neck and approached the restaurant's service entrance, which was propped open. Gethin's girlfriend was on the other side of the screen door, wrapping forks and knives in napkins.

"Sorry I had to run away earlier," Chelsea said. As always, she was ashamed by the cigarette-scorched sound of her voice. "I had to catch a ride to Daytona. Gethin was waiting by the bridge."

Rocky jumped. A spoon clattered to the floor. "What are you doing here?" she said. "What do you want?"

Chelsea pressed her nose against the screen. Her smile wobbled. Snooty Inside People were always backing away from Chelsea, but she couldn't afford to get mad. She needed help. "I thought you wanted to talk to me," she said. "You're Gethin's girlfriend, right? We met on the street, remember? You said your name's Rocky."

"He's back home now." Rocky's eyes darted all around, from the kitchen to the dining room, and back to Chelsea. Was she searching for a weapon, her cell phone, or backup?

Further inside, a teenager in a white chef's hat was hunched over a pot. The steam circling around his head looked blue, from the glow of the gas stove. The salty smell of roasted potatoes made Chelsea's stomach ache. "Oh, I'm glad," she said. "He's not cut out for the gypsy life."

Rocky's mouth fell open and closed again. "I don't need your help," she said.

The cook began ladling macaroni and cheese into a bowl. Still in the shadows, Chelsea swallowed hard. She hadn't expected Gethin's girlfriend to be such a bitch. Was it really too much to ask for a handful of crackers or french fries? "Well, maybe you can help me," Chelsea said. "I mean, if you would, please?"

"I don't have any money." Rocky chained her arms across her chest.

"I have two favors to ask," Chelsea said, ignoring the insult. Of course, people always assumed she was a ten-dollar hooker—even the cops, who had charged Chelsea for having a perfectly innocent conversation with some old geezer in a bar, back in the day. The snobby bartender didn't like Chelsea's short skirt and low-cut blouse, was all. Wanted to pretend he was working at The Ritz or something.

"I can't help you."

A hot bolt of outrage shot up the side of Chelsea's neck. The screen door wasn't latched. Rocky reached for the hook, bless her heart, but Chelsea was faster. In a flash, she was inside, grinning, victorious. "Look, I only want a bite to eat," she said, adjusting the poor sick snake where it was looped over her shoulders. "It doesn't have to be a whole dinner. A piece of bread or a baked potato would be great."

Rocky backed into a shelf full of pots and pans. "You can't bring a snake in here."

"It's just a ball python," Chelsea said, lifting Snowflake's head so that its hooded eyes stared at Rocky.

"I don't care what kind of snake it is. I'm allergic."

Chelsea imagined overturning the stainless-steel table. All the silverware would go flying. What a satisfying explosion of chaos that would create. Instead, she leaned out the back door, picked up the snake's blue carrying case, and stuffed Snowflake into it. "I've never heard of anybody with a snake allergy," she said, latching the box. "There, is that better?"

The sides of Rocky's neck were glistening. She was probably one of those stupid Inside People who hated snakes for being snakes. "Animals aren't allowed in the restaurant," she said. She was obviously trying to sound like a cop, but it came off like a question. "It's a health violation."

Chelsea smiled, remembered how her crooked teeth must look under the bright lights of the restaurant, and frowned. Her teeth were stained brown in spots. The fluorescent light made her blink and blink; she could feel her pupils pinching themselves down to pinpricks. Mercifully, her last hit seemed to be providing a second kick. "Please," she said. "Maybe I could just have a few leftovers?"

"Don't you have a grocery store where you live?"

Looking shaky, Rocky glanced down at the snake. Snowflake flicked her tongue, giving the mesh screen on her box a taste. Poor thing was hungry. Chelsea was hungry too.

"I live in the woods," Chelsea said. Such a stupid question. "My stomach feels like it's on fire. Can you help me or not?"

Rocky adjusted her weight over both feet like she might be gearing up for some dumbass kung fu kicks. Chelsea wanted to slap the sneer right off Rocky's perfectly smooth face. "I have to give you credit," Rocky said. "You have some nerve looking me in the eyes after what you did."

Chelsea looked down at her hands and opened them, silently counting to five. Her fingers were shaking. "Look, sweetie," she said. "I didn't sleep with your boyfriend if that's what you're thinking. Nothing happened. If anybody should be offended, it's me."

From Rocky, more stuck-up posturing. Her chest puffed out. She parked her hands on her hips. "What the hell are you talking about?"

Through the kitchen doorway, the cook was slamming globs of gravy onto fried chicken and waffles. The room seemed to pitch to one side. "I was going to sell those three snakes to my friend in Daytona," Chelsea said. Against her will, her voice was starting to rear up. Once the dragon was unleashed, Chelsea wouldn't be able to hold it back. "You know, make a little cash? Gethin stole them, didn't leave me a dime."

Another waitress slipped in and out of the kitchen, carrying four plates on her arms. Her boobs were pushed up toward her chin. She didn't seem to notice Chelsea, who had always been invisible to Indoor People. Rocky backed up and spoke again. "Gethin didn't steal your snakes."

"Bullshit." Chelsea spit it out as fast as she could. "My friend Brillo Pad told me."

"Gethin rescued those snakes because you weren't caring for them. Anyway, I guess the two of you are even since you stole all his money."

"I didn't steal a dime from him." Chelsea could feel the red dragon splotches blooming on her face. Her volume kept creeping up, notch by notch. "He gave me a little pet food money. That's not a crime."

Like a scared baby, Rocky stepped behind the table. "Right," she said. "The kind of pet food that goes in your arm. You took advantage of somebody with a disability."

The snake bumped against its box. "You're so full of shit." Chelsea clenched her teeth, feeling her mind go blank. Soon, the dragon would shoot flames from its mouth. "I didn't take advantage of anybody."

Rocky crossed her arms again, looking down like she was the queen of the clueless Inside People. She was at least a half-foot taller than Chelsea. "What do you call it, then?"

Tears welled up before Chelsea could stop them. That was always the way it went. She would be furious, then crushed by sadness. "I'm disabled too," she whispered. "Nobody's ever given me a hand in my whole life."

Laughter. Snooty Inside People were always laughing through their noses at Chelsea.

"Oh, really?" Rocky said. "No white privilege at all? Don't you have family?"

Chelsea pictured her sister Trina's sad smile and gray pigtails. Trina had loved brushing Chelsea's long hair on the porch at sunset. The soft, slow brushing had nearly put Chelsea to sleep every time. Against the orange-streaked sky, crickets sang their hearts out. "I have a sister."

"Why don't you ask her for help?"

As quickly as Trina had smiled, she frowned too, the previous summer when Chelsea tried to work at the serpentarium. Trina had yelled and shook her finger. Rummaged through Chelsea's things. So many rules. *Don't you dare bring drugs in here. What is wrong with you? Why can't you act right? Didn't I ask you to change that snake's water last night?* The right side of Chelsea's face kept twitching. She felt like she was floating somewhere above the room. "Well, you know," she said. "I don't want anybody holding me down, judging me."

"Sure," Rocky said, stretching the word out, sarcastic.

Chelsea bounced on her heels and looked all around. Maybe there was food nearby, close enough to grab. "I'd rather be free," she said, talking so fast that her words got mashed against each other. "I don't need you. I don't need my sister. I don't need anybody. You're all a bunch of Brady Bunch bitches."

Again, Rocky laughed. "I thought you needed a favor."

"I changed my mind." Chelsea bounced faster. "Pretty girls like you don't give a shit. Everything's so easy for you."

The cook rang a bell. "I have to close out my tickets," Rocky said. From beneath the table, she retrieved a basket of bread. "Here," she said, shoving it at Chelsea. "Please leave. Take that snake with you."

Instantly, Chelsea shoved a whole dinner roll into her mouth. She couldn't chew it fast enough. "That's the second favor I have to ask you," she said, talking around the bread.

"Seriously?" Rocky said. "You just called me a bitch."

"This is important. It's not about me. Snowflake needs help. She's molting. She can't get the scales off her eyes." Chelsea stepped partway out the door, ready to run. "That's really dangerous for a snake."

"Why the hell would that be my problem? Take her to the vet."

"I can't afford a vet." Chelsea shoved another roll into her face. In a minute, her stomach would feel better.

"Well, you can't leave that thing here," Rocky said. "No way."

"A snake can go blind if it doesn't molt right. Believe it or not, I'm not a monster. For your information, I do care about these critters. Take it home to Gethin. He'll know what to do. You can keep the box."

"Wait." Rocky reached out, but once again, Miss Chelsea Dean was too quick for Snooty Inside People. She slipped back into the alley and around the corner, gone.

❧

Rocky was staring at Snowflake's blue box, trying to slow her breathing when Charlie appeared, finally, looking more stoned than usual. "Where have you been?" he said. "Shelby's been covering for you. Whoa, what's with the snake?"

"Perfect timing," Rocky said. "Snake Lady stopped by."

"That old panhandler? Why?"

"She was hungry," Rocky said. "She left us a present."

"Jesus," Charlie said. "What the hell?"

The cook stepped toward them, craning his neck. "That's a health violation," he said, nodding at the snake. "Man, I hate those things. Toss it out back or something. Burmese pythons are dangerous."

"It's not a Burmese python," Rocky said, exhausted. "It's a harmless ball python. I'm not a fan of snakes either, but we can't go around hating every single thing that scares us."

The cook looked at the saucepan in his hands. "That's deep, man," he said, turning back toward the stove.

Charlie exhaled a long stream of marijuana-infused frustration. "Okay, hide that box for now." He pointed a finger in Rocky's face. "Don't leave it here overnight."

Rocky leaned down, knees shaking, and peered into the blue box. Snowflake stared back, flicked out her tongue, and tucked in her tail. With shaking hands, Rocky placed a kitchen towel over the box.

In the dining room, Rocky's customers had all fled. The older man in the blue linen shirt had left a note and a hundred-dollar tip tucked inside the vinyl invoice folder. "I apologize for those ruffians," he had written in elaborate cursive.

She sat down to read the rest of the message. Her hands froze, holding the words. "In my family," he wrote, "we would never treat the help that way."

Rocky figured she could ask Shelby for a ride to Yanni's duplex. At school, Rocky and Yanni had become pretty good friends. On the way, Rocky could drop Snowflake off at Serena's house, along with a note about the molting problem. Rocky pocketed the old man's cash. The note, she ripped to shreds.

27

Jazz

His mother's ring had felt like a hot coal the whole time Jazz was driving back from Ocala to St. Augustine. Inside Serena's garage, a white snake Jazz had never seen before thumped in a blue box. The snake's tongue flickered through a mesh screen. Had Gethin collected a new pet? Where were the three snakes they had rescued in Daytona Beach?

It struck Jazz as a bad sign. One new snake appearing. Three old snakes gone.

Quickly, he wedged Meghna's ring onto the tip of his pinky finger and tapped on Serena's door. He held the ring upside down, supported by his other hand to show it was a gift, if Serena wanted it. She had to want it. She had to invite him inside and let him stay. Otherwise, the black hole that always seemed to vibrate around his feet would gape open and swallow him whole—shoot him headfirst through a tunnel into outer space, or hell. He might never get back to Earth this time, if Serena sent him away.

He was ready when she opened the door. Except for her eyes, she didn't move. The diamond gleamed between them. Behind her, a tower of toilet paper was wedged beside a crate of canned vegetables and three plastic water barrels. She had told him how she liked to buy in bulk to save money.

Her expression shifted in tiny increments—the slight movement of her eyes from the ring, to his wrist, up his arm, to his face; a barely noticeable uptick of one eyebrow; her lips rising around her teeth. She smelled of deodorant and coffee.

It was all Jazz could do to stand still. Serena lowered her face over the ring like it might give off a scent.

"Wow, it's platinum," she said. Her face had a sheen to it—a light that invited him in. "I didn't know anybody made platinum jewelry anymore."

Jazz didn't move his hand. His arm was beginning to burn from holding it up. He wanted her to know that the ring, like his love, would be available forever—always possessed by Serena. "It belonged to my grandmother. My father's mother. I never met her. She died before I was born, in the old country, Ireland."

Dropping to his knees, Jazz locked his eyes on Serena, not blinking. "My father gave it to my mother. She gave it to me. I'd like for you to have it, for all you've done for me, and because I love you."

Serena's mouth opened. She looked out the kitchen window. Her shoulders collapsed on themselves. Was it a cringe? Not quite a cringe? Something in-between?

He jumped to his feet and straightened his back, embarrassed. He had gone too far. She needed more Cool Jazz, less acid rock, less heat. He could do that. He could be whatever she wanted him to be.

Waving him inside, she turned and walked through the house, to the side porch.

It was a space that looked like Serena might have built it herself, about six feet by five feet, crammed full with two red-cushioned chairs and an aloe plant in a cracked pot. She tossed a newspaper onto the floor, sat down, and lifted a cup of coffee off a tiny wrought-iron table that had rust on its legs. "You'd better keep that ring safe," she said, taking a sip that turned into a gulp, "for whenever your mom gets out of the hospital."

On the ceiling, a fan creaked in slow circles, shifting the air around them. In the yard, a cat stalked a lemon tree. The lemons were still a bright green, as green and tender as Jazz felt, waiting for a sign—a softening of Serena's eyes, or a hand, reaching to let him know he could stay, maybe forever. To let him know he could have a home with a woman who would look at him and see him instead of looking straight through him, the way most people did when they saw Jazz in the park, as if somebody had tossed a cloak of invisibility over his head, turning him into a ghost, unseen and unheard, not even on the margins.

In the yard, the cat's tail was pointed flat and quivering like an arrow, ready to pierce a heart.

Serena's eyes were red. The skin around them looked like a scarf that needed ironing.

Jazz craned his neck and peered through the living room, toward the bedrooms on either side of it. The ring had cut off the circulation in his finger, which was throbbing.

"Where's Gethin?"

She closed her eyes. "I don't know." The dimple in her chin appeared and vanished. "He's supposed to have dinner with Rocky tomorrow night. He's turning it into a big production, like the reunion of the century. I saw him yesterday at the park where you're living."

Jazz removed the ring and sat down.

At the park where you're living.

"He was picking passion flowers," she said. "Remember how you told him about the island?"

Her coffee mug said, *Look like a lady. Act like a man. Work like a dog.* When she raised it to her mouth again, a cartoon version of Rosie the Riveter flexed a bicep at Jazz from the bottom of the mug. He looked at his fist, which was clenched around the ring. "There's a new snake in the garage," he said.

"I noticed." She rubbed her eyebrows. "Rocky left it. Long story."

"The other three snakes aren't here anymore."

"That police officer confiscated them," she said. "He said the snakes were stolen from the serpentarium. He took them back to their owner."

"I'm glad they have a home," he said. "Did you sleep last night?"

Serena laughed like she might cry. She finished the rest of the coffee, set the mug down with a bang, and pinned him with a stare that felt like somebody clinging to a root sticking out of a cliff. "I canceled a paying client. Again."

The words came out like an accusation. Was she mad at Jazz? Maybe he was late returning her car? But no—he was back a day early. He had decided to drive straight back. He hadn't wanted to spend the night in his mother's reclining chair, feeling suffocated by smells as thick as a day-old fish.

"I put a little bit of gas in your car," he said. "I cleaned off the windshield and I made sure there weren't any bugs in the grill."

She smiled with her mouth. Her eyes looked too tired for smiling. "That could be a first for my car."

"I scrubbed it with my toothbrush. I couldn't find a car-wash."

She laughed. Not a sarcastic laugh, but a real one. From her face, a ceramic mask of sadness seemed to tumble off, sliding onto the floor. In his mind, it shattered into a million pieces, all of which instantly evaporated. The pieces rang like a string of small gold bells. Streamers of yellow ribbons, silvery glitter, and pink confetti rocketed around the room behind her teeth and her beautiful, shining face. Outside, the cat jumped and scrambled up a tree. A dog ran through the yard, barking. *Thank you, Lord,* Jazz thought. *She laughed.*

"So now you can't brush your teeth."

"I guess not," he said.

Serena touched his hand where it was wrapped around the wedding ring. Her voice was a choir and a whole stadium cheering while a marching band danced to a drum solo. "Tell me how it went with your mom. Did she seem any better?"

He had told Serena all about Meghna. "She loves you," he said, picking up Serena's hand, which seemed to pulse and expand. Jazz could live with Serena. Everything would be okay. His mother could live with them too. She could teach Serena how to dance with scarves and they would laugh and listen to oldies music every day. He put the ring into Serena's hand as payment up front. *Please let me stay.*

"That's very kind of her," Serena said, "considering she doesn't know me."

"She knew my name. We took a walk. I saved her dog. There

was a turtle. She gave me this ring. She would want you to have it. I told her I love you and you're the most perfect woman I've ever met. This ring is my heart. I'm giving it to you."

Her hand moved over his, warm and silky as a blue spring bubbling up from below a river, infusing his veins in a way that made him forget all about feeling thirsty, hungry, or tired from the long drive to Ocala and back.

Beyond the porch, the dog sat panting beneath the tree. His tongue bobbed up and down through a scraggly grin. Above his head, the orange cat crawled further onto a branch and swatted at a green lemon.

"I have a toothbrush that's still in the package," she said. "You're welcome to it."

"Thank you."

When she stood up, he dropped to his knees and pressed his cheek against her stomach, wrapping his arms around her back, inhaling her, whispering into her skin.

She touched his back.

He squeezed her waist more tightly.

She patted his back—a referee's signal to a wrestler—*release!*

Jazz knew he should let go. He didn't want to come off like some kind of aggressive creeper, but his life depended on whether he could hang on to her. He could feel the black hole yawning open, ready to suck him into space if she turned him away.

"I need to get some sleep tonight," she said, tugging at his elbows. "If I don't get back to work tomorrow, I'll have to sell my car. Look, I can't afford to be unemployed."

As soon as he let her go, she disappeared into the house. There was nothing for him to do but follow. It made him feel like a hungry puppy hoping for a scrap of love.

In the bathroom, she started fishing through drawers. Her shower curtain was torn on one side. The corner dangled down into a sad triangle.

Serena, Jazz, Gethin. Another kind of triangle.

Maybe Serena didn't have time for Jazz because she was too

worried about her brother. "As soon as I'm rich," he said, "I'll give you all my money."

She squatted and opened the cabinet under the bathroom sink. Her knees popped. "Is that right?" Her head was partway inside the cabinet door. Her words echoed around the cave full of face creams, makeup, and extra bars of soap wrapped in plastic.

"I'm going to win the Hacker's Challenge." Hunkering over his ankles, Jazz tried to help her search for the toothbrush. "I'll get a cash prize and probably a job with Google or Apple. They're going to have recruiters there. I'll build a house for you, my mom, Gethin, and Rocky. Everybody can have their own wing. It needs to be on the ocean. I'm going to paint it gold."

A toothbrush appeared—white with a gold stripe—and she handed it to him. "There's some gold for you," she said. "When's the challenge?"

"Tomorrow."

"Where?"

"At the college. I'm going to blow them away."

He offered his hand, to pull her up.

She grabbed the sink and stood up by herself. When she walked into the kitchen, he tried not to step on the back of her flip-flops. "When I start coding, the roof's going to blow off and spin around like a giant Frisbee until it's just lightning bolts shooting in all directions," he said. "Like me. That's the way I am. Nobody knows what I'm capable of."

"Seems like I've heard that somewhere before." Serena lifted her pocketbook off a chair. "I have to say, it kind of scares me when you start talking so fast like that."

The black-stitched strap on her pocketbook took up his entire field of vision. It shouldn't be over her arm because she shouldn't be going anywhere. The strap loomed over him, huge. It whipped forward and sank its fangs into his chest.

"I don't know what you mean," he said. "You want me to talk more slowly? I can talk more slowly. I know my mind moves faster than other people's minds. Most people are super-slow compared to me. It gets kind of frustrating, to tell you the truth, the way I always have to slow down so people can catch up with me."

She tipped her head to one side, smiled, and narrowed her eyes. "Thanks. I didn't realize I was slow compared to you."

Her hand was on the doorknob. The door was opening. He had to stop it. If he could keep the door closed, he would be able to stay.

"I want to cook dinner for you," he said. "I didn't mean you're slow. Not at all."

Serena stared at him, opened the door, and stepped into the garage. Again, Jazz followed. "That's exactly what you just said. Can you understand how that might be a little insulting to me? Kind of like how you compared me to the devil when we were down in Daytona."

"I never said that." The words burst out of him like an exploding can of soda. "Why would you say I said something I never said?" His feet slipped around the edge of the black hole, which kept expanding beneath him. "I wouldn't put words in your mouth. I wouldn't say you said something you didn't say. I love you. You're smart and kind, and I'm sorry! If it sounded like an insult, whatever I said, please forgive me. Beautiful Serena. Forgive me."

Her shoulders curled forward again. She looked at the chipped polish on her bare toes. "Do you have my car keys?"

Beneath him, the black abyss shot open. Jazz moved forward, out of its expanding perimeter. He fished in his pocket, but he didn't pull his hand back out right away. He spoke one word: "Please."

Again, her face slipped behind a ceramic mask. "Listen," she said.

He did, but all he could hear was her breath, which sounded like she was cold, although the garage felt like a sauna and smelled musky as tree moss. "Don't make me leave."

"God, this is hard," she said. It felt like a full minute before she looked directly at him and began speaking again, enunciating every word like the slow twisting of a sadistic dial designed to rev up his heart until it burst into flames. "I care about you. You're a good person. These strange things you say—I know you don't mean it and you can't help it. I wish you nothing but the best in life. But you have—you have a problem. I'm not exactly sure what it is. You don't seem to be dealing with it."

"What do you mean? I deal with everything."

"You need to see a doctor and get on medication or something."

"Like there's a magic pill for everything," he said, as fast as he could. "Because that's what the big pharmaceutical companies tell us, every time a commercial comes on TV during the news."

"Hey, I don't really know." Her shoulders hiked up as if she meant instead, *I don't really care.* "I don't pretend to know."

"Maybe you're not used to someone like me. You might need to open the aperture you're looking through, so you can see more of the world. Expand your horizons."

"Right, right." She laughed a little. "My perspective's all messed up. Fair enough."

"You're telling me I'm crazy."

"Look." First, she had commanded him to listen. Now, he was supposed to look. "Like I said, I don't know what's going on with you. All I know is, I've got my hands pretty full right now looking after my brother. I'm sorry, but one person with special needs is about all I can handle."

The phrase—"special needs"—felt like two stabs to his chest. He handed her the car keys. "I don't need a ride," he said.

"Come on, let me drive you back to your spot."

"I'm okay."

"Please," she said. "It's too far to walk."

"I run faster than anybody you ever saw. I don't need to borrow anybody's car and bring it back early with gas in it, all cleaned up, but get kicked out anyway. I can run like a cheetah. I'm faster than a lightning bolt. People don't know what I'm capable of."

As he walked toward the street, her voice followed him. "Okay, bye-bye, Jazz. Take care of yourself."

From her mouth, his name had a sweet, soft ring to it.

His feet started moving faster and faster. Palm trees, mailboxes, and chain-link fences slammed by, one after another. He ran with one hand on his hip, to keep his mother's ring from bouncing out. The blackness rolled after him, right on his heels like a tsunami, all the way to the park, where he finally sat down. Leaning back, he let the blackness consume him until he was drowning in it.

28

Jazz

Jazz woke with a start, moist from a morning rain that had seeped across the concrete floor of the pavilion. He reached for his phone to check the time, but he already knew.

He knew.

The Hacker's Challenge was scheduled to start at nine o'clock. Registration was at eight o'clock and he could tell from the slant of the sun pushing across the park that he would be lucky to make it. His phone confirmed his worst fears: 8:39 a.m. He had twenty-one minutes to bicycle two miles to the college, get checked in, and find a seat.

Grabbing his backpack, he jumped on his mangled bike and took off like The Flash, a superhero he had seen on TV back when he was eight or nine years old and used to sit in his mother's darkened living room, waiting for her to wake up, waiting for his father to come home. The TV had blared in his ears, always too loud, turning the rest of the world into white noise.

On the sidewalk, Jazz leaned forward over the handlebars, picturing himself in a red leather jumpsuit with a gold lightning bolt over his chest, pointy ears, and sparks flying from his heels. Banging against his back, his pack was heavy with notebooks, pencils, pens, two water bottles, and his mother's ring, which he had zipped into a secret compartment before passing out the night before.

He shot across the bridge and into traffic. Tires squealed. A horn honked.

Jazz kept going. He never looked back.

On the school's grassy quad, he rocketed under a banner emblazoned with the Hacker's Challenge logo, ditched the bike, and banged through a heavy auditorium door. The room was enormous. Curling rows of chairs climbed to the back of the hall. Most of the seats were occupied. Some people were talking together or looking at their laptops and phones. A few people stared at him. Near the entrance, a guy was putting name tags and markers into a box.

"I'm here," Jazz said, pulling hard for air.

On the front row, someone laughed.

The guy with the name tags looked up, smiling through amber-colored glasses. "Good timing," he said. "You're preregistered, I hope?"

Adrenaline surged through his chest. Jazz had looked at the website twenty times. He hadn't seen anything about preregistering, which was probably just as well because he didn't have a credit card. When he shook his head, a big dollop of sweat flew out of his hair and landed on the guy's table. "No," Jazz said, wiping the sweat blob away before the guy could see it. "I've got cash."

A woman wearing a purple woolen shawl walked by the table, stopped, and tapped it. "Carl, the livestream's set to start in three minutes."

"Yep," Carl said, turning his laptop back on. "One more check-in."

"If he's preregistered, just let him sit down. He can find you at the break."

Carl pushed his glasses higher onto his nose. "He's paying cash."

Jazz was trying to open a zippered compartment where he had hidden his money. The wad of bills from his father seemed to be stuck. With every tug, the zipper pushed back twice as hard.

Carl asked for his name, email address, and phone number, all of which Jazz recited while also struggling with his backpack.

"I need to borrow a laptop," Jazz said. "The website said you'd have a loaner."

Blinking, Carl laser-scanned the tabletop and the podium with his eyes. His hands rolled over the desk, searching. "Nobody's ever asked for a loaner before. Most people bring a computer to a computer contest. Um, I guess you can use this one after I'm done checking you in," he said. "What's the name of your team?"

"I don't have a team," Jazz said. "It's just me."

The woman in the purple shawl made a noise. She tapped the table again.

"You have to be on a team, man," Carl said, sounding sad.

Using both hands, Jazz ripped the zipper of his backpack open, breaking it. A wad of damp money fell onto Carl's table. "I'm my own team."

"Yeah, we've got one minute to go here," the woman said. "Give him your laptop and check him in later."

"Okay, look," Carl said. His hands were shaking over his keyboard. He stood up and shouted into the rows of seats. "Team Dark Horse. Raise your hands, please!"

Toward the back, two guys in matching gray hoodies raised their hands.

"You guys are our smallest team. You just got a third person."

A groan rolled down the aisle and punched Jazz in the stomach.

"That's not how we work, man," one of the Gray Hoodie Guys said.

The woman walked toward the stage. She clicked on a handheld microphone and spoke into it. "Our corporate sponsors want to see teamwork," she said. "Let's all give Team Dark Horse a round of applause for accepting—" She lowered the microphone and hissed at Jazz, "What's your name?"

Jazz said his name, feeling weak from running on an empty stomach and because he had broken his backpack.

"Let's have a round of applause for Team Dark Horse for accepting Jazz on their team!"

Feeble claps rose before wilting onto the floor.

Jazz took the loaner laptop, which seemed to be a perfectly

good fifteen-inch, current-model Dell, and he made his way up the auditorium steps.

Team Dark Horse—two guys whose name tags said, Conrad and Enzo—shifted their legs, but they didn't stand up to let Jazz into their row. Once he had clambered over them, he whispered hello. Conrad nodded. He had only one eyebrow that ran straight across his forehead, above bright pink acne pits on both cheeks. Enzo offered a slight smile, revealing a mouthful of braces.

The auditorium lights dimmed.

Below the audience, a soft-edged spotlight rolled across the floor until it landed on the woman who had been hissing at Carl. She tossed off her purple shawl, revealing a black pantsuit, and shouted, "Welcome to the Hacker's Challenge!"

Applause, cheers, whistles, and shouting erupted.

The woman introduced herself as Karen. On a big screen behind her, a close-up of her face appeared. She had straight dark hair with a neon-orange streak on one side and a silver ring in her nose. She kept scrunching up her face and shouting in an excited way, like a kid.

She looked nothing like Serena, with her tired, slightly crooked smile.

Corporate logos rolled across the screen. Most were local computer firms, but when the list stopped moving, it locked on a more famous logo—a partially eaten apple.

"Now, with great pleasure," Karen said, "I'd like you to meet this year's primary sponsor. For the first time in the history of the Hacker's Challenge, let's give it up for Timothy D. Welbourne! Tim's a recruiting manager for—are you ready for this?—your favorite computer company."

To Jazz, the front of the room seemed to be sparkling. Flakes of gold, the same brilliant shade as the towers Jazz wanted to design for his beachside castle, swirled down from the ceiling, floating in circles and sideways arcs. The corporate recruiting manager, dressed in khaki slacks and a blue polo shirt, moved toward the light. Down front, Timothy D. Welbourne held his hands together and rolled strings of words out like long pearly ropes that whipped around the room. *Next generation of innovators. Bright futures in computer science. We value teamwork and transformative thinking.*

At the edge of Jazz's vision, Conrad plucked three hairs from his eyebrow.

Applause. A whistle.

Karen was back in the spotlight, more lit up than before. "Are you guys ready?"

"Yeah," someone said.

"Hell, yeah," another person said.

She snapped her fingers with both hands. "Okay, here's the deal. We've got Black Hat teams and White Hat teams here today. White Hats are defending the Temple. They've got to find and fix a wormhole in the firewall around the Temple. The Black Hats will be trying to find the wormhole before the White Hats can fix it. First Black Hat team inside the Temple wins. Or, if good prevails over evil, the first White Hat team to fix the wormhole wins. We'll be timing all of you. Ready, set, go!"

Jazz cracked his neck and set his fingertips on the loaner laptop. "Okay," he said. "This sounds easy. Let's fix that wormhole, brothers."

Enzo sucked on his braces.

Conrad hunched over his computer until his nose nearly touched the screen. "Yeah, we're Black Hats. Hence the name, Dark Horse Team. We're blasting through that wormhole."

"I've started my scan," Enzo said.

"Scanning in three, two, one, bingo," Conrad said. A sticker on his computer said, "I [heart] my Bots."

Sitting up straight, Jazz tried to control his breathing. The room felt like it was pitching to one side. "I'm not a Black Hat," he said. "I don't work for the dark side. I only work in the light. I'm the light and the way."

Enzo made another noise that sounded like he needed to blow his nose.

Conrad lifted his mono-brow without taking his eyes off the

numbers ticking across his computer. "You're welcome to join another team. We're Black Hats."

Jazz scrambled over their knees. He nearly dropped the loaner laptop. At the podium, Karen stared at a digital timer on her smartphone. "I only work with White Hats," he said.

Without raising her chin, she looked up. It made her eyelids disappear, snake-like. "Ah, yes, Mr. I'm Paying Cash."

"McGinness. But you can call me Jazz."

Karen blinked. "Is there a problem?"

"I only work with White Hats. I like to stay in the light."

"Um." Her eyes scanned the room behind him. "Is that right?"

"Please." His palms were wet. The laptop kept slipping under his fingers. "It's my job to save the Temple. I don't want to force myself into it. That's not my style. I'm the Maximum Champion, protector of Temples."

She set the smartphone on the podium, straightened her back, and whispered. "I'll give you your money back. I can't assign you to another team. The competition's underway. You didn't even have a team when you showed up here. You didn't have a laptop. You weren't preregistered. It's not going to work out for you today."

His weight kept shifting over his legs, left foot, right foot, left foot, and back again. He wasn't doing it on purpose. His body was winding itself up like a top. At the back of his throat, the words piled up, choking him. "What do you mean you can't reassign me?"

"I mean I won't reassign you at this point." She smiled, curling her pointer finger at Carl, the guy who had checked Jazz into the competition. Carl stood up, adjusted his yellow-tinted glasses, and began making his way across the room. He had curled shoulders and he walked slowly, an inch at a time. He didn't look like he wanted to fight anybody.

"You'd be making a big mistake," Jazz said. His words tumbled and crashed against each other. "I'm the best programmer you've ever seen. Sometimes, I wake up and I realize I wrote four apps in my sleep, and they were all these great ideas nobody else could ever imagine, even if they tried for ten years without stopping, even if it was an army of chimpanzees typing away or five hundred Shakespearean clones or a cluster of robots powered by supercomputers. My fingers have a mind of their own, but I only use my powers for good, not evil."

Karen kept her eyes on Jazz and spoke to Carl. "Call security, please."

Carl tapped on his phone and mumbled into it.

"Hey, stop," Jazz said. "What are you doing? I'm not dangerous. I've never hurt anybody in my life. I bring comfort. I bring joy and healing. Why are you calling security? All I'm saying is, my mind doesn't work in a dark way. I think about a line of code and usually it's shining. Do you know what I mean? It actually starts glowing gold from the light bouncing off it. There's nothing dark about what I do, and that's a choice I've made in my life because darkness hurts people. There's pain in the darkness."

That was where his mother had gone wrong, when she turned off all the lights in the house and danced in slow motion through shadows.

As it had at Serena's house, the black hole opened around his feet, trembling at the edges.

"Okay," Carl said, letting out a heavy sigh. "I called."

"Let's step into the hallway," Karen said, gesturing toward the double doors.

The doors were a dark brown color, tall and heavy. Jazz didn't want to go through them. A bottomless pit would be waiting for him on the other side.

"Why are you doing this?" He scanned the rows of faces in the audience. Most of them were looking back at him. He shouted, "Why are they doing this?"

The double doors opened, revealing a tall man in a white shirt with a silver badge.

Karen tried to shove twenty-dollar bills at Jazz. He stared at the money but didn't reach for it.

He handed the laptop back to Carl. "Bye, Enzo," Jazz yelled, waving at all the blank faces in the back rows. "Bye, Conrad. Block the wormhole!"

When he reached the double doors, Jazz walked through them, past the man in the white shirt who put his hands on his hips but didn't move from his spot.

"Wait up," Carl said, but Jazz was moving too fast.

At the campus quad, Carl caught up with him, lugging everything Jazz owned. "Sorry, man," Carl said, sounding winded. He pushed the backpack toward Jazz, offering a weak smile. "We'll be doing another contest in a few months. Try again then. That's going to be all about who develops the best applications. You might like that better."

Jazz nodded, numb. He looked down at the backpack and didn't recognize it. His arms felt too heavy to lift, to reach, to hold onto what was his.

"I put your money in there," Carl said.

For Jazz, no words came.

"Hey," Carl said, nearly whispering, "my dad's got the same kind of trouble as you, I think." It was the first time Jazz had noticed the sad, crinkly lines around Carl's eyes, behind the tinted hipster glasses. "The doctor put him on a plan. He's doing a lot better. I wish you well, Jazz. I hope I'll see you again, okay?"

Jazz didn't have the strength to smile. He couldn't open his mouth to say thanks. Finally, he took the backpack, letting his fingers touch the back of Carl's hand. For a split-second, Jazz locked eyes with Sad Carl.

Jazz was on the move, after that, running faster and faster until he was back at his spot in the park. His mother's ring was still in its zippered pocket. His father's money was there, too, thanks to Carl.

The ground was wet. Jazz was hungry, but he didn't care. He couldn't feel it. He was floating above himself, looking down, saying goodbye. He saw himself curled on the spongy grass by the bush where he had hidden his belongings. He imagined himself gone from that place and all places—disappeared, suddenly, as if by magic. He listened to the soundless sky.

29

Serena

As soon as she saw Gethin, Serena shouted his name. A bloody oval covered his chin. He didn't flinch, look at her, or stop what he was doing. He was setting the table, preparing for his dinner date with Rocky. The wound on his face had a jagged edge.

She dropped her grocery bags by the door, surged across the kitchen, and gripped his face. "What have you done to yourself?"

His eyes, usually brightened by the many strange observations that seemed to tick through his brain like phone poles flashing by a car window, had gone flat. "Please don't touch my skin," he said. "It's quite itchy right now."

Serena released his face and stepped back. "We have to get you to a doctor." She had worked all day, trying to make up for lost time and money. The client, a middle-aged man in a gated community, had huffed and puffed his way through a workout session. After that, she had gone shopping because she couldn't count on Gethin to purchase food, ever. Now she had another job to do: *Chauffeur troubled brother to the urgent care clinic.* "Are you still upset about the snakes? We talked about this. They're going back to a great life at the serpentarium."

"I'm not sad about the snakes being returned to their owner." He turned and began working a corkscrew into a bottle of Zinfandel that Serena recognized as a Christmas gift from a client. "I'm curious about how we acquired Snowflake, Chelsea's white ball python. Inquiring minds want to know."

When Serena touched his back, Gethin flinched. "Rocky brought it here while we were out. Chelsea dumped it at the restaurant. She said it's having trouble shedding its skin."

The cork popped out of the wine bottle. "I noticed," he said. "I'm not afraid of Chelsea."

"I'm not either," Serena said.

Without a word, Gethin turned to face his sister. At close range, the scar on his face looked angrier than before. "Snowflake was dehydrated," he said, with no emotion. "I put her under the reptile fogger. She's fine now."

Serena glanced at the clock. "I thought you were picking Rocky up for dinner."

"She's riding over on her new bicycle. Which is fine. I didn't want to visit Kevin's house anyway."

Serena kept her mouth shut. Gethin was already agitated. He didn't need to know about Rocky's housing crisis. It would only throw him further off-balance. Rocky had called Serena. The news she shared brought Serena to her knees. In a million years, she never would have pictured her father's longtime friend as a sexual creep, and yet, having been subjected to creeps many times herself, Serena didn't doubt Rocky, not for a second. Rocky had moved in with a girlfriend. Serena had been so upset, she forgot to ask the friend's name or address.

"Since I don't need to pick her up," Gethin was saying, "I can complete my list."

"Your list." Exasperated, Serena lifted her arms and let them slap back down against her thighs. The effect was louder than she had intended, like a hope chest slamming shut. Two days earlier, the wound on his chin had looked more like a scratch, as if he had been nervously picking at an ingrown hair or a pimple. She had asked him to stop. Against his protests, she had smeared antibiotic cream on his face. Now, his entire chin looked raw. "Was gouging your face at the top of your list?"

"Unfortunately, I wasn't able to buy a lovebird," he said, ignoring her question. He faced the sink, head down, and set the corkscrew on the counter. "I did wash and press my clothes, and dinner's almost ready."

The oven door was propped open. Inside, a pair of small steaks bubbled in a pan. On the stovetop, steam drifted from two pots. She checked to make sure he had remembered to turn off all the knobs. Sometimes he forgot. "We're going to the urgent care place. Your skin is infected. I don't want you to get sepsis."

"The only remaining items on my list are to spray lemon oil, find some suitable music with a female singer, and light the candles." He set the wine bottle on the table beside two white candles and a box of matches that said, See Historic St. Augustine. He repositioned two glasses, inspected one, polished it with a paper towel, and put it back down. "Oh, and I have two favors to ask. One is a small favor and I think it should be easy for you. The other favor is larger and more important."

"I can call Rocky." The skin around his wound seemed to be turning a brighter shade of red by the second. It looked inflamed. Serena started talking faster. "I won't tell her about your face, I promise. I'll just say you're not feeling well, so we're going to the doctor and you'll call her later. She'll understand."

"No." It wasn't quite a shout, but almost. He picked up a silver bottle of oil, held his arm straight out, sprayed the air, turned, sprayed again, turned, and sprayed again, as if he might be reenacting the stations of the cross. The smell overpowered the room. "The favors I need to ask of you are, first, take Snowflake next door to the neighbor's house for three hours. Rocky doesn't like snakes. That's the smaller favor. Second, go to a movie for three hours."

"Oh, is that all?"

"The tenth item on my list is to convince Rocky to move back here, with me."

His sentence deflated so that the words drifted off at the end. Briefly, he made eye contact and blinked. Was he sad? Scared? Both? It was hard to say. Behind him, the purple passion flowers languished in a vase. Their wiry faces turned upward, hopeful. "You don't really want her to see you like this, do you?"

Gethin's eyes roamed the room, probably ticking off the tasks he had completed and the ones still left to do. "Animals have injuries all the time in the wild. The other animals don't point it out and pass some sort of judgment. We shed our skin. We grow new skin. This is actually how the cycle is supposed to work."

"No, it's not," she said. "Not for people. It's not normal at all."

He looked at the ticking cat clock. "As I said, I need to ask two favors, one small, and one larger—"

"Forget it." Serena was yelling. To hell with walking on eggshells. "I'm not doing those things. You hear me? I've had enough. I need to know what's going on with you. Why did you scratch that hole into your face? Are you doing drugs again? You look like a meth addict."

The clock ticked its tail. Gethin shifted from one foot to the other, back and forth. "I'm definitely not on drugs. There are extremely small fibers growing under my skin. Either small fibers or tiny snakes, too small to see with the naked eye. I can't be sure which it is, but they're constantly moving under my skin. They cause me to feel itchy, to the point that my skin burns even when I'm trying to sleep. I'll have to let a doctor investigate with a microscope, but I can't do that right now. I need to wait for Rocky because she has to come home. She has to get back in the Safe Bucket."

"Stop talking about your stupid buckets. Nobody knows what that means."

"Right now, it's time for dinner. She should be here by now. She's a minute late."

Even though she was near the hot oven, Serena felt cold. Gethin's peculiarities had sometimes been extreme, but she had never seen him acting psychotic. Or had she? She said the word to herself. It bounced around her skull like a bird banging against its cage. *Psychotic.* Her thoughts raced ahead of themselves. She needed to call someone, but who? She would have to get him to a doctor. There was no way she could do it alone. Her father was gone. Her mother had never been any help. She wasn't about to call Kevin after what he had done to Rocky. Serena imagined Jazz giving her a hug as his solution, telling her he loved her, which she believed. She missed his warmth, his smell, and his outrageous declarations, but she couldn't take on his problems too. Not now.

"She's two minutes late," Gethin said, staring out the kitchen window.

Rocky would help. She would take one look at Gethin's face and understand what needed to be done. The two of them could get him into the car for medical treatment. Serena alone would never succeed, but Gethin would do anything to win Rocky back.

"I'm going to the drugstore," she said, thinking fast. "We need more antibiotic cream. When I come back, I'll say hello to Rocky and then I'll read on the side porch for a couple of hours so you can spend time together. I'll stay out of sight. Okay?"

He scratched his forearm. "What about the python? Rocky won't like it."

"Rocky brought the thing here."

"That's a good point."

"She'll understand," Serena said. "Do we have a deal?"

Gethin nodded. "I need to select some music now. Good-bye."

Serena didn't bother to unpack her grocery bags before throwing them into the refrigerator. In her car, she couldn't call Rocky fast enough. Rocky needed to know what she would be facing the minute she saw Gethin. The number rang six times and switched over to voicemail.

30

Jazz

"I don't really need these," Jazz said after he had worked up enough courage to walk into the noisy big-box store and up to the pharmacy counter.

The blank-eyed man behind the cash register offered no reply.

Jazz continued. "People don't understand why I remember my dreams from before I was born or how I can talk to the birds so that they actually know what I'm saying, and why everything that gets said on TV, I've already said."

A minute later, the pharmacist pushed a small paper bag across the counter. "Twelve dollars and forty-three cents. Lucky you. Generic price. Stay out of the sun."

Jazz laughed. He hoped it didn't sound like a mean laugh. "I'm homeless in Florida," he said, counting bills and coins. "There's no way I can stay out of the sun, but thanks for letting me know about the danger."

"Be sure to take all of your medication," the pharmacist said in a flat voice.

Jazz carried the paper bag to a water fountain by the restrooms. He took the first pill so fast he didn't have time to think about it.

On a bench outside the store, he decided to meditate for thirty minutes. It would take that long for the pill to reach his bloodstream, at which point he would probably sprout fangs and horns and have to dial 911. He leaned over his knees, cradling his soon-to-be Zombie-fried brain.

After the Hacker's Challenge debacle, he had walked for hours, around and around the park, across the bridge and back, through the tangled, prickly brush along the river. He had breathed exhaust fumes for five or six miles along King Street. Finally, he had found a store with a pharmacy. He had paced the parking lot, periodically feeling the twenty-dollar bills in his pocket to make sure they were still there. He had stared at the doctor's deeply creased prescription for a good ten minutes before walking into the store.

The world was gaslighting him—making him think the flickering lamps weren't flickering at all, but only dancing inside his mind. Jazz knew better. His so-called problems were never problems at all. He was living in a world where everyone's point of view had gotten squeezed through a single small pinhole that focused the light but turned its edges blurry at the same time. Jazz had a brightness all his own. The light overpowered anyone within his vicinity. It kept getting in the way of his goal to help others walk in the light. They seemed to be blinded or burned by his light, every time. They turned away, like Karen at the Hacker's Challenge, like Corinna, and Serena.

If he couldn't dial down the power of his own light, Jazz would never have his castle with golden turrets, or his mother healthy and by his side, or Serena.

It wasn't fair, but he had run out of options. He was trying to accept it, although the truth sucked so hard, Jazz thought it might rip the clothes right off his body, like when he was in the ocean once, as a kid, and a mean wave yanked him underwater. He had banged his head against the sand, lost his sandals, and barely managed to hang on to his swim trunks. Where were his parents? Jazz had no memory of their presence that day.

After he had walked up to the pharmacy counter, his hands kept shaking while he imagined swallowing a pill that would probably make him drool and convulse, paws up, thoughts stopped, dreams over. Serena's face returned to him, though, over and over. Her gentle, sad face loomed above him. The sweet face he needed to hold in his hands.

He would give the pills a week.

After he had been parked on the bench for twenty-nine minutes, a city bus whooshed to a stop and his ears throbbed with a dance song. It was something about coming out and getting the party started. A woman wearing dingy compression socks stepped off the bus, onto the sidewalk. At the same time, Rocky blazed up, inexplicably riding the multicolored bicycle Jazz had built after his accident with Serena. The bike he had left at Bantam's shop.

"Well, well," she said, rolling to a stop by his bench. "Speak of the devil."

Jazz sat up straighter. The sound of her words, so cold at their center, made his chest hurt. She didn't trust him. She might even hate him. "I'm not the devil. I try to be the opposite of the devil. Are you saying I look different all of a sudden?"

"What?" She swung a leg onto the sidewalk and killed the music that thrummed through a cylindrical speaker in the spot where a water bottle should have been. "Um, no. Listen, never mind. I'm in kind of a hurry. Hope you're doing okay."

The bike he had built was every bit as magnificent as he remembered it—red frame, orange handlebars, chartreuse fenders, teal seat—all the bright colors he had selected for Inca, the neurotic toucan at the bike shop. The tall, looping handlebars and banana-style seat reminded him of a motorcycle. He regretted naming it the Jazz E. Frankenbike on Bantam's website. There was nothing mismatched about his creation. It was perfect beyond comprehension. Why Rocky had it, Jazz couldn't guess, but it didn't seem to matter.

"Who called me the devil?" With a start, he remembered the shell-shocked look on Serena's face when they were in Daytona Beach and he told her that Satan uses fear to blacken souls. Did he actually say Satan had taken control of her thoughts? He couldn't recall his exact words, but whatever came out of his mouth that day had been all wrong. His words had tumbled over each other. He hadn't been able to slow himself down. The more he tried, the worse it got. When she had yelled at him to get away, her face turned red.

"Nobody, it's just"—Rocky lifted her bicycle's front tire onto a rack, next to Jazz's equally colorful bike. "Haven't you ever heard that expression, speak of the devil? It means your name came up in conversation."

"When?" Jazz was pretty sure he could feel the beginning of a chemical lobotomy being caused by the pill he had swallowed. Her words kept echoing, fast and then slow—*yournamecameup, your...name...came...up.* Nobody was sitting in the driver's seat of his mind. His brain had turned into a driverless car without a passenger, vacant. A ghost car. He felt unable to string nouns and verbs together.

Rocky exhaled and rearranged her braids. "The old guy at the bike shop where I went. I asked him if he had a used bike for twenty bucks. He said I could have this thing for ten. He called it a Jazz E. Frankenbike."

"I regret giving it that name."

"He said you're brilliant but crazy. Anyway, hey, I've got to run."

Jazz wondered if Bantam was feeding Inca the Toucan on any kind of regular basis. He stood up and ran his hand over the bike's handlebars. "Bantam can be kind, but he's drunk most of the time, so if I'm crazy, I guess we're even."

She shifted her feet, bouncing like she wanted to take off running. "Would you mind watching the bike for a second? I don't have a lock and I've got to grab a toothbrush, a hairbrush, and a million other things."

"Of course," he said. She was talking too fast—or maybe the pill had slowed his brain down and it only seemed like her words were bombarding him.

"All my stuff is at Kevin's house. I can't go back there right now."

"Why not?"

With her hand, she dusted his question away. "Long story. Old Kevin turns out to be a creeper. Who knew?"

"I knew it," Jazz said. Leaning over his knees, he breathed in and out.

"What do you mean, you knew it?"

"I could see it in his eyes. I saw it rolling off his fingertips, that day he was pretending to help you into the car at the Jester Festival. Don't you remember? I saw it all the way across the parking lot. He had a dark energy. No light at all. All control and entitlement. What did he do to you? Are you all right?"

She laughed in a sad way. "Whoa, man. Yeah, I'm fine. He got a little grabby, that's all, but I got so freaked out, I left my stuff behind. So now I need new stuff. I can't go around without a toothbrush, but I'm running really late. I promised Gethin I'd meet him for dinner, so if you could just watch the bike—"

Jazz pictured the purple passion flowers Gethin had picked for her, in the park. He wanted Rocky and Gethin to be together again, just like he wanted to be with Serena. *One person with special needs is about all I can handle.* That was how Serena had put it when she said goodbye. Rocky watched him, waiting for an answer. Her face looked brittle with impatience and exhaustion. "You shouldn't have to buy things you already own," he said. "I can swing by Kevin's place and pick up your stuff. That way, you won't be late for dinner."

She blinked, looked down the road and back at him. "That's—that's a nice offer. I wouldn't mind saving the money. You'd really go and pick up my suitcase?"

"Of course. Text me the address. I'll bring your luggage over to Serena's house." If Jazz did a favor for Rocky, maybe Serena wouldn't hate him quite so much. Maybe she would be home and he could win her back. Maybe he would have a home with his mother someday.

"Okay, man. Thanks. It's only one bag—a roller bag with a leopard pattern on it, only it's red, so like a red leopard."

"Got it. Red leopard luggage. Your spirit animal."

A guy with a ponytail and a tattoo of a crow on his arm walked by and whistled. "Nice wheels," he said. "Love those colors."

"Thank you," Jazz said. "It's called a Jazz E. Blaster. You can Google it. Not today. I haven't got it named that way yet, but that's what I'm going to call it as soon as I'm near a computer again."

Rocky's laugh was real. "Holy Jeff Bezos—a Jazz E. Blaster? What?"

"It's all about the branding."

She tapped on her phone, thanked him, and pedaled off, laughing. Jazz had never seen her looking so happy and free. His heart was breaking for Gethin, who was surely about to get dumped. Rocky had moved on. Jazz could see it.

It was already six-thirty when Jazz, pedaling hard on his bike, reached Kevin's house. He figured Rocky would be at Serena's place for dinner until at least eight o' clock, but he didn't want to risk missing her. He needed to come through for Rocky, to show Serena he could get things right. He could be a hero and not a burden to her.

He could get a prescription filled, take a pill, and act normal, whatever that meant.

Kevin's house was blue with white gingerbread decorations along the porch roof and upstairs windows shaped like eyebrows that seemed to leer at Jazz like an elderly pedophile.

From the start, Jazz hadn't liked Kevin. It was that day at the Jester Festival when Gethin was still missing and Kevin gave Serena and Rocky a ride home. If anybody had asked him right then, he would have said out loud, "Don't trust this dude." Rocky had been upset that day, curled over herself with her back exposed while they all wondered if Gethin was dead or shooting drugs. Something about Kevin's hand, snaking over to touch her bare spine made Jazz shudder, remembering it. He had met so many guys like that over the years. Guys who thought they owned women and women owed them something. It made Jazz feel sick. It made him want to smash Kevin right in his smug, entitled face.

Nobody answered the front door at Kevin's house. Jazz walked down an alley and through a fence, into Kevin's backyard.

At the top of some rickety wooden steps, one corner of Rocky's red leopard bag appeared through a grime-streaked window in the back door. Jazz could only see part of the bag, parked next to the smallest bed he could imagine, inside the tiniest bedroom he had ever seen. It opened onto the kitchen, as if household workers might have slept there at one time, back before the Civil War, emancipation, and light bulbs.

He rapped his knuckles against the door six times: *bam bam bam, bam bam bam.*

Breathing the perfume of recently cut grass, he waited. If given a choice of staying in Kevin's coffin-style back room or under a bush in the park, Jazz would say, "Park, please," without hesitation. The more he stared through the window at Rocky's abandoned bag, the hotter his cheeks burned. Maybe Rocky didn't trust or like Jazz yet, but she was a woman and therefore a goddess, like all women. She shouldn't be stuck in some old servant's quarters, dealing with a presumptuous jerk like Kevin, with his long shiny fingernails constantly reaching for what didn't belong to him.

Bam bam bam. Jazz knocked louder. He had promised Rocky he would get her bag and bring it to Serena's house. The bag was right there, not ten feet away, on the other side of the door. He was going to get it.

Again, he banged. *Open. Open now.* His chance to prove his usefulness to Rocky and Serena was slipping away with every minute that ticked by. The light in Kevin's backyard had begun to fade. Crickets were screaming their brains out.

"Hello," Jazz shouted. In frustration, he rattled the doorknob. To his surprise, it turned. He gave it a twist. It turned further. "Anybody home?"

He opened the door. Cold air blasted his face. The skin on his arms immediately grew tiny peaks. On the doorsill, he hesitated. "I need to pick up Rocky's suitcase," he yelled. His shouting bounced around the hardwood floors, echoing back to him. Across the kitchen, by a dining room table, a grandfather clock had stopped at 2:35. Beyond the clock, a staircase loomed.

Moving quickly, Jazz stepped into the tiny guest room, which was freezing. He grabbed Rocky's bag and scanned his surroundings for anything else she might have left behind. As he turned back, he nearly stepped on Kevin's foot. Jazz hadn't heard Kevin creeping up on him. The air conditioner was roaring too loud.

"May I help you?" Kevin said.

The answer Jazz gave came out in a long stream that picked up speed. "Sorry, man. I knocked and yelled. Nobody answered. The door was open. I could see Rocky's bag right here. This is exactly the bag she asked me to pick up for her so she wouldn't have to buy a new hairbrush or toothpaste or anything like that because it's all right here, and I—"

Kevin cut Jazz off. "What made you think you could walk into my house?"

"Like I said, the door was open. I could see her bag right there on the floor. I told her I'd bring it to Serena's house, so if you'll excuse me, I can—"

Kevin asked the same question, only he put a period after most of the words. "What. Made. You. THINK. You. Could. Walk right into my house?"

Jazz still had his fingers wrapped around the handle of Rocky's bag. She was waiting to get her things back. He was moments from being crowned a hero. "Come on, man," he said. "Rocky works hard. She needs her stuff. I'm only trying to help her out. It's not like I'm stealing your silverware. Let me out and I'll be gone."

With one hand, Kevin braced his weight against the door frame. Jazz looked left and right, as if an escape hatch might open up, but unless he wanted to crawl through Kevin's legs like a scared rabbit, he was trapped. "If she wants her luggage back," Kevin said, "she should stop by herself and get it. I did her a favor, gave her a place to stay and she ducked out of here like a thief, didn't even say thanks. Where I come from, we call that rude."

Kevin's arm, where it wasn't covered with white hair, was as spotted as an old banana. Jazz imagined him pulling the same crap on Rocky, blocking her way out. His voice dropped, hitting decibels deeper than death. "Look, man, you scared her. You scared a woman. Where I come from, which is God's kingdom, that's what I would call pretty freaking rude."

A sneer contorted Kevin's face until he looked like a wrung-out rag. A red film covered his eyes. Inside the doorway, he shifted his weight and locked his knees again. He never seemed to blink. His cheeks kept trembling. "Are you actually lecturing me? A homeless con man like you?"

"Wow," Jazz said. "Are you okay? Why are you acting like this?"

"That girl came on to me," Kevin said.

"What?" Before he could stop himself, Jazz laughed. He couldn't picture it.

"When I turned her down, she lifted money out of my wallet." Kevin was smiling, although nothing he said was funny. "Next thing I knew, she was gone."

Jazz didn't hesitate. Enough was enough. "You're lying. I can smell it. People don't realize that lies stick to your pores and start to decay. Liars start smelling like a rotting piece of meat. They smell like death after a while. That's how you smell."

A toxic red tide swept up Kevin's collar and under the thin, pale skin on his face until the tips of his ears were crimson. "Who do you think you are, breaking in here and insulting me in my own home? I should report you for trying to scam Serena."

For a second, Jazz felt the weight of Rocky's bag in his hand and he listened to his own breath. Kevin had one hip cocked so that his boots pointed in opposite directions. "You're a fake," Jazz said. He didn't mean it in a hurtful way; it was a statement of fact. "You like to pretend you're better than everybody else. What's wrong with you, trying to jump on Rocky like that? That's Serena's best friend. You're supposed to be like an uncle to Serena."

"That's right, I am," Kevin said, "and I don't appreciate some little punk like you sniffing around Serena. She's as good as they come. You need to leave her alone. I'm warning you."

Jazz stared at Kevin sideways. "Whatever, man," he said. "Step aside, please."

"You ever heard of a thing called the Stand Your Ground law?" Kevin said. "That gives me a right to protect myself."

The gun, pulled from Kevin's waistband, was small and dark gray.

Jazz looked at it. The hole at the end of the gun looked back at him, surprisingly doe eyed. Jazz felt no fear. He had a weird urge to laugh. He had never felt more courageous in his entire life. "How did this happen?" He meant to ask, How does someone become infected with so much hate and evil?

"You broke into my house," Kevin said. "Leave that bag right there. She can come back if she wants it. I'm sick to death of women like her and little bleeding-heart snowflakes like you turning everything into one big politically correct drama like you're—"

The punch landed true, square in the middle of Kevin's face and so fast, his eyes seemed to rattle in their sockets. The pistol slammed to the floor. Blood surged from Kevin's nose, but he didn't fall. Jazz swung again, made contact, and in an instant, Kevin went down.

Jazz lifted Rocky's bag and stepped over Kevin, who was groaning and therefore not dead, thank god. For a second, Jazz froze by the back door, listening to Kevin's breathing. What had he done on the first day of his Journey to Normal? Jazz had never hit anyone before, not even in grade school. The kitchen spun around him, black and lined with steel teeth.

Kevin's eyes popped open. "Pack a bag," he said. "You're going to prison."

Jazz tried to swallow, but his throat felt like it was lined with cactus spikes. "Nobody knows," he whispered. "Nobody knows what I'm capable of."

As he bolted, Rocky's bag—his ticket back to Serena—bumped down the crooked wooden steps behind him.

31

Rocky

Walking through Serena's damp garage, where the white ball python was still sitting in its blue box, Rocky felt more certain than ever about the decision she had made—dead set on putting Gethin in the past. She didn't want to see him again, dreaded being sucked into another long, crazy-making conversation, but she wouldn't feel right about ghosting him. Ignoring someone as if they were invisible and mute seemed cruel. She could sit down with him, explain herself, and wish him well. That way, she wouldn't have any regrets later.

Inside Serena's house, the smell hit her first—so much lemon-scented room spray. She coughed and started to laugh until Gethin turned from the stove. His face, with the deep, raw wound on his chin, looked inflamed and wet. Her mouth, frozen in mid-laugh, felt too heavy to close. Her eyes filled. Her heart raced.

"Who was it?" she said. "Who sold you the drugs?"

At the sink, Gethin dumped a pot of steaming asparagus into a strainer. "I don't have any drugs, except for some Advil, but I haven't had a headache in a long time. The bottle may have expired. I'll have to check."

"What's wrong with your face? I damn sure know meth mites when I see them."

He transferred the asparagus into a bowl, using tongs to move one stalk at a time. Rocky stared at his back and waited. "I'm sorry I look this way," he said finally. "I've had little nematodes or fibers under my skin for about a week now. They're quite active and I'm constantly itchy, but not like a regular itching—I'll bet you know how that feels—like my skin is burning. I always have to scratch. Serena went for antibiotic cream."

More than she had ever wanted anything, Rocky longed to run, jump on her new bicycle, and get as far away from Gethin as possible. What had she been thinking by staying with him for so long? How could she have loved someone so impaired? It wasn't his weird habits. It was Gethin. She felt trapped inside a tangle of steel wool, lost in the maze of his strange way of thinking. "I don't believe you," she said. "This is emotional manipulation. You want me to feel sorry for you so I won't leave, but I can't stay with you anymore. That's all I came to tell you."

The silver tongs clattered to the floor. Gethin took a step toward them and seemed to lose his balance. "This isn't on my list. I have a whole list for this date and it ends with you getting back into the Safe Bucket with me."

"Oh, for god's sake," she said. "Cut the crap about your stupid buckets. I'm sick to death of your games."

"I know you love me." Gethin's chest heaved as if he couldn't catch his breath.

Rocky pictured her father's sad, yellow-rimmed eyes, and her mother packed into a desperate-looking miniskirt. She saw her future self in a college graduation robe, behind the wheel of a car, mowing the lawn outside her own house. Her mouth had gone dry. "I don't love you anymore," she said. "I'm sorry."

It happened so fast, she didn't have time to react. He yanked Serena's largest butcher knife from a wooden block by the stove and ran across the living room, into the bathroom, where he slammed the door.

Rocky howled his name.

Through the door, water splashed into the sink. Something fell, shattering. "I have to get these things out of me," Gethin shouted. "The itching makes me crazy."

"Open the door now." Rocky tried the door handle, but it was locked. She pounded on the door. "What are you doing? Stop!"

His voice sounded contorted by pain. "I've got snakes under my skin. Little snakes. I've got to get them out so they can be free. I have to make you love me."

"Oh my god."

Her phone. She had left it in a zippered pouch strapped to the handlebars of the Frankenbike or the Jazz E. Blaster, or whatever Jazz's invention was called. Charging through the kitchen with her head down, Rocky nearly collided with Serena, who was stepping through the door with a white pharmacy bag. "He's in the bathroom with a knife." Rocky's voice sounded like a ragged piece of metal, see-sawing back and forth. "I'm afraid he's going to hurt himself."

Serena's eyes looked out of focus for a second. "Why, what are you saying?"

"He locked himself in the bathroom. He's got a knife. He says there are snakes under his skin. I think he's high."

Serena dropped the white bag and her pocketbook. "Call the police."

32

Jazz

Spinning lights illuminated the whole block, blinking red, white, blue, and red again in a repetitive pattern like some patriotic nightmare as soon as Jazz turned onto Serena's street. Before his eyes, her house seemed to expand to massive proportions, zooming at him in an instant, its open windows wailing in despair. *They're coming for me,* was what Jazz thought. Kevin had called his cop friends. They were waiting for Jazz at Serena's house—why on earth had he told Kevin where he was going?—and now Jazz would go to prison. Assault and battery, maybe breaking and entering. At the dawn of his so-called pharmaceutically induced Journey to Normal, Jazz would fall into the blackest of all black holes, the bottomless chasm that had been waiting for him since puberty, always lurking at his feet.

He had accepted his condition. He had taken the pill, but it was too little, too late. The hole was determined to swallow Jazz alive, still twitching.

Rolling without pedaling his bike, he repositioned Rocky's suitcase on the handlebars and eased off the street, across someone's yard, and around the back of a darkened house. Lizards streamed across the grass, racing out of his way. Behind the row of houses, he could make his way closer to Serena's house without being seen. Remaining invisible had been his superpower ever since he started living in the park. People looked right at him but never saw him. He could make himself invisible to the police too.

At the rear wall of Serena's garage, Jazz stood on a hose spigot so he could peer through a small window. Words squawked from the flashing police car. *Psychiatric.* A balding, older police officer was in the car and talking into the radio cupped to his mouth. *Backup requested.* A second cop—a small woman with her hair slicked into a bun not much larger than a walnut—stood alert by the car's bumper with her thumbs latched under her belt. Names were tossed back and forth. *Foster. Jefferies.*

The second cop, Foster, started pacing, turning in a slow circle. Her eyes fell directly on Jazz, but she continued scanning, leaving him unseen. His cloak of invisibility remained intact. His superpower was in full force.

Serena's voice drifted toward him, pulsing with fear and grief, and he didn't catch everything she said, but from her tone, Jazz knew the police had not come for him. They had come for Gethin.

33

Gethin

Behind the closed bathroom door, Gethin released his thoughts, dropping them into a river with an imaginary weight the size of a runaway truck. The butcher knife lay on the tile in front of him. He didn't want to cut into his skin, and yet he did, to set the snakes free. He repositioned himself and bumped into a laundry basket, toppling it. Out fell his dirty jeans. Something was poking out of the back pocket, the same pocket that Brillo Pad had tugged on when Gethin was leaving St. George Street.

The plastic bag was tiny, about the size of a quarter with an even smaller rock of meth inside of it, glistening. Gethin hadn't had any meth for a long time. Rocky and Serena didn't seem to believe him, but it was true. He had stayed in the Recovering Bucket. The rock laughed at him through its plastic encasement. Picking it up with two fingers, Gethin held it to his nose.

Rocky's voice stabbed at the door. Serena shouted his name, rattling the knob like she meant to squeeze venom out of it, but in the bathroom with the door locked and his back braced against it, Gethin only saw the bag containing the white rock, which he tapped lightly between his thumb and forefinger. Not having a lighter, a spoon, or a needle, he would have to eat it and let it sweep him away to wherever it would, into the chaos of the nonbinary world, through a trap door from which he would never return this time.

In his hands, he rolled the baggie until the meth formed a curling cylinder like a sly smile, seducing him. The bag formed a poisonous grimace.

Gethin had always preferred the needle method, but he had long since thrown his stash bag away. The needle had to be clean. Nothing had been clean in Chelsea's tent, where the boundaries between what was his and what was hers got blurred until they evaporated with the mist over the river every morning. He had managed to stay in the Safe Bucket the whole time he stayed there. He didn't want to catch her germs.

Bang. The door talked to him. "Open up, Gethin! Gethin!" The door's voice sounded like his sister, Serena with her sad eyes, which were shaped like a constant apology for taking up space. The meth, if he took it, would numb his mouth and throat. It would race through his bloodstream, pushing a scorching wave of relief into his veins. Gethin would no longer be in the Safe Bucket. He would be in the Death Bucket, along with his dad, and his mother's lovebird, eaten by a snake, killed by Gethin Who Left the Cage Open. Rocky had left a long time ago, before he had joined the Hidden Hundreds by the river, maybe the day she met him and noticed his fingers tapping out a rhythm she couldn't hear.

Gethin's heart banged and banged. His teeth clicked off a fast rhythm. To slow them down, he closed his eyes, accepting the darkness that would never change because he was buried, barely alive, locked in a tiled cage with a toilet and the overturned laundry basket that had delivered Brillo Pad's unwanted gift. He was too different for the world; he was alone. He felt no sorrow about this; he didn't cry. From a great distance, he saw the open cage, the blood and feathers, his mother's mouth open, the dark painting of his life.

More rattling. More knocking. Someone's voice vibrating, spinning, cutting through the door faster than a table saw. *Rocky.* "What are you doing in there?"

Floating while his brain vibrated, looking down at himself in the cage of his sister's small bathroom, Gethin propped himself higher on the door and tried to laugh, but it sounded fake. He hated fakers. "I'm staring into the Death Bucket," he said. His words came out too quickly. They echoed, circling around until they consumed themselves.

"You're scaring us," Serena said, still banging. "Open the door right now."

Beyond the tiled cage, Rocky was whispering to Serena, a sound that reminded him of wind rushing through saw palmettos or a cottonmouth whipping across grass, ready to strike. "What should we do? Oh my god. I'm so sorry. I just couldn't do it anymore."

Again, Serena spoke through the door hinges: "Why won't you let us in?"

A lightning bolt boomeranged from his toes and his fingertips and ricocheted around his brain. It really had become tiresome, attempting to explain his thoughts to other people. Was it so difficult for them to comprehend? "I'm. In. The. Death. Bucket," he said, louder. "I'm. Shedding. This. Skin."

His name, twice.

"Goodbye," he added, hoping they would take the hint and leave him alone. Gethin dumped the meth into the toilet, flushed it, and picked up the knife again. If he was going into the Death Bucket, he would do so with his eyes open and clear. "Goodbye and be well, all those who have known me. Ha ha."

A murmuring. A low wailing. The river of his thoughts had turned stagnant. Through the muck, Serena's voice returned—not from that moment, but from a time many years earlier when he was hiding in a garage, listening to his mother howl because her bird was dead. Someone had left the cage open. Someone had let the snake in. Someone had killed her bird. Serena found him, reached down and touched his face, pulled him up and held him, rocking. "It's okay," she had said. "It's not your fault. You're a good boy." He would miss his sister, wherever he was going.

The words "police" and "here" rose from the depths of his consciousness like spring water, breaking the river's surface. Feet clicked across the linoleum. He wiped a string of drool off his lip. He would wash his hands later, if there was time after he had removed the snakes from his body once and for all. He bobbed on the accelerating current of his grief, moving so quickly, surely it would carry him away.

34

Fletch

From Gethin's sister, Fletch had heard the same thing at least four times: "I need help getting him to the hospital."

Every time she said it, Fletch felt the sweat surge and pool in a ring around his neck like a noose. Retirement was a big tease, so close he could taste it. Fletch and Kala Foster weren't even supposed to be working nights. Once again, the boss had scrawled all over the patrol schedule with a red marker, posted the new rotation on the bulletin board like a kid proud of his latest crayon creation. The boss was trying to torture Fletch. The mental health calls were always the worst too—unpredictable and dangerous—but Serena Jacobs kept laser-beaming him with her sad eyes, begging for help as if Fletch could magically fix her strange brother. The police department didn't have any social workers or shrinks on staff, and there weren't enough Tasers for every officer. The department had requested more Tasers, but before they could be ordered, the funding got pulled amid some stupid political dispute. Even the community outreach department, otherwise known as the "Officer Friendly" force, had been downsized.

Buying time, Fletch mopped his neck with a bandanna and looked down.

Serena tried again. "I believe he's had a psychotic break," she said. Her face kept flashing red, from the lights on the patrol car.

Standing beside Fletch, Foster leaned her small frame forward. "Is he on drugs?" She had her thumbs tucked in her belt and her elbows out like she meant to take charge, well-meaning and misguided as ever.

"I'm not sure," Serena said. "I mean, no—I don't think so.

He said he's in the Safe Bucket." Her eyes kept shifting back and forth.

"The Safe Bucket," Fletch said. "Is that something from a twelve-step program?"

Serena pressed both palms against her mouth, removed them, and folded her fingers together in prayer. "Honestly, I'm not sure what's going on with my brother, but he said he was clean. That's all I can tell you."

Fletch surveyed the cluttered garage and the open kitchen door behind Serena Jacobs. He would need to move things along. He could hear another woman inside the house, pleading with Gethin to open the door. Fletch shifted his weight and tried again. "You said he's got mental health issues. You want us to Baker Act him?"

"I don't know what that means," Serena said.

Fletch exhaled, maybe a little too loudly. He could Baker Act somebody in his sleep. He had done it so many times. It was always a huge pain in the ass. Mountains of paperwork. "It means involuntary psychiatric assessment. Should we do that?"

Foster wandered off, heel-toeing it across the garage, looking around in an overly casual way while Fletch kept talking. She was assessing the scene. Thorough police work. "I'm not sure about that," Serena said. "Can't you just talk to him? I think he would listen to you. I just want him to come out and go to the hospital."

"Is he a danger to himself or others?" Fletch stepped closer until he was looking down at her, keeping Serena's eyes focused on him. It was one of the tricks he had learned for deescalating tense situations. He kept his voice flat and low, like somebody reciting a checklist, letting her know he was in charge and this was a standard procedure he knew how to do. To avoid banging his bald head on the garage door, he had to stay hunched over. It hurt his back, standing at half-mast.

"He's not a threat to others—but I mean, I'm not sure what he's doing in there." Her voice got shaky. "Like I told you already, he's locked in the bathroom with a knife."

"Do you think he's suicidal?"

"He says he's got snakes under his skin and he's in the Death Bucket." Serena was talking faster and faster, trying to explain it, but with every word, the story made less sense to Fletch. "That's what I mean about him acting psychotic."

From the back wall of the garage, Foster whistled. "Look at this snake, Officer Jefferies. Looks like the same one we saw downtown."

Fletch scanned the over-packed garage, with its rows of rusty rakes and shovels hanging along the walls, an ancient push mower in one corner, and Christmas and Halloween decorations jammed into clear plastic bins. So much clutter could pile up, over the course of a lifetime. After his wife died, Fletch had left their garage untouched. He couldn't bring himself to go through her piles of fabric and thread, which she had used to make clothing for people at the church shelter. He stepped under the garage door, eyeballed the snake, and turned back to Serena Jacobs. "I cleared all the reptiles out of here," he said. His cheeks felt tight to the point of bursting. His blood pressure was rising. "What's Snowflake doing here? Where'd you get that animal?"

Serena's shoulders rose and fell. Her head tipped back. "It's kind of a long story."

"Try me," Fletch said.

"Chelsea had it." Serena glanced into the kitchen and back at Fletch. "That woman who took advantage of Gethin after he ran away. She confronted Gethin's girlfriend."

"Which means it's been trafficked." He damn sure knew Chelsea didn't purchase the animal with papers through a responsible breeding program. "Wonderful."

"We rescued it."

Fletch repositioned his feet, which were beginning to swell over the tops of his shoes, one of the many joys of having diabetes. "Where did you last see Chelsea? I need to talk to her."

"She was downtown at The Spindle restaurant. Look, I'm sorry, but what does all this have to do with my brother being locked in the bathroom with a knife, saying he's in the Death Bucket?"

Through the kitchen door, Gethin's girlfriend appeared. Fletch couldn't remember her name; he only remembered the tough-talking attitude, from the day she tagged along with Serena to fill out a missing person report at the police station. "What's taking so long?" she said. "Why are you talking about the stupid snake?"

Foster intervened, pulling out the small spiral-bound notepad she always carried around like she was Inspector Gadget. Turning to Serena, Foster fired off a series of questions. "Excuse me. Who is this? How many other people are inside the home? You mentioned a knife. Are there any other weapons we need to know about?"

Gethin's girlfriend made a noise like air leaving a tire in a hurry. "Are you kidding me?" she said. "We called you for help. There's a man locked in the bathroom. He says he's dying. He needs a doctor. He won't come out. My name's Rahkendra. Rocky for short. Last name Wright. Can you help us, or not? If not, I need to call a lawyer."

Fletch closed his eyes and smiled. He had heard that one so many times. "Okay, okay, fair enough," he said. Later, he could worry about finding Chelsea and getting Snowflake to Trina for safekeeping. "Forget the damn snake. Let me ask this again. Do you want us to Baker Act him? There's a procedure for involuntary assessment. I know how to do it, but it's a serious step. I'd like some reassurance that we're in agreement."

The spinning lights on the police car found Serena's face, making her blink. Fletch knew the look. He had felt the same way, sitting by Farah's bed in the hospice care place. Serena was cycling through all the years of her life with her brother, picturing him as a kid, maybe with Lego blocks or playing catch in the yard. It was almost like Fletch could see the gears turning inside Serena's head as if he had X-ray vision. "I know how to bring him out," she said. "Could you wait here a minute? Please don't leave."

Before Fletch could answer, Serena darted into the house. A jolt of adrenaline made him feel dizzy. *Here comes the unpredictable, dangerous part,* was what he thought. People moving in and out of a house, someone else inside doing god knows what, a knife somewhere in the mix, and Fletch and Foster standing there like targets. Foster jammed the notepad into her pocket, backed up, and put one hand on her gun—her only tool—without unclipping the holster. Her fingers were so small, she looked like a kid playing cowboy.

From inside the house, Serena was shouting. "They're taking Snowflake," she said. A metallic bang rang out. Glass cracked, as if someone had smashed a mirror, but it was muffled by the bathroom door where Gethin was holed up. "They're confiscating the snake," Serena continued. "You'd better get out here and talk to these officers or this snake will be gone, and you'll have no snakes left."

"No," Gethin said. "Noooooo."

More banging. "Open up right now," Serena said.

Beside Fletch, Rocky piped up. "Do something," she said, looking defeated.

"Okay, that's it," Fletch said in a soft, sing-song voice intended for Foster. "I'm calling for backup. If he comes out, be cool, please. We'll give him a nice little ride to the hospital."

Fletch was inside the patrol car, on the radio when Gethin ran into the garage with a knife in one hand and blood streaming down his arm. Dropping the microphone, Fletch popped the car door open. He wasn't as fast as he had been in his younger days. He saw one swollen foot hit the driveway and his hands on the car's frame, tugging himself upright, which caused all the blood to rush from his head. On his feet at last, Fletch locked his knees to avoid falling over at the sight of Foster, braced with her gun drawn. He called out "stop" and "no," but she was yelling and Gethin kept moving toward her.

Serena flew through the kitchen door and froze.

Rocky screamed.

Gethin waved the knife. "Look at me," he said, roaring. "Look at me."

"We see you," Serena said. She was whispering it, seemingly paralyzed. "I see you, Gethin. I see you. Drop the knife."

"Don't," Rocky said. "Please."

"Foster," Fletch shouted. "Step back. Secure your weapon."

Foster stared at Fletch, wide-eyed, and holstered her gun. She stumbled away from Gethin, bumping her shin against the blue bin containing Snowflake.

From behind Fletch, another voice caused his heart to bounce around in his chest. "I am the light and the way," the voice said. A man with long reddish hair stood at the edge of the garage with his hands in the air. He looked like a ghost, or maybe the archangel Michael.

"What the hell is this?" Fletch said, spinning in all directions. "Stop! Nobody move a muscle. Keep calm." He kept saying it, mainly to himself. "Everybody keep calm."

"I can talk to him," the man said, motioning toward Gethin, who was still shouting, "Look at me."

"Jazz," Serena said. "Stay out of this."

Near Foster's ankles, the white snake stirred inside its container, turning over with a muted thump. "Get away from her," Gethin said, staring at Foster. He lunged forward, still holding the knife, although it was facing down and backward.

Before Fletch had time to think, rocket-powered by adrenaline, he drew his gun, certain his trainee was about to get stabbed. Fletch couldn't disappoint Foster's dad and all those crazy brothers, and worst of all, Farah, the love of his life. The gun was all Fletch had to protect Foster, who was so young, she hadn't even had time to screw up her life yet. The rules for use of lethal force scrolled at warp speed through his brain. When the gun lurched in his hand, twice, the long-haired ghost angel was already in motion.

35

Jazz

Bathed by the spinning red police lights, Jazz had eased Rocky's suitcase onto the grass before propping his bicycle against Serena's garage. On the other side of the cinder-block wall, the voices surged, growing louder, filled with venom. Thick patches of sweat kept popping through his thin cotton shirt, but Jazz wasn't afraid. His body was gearing up for the most important moment of his life. He had pedaled his bike all the way across town on an urgent mission, wanting so badly to deliver Rocky's suitcase, to show he could stand up to a bully like Kevin, to open Serena's heart again.

Inside Serena's garage, a mission more crucial than the suitcase was presenting itself. In his mind, Jazz saw Gethin teetering above a black abyss from which there could be no return. Jazz felt it in Gethin's long, wailing protest—the word "no" drawn-out like a train's whistle, passing in slow motion. The thin, trembling cord of Gethin's life was waving goodbye. Jazz caught the cord. He held it and pulled it toward him. Stepping forward, he moved into the garage with its red police lights trapped and strobing.

The contents of Serena's garage snapped through his mind like a series of photos, clicking off, one after the other. The younger police officer, the one called Foster, backing up, bumping a blue bin with her leg. Inside the bin, the white snake, tightening its coil. The older cop, Jefferies, with his gun raised and his mouth open. Rocky's voice. Serena's face heavy with grief. Gethin's bloody chin and his empty eyes, which were rolling all over the place. His long, thin legs on the move. The blood pouring down his arm, pooling around his hand. The knife.

Jazz heard the blast before it happened. He saw it roar out

of the gun before it flew through the air. He bolted, faster than lightning, reaching with outstretched hands. Under his feet, a glowing path seemed to form, pulling him toward Gethin. Jazz was a force of nature, a supernatural being, even now, one day into his Journey to Normal. He could outrun a bullet. He could save Gethin because Jazz loved Serena and he always had loved her. He would never stop. Nobody knew what Jazz was capable of.

"I am the light and the way," Jazz said, flying forward. "I can talk to him."

When the bullet hit Jazz, his bicep split open. He felt it in slow motion. The cold concrete rose to meet him. He fell so that his body was partially covering Gethin, who opened his hand, dropping the knife.

Jefferies shouted the same instruction three times: "Stay down."

Serena, screaming.

Rocky, shouting.

Foster, yelling. "What the fuck, Jefferies? What the actual fuck?"

A warm river ran out of Jazz and onto Gethin, who had gone rigid beneath him. The river pooled under Jazz. It seemed to lift his neck and head until he was floating.

"You're okay," Jefferies said, sounding shaky. "You're okay."

"Get out of my way," Foster said, pushing past him, leaning down so her green eyes glowed under the fluorescent lights. Rocky's braids brushed his cheek and Serena hovered, illuminated. They were all staring and touching, a trio of women leaning over him as Jazz lay bleeding and stunned with Gethin pinned beneath him. A trinity of love and understanding as Serena brushed his face with her warm, smooth hand.

36

Serena

The night replayed itself, again and again the next day, back and forth on an endless, slippery loop so it seemed to be carving a painful new groove in Serena's brain:

> The heat and the glare of police lights.
> The snake, rustling in its bin.
> The ripping sound of the gun.
> Screaming. So many voices.
> Jazz, wide-eyed, tossing out mysterious fragments of speech.
> Foster's eyes rattling around in her head.
> Jefferies pacing. His tremulous shouting.
> Rocky, yelling at Foster: "Call an ambulance."
> The police radio buzzing without words.
> The dark outline of her brother on the garage floor.
> Falling, hitting her head. Her screams spiraling up.
> The ambulance driver looming over her, sweating: "Hold still, please."
> Blood rolling across the garage floor.

When Serena had finally awoken, hours or maybe a day later, her head felt leaden. Her eyes, crusted over from crying, creaked open with heavy reluctance, only after Serena dug at them with her fingernails.

What had happened? The paramedic's sweaty face came back to her. He had held her flat. Something seemed to bite into her arm. Instantly, her veins had felt scorched. In her bed, she struggled to find the spot on her arm and winced. Her violated skin, beneath the bandage, recoiled.

Where was she? Serena tried to sit up, but she couldn't. The gold-colored quilt slipped off the bed. Rolling to one side, she tugged at it. Her legs felt refrigerated despite the heat. Her shoulder bumped against the wooden nightstand she was constantly trying to prop up with bits of cardboard because one leg was shorter than the rest. A photo, yellowing in a frame of fake turquoise jewels, fell over with a smack. She righted it, touching an image of Gethin as a baby in her arms when she was still in grade school. Immediately, she began to cry again.

In the doorway, Rocky swayed on bare feet, inhaled, and padded across the room. She pulled the quilt back onto the bed and climbed under the covers with Serena, wordless and warm, offering only her breath.

"I need to get to the hospital," Serena said.

The back of Rocky's hand was pressed like a flower against Serena's cheek. It felt cool and smelled sweet.

"I called." She smoothed and rearranged the wet vines of hair from Serena's face. "He's fine, still in shock, is all. They kept him overnight. They'll evaluate him and give us a call when they're ready to release him."

Gethin's face, pale and staring into a terrifying void, looped back around a corner of Serena's brain, got deflected by fear and made a U-turn. *Gethin needs me.* "He didn't die," she said. "Thank god, he didn't die. My brother needs me."

Rocky's grip tightened around Serena's arm like a slow-burning fire, picking up heat. "Just breathe. I'll take care of everything."

The words came at Serena from a cold depth, as if they were traveling up the walls of a stone well. She was squeezing her eyes shut and opening them, working to remember. "Jazz was injured. He took the bullet." Her voice sounded alien and blurry. Rubbing at her eyes, she fought to keep them open, but the room kept going black. "Jazz is a good guy."

"He's a great guy," Rocky said.

"Why do I feel so strange?" Serena's words were all mashed together.

"Try to relax. The paramedic gave you a sedative."

Serena turned on her side, letting Rocky massage her shoulders, neck, and back. Her skin tingled, going slack, and Serena let go, spiraling down, sliding past her worst fear without even glancing at it.

The room was dark and Rocky was gone when Serena opened her eyes again. Finally, most of the pharmaceutical haze had cleared from her brain and she managed to weave her way into the bathroom, where she squeezed toothpaste onto both the floor and her toothbrush, remembering, suddenly: Gethin lifted onto a gurney, being loaded into the ambulance. She needed to see him.

In the mirror, his face stared back, white and turning blue, hollow-eyed and scarred, nearly unrecognizable. Dark purple flowers bloomed under his eyes, which were swollen into slits like gun turrets in a fortress, mute and ominous.

"I see you," she whispered, remembering her words to Gethin. *I know you.*

Still in bloody clothes, she barreled into the living room and found Rocky on the couch. Fast asleep and slack-jawed, Rocky jumped at the sound of her name.

"I want to be with him," Serena said. She needed to touch her brother's face, to hold him, even if he didn't usually like being held. "Where is he?"

Rocky's beautiful eyes retreated into their sockets, shrunken and watery, and in the new lines around them, a vivid map of sadness was taking shape. "I talked with the counselor at the hospital," she said, looking groggy and confused. "She's helping me with the arrangements."

Stepping back, Serena stared. "What arrangements? You said they'd call when it was time for us to pick him up."

"Right." Water ran from Rocky's right eye, as if she didn't have enough tears to cry with both eyes anymore. "I meant Jazz."

Maybe it was a sedative hangover, but Serena felt a flash of anger. Gethin was alone in the hospital. She pictured a clipboard attached to the end of his bed, a parade of people in face masks coming in and out of his room, police questioning him repeatedly. "He can't stay there by himself," she said, turning. "I'm going to see him."

"I called your mom. The Texas State Police tracked her down."

Serena's purse was on the kitchen counter. Her car keys drooped from a dolphin-shaped hook by the door. "Ha. I'm sure she'll change her plans and get here right away."

"Wait."

The keys slipped from Serena's fingers and clattered to the floor. She picked them up and dropped them again. "Shit," she said.

Rocky retrieved them. "Look, you're in no condition to drive."

"Why do I feel this way?" Stepping back, Serena stumbled.

"It's the ketamine. I told you. The paramedic gave you a shot."

"What?" Serena banged her fist against the refrigerator. All her colorful magnets clattered to the floor. A long to-do list fluttered across the room, pointless. "Why would they do that to me?"

"Honey, you were really—"

"I want to see my brother." Serena was wailing. She hated herself for it, couldn't stand feeling like a helpless toddler.

"You want to go to the hospital right this minute?" Rocky held the keys up like a dare. "Okay, I'll drive you. Let's go. You can ask them whether they'll let you see him yet. They told me he wouldn't be ready until tomorrow."

"What do you mean, he won't be ready?"

"I mean." Rocky closed her eyes without finishing the sentence.

Serena pictured tubes attached to her brother's arms, maybe an oxygen tank beside his bed, pumping up and down. "I have to see him," she said. "I don't care what he looks like."

Rocky exhaled, looking Serena up and down. "Let's get you into some fresh clothes."

At the hospital, Rocky guided Serena down a pale blue hallway that reeked of bleach. Serena pushed on a hospital room door that opened without a sound. Gethin wasn't there. Propped in a bent bed, Jazz gave her a woozy, sad smile. His left arm was in a cast attached to a metal hook, which made him look like someone constantly waving hello. On the wall, a TV news announcer droned on about a three-car accident on I-95.

"Jazz," Serena said, confused. She searched Rocky's face for clues. "Where's Gethin? Where's my brother?"

"Remember, honey," Rocky said. "I told you he's not ready for us to see him yet. We can visit with Jazz while we're waiting."

"I'm so sorry," Jazz said. His face, always transforming from youth to adulthood and back again like someone in a funhouse mirror, looked surprisingly lifeless.

"I know he had surgery." Pressed against her chest, the zipper of Serena's purse bit at her skin. "I know he'll look scary. I just need to see him. Why do you keep stalling?"

Rocky touched Serena's arm. "Sit down, okay? You're still drugged."

People on the TV chattered away, infesting the room with a constant buzz.

"I tried to push him out of the way," Jazz said. His eyes reflected the TV screen's blue light. "I saw the knife and the gun, so I ran. I don't know why I wasn't faster. Usually, I'm faster than anybody you've ever seen."

Serena stared through the door, into the hallway. "Which room is he in?"

"In other news," a TV reporter announced, "shots were fired last night after police responded to a mental health emergency at a St. Augustine home."

Turning her head toward the sound, Serena winced. Her eardrums popped. It felt like two balloons had exploded inside her brain.

Rocky's arms became a brace, fastened around Serena's waist, holding her upright.

Gethin's blurry online profile picture appeared on the TV screen. "Police said Gethin Jacobs, who reportedly suffered from mental health issues, charged at police with a knife."

"Oh god," Serena said. "He's going to need a lawyer."

"Officer Fletcher Jefferies fired two shots, killing Jacobs and wounding a second man, Jaswinder McGinness, who apparently tried to intervene in the conflict."

A photo of Jazz flashed across the TV screen. When Serena went limp, Rocky lowered her onto a chair.

"Officer Jefferies, who was said to be nearing retirement after eighteen years on the force, has been placed on administrative duty pending an internal investigation."

Serena felt as if she had been pulled inside-out.

"Official details are pending. Sources told us McGinness tried to shield Jacobs so that he took the first but not the second bullet. In a seemingly unrelated development, a white ball python was confiscated from the home on West Riverside Drive. McGinness is reported to be in stable condition at the hospital."

The room collapsed around Serena.

"Sweet Serena," Jazz said. "We love you so much."

There were two bullets.

"They worked hard," Rocky said. "They did everything they could."

But no. He didn't die.

"I hope—I hope you don't blame me," Jazz said. "I ran as fast as I could."

"Hush," Rocky said to Jazz.

Leaning across the bed with his good arm, Jazz tried to touch Serena. "I thought I could push him out of the way."

"It wasn't your fault," Serena said, mumbling, barely forming the words.

She saw her brother, rigid on the concrete, already turning cold, slipping away, not Gethin at all anymore. It was only the frail shell of his body, bleeding out. The blood, pumping from a vein in his leg, pulsed in an arc, spraying Serena's face, blouse, and hair. He clearly didn't have much time. Jefferies was pacing back and forth, crying. Foster kept shouting into the police radio, obviously unsure of what to do. Serena had taken a class for her work as a fitness trainer. She knew how to stop the bleeding. Grabbing one of her workout towels, she twisted it tighter and tighter, wrapping it and tying it around a wrench Rocky had pulled from a pile of tools. The blood below the tourniquet kept flowing. No matter what Serena did, the blood wouldn't stop. By the time the ambulance arrived, Gethin's open eyes had quit searching Serena's face and his skin was turning gray, then blue.

Gethin was gone. Her brother had died.

37

Jazz

From the hospital bed, Jazz had reached for Serena, but his one good arm hadn't been quite long enough. She had looked confused and scared, like a small child lost in a shopping mall. His face, soaked with tears, had felt heavy. "Hey, man," Rocky had said, giving Jazz a sad smile, "I need to get her home. We'll talk later, okay?" Rocky had taken Serena by the shoulders, guided her out the door, and they were gone. If his left arm hadn't been attached to a metal pole, Jazz would have run after Serena.

He had wanted to tell her about the prescription, his Journey to Normal, his plan to try again at the next Hacker's Challenge, his mother's progress with her illness, and the love that kept flooding his heart until he felt like it might burst. He hadn't been able to tell her any of that because her eyes wouldn't focus. Her knees kept buckling and her face looked drained of blood. Rocky had steered Serena out of the room. For a while, he thought she might come back, but hours had passed. Behind the window blinds, all the daylight was gone.

Once she was feeling better, maybe months in the future, Jazz would ask Serena for a date—*a proper date,* as his mother would say. He would shower at the community center, wash his clothes in the sink, buy a few flowers, and take Serena out for a meal.

First, he needed to get back to school. He had missed far too many classes lately. If the hospital didn't set him free soon, he might have to forfeit Computing 401.

Another day passed and nobody removed his arm from the metal pole.

A lawyer with a bright red face and a too-tight gray jacket stopped by to recommend a lawsuit. He dropped a business card, all exclamation points and primary colors, onto the bedside table. Billy Daniels. The lawyer's nonstop talking made Jazz feel queasy, as if Gethin's life could be reduced to dollar bills. Jazz pictured Gethin's eyes, so empty before he died. "Don't be fooled by others," the lawyer said, reading from his card. "Only Billy D. can show you the money."

A police detective stopped by. Officer Muldoon. His questions, outlined on a yellow notepad, were surprisingly brief. With shaky hands, he cleaned a smudge off his thick glasses. He tucked a pen into his pocket and pulled up his navy-blue socks, one at a time. To each question, Jazz offered the same response: "Officer Jefferies shot us. He made a mistake." Clicking his pen, Muldoon said he would be in touch.

But why? What else was there to say? "Tell Mr. Jefferies that I'm okay," Jazz said. He didn't like to think of the old guy crouched beside him, crying after Gethin got shot.

Officer Muldoon flashed a tight-lipped smile and slipped out the door.

A nurse named Lindsay rolled into the room. Her lavender uniform smelled of starch and laundry detergent. "The doctor signed your discharge papers," she said, clipboard in hand.

"Thank you," Jazz said. "I need to get back to school as soon as possible."

"Who's picking you up?"

He could have called Serena's cell phone. Hearing her voice would have felt like stepping into a warm bath, but he wasn't going to make that call. He had offered his mother's ring to Serena. She had told him to keep it. If he kept hounding her, he would be no better than a stalker—*no better than Kevin.* His heart felt like a wishbone somebody had pulled apart. He had spent enough time making pointless wishes. At least she didn't blame him. She had told him it wasn't his fault. "Nobody," Jazz said, smiling his best smile at the Lavender Nurse. "I'll take the bus."

Lindsay's gold name tag identified her as the Head of Nursing. She looked at him sideways like she knew a secret. "A bus to where? You never gave us your address."

"I can go to the park."

"Are you homeless?" Nurses tended to get straight to the point. Jazz had noticed this about them.

Outside, the rotors of a helicopter *chop-chop-chopped* the sky before landing on the roof of the hospital. "I prefer the term, 'Citizen of the World.'"

"Got it." Lindsay scribbled one word on the clipboard and attached it to the end of his bed. "Couldn't you stay with your friends who were visiting you before? Gethin's family? You need to keep that wound clean."

In the hallway, a message warbled indecipherably over the intercom. More than anything, Jazz wanted a castle with turrets so he could invite Serena to dinner by the sea. He couldn't be begging her for a free place to stay. Her brother had died. "My friend has her hands pretty full right now," he said, echoing what Serena had told him about not wanting to deal with more than one person with special needs. "I can take care of myself. Please. If I'm not out of here by tomorrow, I'll miss an important class at school. I'm on a scholarship."

The word *scholarship* caused his chest to puff out. It was a small scholarship, but it was based on his grades, not poverty. The school knew Jazz was smart.

"I don't want to release you to the streets. I'll have a social worker stop by."

"I already have a social worker." The words exploded from him at warp speed. Jazz didn't feel like telling his whole life story to somebody new. "Her name's Corinna."

Lindsay asked for Corinna's phone number, which Jazz knew by heart. "I was supposed to turf you today," the nurse said, eyeballing her enormous wristwatch that looked like it belonged on a scuba diver. "You don't have insurance. I'll need to call Corinna."

After telling him to take care of himself, Lindsay left.

Day turned into night.

Jazz fell asleep, which was a new thing, courtesy of the lithium. Glittery sheets of sleep kept enveloping him.

When his phone jangled, he woke with a start. It was Corinna, sounding unhappy. "I got a call from a nurse named Lindsay. This is what happens when you're bipolar and you don't take your medication," she said. "All the time with the high-risk behavior, and I understand you were trying to help your friend, but it's still high-risk behavior, and that's how it works out, every time, when—"

"I'm sorry," Jazz said, but before he could tell her about the pills and his Journey to Normal, Corinna kept going.

"I've been trying to find a home for your mother. Now, I'm supposed to find a placement for you, ideally a two-bedroom so Meghna can move in with you soon, but do you know how hard it is to find a subsidized two-bedroom apartment?"

"I imagine it's—"

"It's impossible," Corinna said. "Wave a magic wand, bribe somebody—it's still impossible. I've been on the phone nonstop for hours. What happened to your girlfriend, anyway? I thought you were living with her. Why can't your mother move in there?"

His fingers, sticking out of the cast, had turned blue and felt cold. "I'm not living with Serena," he said. "She needs her space right now."

"Let me guess," Corinna said. "She couldn't handle your mania. Most people with bipolar have a very hard time maintaining a romantic relationship because—"

"I got that prescription filled," Jazz said, quick as a sand crab, mainly to change the subject. "I'm taking the lithium, doing what the doctor told me to do."

For a minute, Corinna didn't say a word.

Jazz waited, enjoying the silence, feeling smug.

Finally, she exhaled into the receiver. "You didn't tell the nurse that."

"She didn't ask me."

"Fair enough," Corinna said. "How do you feel?"

Jazz blinked and looked around the hospital room. "The bullet wound hurts," he said. "How are you feeling? Any better?"

Corinna paused another beat. Had Jazz said something wrong? "Listen to me," she said, as if he had any choice in the matter. "What you're doing by getting on this medication is a huge step in the right direction. It could change everything for you. You hear me? Everything."

Inside the cast, Jazz felt an itch he couldn't scratch. He didn't like to think about taking a drug for the rest of his life. "I'm trying it out for a week or two. I'm going to see how it goes."

Once again, she went quiet. He pictured her piercing eyes bearing down on him. "You need to stay on it," she said. "People with psychosis are a lot more likely to get mugged or raped or shot than a so-called normal person. Did you know that?"

At the Jester Festival, Serena had saved Jazz from getting arrested. If the pointy-haired cop had shot Jazz that day, would Gethin still be alive? No matter what, Jazz wasn't going to cry on the phone with Corinna. "People don't understand," he said, trying to sound agreeable. Without Corinna, Jazz would never get out of the hospital in time for his computer class. "They see somebody acting weird and they think we're dangerous."

"Exactly," she said. "Like Gethin, scaring that cop. Your nurse told me all about it. I got the report from the police department too. He had a knife. Even if he didn't mean to hurt anybody, it must have been pretty scary. The police are in constant danger every time they answer a call. They get paid to be hypervigilant, and they carry guns. Mistakes happen."

"And sometimes the cop's a racist," Jazz said, thinking about all the brown men and sometimes women who got shot by the police for driving to work or the store.

"Yes, but that's not what happened here," Corinna said. "You don't get to lecture me about police brutality and systemic racism. I've had family members who lived it. Your friend wasn't Black. He was a kid with mental illness, running with a knife."

"He wasn't pointing it at anybody." Jazz could feel his head heating up with anger. "It wasn't even facing the right way."

"We don't have any way of knowing what Gethin meant to do. He wasn't in his right mind."

"I should have pushed him out of the way faster." Jazz was surprised by the scratchy sound of his voice. "He wasn't a bad guy. He had trouble connecting with people."

"My point is, people with mental illness are more vulnerable," Corinna said. "Stay on your medication. Schedule a visit with the doctor. People on lithium need to have regular blood tests. Do you understand? Do your part. Your mother needs you."

"I took the first bullet, but the cop fired again. I don't know why he did that."

"He panicked," she said. "Listen, you did the best you could. You were very brave, son."

"I'm the Maximum Champion."

"Keep taking the lithium."

He didn't want to agree with her out loud. "Can you get me out of here? If I have too many absences, they could withdraw me from my classes. I don't mind sleeping in the park. I need Computing 401 to graduate."

"I'm going to make some more calls," she said. "You do the same. Let's touch base first thing in the morning."

"Corinna?"

"That's my name. Don't wear it out."

"You sound better. Is your cancer in remission?"

She laughed. "You're psychic," she said. "Yes, son, it is. Thank you for asking. Now try to get some sleep."

Jazz closed his eyes, thinking he would rest for a second, but sleep pulled him down hard. When he awoke, it was dark beyond the window blinds. By his bed, a woman with gray pigtails was holding Billy D.'s card under her nose, reading it with a look on her face like she felt sick to her stomach. Her aura seemed blue, but not a vibrant blue like the deep sea rolling on the horizon. It was more of a muted, gray-blue—the color of Gethin's lips the night men hoisted him onto a gurney. The color of the gun that killed him.

"Are you a nurse?" He asked the question to be polite. He knew she wasn't anybody official. He could tell by the mud on her boots and the safety pin holding one side of her coveralls that she wasn't a lawyer, either.

Her eyes, heavy-lidded and syrup-colored, offered a kind of answer, although she didn't speak. She didn't have to say she was sorry. Jazz could read the SOS in her expression. He could feel her sadness, especially when she gripped the sides of her chair and held her breath, mouth trembling, like somebody who had realized it was too late to jump off the roller coaster.

He tried again. "Were you Gethin's friend?"

"I met him a few times. He used to visit me at work."

She touched her hair, pulled out a clip, and slid it back into place. At the end of the clip, a plastic snake sparkled, pinkish-purple and coiled. The color reminded him of the tent along the river where Serena had talked to a man named Julee and picked up a snake without flinching. Jazz squirmed on the bed's noisy pee-proof cover. "Is your name Chelsea?"

The woman smiled in a way that made Jazz want to cry. That had been happening a lot lately. Maybe it was the lithium, or Gethin getting shot, or Serena's absence. "No," she said. "I'm Trina."

"Nice to meet you," Jazz said, although he wasn't sure yet.

A nurse clicked by the open door. Trina leaned over her knees and sat up again, shaking her head, tapping her hands together. If his mother had died and somebody had sent Trina the Farmer to tell him, Jazz was going to yank his sliced-up arm off the pole and run far away. "I like your hair clip," he said.

Trina touched the side of her head as if she had forgotten she had hair. "How is Serena holding up?"

The question gave Jazz another idea. The resemblance wasn't strong, but there was something around Trina's sad eyes, which kept scanning him. Maybe Serena's mom had shown up, after all. Maybe she had come for Gethin's body and didn't even know how to find Serena's house after so many years. "I'm not sure," Jazz said. "I could give you her number."

Again, Trina picked up Billy D.'s card. She turned it over in her fingers. "I can understand why you might want to file a lawsuit," she said, tucking the card into a pocket near her breast. "I sure wouldn't blame Serena, either, but for whatever it's worth, Fletch is a good guy. He served his country for a long time, but he's been sick—high blood pressure and what they call police fatigue. He should have retired a year ago. He couldn't afford it."

As best he could, Jazz sat up straighter. The gears in his head sprang loose. "You're his wife," he said.

"No, just a friend. His wife died a year ago. I've been looking after him."

Jazz tugged at his tethered arm and winced. She didn't seem dangerous, but he didn't like being pinned to the bed. It occurred to him that Kevin could waltz into the hospital anytime too. "Why did you come here?"

Trina clenched her teeth and shook her head. "I don't really know. I guess I wanted to make sure you've got everything you need. Is there anything I can do for you?"

Outside, illuminated bugs were buzzing around a streetlight. "Not unless you've got a beachfront castle with golden turrets," Jazz said, half-laughing at his manic dream.

She leaned forward and smiled a little. "What do you mean?"

"I was joking," Jazz said, deadpan. "They won't cut me loose until I have a place to stay. I'm kind of between houses right now. I need to get out of here."

"For some reason, I thought you and Serena were—"

"It's complicated," Jazz said.

Her head hung from her shoulders, looking defeated and heavy, but her eyes brightened. "I don't have a castle," Trina said, "but it so happens I've got some big old barracks where I work—twenty-four beds and they're all empty."

Jazz looked out the window, confused. "Military barracks?"

"I used to run summer camps for kids. I'm too old now. If you don't mind pitching in with chores, I won't ask for rent money. Buy your own groceries and we'll call it even."

Jazz kept his mouth shut about his mother. Asking about a place for Meghna might be a bridge too far, too soon. "Why would you do that for me?" He looked down at the hand on his good arm, which was scraped from sliding across Serena's garage.

"I've been called crazy," she said, looking serious.

"Me too," Jazz said. "Um, so you don't get the wrong idea, I should probably mention that I'm—you know, my heart's taken."

Trina exploded with laughter, startling him. "Oh my god, son," she said, "you've made my day, but trust me, it's nothing like that."

"Then why would you ask me to live with you? You don't even know me. I might be a serial killer, for all you know."

Her jaw snapped shut, forming a hard line. "You're not even remotely dangerous. The newspaper says you're a damn hero. I'm afraid Fletch might kill himself. He hasn't stopped crying since it happened. Please don't sue him. He's already punishing himself worse than you could imagine."

"I don't like to think about anybody suffering," Jazz said. He couldn't even stand to see bugs suffer, much less grown men.

"He'd do anything to bring Gethin back, but he can't."

"I'm not going to sue him," Jazz said. "I didn't like that lawyer's aura."

Trina closed her eyes and opened them. "Would you talk to Serena? Please?"

Jazz tried to imagine having the same awkward conversation with Serena. Her eyes had looked hollow and far away before she left his room with Rocky. "I'll try," he said. He wasn't sure if he would ever see Serena again.

Trina told him about the serpentarium and the work he would need to do. She said she would be back for Jazz in the morning. His eyes were closed again before she reached the door.

The next morning, Bantam called Jazz's hospital room phone. "I seen you on TV," he said. "What the fuck happened?"

Turning his head sideways, Jazz read what the hospital staff had written on his cast at breakfast to try and cheer him up: *Use your superpowers to heal quickly*, one nurse had written. *Don't break any legs*, was another one. Nurses could be funny. "I was trying to help my friend. I got shot."

"No shit, Sherlock," Bantam said. "How'd that work out for you?"

Through the phone line, Inca the bird chimed in. "No shit!" the bird said. "Go to hell."

"It was only my arm." Jazz slipped a drinking straw under the cast to scratch his itchy skin as best he could. The wall clock said eight-thirty. Trina Leigh Dean had promised to be back for him by nine. Lindsay had agreed to spring him. Corinna was thrilled to hear he had a place to stay. She said that would be much easier to find a subsidized one-room apartment for Meghna. His class was at one o' clock. He was going to make it.

"I can't believe you took off on me. I didn't even know where you went."

Although Bantam's words were less slurry than usual, they were trembling. His industrial-grade drinking usually didn't start until later in the day. "You kicked me out," Jazz said. "You told me I was talking too much and driving you crazy."

"Yeah, whatever, so you talk too much. You're crazy as shit. You still got that phone I gave you?"

"Yep." The phone was on the bedside table, next to a pan for puking and a plastic pitcher filled with ice chips. It had been in his pocket when the bullet hit his arm.

"So you could have called, you dipshit. Just because I tell you to shut up once in a while, you go missing like one of those kids on milk cartons? I had the guys looking all over for you."

"Shut up, shut up," Inca said. "Go to hell."

One of the nurses had opened the window blinds all the way. In the parking lot, a young man in a red T-shirt was helping an old woman push a silver walker across the asphalt. The walker had yellow tennis balls under its legs. The old woman reminded Jazz of his mother. Corinna said they had gone grocery shopping together to help Meghna "reintegrate " into the community. "Hey, man, I need to tell you something." Jazz had never heard his voice sounding so small. "I have a condition. I get manic sometimes. That's why I was talking so much and not making any sense. I'm getting better now. I've got a prescription."

For a minute, Bantam's raspy breathing filled the phone line. "Oh, boo hoo," he said at last. "You got a condition. Everybody's got some shit to deal with. You think you're so special?"

"I know, but I wanted to say I'm sorry if I—"

"Look, shut up already. The reason I had the guys looking for you, it wasn't because I was missing my bat-shit Jazzy boo boo, it was because of that stupid bike you made. I need another one. Lady offered me four hundred bucks."

On Bantam's end of the phone line, Inca let out a cry of outrage.

"Four hundred? Who? Why?"

"Who? Why? You sound like a barn owl. I guess you put a picture on the World Webs and somebody named Rocky Reactions sent it around on that Twitters thing. I got three calls and one solid offer. You wanna work on commission? Fifty percent?"

"Sixty." Jazz said it before he lost his nerve. "It was my idea."

"You asshole. What happened to, oh, I'm so sorry, Bantam?"

"Asshole," Inca said. "Shut up."

"Fifty's okay," Jazz said. He could make bikes and do chores for Trina too.

"Okay, sixty percent, only because some of the guys missed your crazy, stupid face around here. Your cot's still set up by the Buddha. Come over when you get out."

"I've got a place to stay." Jazz said it as quickly as he could. He would sleep in the park again before he laid down on Bantam's stiff, grease-covered sheets. "I'll need to borrow some tools."

The phone went silent. Even Inca was quiet. "A place? Where? You got a girl?"

The question hurt. Was Serena his girl? Probably not, in her mind. "I got a job at the serpentarium out past the county line."

"That snake place?"

"Yeah, my new boss said I'd be taking care of snakes, raking leaves, cleaning up, stuff like that," Jazz said. "I can still make bikes for you, though. I mean, if you want."

"That's weird." Bantam was sounding wobbly again. "You got a bed there?"

"Yeah, sounds like a nice one."

"Good for you." Through the phone, a cigarette crackled. "I know that place. I'll bring some tools and stuff over. Hey, you little shit, you know what?"

"What?"

"I'm proud of you."

Feeling his eyes grow heavy, Jazz managed to croak out a thank you.

"Yeah, yeah," Bantam said. "Shut up. Oh, I got one more thing for you."

"Shut up," the bird said again. "Asshole. Go to hell."

Over the phone, a bang. "Be quiet, you stupid psycho bird! Listen, Jazz, I can't handle this crazy animal."

"He's hungry. Just feed him. What was the one more thing?"

"A guy named Bruno called. Your dad saw you on TV. He's looking for you."

The sudden memory of his father's poisonous mouth and dead eyes gave Jazz an unpleasant jolt. "He can keep looking." Jazz said it without hesitation. "Hey, do me a favor? Don't tell him where I am."

"What, you don't get along with the old man?"

"My dad's not a good guy," Jazz said. For the first time in his life, he was certain of it. "He's a real jerk, actually."

"Yeah," Bantam said, blowing smoke, "I had one of those, too, back in the day."

"If I never see my dad again, that'll be okay." It didn't hurt to say it, which was both a surprise and a relief.

"Bruno wasn't so nice when he called," Bantam said. "If

your dad wants to know where you are, he can suck my dick."

"Perfect," Jazz said. "Thanks."

"See you at the snake pit, kid."

38

Serena

Serena was sitting cross-legged on her living room floor when Kevin appeared, unbidden, in his bejeweled trousers and ridiculous string tie as if he owned the place. She had been sorting old photos of Gethin. As soon as she saw Kevin's boots, Serena dropped her brother's third-grade school portrait back into a box. Instead, she picked up a yellowing envelope she had discovered earlier—photos of her mother in a surprisingly short, sparkly dress. Popping onto her feet in one swift, hands-free movement—one of her signature moves—Serena asked a question that came out thick and tangled, filtered through a swamp of grief. "What are you doing here?"

All around the room, images of Gethin were arranged in chronological order, from baby photos to awkward school portraits that showed off his crooked bangs and missing teeth, to candid shots of him as a grown-up, hunched over, never quite looking at the camera. Kevin surveyed the pictures and stretched his mouth around his teeth in a dramatic way, as if speaking caused him agony. "I saw it on TV," he said. "Oh, honey, I still can't believe it. Why haven't you called? I've left you three messages."

"Again," Serena said, bouncing on the balls of her feet, thinking how fun it would be to unleash a spinning kick, Bruce Lee-style, "why are you in my house?" The thought of Rocky trapped in Kevin's icy guest room felt like it was burning a hole through Serena's temples. Rocky had spared no details in her retelling of the tale.

Kevin stepped back, eyeballing Serena, and he touched his string tie in a spot near his heart. "I know you're in terrible grief, but I don't much care for this attitude, young lady. What's gotten into you?"

Serena started to make a fist, but she was holding the envelope containing photos of her mother. The corners of it dug into her palm. "Don't you dare scold me." She stepped forward, which forced him to back up again. For her training videos, she had perfected a certain move that involved running full speed up a wall before flipping over into a pounce. She would have launched into it right then, just to see the look on his face, but there were too many framed items on her living room walls, including her parents' wedding photo—her mother in a crown of white flowers—and a shot of her dad in his uniform. "You're not in any position to lecture. Rocky told me what you did."

A few blocks away, a train thundered through the neighborhood, letting out a low moan, as it did twice a day. Kevin looked away, pretended to laugh, and rubbed the back of his neck. "Oh, she did, huh? Did she also tell you about the money she took from my wallet?"

Serena tightened her fist around the envelope. "That's a lie. Rocky's not a thief. You preyed on her and now you're making up a story, trying to gaslight us."

Kevin pointed his finger at Serena, who was standing almost under his chin, the better to head-butt him if it came to that. Maybe he had been friends with her father once, years before, but Serena didn't care. "Somebody's covering their tracks here, but it's not me," he said. "That girl forced herself on me, I turned her down, and she took all my cash. That's the thanks I got for giving her a place to stay."

For a second, Serena felt paralyzed. It was as if her brain wouldn't process his words. He continued to stare down at her. Why had she remained passive for so many years, like an obedient dog listening to his many unsolicited lectures, thinking he deserved respect? He wasn't a trusted family friend—a stand-in for her father. Kevin's craggy, slightly yellow face no longer even looked familiar. "Wait," she said, shaking her head like somebody trying to make a bunch of marbles fall into the right holes. "I don't understand. You're saying Rocky was the one who hit on you?"

"That's exactly what I'm saying."

Laughter shot out of Serena so hard it hurt and sounded more like a scream. She laughed until she was crying over Gethin again. Her old stationary bicycle lurked in one corner of the room, gray and menacing. She leaned against it to catch her breath and laughed some more.

"I don't see what's funny," Kevin said. "All of this is very sad."

"Yes, it's s-s-so sad," Serena said, stuttering through convulsive laughter, struggling for air. The more she tried to regain her composure, the hotter her face felt. "It's fucking tragic. I mean, look at yourself. Do you seriously think anybody's going to believe a woman like Rocky tried to have sex with you? What the hell's your problem? Why are you saying these things?"

Kevin parked his hands on his hips and made a face like he smelled something rotten. With her head down, Serena paced to the far side of the room, buying herself a few feet to maneuver. In her mind, the marbles kept rattling around and around until they finally triggered a jackpot of an idea. She pulled her foam workout mat from a shelf and tossed it onto the floor, getting ready. "She's not who you think she is," he said through his teeth. "Gethin was a fun romp for her, that's all."

"I'm warning you," Serena said, unreasonably giddy at the thought of dominating Kevin. She turned and sized up his lanky, limp frame, smiling, certain she could take him without breaking a sweat. "Don't say one more word about my friend."

"Or what? Are you going to punch me like your crazy friend Jazz?"

The room felt like it was ringing and flashing, too bright and loud, like a pinball machine on tilt. Again, she laughed. From the couch, she removed a large cushion, which she threw onto the workout mat. Her goal was to scare him, not cause a spinal cord injury. She would need to aim carefully. "This story keeps getting better. You're saying Jazz punched you?"

Kevin kept going without answering her. "Really, Serena, you need to stop surrounding yourself with these sketchy people. You're a sweet kid, but they're only sponging off you. Your old man would be disappointed."

Serena sat down on the sofa, keeping her back straight, and she set the envelope on the coffee table in front of her. Around the room, Gethin's face in all its incarnations stared up at her: pink and slightly plump in his pre-teen shots, or later, tall and pale, lost in his own thoughts, staring into the distance, into his dark, empty future, somewhere beyond the flat horizon where his life would eventually run straight off a cliff, leaving her alone. Against her will, Serena's eyes filled. She swiped at them, cursed under her breath, and laughed. "Jazz really punched you? Why? Where?"

"In the face," Kevin said. "At my house. He had a whole story about picking up Rocky's suitcase, but the fact of the matter is, he broke in."

"He was trying to help Rocky." Serena was talking mainly to herself, imagining the startled look on Kevin's face after Jazz walloped him. "I love that, and you know something else? I love that guy. I've been afraid to admit it. He's got problems, no doubt about it, but he's got a good heart."

Kevin clapped his hands together. "Okay, that's it," he said, like somebody taking charge of a kindergarten class. "I want you to lie down. You're not thinking straight. Lie down right there. I'll bring you some ice water. You're in shock."

When she told him no, Serena's whole face warmed up from grinning. "I'm not going to lie down." Her hands shook when she opened the envelope, pulled out all the photos she had found, and set them down one by one, like playing cards on the coffee table. "I'm not listening to you anymore. You've been lying to me for years. I didn't realize it until I saw these pictures. Remember these?"

He stuffed his hands into his pockets, stepped sideways, and leaned over the images, squinting. "Your mother was a beautiful woman," he said, straightening up. "I'm not sure what she has to do with all of this."

With her fingertips, Serena pushed the images around the table—so many shots of Gladys laughing, kissing, being kissed, raising her glass, with Kevin, with a group of other people, all of them looking glazed-over drunk. "See this one?" Serena picked up a photo of Gladys and Kevin bathed in the blue light of a bar. Gladys was wearing a sequined purple dress, laughing into the camera with one strap off her shoulder. Her long dark hair was piled high on her head, topped off by a glittery silver tiara that said, Happy New Year's. Kevin had his arm around her waist and his face buried in her hair.

Kevin opened his mouth, closed it, and opened it again. "Your dad was there too. I was still drinking back then. What's your point?"

Serena picked up the photo, stood up, and stepped toward him. The hardwood floor creaked under her bare feet. "My dad wasn't there," she said, turning the image over in her hands. She ran a finger over the photo's white edges. "He's not in any of these shots."

"Now, look," Kevin said, peering down at her again. He was at least a foot taller. Serena kept moving forward until she was staring into his cavernous mouth, unafraid. "Your dad was taking the pictures. He was behind the camera."

"I don't think so." She held the photo up for him to see the faded cursive writing on the back. "January 1991. Looks like a New Year's Eve party. My dad was in Dhahran, Saudi Arabia. He died there a month later. You always told me you survived the missile attack that killed him, but you weren't even there."

"That's enough," Kevin said.

"You weren't there because you were back home, sleeping with Gladys while my dad was serving his country. I guess the party ended kind of hard when he got killed. Did you dump her then? That's the only part I don't understand. What made her go crazy and leave us?"

"Stop it."

"Pretty sure you had something to do with that. I'll bet you were too much of a coward to step up and take responsibility for a wife and two kids, so you broke it off. She couldn't handle losing you and my dad at the same time."

"Not one more word," Kevin said, shaking his long finger in Serena's face.

Seeing her opportunity, Serena dropped the photo, grabbed his arm with both hands, turned hard, and yanked his whole body over her back. Kevin's feet flipped toward the ceiling and he came down with a loud bang, onto the couch pillow and Serena's foam workout mat, just as she had choreographed it. He cried out and lay on his back, stunned, arms and legs flailing like a partially squashed bug. Serena leaned over his face, got one hand around his neck, and spoke in a hoarse whisper. "Give me your key."

"Oh my god," he said, pushing against her. "You've gone psychotic."

Serena dropped onto his chest and tightened her grip around his throat. "Give. Me. Your. Key," she said again, springing back to her feet, releasing him before any actual damage was done. "Now."

Kevin pulled her house key from his pocket.

She plucked it from his hand, waited for him to struggle back onto his feet, and pointed toward the door. "Don't even think about coming to Gethin's memorial service," she said, welling up at the thought of cremating her brother's body, which turned out to be her only affordable option. The funeral home director had recited a jaw-dropping list of coffin prices. In hushed tones, he had carefully enunciated all the memorized numbers for "embalmment of the deceased," a viewing complete with a "memory video" that would play on an endless loop if Serena could ever select the photos, the hearse (extra for a white one, the color of angels), flowers (lilies or carnations?), and an inscribed plate for the urn. Sadness and horror overwhelmed her in crushing, repetitive waves.

In the center of the room, Kevin brushed off his pants,

straightened his tie, and watched her for a second without speaking.

Serena walked through the kitchen and held the back door open. "Goodbye," she said, waving a hand in front of the exit.

When he walked out, Serena couldn't slam the door fast enough. Immediately, she was on her phone, mapping a route to the serpentarium. Rocky had said Jazz was living there. He would help her with the photo tribute—all the random fragments of Gethin's life now stored in a crumbling box, which she picked up and clutched against her chest. Her heart felt like it was banging against her ribcage in double time, insistent, too painful to ignore.

38

Serena

Three times on her way to see Jazz, despite her best intentions, and no matter how many times she recited the three P's—Perseverance, Patience, and Pluck—Serena had to pull off the road to compose herself. She should have waited for Rocky to get home, especially after the confrontation with Kevin, but Serena couldn't wait. She wanted to see Jazz, needed to be with him.

Beyond the edge of town, trees and cow pastures flashed past her windows. The constant loop of Gethin's death rewound itself and started to play for the millionth time—the blood and the screaming, the pinch on her arm followed by blackness, loss, nothing. Serena blinked hard, shouted through the open windows, and kept going. She had a job to do. If she couldn't assemble his photos, Gethin would have no video tribute. She couldn't even afford a memorial service at the funeral home. If her brother had any friends other than Rocky, which Serena doubted, they would have to gather inside her tiny house.

At last, a roadside sign appeared with a red arrow pointing toward Snakes of All Kinds. She bounced down a gravel lane to find the main serpentarium building. It was long and squat, tucked into a scrub pine forest, its perimeter adorned with a few forlorn-looking marigolds. Another narrow aluminum-sided building sat off to the left, partially hidden among the winding forest trails. Years earlier, Serena and Gethin had been there to look at an assortment of snakes, gopher tortoises, iguanas, and a Burmese python in an enclosure that made Serena think of Fort Knox. Rocky had said the owner was a nice older woman, Trina Somebody, who had seen Jazz on the news. Trina had remembered Gethin from all the times he stopped by to ask endless questions about the different species of snakes. She had offered Jazz a place to stay. The kindness of strangers turned out to be a thing.

Not knowing where else to go, Serena parked her car and stepped through the creaky front door of the main building, into its cool, silent interior, which reminded her of the funeral home where Gethin would be cremated as soon as she had said her goodbyes. The air was crisp and quiet. Serena walked down a dark hallway lined with exhibits and there he was—Jazz, standing under a track light so that the top of his head appeared to be glowing orange. His broken arm was encased by a cast and a sling, positioned across his chest. He extended his good arm and she stumbled into it, collapsing again, angry with herself for letting go, yet grateful not to be in charge. She didn't have the strength to be brave, stand up straight, and smile for the camera. She didn't want to do so.

"I'm glad you're here," he said.

"It feels like a bad dream." She mumbled it against his shoulder. "I've been trying to put his photos in order for a video. I can't stop crying. Will you help?"

"Of course." Jazz stood back and took her hand. "Come with me."

He guided her around a corner, through an empty classroom, into a fluorescent, tiled lab that looked like a library with many tall stacks of plastic drawers. They walked through a maze of filing cabinets until they reached a kitchen with a round table under a yellowish light bulb. The refrigerator and stove were olive green, clearly from the 1970s. The sink was white porcelain with gold-colored knobs. A curtain patterned with bowls of cherries framed a large window overlooking a dense pine forest. Jazz took the photo box from Serena, set it on the table, and pulled out a chair for her. With one hand, he poured water from a pitcher and set a blue cup by her wrist. He watched her take a sip before he opened the box.

Compared to his usual pace, Jazz seemed to be moving in slow motion, as if he didn't want to startle her. Serena touched the back of his hand. "Did they give you some pills for pain?"

He wrapped his fingers around hers. "They did, but I haven't been taking them. My arm feels itchy, is all. It doesn't hurt much."

"That's good." Serena had to concentrate on blinking at normal intervals. It felt surreal to be talking to Jazz in a strange kitchen, knowing Gethin would never be back. She imagined herself floating above the room, looking down on the box of photos, the table, and Jazz.

He squeezed her hand, let it go, and reached into the box. "I started taking lithium for my bipolar." He spoke in a bright voice like somebody saying, *What nice weather we're having!*

"What?"

The first photo showed Serena applying Halloween makeup to Gethin's face when he was six or seven. She had painted his face white, but with a ring around one eye and whiskers like a puppy dog. The memory made her heart hurt. When he had looked at himself in the mirror, Gethin burst into tears, saying people would laugh at him. He didn't understand the whole idea of Halloween costumes. "I have bipolar I," Jazz said. "It makes me talk and think too fast, to the point that nobody can understand me. I guess I've always known that, but I didn't want to admit it. My mom's social worker sent me to a doctor a while back, but I didn't get the prescription filled until this week. I'm taking the medication now. What you said helped too."

Serena turned her face away from the photo, not remembering what she had said that could have helped him. She didn't want her eyes to spill over again. "I'm happy for you," was all she could muster. Did she have a flashing beacon on top of her head that lured damaged men into her orbit? Would Jazz be okay? At least he was doing something about his issues. If only Serena hadn't called the police that night. If only she hadn't threatened to take Gethin's snake away. She had only wanted to get him out of the bathroom. He might be getting help, like Jazz, and not lying on a refrigerated tray, dead.

If only.

Jazz wrapped his arm around Serena, pulled her in and

rocked her. "You're going to survive this," he said. "He won't be forgotten."

"I can't even make the arrangements." Serena had surrendered to her tears. She pulled a dirty wad of tissue from her pocket and blew her nose. "I've been shuffling these photos around for three hours."

Exhaling, Jazz emptied the box and spread the photos in front of them. "Let's put them into categories. To start, how about one group for the photos of you and your brother and another one for his school mug shots?"

Serena nodded, exhausted, and watched Jazz arrange the images. His one good hand moved deliberately, like a blackjack dealer. Every now and then, he stopped and adjusted the sling around his neck. "I never knew funerals were so expensive," she said. "I wanted to have a memorial service, but I can't afford the funeral home fee, and my house is so small."

"Why don't you hold it here?" He had started a third group of photos—baby pictures. Gethin's dark, bright eyes were wide open in every shot so that he appeared to be continuously startled. "He loved snakes."

"It's an interesting idea," Serena said, "but it's a lot to ask. I don't even know the owner."

"She's really nice," Jazz said, taking a break to kiss Serena on the cheek. "I know she'd be glad to help. I could ask her."

Serena picked up a shot of her mother beaming down at Gethin as a baby. It was Gladys during the brief period of her life when she was a normal, happy mom, someone Serena could barely remember. Serena still hadn't heard from Gladys. "Rocky said Trina saw you on TV and she knew Gethin. What's her story? Why is she doing all this?"

Jazz stopped shuffling the photos. "Is this how you want them, in these categories? What if I put them in order by his age, so the baby photos would be first, then elementary school and high school, his time with Rocky, and the shots with you and Gethin together. Would that be better?"

"No, I liked your first idea," she said.

"Or, I could put them in reverse order, with the recent shots first, back to high school, grade school, until he was a baby." Jazz kept picking up photos, staring at them, and setting them down. His face had turned shiny with sweat. "What do you think? What else is in this box? I can do whatever you want. I was on my high-school yearbook committee, you know. I'm probably the best video producer you've ever met. I'm the Maximum Champion of photos."

"Stop," she said. "Why are you stalling? What's her story?"

"She knows him." Jazz sat back and stared at his swollen fingers. They stuck out of the cast like a pack of sausages. "Trina knows Fletch, the cop who shot Gethin. They're friends."

Serena gripped the edge of the table, to keep it from spinning. "So she's not just a Good Samaritan. She's got an angle."

"She doesn't want you to sue him."

Fury jumped into Serena's throat, so strong it startled her. "I can't even pay for the funeral." The words came shaking out one at a time like rotten grains of salt. "I'll do whatever I think is right. I haven't made up my mind yet, but it's my decision."

"I know, and listen," he said, pulling his chair closer, taking hold of her. "I'll back you up one hundred percent, whatever you decide, but you should know he's suffering too. Trina's out looking for him right now. He's not at home and not answering his phone. She's afraid he's going to do something stupid."

"He already did."

"He knows it," Jazz said. "He thought his partner was about to get stabbed."

"That's bullshit."

"His wife died last year. He was in the service, same as your dad."

"I have to go," Serena said. "Do you have envelopes or plastic bags or something, so the photos won't get mixed up again?"

Jazz stood up and pulled kitchen drawers open until he found a box of plastic food bags. Without a word, he slipped each grouping of images into a different baggie, one-handed. "Let me drive you."

"No, thanks. I can make it." She took the photos from him.

"Please wait. I didn't mean to—"

"I'll call you tomorrow."

When she saw the man who killed her brother, Serena was stopped at a red light by the bridge with the train tracks below. It was the spot where she had often seen people hunkered down in the shade of the bridge.

From a distance, someone cursed. Serena turned her head and saw him: Fletcher Jefferies in blue jeans and a brown shirt. He had one paunchy leg hoisted over the bridge railing. He was struggling to get the other one over. With a grunt, Jefferies stepped across, looked around, and lurched down the embankment, kicking up a cloud of dust.

Had he seen her? Serena couldn't tell. Her face flashed with heat. So what if he was a veteran? He looked like a trigger-happy loser with his wild eyes and two white strands of hair plastered over his sweaty, bald head. What the hell was he doing, anyway? She damn sure knew he wasn't going for a sunset nature hike. He was probably headed under the bridge to get drunk with the homeless people who lived there, in a place where Trina would never find him, as if nothing had happened, as if he hadn't murdered Gethin. Serena wanted to leap from the car and rip out his heart, the same way he had gutted her.

A cool wind blew through the open car windows. Serena's breathing slowed. The light turned from red to green, but she didn't move forward. There was nobody behind her. Something wasn't right. Overweight older men didn't vault over bridge railings to reach the green space below, even if they were trying to hide. Jazz had said Trina was looking for Jefferies. In the waning orange light of a sickly sunset, the sky let out a low, distant moan, and she remembered. The Florida Railway service. Her dashboard clock said 5:56. In four minutes, a freight train would thunder through St. Augustine.

Serena didn't stop to think. She shut off the car, jumped out, and hurled herself over the bridge so that she half-ran, half-slid down the scruffy embankment. Bits of gravel got jammed between her toes and her sandals. She banged her chin and started to roll but managed to grab a tree root before tumbling to the bottom of the hill. "No," she said, as loud as her lungs allowed. "Stop!"

Standing by the railroad tracks, he turned, staring with his mouth ajar. He nodded, acknowledging her, but didn't speak.

"So, this is how you deal with it?" Serena said, furious. "Instead of facing the consequences, you take the coward's way out?"

His shoulders were shaking. "I could say I'm sorry a million times and it would never be enough," he said. "I wish I could trade places with Gethin. I'd give anything to bring him back."

"Well, you can't." She was yelling at him and plotting her next move at the same time. Shoving him to the far side of the tracks at the last minute would take more effort than yanking him closer. "You'll only cause a lot more pain if you check out. Seems like your friend Trina cares about you. Can't imagine why."

A rumbling noise grew louder. "I can't, either." The tracks started to hum, nearly drowning out his voice. "The shame is… so deep, it…I can't."

Serena widened her stance, making sure her hips, knees, and feet were aligned. She inhaled, held it, and exhaled. "You made a mistake," she said.

"Yes, stupid, stupid." He was mumbling. Through the trees, the train appeared and blasted its horn. "I could have tackled him. I could have fired into the air."

"It was an accident," Serena said and flinched. With a pain like a stab wound, she realized it was true. *It was an accident.* "He had a knife. Your partner was in danger."

When she extended her hand, Fletch took it, stepping away from the tracks a second before the train roared under the bridge, each car pounding out a rhythm like a heartbeat.

40

Fletch

Months later, Fletch still jumped at every sudden sound or movement, but it was a big day for Rocky and Jazz—their college graduation—and he had promised Trina. Rocky had made dinner reservations. It was an Italian place she liked that they could all afford. Jazz had even brought his mother, Meghna. Fletch sat at a far corner of the long table, nibbling buttery breadsticks while Serena pretended to arm wrestle Jazz. "I thought you were the Maximum Champion," she said, laughing. Fletch could see she was holding back. "Is that the best you've got?" After a pause, Serena slammed her opponent's arm onto the table, which nearly caused Fletch to choke on his appetizer. His eardrums wouldn't stop ringing.

It was the first time Fletch had been out in public since the incident by the railroad tracks. He had moved in with Trina, who never let him out of her sight.

"My son," Meghna announced. She pulled the straw from her soda and knighted Jazz with it. On her hand, a large diamond ring sparkled under the fluorescent lights. "The Maximum Weakling."

Trina scooched her chair closer to Fletch and wrapped an arm around his waist. "You okay?" she said, talking into his ear.

Fletch nodded and winked at her. She was warm and smelled like soap, and once again, in his mind, Fletch rifled through the remarkable collection of blessings that had somehow befallen him. Farah would have been happy to see Fletch with Trina, who had been so kind ever since the Black Night when Gethin died, an episode he only remembered as shards of sight and sound. The shame burned his pores, every time he relived Gethin's last moments.

"Hey," Jazz said, wiping a drop of soda from his chin, "I can't help it if my girl's an Amazon warrior."

"To Serena," Rocky said, raising her glass. "The original Savage."

"To Serena the Savage," everyone said.

Trina, bless her, had been working hard to include Meghna in the gathering. Every few minutes, Trina would bend forward and ask Meghna a question about her new apartment, which was close to the serpentarium, or her daily walks along the river, or her quiet little dog, Pandora. In response, Meghna waved her paper napkin over her head, swaying as if she might break out some Mardi Gras moves. "I have my handsome son, the college graduate," she said. "Inventor of bicycles. Charmer of snakes and beautiful women."

Jazz gave his mother a sideways shoulder hug and smiled at Serena. "She is beautiful, isn't she, Mama? Aren't we lucky?"

Serena patted Jazz on the knee and grinned. Fletch was glad to see her looking relaxed and happy. Still, he secretly hoped Jazz wouldn't move out of the serpentarium and into Serena's house anytime soon. Like a perpetual motion machine, Jazz never stopped raking, mowing, caring for the animals, and making life easier for Trina—all in his spare time, when he wasn't building bicycles. Serena visited nearly every day. Sometimes her old car was outside the barracks the next morning.

"I have my own home again," Meghna said, rocking on her chair. She waved a hand at the ceiling, causing her ring to sparkle. "There's a rectangular courtyard with grass and four white chairs. Pandora likes to watch the sunset."

A woman with gold hoop earrings dropped two trays of deep-dish pizza on the table. The smell of steaming sausage and onions rolled down the table until it reached Fletch. He inhaled the aroma, hoping to feel a familiar pang of hunger, but as usual, his appetite was missing in action. Mainly, he wanted to leave the overly bright, noisy restaurant. Behind him, a toddler in a high chair kept banging a spoon and screaming at unexpected intervals.

I promised Trina, he thought. *Man up, Jefferies. You can do this.*

At the other end of the table, Serena's face had lost its color. "Okay, you said it would be a surprise, and it certainly is," she said, fixing Rocky with a look of mock accusation. "What do we call this, exactly?"

"Lasagna pizza!" Rocky said. "My favorite."

"Jesus, take the wheel," Serena said. "Who's got the defibrillator paddles?"

"It's world-famous," Trina said, grinning at Meghna, motioning for her to take a slice.

"It's going to be way too hot to eat," Serena said. "Why don't we give it another minute—or an hour?"

"Another toast," Trina said, raising her glass of iced tea. "To the graduates, Jazz and Rocky."

"To the graduates!" everyone said.

"To Rocky's new job in Jacksonville," Serena said, launching another round of toasts. "I've always wanted to know a real chemist."

"To Trina and Fletch!" Jazz said.

"And Meghna!" Rocky said.

The longer they celebrated everyone at the table, the more vivid Gethin's absence made itself known. He was right there, slipping from spot to spot around the table, unseen but touching all of them. When Serena's eyes took on a sudden distance, Fletch knew she was feeling it too. He wanted to offer a toast to those deeply loved and gone too soon, but he was afraid Serena might cry. Her spells of grief could be unpredictable, triggered by a song, a smell, a memory, or a word.

Fletch leaned into Trina and whispered, "I need a minute. I'll be right back."

She squeezed his hand and craned forward to lob another question at Meghna.

Outside, Fletch hiked his slacks up higher. His pants were too baggy. His appetite had moved on to greener pastures. If the nightmares ever stopped, maybe he would be able to eat a whole meal again someday. Fletch propped himself against the building and tried to exhale. St. George Street churned with the usual river of tourists, dogs, street musicians, and drug addicts sprawled across benches. He wasn't in uniform anymore, having turned in his gun and badge the day he retired. At least the investigation had turned out to be a nonevent, thanks to Serena's lengthy written statement, also signed by Rocky. She had walked into Trina's kitchen without a word and handed Fletch a copy.

Cancer had stolen Farah. A bullet, misguided, had claimed Gethin. Yet somehow, for Fletch, grace had persisted. His eyes filled at the epic improbability of it.

To his right, through the constant, random chatter of pedestrians, a familiar sound rang out: a tambourine. He recognized the sound before he saw Brillo Pad and Melon Ball a half-block away, begging for change with a jester hat at their feet. Fletch stood up straighter and squinted. Around her neck, Melon Ball had another ball python, a spotted brown and tan one this time. Had they gotten it from Chelsea? Were they running a wildlife trafficking ring? Trina would know what to do with a possibly stolen snake, but he wasn't about to haul her outside and spoil the celebration for Jazz and Rocky.

Fletch fingered the phone in his pocket. He could call his former partner, Parson, and report it. Maybe Parson or even Foster could pick up where Fletch had left off and track Chelsea down. Maybe Chelsea would even agree to visit with her sister sometime.

Someone dropped a few coins into Brillo Pad's hat. The boy danced on the tips of his toes and bowed with a skeletal flourish. Melon Ball gave the tambourine a few extra victory bangs. Fletch turned and walked back inside the restaurant, into the bright, loud circle of his family.

Acknowledgments

To those who marvel at, and refrain from killing native snakes, thank you. To anyone living with neurodiversity who bravely tells their story, many thanks to you as well. Your courage will help stop the stigma that too often turns those with differences into "The Others."

Many friends, family members, and colleagues supported me in writing this book.

First, for giving my story a chance, I'm deeply grateful to the talented, compassionate people at Regal House Publishing (RHP), who reviewed an unsolicited manuscript about stolen snakes and malevolent jesters, yet did not block my emails. Many thanks to RHP founder and editor-in-chief, Jaynie Royal, and managing editor, Pam Van Dyk, as well as everyone at Books Forward.

Thanks also to my wonderful writing group: Jennie Erin Smith, Sandy Smith Hutchins, Derek Catron, and Jeff Boyle. They read every word of this book, chapter by chapter over many months, offering keen insights and invaluable suggestions.

For moral support above and beyond the call of duty, I'm indebted as always to my biological and honorary siblings: Katie and Maggie Pinholster, Carrie Wisniewski, Jessica Handler and Mickey Dubrow, Gerry Landers and Greg Causey, Eva Sotus, Michaela Jarvis, Teri Barwick, and Carol Longacre and family.

For providing me with a sense of community, purpose, and belonging, thanks to all Volusia-Flagler Turtle Patrol volunteers as well as many Ponce Inlet neighbors, too numerous to name. I'm also grateful to my dear colleagues at Embry-Riddle Aeronautical University.

Although there is a real St. Augustine Police Department, the police officers, facilities, technologies, and operations depicted in this novel are entirely fictional. Certain operational details and character traits had to be invented in order for the plot to work; those literary choices do not imply any disrespect for law enforcement. In fact, I have been impressed to read about community outreach efforts by the St. Augustine Police Department.

Blessings, gratitude, and much love to my partner, Michele Amato.

All my heart to my brother, John Roberts Pinholster, who left too soon.

To my daughter Caroline—love always, to the moon and back.